Dying Days

Dying Days

A romance about finding love,

family, and redemption.

Gillian Long

Dying Days

Gillian A Long © 2015

revised edition
First published 2015
ebook ISBN: 9780994267108
& 9780994267122
Paperback ISBN: 9780994267115
& 9780645576047
Millaa House Publishing
PO Box 89
Millaa Millaa
Queensland 4886
Australia

This book is dedicated to John Murphy,
my friend and inspiration for this story.

History will mark the course of events, but our
imaginations may conjure a different reality.

Table of Contents

PART ONE ....

Chapter One — 1
Chapter Two — 14
Chapter Three — 23
Chapter Four — 31
Chapter Five — 37
Chapter Six — 46
Chapter Seven — 57
Chapter Eight — 66
Chapter Nine — 77
Chapter Ten — 86

PART TWO 100

Chapter Eleven — 101
Chapter Twelve — 111
Chapter Thirteen — 120
Chapter Fourteen — 127
Chapter Fifteen — 136
Chapter Sixteen — 146
Chapter Seventeen — 158
Chapter Eighteen — 165
Chapter Nineteen — 170

PART THREE 185

Chapter Twenty — 186
Chapter Twenty-One — 194
Chapter Twenty-Two — 211
Chapter Twenty-Three — 221
Chapter Twenty-Four — 231
Chapter Twenty-Five — 246
Chapter Twenty-Seven — 251
Chapter Twenty-Eight — 264
Chapter Twenty-Nine — 270

PART FOUR 275

Chapter Thirty — 276
Chapter Thirty-One — 288
Chapter Thirty-Two — 293
Chapter Thirty-Three — 309
Chapter Thirty-Four — 316
Chapter Thirty-Five — 321
Chapter Thirty-Six — 332
Chapter Thirty-Seven — 346

Prelude to Disaster

It was August 1953 when it all started, and it didn't end until the nation died. The air was a crisp champagne yellow in the dying light of day, its temperature hovering between the lingering cool dry winter without a hint of the torrid summer to come. Government House was bustling with anticipation as guests from all over the world gathered to celebrate the birth of the British Central African Federation.

Flight Lieutenant Dennis Ryder helped his companion from the car and followed his parents into the ballroom. He was a tall, handsome fellow with a rangy physique, light brown hair, regulation short, and a glint of the adventurer in his eye.

As they entered the ballroom, a small orchestra broke into Percy Faith's *Where is your Heart* and his companion, Julia Baker's hand tightened on his extensor carpi radialis muscles. He was glad of his uniform sleeve; those red nails were lethal.

With her other hand, she touched the feather fascinator affixed to her blonde hair marshalled into tight rolls on her head. Then her gloved fingertips brushed the Kimberly diamonds at her throat as if for reassurance. 'There's Major-General Sir John Kennedy talking to your father.'

Dennis followed her gaze, wondering who he might recognise. He'd been away for so long. Like him, many of the men were in dress uniform. Others, like his father, wore evening dress, white tie, and tailcoat. Some, like Julia's father, wore the more modern tuxedos.

The women wore elegant, full skirted gowns that swept the air just above floor height. Like Julia, they too had adorned themselves with jewels and feathers to match the grandeur of the occasion. Dark-skinned waiters in uniforms, white coat and red fez, manoeuvred expertly between the small round white-linen-covered tables, trays of drinks and canapes held high.

Why the staff wore the fez Dennis hadn't a clue. It certainly had no local cultural relevance. He took two glasses of champagne off the tray of a passing waiter and handed one to his date.

She shook her head. 'Really Dennis, you should know better!'

'I should?' He glanced at his feet with a puzzled frown.

Julia sighed. 'Darling, a lady can't be seen walking about with a drink in her hand.'

He blinked and bowed slightly. 'My apologies.'

'You've been away too long, that's all.'

'Three years is not so long.'

'Mummy said war turns men into savages, and perhaps she is right.' Julia arched a pencil thin eyebrow.

'I say! That's jolly unfair.'

'It's all right, dear. Now you're back... Oh, there are Mummy and Daddy with your parents. Come along Dennis, I want you to say hello.' You haven't seen my parents since you've been back.

Dennis had met Julia's parents, Don and Elizabeth Baker, many times before. They were old friends of his own parents. Some liked to joke the Baker's farms covered one half of the country and the Ryder's held the other part. It wasn't true, of course, but between the two families, they held extensive acreage. Now his father was in a delicate negotiation for a stretch of Don Baker's land.

For years, Dennis had been carrying out his duty as Julia's escort, although he took every opportunity to volunteer abroad. First to the Malayan Emergency, and from there he had managed a short stint on loan to the Royal Australian Airforce's 77 Squadron in Korea. Tonight, he hadn't a choice on who his date might be. It was all arranged before he arrived home.

He followed Julia to the table reserved for their families. A little while later, Julia suggested they dance. He obliged, but when they returned to the table, another couple had pulled up, the man speaking to Don Baker.

With him was the most stunning woman Dennis had ever laid eyes on. Tall and willowy in a mid-calf length emerald sheath, exposing a long neck and golden shoulders arising from the delicate swellings high on her chest. The extremities below the dress showed neat, bronzed calves and ankles, above long, elegant feet with red-painted toenails, encased in high-heeled golden sandals.

She turned towards him, a ribald grin on her wide red mouth. She was sucking on an olive, or perhaps it was a cocktail onion, taken from the glass in her hand. The toothpick still poked from between scarlet lips. Light caught her eyes, and he swore they were the same emerald as her dress. Dark hair, with more than a hint of auburn, curved in a swoop over an attitude that said come hither if you dare.

His pulse quickened, and he hurried Julia towards the table, intent on nothing more than standing within this gorgeous creature's magnetism.

Julia's hand flew to her mouth. 'Oh, my goodness. She's so inappropriately dressed and that nail varnish. It's so vulgar.'

Dennis said, 'You know her?'

'Good lord no. She's some dreadful coal miner's daughter from the Wanki mine, a rabble-rousing union thug giving the natives ideas above their station. I'm acquainted with her escort, the man she is engaged to. He's Robin Harrison, the new chief inspector with the BSA Police, not long out from England. That woman managed to snare him very quickly, some say bewitched.'

They approached the group. Dennis tried not to focus on the woman as Don introduced him to Robin Harrison. A moment of awkwardness followed the introduction.

'And I'm Dolly.'

Robin cleared his throat. 'Julia, I don't believe you have met my fiancée. May I introduce Miss Dorothée Betham?'

'Dorothée. What a lovely name. It's French isn't it?' Julia gave her most superior smile, one that left her eyes to slide down her sharp nose and freeze the object of her focus.

The woman shrugged, her eyes like green glaciers. 'I prefer Dolly.'

Robin grimaced in apology. 'Dorothée's mother was French. She died when Dolly was a baby. Her father's Welsh and has always called her Dolly. Isn't that right, darling?'

'You know it is, dear.' Dolly turned towards Dennis and thrust out her hand. 'And you are Dennis Ryder, the famous ace. Why don't you join us at our table? We can leave the old folks to chat, and you can regale us with exploits of your daring-do with the Australians in Korea. What do you say?'

Dennis's ears were on fire as he took her hand, cool and dry in his burning slab.

His father intervened. 'What a jolly, splendid idea! You young'uns sit together and leave us old folks to codger over dinner. We have some rather pressing business to discuss with your parents, Julia.'

Julia's voice was too bright, her eyebrow spitting cats. She glared at Dolly's hand resting like a precious bird in Dennis's large hand. 'Are you sure you won't mind us barging in, Robin? You must have other plans. There are probably all sorts of people you want to chat with without us in the way.'

'Not at all. I would be honoured if you would join us.'

Dennis adjusted his shoulder creating a private space to give Dolly a conspiratorial wink. Had he imagined it, or had he seen Robin frowning at Dolly? Perhaps it was the light playing on the man's very British reserve. Too bad. If he could put a wedge between man and woman, he'd do it in a heartbeat.

Part One

Chapter One

Matt Reid leaned forward with his forearms resting on the steering wheel of his rented car. Despite the heat, a shiver ran across his shoulders as he surveyed the house at the end of the steep driveway. A cooling breeze was blowing through his open car window, drying his sweat, and bringing back memories of eucalyptus flu inhalers from his childhood. He shifted in his seat to loosen his shirt.

A radio announcement that morning had claimed that January 2013 was Australia's hottest on record, but that was okay. He had dealt with worse. His fingers clenched and unclenched as he recounted the mental drill of close target reconnaissance, forcing his muscles to relax and reminding himself that there was no physical danger in this mission, even though he didn't want to have any ties or displays of emotion.

He had only arranged to meet the man to get the truth. Now he wasn't so sure he wanted it, especially if it meant exposing his own personal story, although he could always fall back on his cover. The man he was about to meet had struck him as being a little eccentric when he called from London.

A week ago, Alan Fletcher had listened to Matt's request on the telephone and agreed to see him. At first, the man had seemed normal until he gave directions to his house, which he explained was in the hills north of Brisbane.

'When you find the right street, you'll see an old Queenslander,' he had said.

Matt had been sceptical. 'This Queenslander... How will I recognise him? Will he be there waiting for me?'

There was silence at the other end of the phone, and then a strident intake of air, followed by the sound of a braying donkey. 'Sorry,' Fletcher said, 'a Queenslander is a house. When you turn into my road, you'll see my house down the side of the hill. It's two stories, white with weatherboard cladding, a corrugated iron roof, and three-sixty verandas.'

The house Matt could see was at the end of a driveway. Colonial and gracious, with bone-white walls and an iron roof, set into a hillside above a forested valley just as Fletcher had described. Matt couldn't see beyond the house, but the map he had consulted earlier showed the hillside fell away steeply.

The house was raised above the ground to catch the cooling breeze and had a white paling skirt modestly covering the gap between earth and floor. Verandas at different levels with white banisters framed the staircase. A mechanical wheelchair lift on the stairs marred an air of purity. It seemed an odd choice of home for an old war correspondent.

The garden bustled with flowering shrubs, many of European descent, but many Matt didn't recognise. Garden beds crouched below towering eucalypts. They had cut blue hydrangeas back to prevent the chair lift's entanglement. The whole place was a rural idyll just beyond the creeping grasp of Brisbane.

He released the handbrake and let the car roll forward down the driveway.

Inside the house, Alan Fletcher slouched in front of a large window, using its light to read a newspaper. He was uncomfortable in his borrowed wheelchair, and it wasn't helping his temper. In growing fury, he read that the Zimbabwean president Robert Mugabe and his ruling elite ZANU had approved a new constitution enshrining their right to steal property. The next article covered North Korea's threats to launch nuclear weapons against imperialist Americans. He muttered, 'Bad as each other, but does anyone care...?'

Outside, the wheels of a car crunched on gravel, alerting him to someone's arrival. He folded the paper. It must be him, although he didn't believe the man's tale. An author? Bullshit! Fletcher searched the web for his name and found nothing.

He rolled along the passage to open the door as the young man walked up the steps. The way he moved was familiar.

'Morning sir, thank you for seeing me.'

'Mr Reid, I take it?' Fletcher held out his hand.

'Call me Matt, please.'

'Matt it is. Come in. We are through here.'

Fletcher maneuverer the wheelchair to turn around, knocking paint off the doorjamb. 'Bugger the bastard.' He muttered.

He shot back along the hallway and turned into the sitting room, scraping past a leather sofa, and leaving scuff marks along its side, before stopping in front of a large window. Beyond the glass pane he could see the forested hills, lush from the recent rain, as they rolled away into the hazy blue distance. He never tired of the view.

'Take a seat.' With a sweep of his hand, Fletcher indicated an array of options.

Matt followed behind Fletcher, wincing at every collision. The sitting room he entered was large and airy, with a comfortable, lived-in feel. The morning sun, flooding through the glass, shone through Fletcher's thinning hair, but his face was in shadow.

The room smelled like a stationary cupboard with mounds of books, newspapers, and magazines piled on every available surface. Battered leather lounges and old armchairs wore their injuries with pride. Persian carpets, almost hidden by the clutter, lined up next to each other to cover the wood plank floors. Asian wall hangings, interspersed with African masks and unframed paintings, filled any remaining wall space.

The cluttered decor of competing cultural artefacts told Matt of a life of travel. His eyes lingered on the paintings, Australian scenes, mostly scenic realism. A desert scene captured his eye, its rocky orange outcrops seeming to pulsate against a deep sky, and he wondered who the artist was.

He pulled up an upright wooden chair to sit opposite and on the same level as Fletcher. Too late, he realised the old man had manoeuvred him into facing the flooding light. He smiled and glanced down at his shoes.

For a moment, neither man spoke, until Fletcher said, 'So, you want to know about the Rhodesian war? Surely you haven't flown sixteen and a half thousand kilometres to get my perspective just for some book?'

Matt's fine angular features, his clothing and hairstyle all spoke of his native British reticence. He shifted on the hard seat, recognising his disadvantage in front of this forthright and cranky old man. 'What you have to say will be valuable, but that's only partly why I'm here...'

Fletcher interrupted. 'They couldn't win. It was a foolish gesture ever going down that path. They were tilting against an unstoppable avalanche of colonial remorse. The Americans made sure of that, insisting Britain honour her deal to de-colonise in exchange for their help in the War. That was before the Japanese bombed the crap out of them and they had no choice but to retaliate.' He paused and his hand crept towards a small tear in the plastic coating of the wheelchair, then dropped back to his lap. 'Their meddling exchanged the benign, if paternalistic, British for colonisation by a tyrant.'

Matt sighed. 'You mean the Chinese?' He hadn't come all this way to debate Zimbabwean politics or deal with the old man's hackneyed prejudice. Politics were not his game. Facts are what he needs. Facts either for his thesis or about his heritage he hasn't decided yet.

'No, not the Chinese. They're just collecting their pound of flesh for helping Mugabe seize power for the Shona people. MaShona are the new colonial masters who stole the land from the BaKalanga.'

'I read about it. It's interesting.'

Fletcher glared at him. 'Interesting! You think it's merely interesting that people from another country invade and colonise in this modern day and you Poms helped them?'

'Well, no, but is that an invasion or colonisation? It's just a different African tribe moving in—three hundred years ago.'

'I'm sure you don't mean that, although it sounds incredibly racist to me.'

Matt had not missed the irony of referring to the British as Poms and yet implying he was the one being racist, but he kept his own counsel.

Fletcher said, 'You may as well say the Nazis were right to invade and colonise France because they are both white skinned Europeans. If the British were wrong to colonise Rhodesia, the Shona were wrong to colonise Zimbabwe. You can't have it both ways.'

Matt wished he had kept his mouth shut. The man was a nutter, but he couldn't let that go. 'The Rhodesian war wasn't about colonisation, though, was it? It was about every man having the right to vote.' Should he mention Australia's colonial past? Probably unwise. 'But I'm not here to discuss the rights and wrongs of war. My research is concerned with the tactics of twentieth century guerrilla warfare in Southern Africa.'

Fletcher pressed his mouth into a thin line. 'You can't dismiss it when examining the tactics of war. It's who we humans are. Greedy bastards. Even the BaKalanga took Zimbabwe from the !Kung territorial hunting grounds.'

Matt ignored Fletcher's strangled, clicking pronunciation and asked, 'Who are the Kung?'

'The Bushmen, hunter gatherers of the Kalahari called San by some.' Fletcher paused.

A narrow shadow, cast by the window's crossbeam, shaded Matt's eyes as he leaned forward, elbows resting on thighs, hands hanging between his knees. He wished he could smoke, but he'd given up. He pressed his fingertips together to regain control.

'My research isn't so much about background politics but about espionage. I've read a lot of different accounts about British spies in the ranks of the Rhodesian armed forces, and I wondered if you had an opinion given your time covering the war.'

Fletcher's face took on a pensive wariness. 'It's all so long ago I'm not sure I can remember anything worth telling you. Those were the dying days of war with a country in chaos. There were rumours of something shady going on. None of it made sense to me then and still doesn't. Some people thought there were spies in the ranks. Others said they merely switched sides at the last minute to survive the inevitable world of black independence.'

He pulled a palm across his mouth and down the wrinkled leathery folds of his neck. 'The whole sorry affair was the product of rampant cold war paranoia. The thinking that propelled the Americans into war with Vietnam. Bureaucracies full of compromise and competing interests, perpetuating a war nobody wanted. My view was that the British and American intelligence agencies' office politics dictated foreign policy rather than any conspiracy, if that's what you are implying. Remember the old saying, *cock-up before conspiracy*.' Fletcher gazed off into the distance. 'Look at the legacy. The misery caused since Zimbabwean Independence, both to those who remain in the country, and to a diaspora of lost souls trying to adapt but unable to forget. If the Brits had honoured their deal with Smith in 1971, none of the slaughter would have happened.'

He picked at a small tear in the arm of his wheelchair with a nicotine-stained fingernail. 'The Americans and the British have a lot to answer for. It was the British who created MaShona?'

Matt shook his head, wondering how he could answer. They blamed the British for everything, along with the Americans. Who was this white Australian man if not a product of Britain?

Fletcher's eyebrows drew together, stray hairs spiking at angles. 'They lumped all the tribes together just to produce a bible for the savages. Their words. Not mine. Idiots! Anyway, they called the language chiShona. Unfortunately, the British lumped the iKalanga language in with all the other dialects of the so-called MaShona. That was despite academic views that the iKalanga language of the BaKalanga was a different language group with different ancestry. The BaKalanga built the Great Zimbabwe and lived in that region for more than a thousand years? I think Mugabe underestimates them and unless he grants them concessions, he might well see a revolt.'

Matt watched Fletcher reminisce, using the moment to examine his features, the nose, pitted and bulbous, the nose of a drinker. Glasshouses and throwing stones came to mind—he was as bad. War does that to a person, drink, or drugs or both, obliterating memories.

Fletcher's lips are those of a heavy smoker, thin with radiating cracks running into sagging folds at the crease lines of his smile. His hair was a nondescript, wispy grey, or at least what he had left. His eyes were his redeeming feature, alert, intelligent and a startling light blue. Matt hadn't inherited the eyes.

Fletcher jutted his chin out.

Matt realised he hadn't heard what he'd said. Although it didn't seem to matter.

Fletcher continued with his rant. 'America was paranoid over the Russians at the height of the cold war. Cold war politics caused the Rhodesian downfall. Mugabe exploited dissent and division in the government ranks of both the Brits and the Yanks. To the Brits, the Rhodesian rebellion was an embarrassment, but the Americans saw it as a sinister backdoor Russian takeover of Africa. They gave into the Chinese and backed Mugabe out of expedience.

Once Rhodesia caved to the political pressure, the Yanks moved on to their next crisis, as they do. When it was all over, the Brits walked away congratulating themselves for their cleverness. While Mugabe, that cunning Jackal, thrust Zimbabwe into the current chasm of chaos. What for—his own North Korea style government?

Mugabe will never let another tribe survive unless they are subordinate. He wants Zimbabwe for MaShona exclusively, and his family particularly. In his mind, he is the hereditary chief, its king. He has begun his dynasty. That's Mugabe's blueprint even though his ancestors were interlopers, and the so called MaShona are a British colonial construct.' Fletcher chortled at the irony.

Matt said, 'I don't suppose Mugabe would like to hear that.'

'The victors always write the history.' Fletcher's eyes became rheumy in reflection. 'He admired them, the North Koreans.'

Perspiration trickled down Matt's back, but after the grey London winter, at least he was warm. This was his first trip to Australia, and the sun's intensity had surprised him. It was not the warmest place he'd been, but it seemed brighter, as if someone had turned up the volume a notch. Perhaps the clear sky made the light so intense, or it's depleted ozone. Perhaps, unlike Africa and the Middle East, there was less dust, or perhaps it was the lower altitude. Whatever the meteorological explanation, he would have to buy sunglasses when he returned to Brisbane, and perhaps a pack of fags. No, he had quit. He refocused his attention, waiting for the old man to finish speaking, watching the nicotine-stained finger scratching at the plastic armrest.

'I was only there for five years.' Fletcher looked up from his scratching, 'writing a book on the so-called Australian mercenaries, who saw themselves as capitalist ideologues. They were fighting communism, you see. At least, that was how they justified their actions. After the dismal failure of politics in the Vietnam conflict, they believed they were doing some good.'

Matt leaned forward. 'Did you ever write your book?'

Fletcher shook his head. 'No. Not that book, anyway. After the Rhodesian war, I chased other wars and never got around to it. In reality, I was a free-lance journalist trying to sell stories to whoever would buy them, BBC mostly. I didn't want to piss in my nest.'

A shame. A book like that would have made an interesting read. Matt turned his mind back to his purpose for being there, noticing that Fletcher was examining him with strange intensity, as though trying to see something hidden behind the fabric of Matt's presence.

Matt's gaze slid away from the scrutiny. How the hell could he ask the question? It should be easy, but he would feel a fool. Can one ask a complete stranger something so personal? It would be like betraying his family, at least his mother. Once uttered, the question comes into existence and cannot be undone. You can't withdraw it, and there was still no guarantee he would get the truth.

Fletcher's chin jutted again. 'You're not here to write a book, are you?'

Matt flinched. 'As a matter of fact, I am sir, but it's not a commercial publication. I'm researching the history of guerrilla warfare in British Colonial Africa for my doctorate. I know you were one of the few outsiders who covered that period until the Rhodesian war ended in '79. Everything I read has an allusion to British intelligence, having infiltrated the Rhodesian command. But there's another thing'

'Bullshit! As I grow older, people look younger and younger, but even I don't buy that you are just an English Uni student.'

Matt chucked. 'You're right. I'm thirty-two, and I was in the British Army. This is part of my retraining. My re-entry to the civilised world, I guess. If I have a PhD, I can lecture in Military History.' Matt's mouth scrunched to one side in wry self-depreciation. 'It's better than a job as an insurance salesman or security guard, and even those are a little scarce at the moment with the current financial crises.'

'Are those the only jobs open to ex-soldiers in Britain?' Fletcher paused. 'But I still don't get it. You're telling me you've come all the way from London to speak to me about the history of a conflict the world has forgotten? That sounds like a load of old horse cobblers. There must be men living in the same damp English borough as you who actually fought in that war. They could give you a firsthand account of some things they saw. Anyway, there are dozens of books on the subject, from factual histories to personal accounts of war experiences. I know I've read most of them.'

Matt saw the challenge for what it was, and he felt a little sorry for the old man. The spiky eyebrows reminded him of his father, and he leaned back in the chair to dry his palms on his jeans. It's that legacy that started the doubt.

A sound of a car pulling up in the driveway caused Fletcher to glance at the clock on the mantle. 'I'm sorry, but Polly's home. I have an appointment.' He paused. 'Can you come back tomorrow? I will try to remember something of more interest to you.'

Matt hid his disappointment, but at least he would get another chance tomorrow. 'What time?'

'Come for lunch, and Matt, try to be more forthcoming.'

What a bizarre thing to say. 'Yes thank you sir, I'll look forward to it.'

'Sure. Call me Alan, or Fletcher, none of this sir nonsense. This is Australia, not the bloody British Army.'

'Thank you for seeing me sir. Alan.' He turned to walk out. He had missed his opportunity, but tomorrow he would just ask outright whatever might happen.

A girl, or rather a young woman, swung into his path and stopped abruptly, blocking the doorway and his way out. Her clothes were a mess. Stains streaked her jeans, and she had dried paint on her tee-shirt. A seam on her shoulder had lost its stitching, leaving pale freckled flesh exposed. The light blue intensity of her eyes was startling, like Fletcher's, but framed by her long dark hair the colour appeared psycho.

'Who the hell are you?' She said.

'Ah..., I'm just leaving'. Matt tried to get out of her way, stepping aside so she could get into the room.

'I can see that, but that's not an answer to my question. I asked who you are. And when you have answered that, you can tell me what you are doing here.'

She peered around Matt. 'Poppa, you okay?'

Matt retreated, thrown by the girl's brusqueness, and glanced back at Fletcher. The old man was grinning his crazy head off.

Hands on hips, she said, 'Well?'

'Well?' Matt felt his brow furrow in bewilderment. 'Ah, um, I'm Matt Reid. I arranged to speak with your father.'

'Grandfather.'

'What? Oh, yes, I see—your grandfather.'

'What about?'

What could he say to this rude woman? He was about to tell her it was none of her business when Fletcher intervened.

'Polly, this is Matthew Reid, and he's my guest, so stop terrorising him.'

To Matt's relief, Polly pushed past him to get through the doorway, leaving a trail of turpentine vapour in her wake.

'You're a difficult man, Poppa. What have you two got to talk about? He's not your usual type.'

She appraised Matt as if he were an inanimate object. 'He's too young for one of your old journo mates and he hasn't been feeding you gin and cigarettes, so what's up?'

A cunning expression crossed Fletcher's face. 'Make us lunch tomorrow and you'll find out.'

'God Poppa, I have so much to do.'

'What? All you do is hang about in that grungy shed, squirting paint at things.'

Matt hurried to the front door, feeling chastised like a small boy. Blood had surged into his neck, making his pulse thud, but he was relieved he was no longer her target.

He let himself out of the house before she revoked his invitation to return tomorrow. As he got into his car, he realised his hands were shaking, and he concentrated on settling them.

The encounter had rattled him, letting the damn woman's rudeness get under his skin. But if he had known Fletcher was partial to cigarettes and gin, he'd be sure to oblige and bring a bottle when he returned tomorrow.

Chapter Two

In his study later that day, Fletcher hunched over his desk. Daylight faded outside the window, spreading dark corners throughout the room. In front of him lay an old photo album he hadn't opened for years. The cellophane separators stuck together, and with his fingers he released them one by one. The sucking screech of crackling pages was loud in the stillness.

God, it was all so long ago. Did he want to bring back all the pain and disappointment? He leaned forward to snap on a desk lamp and took a breath, hesitating on the precipice of memory. Matt Reid was the spit of Jake Ryder. It was quite a shock. But it was probably a coincidence. It had been a long time and memories got muddled. Both men were soldiers, which might account for the resemblance.

Perhaps it was the eyes. Eyes that had seen what ordinary people shouldn't see. Combat soldiers share that knowledge, a tacit silence of the initiated. Matt had that same aspect. The eyes of men to whom society allocates the role of God. In determining life and death, they saw the world differently.

But it was more than that. That lopsided grin. What did it matter now? Why was he chasing ghosts? The world made its judgement and put the issue to bed. No one admitted responsibility for the terrible damage allowed under their watch, nor for the unspeakable horrors perpetrated against those left to fend for themselves against the might of a man, whom they helped into his reign of terror.

Fletcher smoothed his palm over the open photo album, a Pandora's Box of escaping memories. The map, glued inside the front cover, jolted him back in time to his flat in Montague Avenue, Salisbury, Rhodesia, a country lost in the haze of history.

It must have been about 1978 when he drew it. There was a newsagent across the road. The glue was little better than flour and water. With sanctions biting, the shop sold nothing better. Fletcher remembered cutting out the map with cheap nail scissors, taking pains to copy the operational areas, drawing black lines with a clothing marker pen. He had spilt the glue and, for weeks afterwards, he had picked white scabs of dried glue from his dining table. The map he had made had allowed him to track rumours and reports on where the latest fighting was taking place.

Now, running his fingers over the map, he recalled the old-fashioned colours and typeface. The paper was acid based. It had become crazed with time and deterioration, but the details were still clear. Names long gone, now reminded him of a past he wanted to forget.

On the map, his finger found the town of Chiredzi and traced a line east to the Ryder's farm. The farmhouse with its tall, thatched roof and wide verandas would be gone now, lost with the other land seizures. His eyes glazed as he recalled the first time he had visited.

Until now, Fletcher had forgotten that trip, although Rhodesia stood at the fulcrum of his life. If he hadn't taken that assignment, he wouldn't have met Celia. Would his life have been different? There would have been less pain. Yet, if he hadn't met her, she would never have met Jake. He flicked over pages, hunting for a photo of Celia, the woman with a face and body that made men stare. He didn't think about her so much now. Tried to avoid memory ambushes. But sometimes they came unbidden. Celia's eyes, or Cee as they called her, were a fathomless blue like the pools in Sinoia Caves, whatever the caves were called now.

Polly reminded him of Cee although there was no reason for it except they had the same colour hair and blue eyes, although Polly's are light blue like his. He liked to claim Polly got her attractive qualities from him, although it was probably her mother's genes that made her the way she was. He had married Polly's grandmother on the rebound because she reminded him of Celia. What a disaster that turned into. Yet the union had given him his daughter and Polly.

He rubbed his hands through his own sparse hair as he remembered the once luxuriant dark mass. When he had arrived in Rhodesia, his hair had brushed his shoulders, although he soon cut it short to avoid provocation. Long hair showed you had avoided military call-up and men, particularly, didn't take kindly to that.

A surge of nostalgia threatened to swamp him. Christ, he had loved her. He threw away two good marriages because he couldn't forget, and she still popped up in his dreams. All this talk of Rhodesia was stirring up the muddy waters of his memory. He found the photo. The image had faded, but every contour of her face remained vivid. He didn't need a photo to remind him.

Fletcher's eyes misted at the memory. He flicked over a few more of the album pages. There it was. A large glossy black and white print showing men in skimpy shorts and tee shirts, others in combat fatigues. They were standing in a burnt-out village.

He remembered taking this picture. It was his first time covering a contact, and it hadn't been easy. The scene had made him vomit, throwing up in a Jesse bush, wiping his mouth, and trying to take shallow breaths against the smell.

The nausea hadn't lasted long. Once behind the lens, he had forgotten everything except the shot. The yellow dust smudged horizon visible through thorn scrub. The smouldering huts, the smell, always the smell of sweet garlicky death, dust, burning flesh, animal dung, lingering cooking smells that merged in his mind until he could smell it still.

In the photo's background, bodies lay where they had fallen little more than burning rag and bone bundles. Their outstretched arms, covered with suppurating veldt sores, reached for deliverance. The Russian supplied AK 47s flung to the ground beyond the reach of their lifeless clutch. He shuddered at the memory.

The soldier he was searching for was half in frame back to the camera. He stood with his shoulders hunched, shielding his lighter from the wind as he lit a cigarette.

Yes, the resemblance was there. He hadn't imagined it. The same rangy stance, lithe and fit, younger than Matt but with the same broad shoulders. Even though his back was to the camera, Fletcher could see the similarity. He really needed a photo of Jake's face, to be sure.

In those days, Fletcher had framed the shot by design to avoid exposing their faces. The rules didn't apply on social occasions when they were not associated with C Squadron. He was sure he had photos of Jake on the farm. This was the wrong album.

He wheeled out from the study down the hallway to the sitting room. Polly was curled up on the sofa, headphones plugged into her ears. The television was babbling in the background, but she concentrated on the tablet on her lap. He blamed all this multi-tasking for the diminishment of people's ability to concentrate. *Distracted by shiny things*, Polly called it.

'Polly—Polly.'

She tilted her head to take out one earbud.

'Where are my old photo albums?'

Polly spoke louder than necessary, competing with the Arctic Monkeys blaring from the earpiece. 'They're at the studio. Remember, you said I could borrow them for the photomontage I want to do. I haven't had time but the soon as I get a chance, I'll scan them and bring them home. Is that okay?'

'I need them back.'

Fletcher can't remember her asking for the photo albums. It's another thing he'd forgotten. He remembered things from years ago but forgot things from yesterday. The doctor said the flu affected his short-term memory, and it wouldn't last. It had left him weak and forgetful, which was why he fell. He'd cracked his pelvic bone, although Polly insisted that climbing on the roof to clean gutters caused it, not the flu.

She'd taken the ladders to her studio, forbidding him to climb again. Damn cheek. Since when did kids have the right to tell their elders what they could and could not do? Overnight, their roles had seemed to reverse. One minute he cared for her, the next she was dictating terms, although he was relieved to find she had the albums.

'Okay, I'll bring them back tomorrow. I can always scan them here, I guess.' She screwed the earbud back into her ear.

His mouth inverted, but he turned to head back to his study. As he neared the door, he stopped. 'You will be here tomorrow, won't you Polly? Polly! Can you hear me? I want you here when that young man comes back.'

'Yeah—yeah, I'll make lunch.' She bobbed her head. 'Just something simple because I don't have time. I'll make it in the morning and leave it in the fridge for you.' She turned back to focus on her tablet.

'No, Polly.' He waited for her to unplug the earpiece again, his finger picking agitatedly at the tear in the wheelchair arm. 'I want you here when he's here. I want you to stay for lunch. To listen to what he's got to say.'

'Poppa why? I have to get the last few paintings done for the exhibition. It's less than two months away and I don't have enough pieces to hang as it is. If I don't get them finished, the Gallery will be furious.'

'You have to be here, Polly. I need you.'

Fletcher hesitated. Why did he need her here? Intuition, that was all a gut instinct, and he always followed his gut. That's what had made him a good reporter. That, and tedious perseverance. But she has to be there with her sharp-eyed artist's observations, seeing the real shape of things.

'You don't need me here. You can manage perfectly well by yourselves. Surely the man can help you get the lunch. I'll make sure everything's done before I go, don't worry.'

'Please.' Fletcher had a flash of déjà vu, remembering the same conversation with Celia all those years ago. She hadn't wanted to go with him, but he'd pressured her. Now he is doing the same to Polly. Perhaps he should back off. He had caused so much grief then. If Cee hadn't gone with him in the first place, none of it would have happened. No, this was different.

'I do need your instincts. I need to know if he's lying. You are so good at cutting through the bullshit and spotting stuff I might miss.'

'Yeah, I don't think I did too well today. Perhaps I was a little too direct with my accusations. I think I offended him, but....'

'What? What did you think of him?' He respected his granddaughter's opinion but often forgot to ask for it. Not that such an omission ever deterred her.

'I don't know anything about him.' She pursed her lips. 'Two things. He's a Pom that's certain, and he's not bad looking if you like the conservative stuck up type.' She laughed at the disappointment on Fletcher's face and relented, holding up a third finger. 'He's sad.'

'Sad. How do you know he's sad?' Fletcher racked his memory for tell-tale signs of sadness in the man. There's a serious intensity to him, but is that sadness? He didn't think so.

'I don't know. Call it intuition. It's like someone died, like I felt when Mom and Dad died. His eyes were sad, nice eyes the colour of a stormy sea, but still sad.'

'Okay.' Fletcher was prepared to go along with the idea. Perhaps sad people recognise sadness, although Polly can't be sad still, surely. Her mother and father died thirteen years ago. Fletcher still misses them, but he wouldn't call himself sad. 'So, you can tell me three things about him in the space of a few-word meeting, even if two of them were obvious. What will you be able to tell me if you stayed for lunch? You will stay for lunch, won't you? Please, Polly.'

She sighed. 'Oh, all right. What's it about? You better fill me in on the details, and what left-field questions you want me to ask.'

'Nothing like that this time.' Guilt pricked his conscience. 'I just think he's lying that's all, but I am not sure about which bit. He's ex-British Army, says he's doing a doctorate on colonial guerrilla warfare, says that's why he's here, but I don't think it's true.'

'Which bit?' Polly chuckled. 'That a combat veteran has enough of a brain left to do a Ph.D. or that he's doing one at all? I am sure he's a soldier. He's got the walk, like walking across eggshells.'

Fletcher had another flashback, remembering how Celia disparaged the soldiers in the regular army. She avoided talking to them, particularly the foreigners. Especially not anyone who served in the Rhodesian Light Infantry, or the RLI, which was considered worse than being seen in the pinball arcade. Nice girls just didn't do that, she had said. Fletcher had seen plenty who did and thought Cee naïve.

'I just want you to suss out his real reason for being here.' Fletcher said as Polly's hand hovered with the earpiece at her ear.

'Really Poppa, how am I supposed to do that—water boarding?'

It's a dig at him about their last argument over the war in Iraq and Afghanistan, where she argued the politicians who started wars had lost all morality. But he had countered with the fact that war had nothing to do with morality, just power and propaganda, and of course, she got angry.

He had argued that sometimes there was justification, particularly for a defensive war. She had accused him of bias because war made his career. Not wanting to begin that argument again, he resorted to begging. 'Please Poll, please for your old Poppa.'

'Oh, okay.' Polly rolled her eyes and replaced the earpiece. 'I will stay until lunch is over.'

Chapter Three

The Brisbane River snaked through the city as Matt gazed at it, thinking about his meeting later that day. He was naked, standing at the window of his hotel on the eleventh floor, revelling in the caress of early morning sun on his body. He ran his fingers over the puckered skin that cut a jagged line over his shoulder.

The sun on the eastern horizon heralded a cloudless summer day, and he needed a run. As he dressed, he wondered how he might find the right words to ask Fletcher the question that had brought him halfway across the world. It was tricky, and he'd chickened out yesterday, but if he could finish the job today, he could go home and get on with his life. Christ, he hoped that crazy woman wouldn't be there. Asking Fletcher was hard enough without having her listening in.

He tied his laces and cleared his mind, focussing on his breathing. Outside, the corridors were deserted, the remains of room service trays and newspapers the only evidence of shared occupancy. The place smelled of old food and over-cleaned carpet musk, and he wrinkled his nose. By the time he got downstairs and out into the street, the early morning traffic was already building.

If he'd known better, he would have found somewhere to stay nearer to Fletcher's place. When he had arrived in Australia three days ago, he had told the cab driver to take him to a decent hotel in the city. This was it, but it wouldn't be for long. Perhaps the entire journey hadn't been such a smart idea. He could have asked on the phone or even written a letter, but he needed to see the man's eyes when he answered. The eyes showed the truth, and lying was too easy on the phone. With a letter—well, the old bloke might have answered. He was the literary type, but no one writes letters these days, not the way people did before email. Yet, if it wasn't for the old letters in the suitcase, he wouldn't be here now.

A truck laboured up the hill and backfired. Matt flinched, but at least he didn't dive into a ditch this time. Old habits. He rubbed his shoulder, then relaxed into the run.

As he lopped along the pavement, he mulled over what Fletcher had said yesterday. Of course, the Rhodesian soldiers' reputation was legendary, but war was an odd beast. Since he had stopped fighting to take up research, his thought processes sometimes bewildered him. When you stand back, war is irrational, so destructive, and yet it can be innovative. There is nothing like the threat of death to focus minds.

It occurred to him that war might be a necessary evil to motivate cultural evolution. Would hunter-gatherers have settled, farmed, and grown cities, if not for war? Or did war escalate because humans settled in shared space, accumulated excess and then needed to protect their possessions? Perhaps Eve sinking her teeth into the apple was a metaphor for war, not sex, as his old squadron padre argued.

Since the earliest time, humans had fought wars. The tribal conflicts Fletcher had spoken about were no different. War equated to a need for power. Only the spin-doctors claimed ideology—good and evil, values versus values. If he'd only understood that when he was younger, although he doubted it would have changed anything.

Next, someone would accuse him of being a pacifist. He would never have lived down a statement like that, not from his men. War is war. It was not good or glorious. It was a job. He was a trained killer, sanctioned by the state, but he never saw himself as being a bad person. He did his job and tried to do it according to the rules. Besides, someone had to stop the evil bastards.

The terror in her eyes flashed into his mind and he shut it down, but the shrink's voice droned in his head. *It's always you or them. Going to war is not your decision and therefore not your guilt.* That was bullshit, although it was helpful to think that way. If only he could convince himself.

The adrenalin high of combat was addictive, or it was in the beginning until guilt and grief set in. Adrenalin and camaraderie made it worthwhile, but after twelve years, camaraderie was all he had. The adrenalin faded. The high of combat no longer kicked in. Killing sickened him, in particular those killings the Americans called collateral damage.

He didn't want to have men in his command killed, didn't want to face their families knowing their deaths were his responsibility. Knowing that their husbands, fathers, or sons were no longer with them because of decisions he had taken.

But that was the nature of war. Once he began obsessing about decisions he had made after each mission, he had to resign. If he hadn't left when he had, he feared he'd either have become a dithering fool or have lost his nerve. That was what got men killed, poor planning, poor intelligence, and hesitant men in charge. It was bad enough when soldiers bought it, but worse for civilians caught up in the horror, as she was. Fuck. All she was trying to do was protect those kids.

Matt forced away the image. No decision was worse than a bad one, and that's why she had died. He hadn't made the call. That was the second time Dog had saved his life. He shook his head. No good came from dwelling on the past.

The road curved ahead, in a bend that obscured his direct line of sight, but his mental map of the landscape told him he had half a kilometre to go before he reached the river boardwalk.

At the top of the rise, he began the final length of his run down to the river. The road fell away, making a straight line through high-rise buildings. A car pulled into a parking space across the road and the driver's door opened. A woman swung out, her skirt riding up to expose her thighs as she turned to reach for something on the passenger seat before she got out to lock the door. He admired the view, chic dresser with a stylish blond bob framing her face, nice legs. Shit, he realised she looked like his wife.

He shook his head. Another memory that needed suppressing. Her betrayal was still acid in his mouth. She had been content to marry a soldier, but as soon as he was out of the country, she needed to fuck someone else. He had almost killed the man; such was his rage. Instead, he had left the house with only his Bergen, leaving the front door wide open. What gave him the strength to walk away he never knew, but he had never gone back, ignoring her emails, the entreaties, and phone messages. He hadn't spoken to her again except through lawyers.

The bastard in her bed hadn't known how close he'd come to death. Matt had killed so many others in the preceding weeks; one more wouldn't have fazed him in the slightest. The law stopped him, not concern for killing the bloke. People like that deserved it, screwing another man's wife while he was off doing duty for Queen and country.

His breathing sped up with the memory, and he picked up his pace. It was hard to get up a sweat in the city. As he reached the boardwalk, he slowed to a stop. A passenger ferry made its way upriver, leaving a churning wake that rippled to the banks. What would it be like, commuting to the same office day after endless day? It mightn't be too bad in a place like this, in the sunshine. Better than dreary London.

When he had left the Army, Lloyd's had made him an offer. A few international security agencies contacted him, but he avoided them all, not wanting to get involved with the circuit, sick of the game, sick of killing, sick of clandestine and black ops.

The final straw was that last mission. Poor Bennet bought it, and Brander got a load of shrapnel in his back. If it hadn't been for Dog, none of them would have got out. Even worse, the CO made him lie to his men. He was too old for that shit. Just wanted a normal life, a home, a job, maybe a couple of kids, although when he mentioned it to his girlfriend Nikki, she wasn't keen.

Matt returned to the hotel. The traffic was increasing, and the pavements filled with pedestrians. It took almost twice as long to get back. When he arrived, he ran up the fire stairs, taking them two at a time, and let himself into his room to shower and change for breakfast.

Half an hour later, he idled in the doorway, surveying the restaurant. The usual smattering of people were eating breakfast, reading newspapers, or chatting with colleagues. This was a business hotel. There were no families on holiday, and just one woman sat alone, thirtyish, blonde hair loose around her shoulders. Perfect.

He shook his head at the maître d'hôtel. 'I'm joining someone. Bring me your full breakfast, will you, and black coffee and orange juice.'

'How would you like your eggs, sir?'

'You choose.'

Matt pulled out a chair at her table, sat down, shook out his napkin, and straightened his cutlery.

The startled eyes showed her fluster. He smiled slowly and held her gaze.

She picked up her newspaper and phone to leave.

'Don't go. I need advice.' He fiddled with the spoon next to his plate.

'Excuse me?' Her mouth twisted.

He shifted his focus to her mouth. 'I need help. I'm new to the city and I need advice.' A smile played at the side of his mouth.

She laid down the newspaper. 'I don't live in Brisbane. Why don't you ask reception?'

He gave her the full, lopsided smile. 'I could, I suppose, but I am sure you'll be able to help.'

Now she was curious—good. Wedding ring—check. 'Are you here on business?'

'A conference.' She glanced at her watch. 'I should get going.'

'What's it about?' Elbows on the table, he rested his chin on the heel of his hand, waiting for her to respond.

Her eyebrows arched. 'It's a government thing. You wouldn't find it very interesting.'

'Try me. You'd be surprised at what I find interesting.'

The waiter brought his eggs and bacon and hovered, waiting for Matt to remove his elbows.

He sat back. 'You wouldn't let a man eat his breakfast alone, would you?'

The waiter said, 'The orange juice and coffee are at the buffet, sir.'

'Get it for me, will you?' Matt turned his attention back to his challenge. 'And another of whatever the lady is having.' His gaze enveloped her until a light pink stained her cheeks.

'I'll have another coffee then, milk, no sugar.'

Matt was exultant. Once more, the magic had worked. Sometimes he even amazed himself, but it seldom failed. The waiter mumbled as he walked away to get the coffee, but Matt ignored him and leaned toward her again.

'So, what is it you do with the government?'

Five hours later, he turned into the country lane on which Fletcher lived. He was late for lunch. Christ, the woman had been hard work, or he had lost his touch. When he had realised how late he was, he agreed to have dinner with her, just so she would go. He had broken his own rule, and she was now another complication.

He couldn't understand the compulsion, but as soon as he saw a woman of a certain type, he had to get her into the sack, especially if she was married. Meaningless conquests over which he seemed to have little resistance. When he had met Nikki, he promised himself he would stop, but here he was again. The shrink had told him he was compensating for his wife's betrayal, but this was one area of his life he had not yet controlled.

Chapter Four

The mad woman opened the door. This time, her hair was sleek like seal fur, and he had an urge to touch it. Make-up hid her freckles, and he wished she hadn't bothered. They were her best feature. And her eyes, and her hair and... They were nice eyes, not as psycho bright as yesterday. She was wearing a dress, ironed and neat, and she smelled of flowers instead of turpentine. He followed her into the sitting room.

Fletcher looked up from the book on his lap. 'Ah, Matthew lad you're here. I was wondering if the thought of my granddaughter's cooking had put you off.'

'Poppa!' She didn't seem offended and smiled. 'What can I get you to drink, Mr Reid?'

'Matt, please.' He paused.

'My name is Polly.'

'Yes, sorry' Heat rose in his neck. Christ! She scared the pants off him. He hadn't blushed like that since he was about twelve.

She was staring at him, her eyebrow raised. 'Well?'

His mind thrashed. Well? What did she mean, well?

Fletcher came to Matt's rescue. 'What'll it be, lad?'

The air released from Matt's lungs. 'Whatever you're having, sir.'

'Good, gin it is.'

Bugger, he had intended to buy a bottle.

'Poppa, it's too early to drink, and there's a nice wine to go with lunch.'

'We'll just have an appetite teaser then, my girl. Besides, we have a guest.' He glanced at Matt and back to Polly, his brow furrowed, and his lips pursed into weathered cracks as if to say now is not the time to nag. 'We'll have it out on the back veranda. There's a good girl.'

Matt saw the irritation on her face as he followed Fletcher out of the room. The veranda was a couple of meters above ground level and overlooked sprawling gardens. A broad shallow stairway descended a dozen steps, to meet a shaggy lawn sloping towards a border of azaleas, beyond which the land dropped away into the valley. Strangely shaped blue hills broke up the horizon.

'Glass House Mountains,' Fletcher pointed at the hills, 'Eroded now, but old volcano plugs. Take a seat.' He indicated the cane and floral linen covered sofa and two chairs which were clustered around a cane and glass table. 'Want a cigarette, Matt?'

Matt shook his head. Fletcher lit up, exhaling a long stream of smoke into the clear air. The smell tempted Matt to change his mind.

Polly kicked the screen door open with her foot and the glasses on the tray she was carrying, rattled. Matt rose to help and offered to take the tray from her. She shook her head and placed the tray on the table, revealing a tantalizing glimpse of flesh as her dress gaped.

She asked, 'How do you have it?'

Matt saw Fletcher watching. 'Straight up please.' He wished the damn woman wasn't so confusing.

Fletcher watched the tension between his granddaughter and Matt, and it triggered another memory about a weird picnic he'd been to 38 years ago. The picnic was at Cleveland Dam. Fletcher had sat propped against a rock, smoking, and sipping gin while Jake built a fire mere meters away and Celia sat with her back to both of them.

Jake, tanned, and supple glowed with youthful vigour. Fletcher, almost a decade older, couldn't compete.

Jake continued building a fire and then placed a camp kettle on top to boil. The silence between them was palpable, and Fletcher couldn't take it any longer. He excused himself and walked down to the dam.

When he returned, he found Cee with grass in her hair and a radiant expression on her face. Fletcher couldn't help but curse himself for introducing Jake and Cee to each other.

They had first met Jake at the Round Bar, a favourite watering hole for RLI soldiers. He had hoped to gain information for his book from the man, but Jake had focused on Cee, ignoring Fletcher.

After waiting six weeks for Jake to follow through on his promise to provide information for Fletcher's book, he had received this unexpected invitation to join them on this goddamned picnic. Jake only invited him because Cee wouldn't go alone, and at the end of the day, he still had nothing for his book.

Now, Matt's voice interrupted his reverie. Fletcher pulled himself together. He was becoming an old codger wool-gathering. He said, 'Pardon, sorry I was miles away.'

'I asked if you knew my mother.' Matt cleared his throat. 'Your mother?' Fletcher frowned. 'No, I don't think so. Why?'

Matt remained silent; his gaze fixed on the valley. He raised his glass and swallowed most of his gin. 'My mother was Celia Reid, but her maiden name was Harrison.'

Air shot from Fletcher's lungs as if winded. He couldn't breathe and gasped like a stranded fish.

'Poppa, are you all right?' Polly half rose from her chair, but Fletcher waved her away, and gasped, 'You're Celia's boy?'

It made sense now, but he hadn't known. Why didn't it occur to him? No wonder she had disappeared. But yes, he can see it, the resemblance. His light brown hair, greenish eyes, and olive skin made him think of Jake, but he has Cee's mouth, harder and more sculpted than hers, but the resemblance remained. He felt it when they met yesterday. It was the overt similarity to Jake that led him astray. A thrill ran through him.

He will find her. She'll be in her late fifties. It didn't matter. He would see her again. With an effort, he pulled himself together. 'Where is she—how is she?'

The words fell from Matt's mouth like stones. 'She's dead.'

The renewed shock wrenched Fletcher's gut. He felt ill.

Tears blur his vision and he wheeled himself inside. It was too late to cry, and he was too old, but still tears coursed down his weathered cheeks.

Polly followed him. 'Poppa, what's wrong? Are you sick? Shall I tell him to go?'

Fletcher shook his head. 'I just need a minute. Go back outside Polly.'

Polly returned to the veranda and Matt rose; his forehead creased with concern. Who would have known the old man would react like that?

Polly said, 'Sit down please and finish your drink. Poppa will be out in a moment. Your Mum's passing must be a terrible shock for him. And you—I'm sorry for your loss.'

'I should go, shouldn't have come. What a cock up. Ah, excuse me Polly.'

'Let me top up your drink and we'll wait for Poppa to recover. He'll want to talk to you, I'm sure.'

Matt wanted to escape, but he hadn't come all this way to stop now. The pack lay on the table, he helped himself to one of Fletcher's cigarettes and picked up the lighter before going down the steps to the lawn.

At the edge of the garden, he cupped his hand around the lighter to protect the flame. The smoke seared into his lungs, calming him as he stared across the valley, well aware that his weeks of abstinence had been undone.

The world suddenly seemed vast, the sky a fathomless dome that stretched forever across the mountains. Wisps of ragged cloud floated up the valley, making the scene somehow primordial. He heard Polly go indoors, and minutes later the sound of Beethoven's Moonlight Sonata drifted from the house.

The music reminded Matt of his mother. It was her favourite piece, and memories flooded his mind.

Celia Reid was sitting on the floral covered sofa, her head laid back and her eyes closed. Matt was twelve and had learned this piece at her request. He sat at the upright piano in the drawing room, his fingers stumbling over some of the trickier parts.

'Open your eyes Mum, you can't see me.'

'I don't need to see you, Matthew. I can hear you.'

He stopped playing. She opened her eyes, clouded with tears, and said, 'Don't stop, darling. Play, please play, and let me close my eyes so I can listen.'

Her eyes were always sad. When he asked her why, she laughed, and for days after she would smile to show him she was all right, but somehow the smile never reached her eyes.

He thought it was his fault and tried to compensate when his father was away. He stayed home, helping her and playing the piano whenever she asked. When his father came home he had to leave, staying out late roaming the streets to keep out of the house. When he arrived home, she clung to him, trying to keep him close. He pulled away, unable to deal with the emotional intensity and fearful of enraging his father.

Anger rose in his throat, and he flicked the stub of his cigarette at a bush. Why did he keep thinking of her? She didn't deserve it. She shouldn't have done it. Why did she do it? None of the explanations made any sense. He pushed thoughts of his mother aside and walked back to the house. Polly had topped up his glass, and now a tiny insect floated on the gin. Protein. The liquor slid down his throat, warming the cold ache inside.

Chapter Five

Fletcher stared out the study window as he tried to come to terms with the news of Celia's death. An image of her lovely face filled his vision, and he had tried unsuccessfully to erase the memory by shaking his head.

Matt and Polly's low voices drifted through the window. A moment later, Matt crossed the lawn, stopping at the azalea boarder to turn his back to the wind, and light a cigarette behind cupped hands. Fletcher inhaled sharply. The man was a dead ringer for Jake. Fletcher had never known that Celia had Jake's child. When had that happened?

The sound of Beethoven's Moonlight Sonata drifted along the hallway, taking him back to 1975. Celia had been kneeling beside a record player, her eyes closed, swaying to the music. She had loved this piece—said it was like falling in love.

Celia and Annie had invited him upstairs to a lunch of cheese and South African wine. Annie had been kneeling at the battered coffee table buttering a French stick, its flaky crumbs sticking to the cold butter. She was murdering the sandwich. Her long blonde hair tied back in a ponytail made her seem vulnerable.

Annie had had a crush on Fletcher. He didn't want to tell her he was in love with Celia, so he played the married card instead. It was the truth, but he figured it wouldn't be for long.

Annie said, 'We may have to give up the flat, Fletch.'

'Why?' He stared at her hands, fascinated by her inability to spread butter on bread.

'Ask Cee,' Annie said, giving up on the butter. 'Her father thinks it's not becoming of a young lady to live here. Tell him, Cee.'

Celia shrugged, and Annie continued. 'It's not like you're not earning your own keep or anything. It's just cruel, and if Cee goes, I can't afford this place on my own.'

Celia said, 'You can get another flatmate, Annie. There's a queue waiting for a flat here. Or you can come home with me. The house is enormous, and I never see Mum and Daddy. They're always out somewhere or another. It's easy to get into town, but I'm sure Mum will let us use her car.'

A knock at the door interrupted their conversation. Annie glanced over at Celia. 'Are you expecting someone?'

Celia shook her head.

'You?' Annie asked Fletcher.

'Nope, but I'll get it. It's probably someone buying second-hand clothing or selling something.'

But it wasn't and when Fletcher opened the door, Jake was outside, dressed in camouflage and webbing, his FN

FAL rifle in his hand, a browning nine mm pistol stuck into a holster on his chest.

He acknowledged Fletcher with a slight nod and said, 'Is Celia in?' He spotted her sitting on the floor and pushed past Fletcher, and ignoring Annie, he pulled Celia to her feet and guided her towards the short corridor that led to the bedrooms.

Pale-faced, she at first resisted his pull, but not enough to stop him. They disappeared into her bedroom.

The door shut and all Fletcher could hear was murmuring then silence. That Jake knew which bedroom was Celia's, wasn't lost on him.

'Who's that?' Annie whispered in a voice that sounded like a cat spitting.

A noise from outside drifted in through the open French doors, and Fletcher walked out to the balcony. Below him, was a Bedford truck full of soldiers parked across the entrance to the flats.

One soldier glanced up and, seeing Fletcher, called, 'Tell the Lieut we have to go.'

Fletcher walked back inside, afraid to approach the bedroom. He cleared his throat, glanced at Annie, and used his most authoritative voice. It seemed to have worked, because seconds later Jake walked out of the bedroom, pulling Celia into a last-minute embrace. He kissed her slowly before staring into her eyes as if trying to engrave her image in his memory. He pulled away, nodded to Fletcher and Annie, and left.

Celia smoothed her hair, walked back to the gramophone, and continued flipping through album covers as if there had been no interruption, but her eyes were glittering. Through the balcony door, Fletcher heard a cheer, and the truck took off, its wheels spinning up gravel as it left.

Annie sat back on her heels. 'Who was that Cee?'

Celia smiled, that secretive smile that infuriate Fletcher, and said, 'No one, just a friend. He's going away for a few weeks and wanted to say goodbye.'

Fletcher felt a pain clench his stomach. She gazed at Jake the way Fletcher looked at her. She was in love.

Polly's voice interrupted Fletcher's reverie. 'Poppa, lunch is on the table. Are you ready for it?'

His face felt like it was hanging in loose folds, and he rubbed it to force life back into his skin. As he entered the dining room, he heard Puccini's Madame Butterfly. Vinyl was always Polly's thing.

Matt stood at the window, and said, 'Sir, I am sorry. I can go if you prefer.'

Fletcher waved his hand. 'No, sit down. It's a shock, that's all. Sit and tell me, but slowly. I can't take much more today.'

'Well, sir'

'Fletcher, please, or Alan, even Fletch - not sir, okay?'

'Okay Alan. Well... my mum died a few months ago. Last November. After she died, I found letters from you. I did some research and found you were a war correspondent in Rhodesia in the late '70s before my mother left. So, I thought I would pay you a visit. Sorry, I should have said.'

'Letters, my letters?' Fletcher searched Matt's face, checking to make sure he was telling the truth. She thought of him all those years and yet never contacted him. What a waste, what a terrible waste.

'Yes, I thought you two might have'

'What?'

'Well, I wondered...'

He knew what the man was trying to say, but how would he respond? Will he tell the truth, or lie? He glanced at Polly, but she was cutting slices of quiche. He wished now she wasn't here to hear this. 'Wondered what?' Fletcher was making Matt squirm, but he didn't dare help him out.

'Did you have a relationship?' The air rushed from Matt's lungs.

Fletcher leaned back in his chair, pursing his lips. Polly stopped cutting the quiche, knife poised as she waited for Fletcher's response. The recording ended and the tch, tch, of the needle arm bumping against the centre, was the only sound in the room.

Fletcher picked up his napkin and shook it. 'No, we never had that kind of relationship. We were friends, nothing more. Is this what your visit's about?'

Matt remained mute. Polly put the knife down. It clattered against the flan dish. She walked to the record and lifted the needle. The room was silent as she turned back to the table, but Fletcher stopped her.

'Put on another one, Polly. Bit of background music for the digestion.'

Matt drew in a breath. 'I thought from the letters...'

Fletcher interrupted. 'So, you came here to ask if I had a relationship with your mum? It seems an odd thing to do. You could have written.' This wasn't it. Fletcher knew there was more.

Matt retreated. 'Yes, ah no. That's not it. I wanted... What I mean is that I was writing my thesis on the Rhodesian war. I wanted an observer's account, one whose opinion wasn't clouded. Soldiers are biased. They wouldn't fight unless they believed they were in the right or forced to. What I'm trying to say is that just by participating, they would have made their views open to criticism. The same goes for the politicians and people who lived there, black and white. It doesn't matter what side they took. I know. I've been in a similar situation, and I know that there's nothing definite about war.'

'There were other correspondents....' Fletcher remained sceptical.

'Yes, but you were close. She trusted you. I thought'

Fletcher challenged him. 'There was other research on this subject. Someone at Oxford I think, but there was criticism about bias there too. Can you be impartial about such an emotional topic? I don't think I was. I became too close to the people there.'

Polly interrupted. 'Take a break, you two. Have some lunch. Wine Matt?'

Matt scrunched his mouth to one side and rubbed his shoulder.

Polly said, 'Are you all right, Matt? Is there something wrong with your shoulder?'

He dropped his hand, almost like he was unaware of the action. 'No, I'm fine thanks. This quiche is delicious. Thank you.' His voice sounded guarded.

They ate in silence with just the sounds of music, the scraping of cutlery, and the occasional clink of a glass the only sounds.

Polly broke the silence. 'So, Matt, tell us about yourself. Where are you from etcetera?'

Matt glanced at Fletcher.

Polly's voice added ice to her words as she said, 'It's actually a simple question. For me anyway. I was born here in Brisbane in March 1989. Did my schooling and Uni here. I've travelled, been to Bali and New Zealand and U.K. Hated the U.K. It's so bloody cold, and New Zealand isn't much better, let me tell you. That's it. Not so hard, is it?'

'Polly!' Fletcher frowned at her.

Polly ducked her head. 'Sorry, that came out tetchier than I intended.'

Matt grinned, rubbed his palm across his face, and said, 'Okay, potted history. I was born in London, one gloomy winter's day in February 1980. I went to school in Kent, did my training in Berkshire and university in London. I travelled to Australia.' He gestured at his surrounds. 'Aside from that, I've been to Libya, Ireland, Iraq, Afghanistan, Sudan and Kenya, Uganda, Spain, Portugal, Gibraltar, France, and Germany.' He stared at the ceiling for a moment. 'Oh, and Hong Kong, America, Bosnia... Oh yes, I've been to Mali, Libya, Pakistan, and Uzbekistan, and'

'Okay, okay smarty pants, you win,' Polly laughed. Fletcher was grateful that the atmosphere had lightened. He said, 'Well, I've been'

'No' Polly put her hands over her ears. 'Enough, you've been everywhere. I know I'm the little homebody here, but yours wasn't tourism - either of you. I bet you just travelled as a soldier to war zones, didn't you, Matt? That's not proper travel.'

'I've been a tourist. I've been to' he counted his fingers and grinned at her again.

Polly laughed, and Matt reached across the table for the wine bottle. 'May I?'

She shivered and nodded. 'Screw it. Work can wait.' Matt filled her glass and then Fletcher's and then his own and leaned back in his chair. 'That was a delicious lunch. Thank you, Polly. You're an amazing cook, but you've eaten nothing.'

'Have some more,' she said.

'I thought you'd never ask.'

Fletcher watched the man flirting with his granddaughter. Damn cheek. Then he relaxed. Anything was better than silence.

Matt said, 'Where were you born, Alan?'

'Perth.'

'Oh yeah. I hear they have great beaches. Tell me, why did you stop writing to my mum in 1979?'

Fletcher recognised the clumsy attempt to ambush him but answered evenly. 'I don't know. She disappeared, and they returned my letters. I didn't know she was in London, but it sounds like she was having you. She was marrying some joker from U.K. Ah, sorry. I heard he was in Zimbabwe-Rhodesia to monitor the transition to independence in 1979, but I never knew she was expecting a baby.'

'You met my father, George Reid?'

'No, I didn't. She told me about him, a whirlwind romance. I must admit, it surprised me.'

The words of the letter flash into Fletcher's mind; *please Alan don't contact me again. I'm happy and I don't want you in my life anymore.* They were typed, unlike her usual scrawl, and she called him Alan, not Fletch, which was odd. He had engraved the words deep in his memory. For months afterwards, his grief had nearly driven him crazy.

'Why did it surprise you?' Matt asked.

'Well, Celia couldn't have known him for long.' Fletcher hesitated. He couldn't tell a man about his parentage and anyway, he wasn't sure. It might be a coincidence, although he can't account for Matt's resemblance to Jake. It never occurred to him that Celia may have been pregnant. Perhaps that was why she married the English bloke. But why not Jake? Christ, if she needed someone to marry her, why didn't she ask him? He would have done it in a heartbeat.

'Did you know George Reid, my father, was twenty years older than my mother?'

'No. After I left, I travelled to London and stayed for almost a year. My wife was divorcing me. When I returned, Celia had already gone. I sent letter after letter to her parent's home, but they were all returned. I even visited their house, but someone else was living there. They had sold the house and disappeared. I thought at least her grandfather would have stayed to see everything through to the end, but he didn't. Sorry, I'm getting a little emotional.'

'Did you love her?'

'Yes, damn it, I loved her. Are you happy now that you've wheedled that out of me, even though I do not know what difference it makes to you?'

Fletcher pushed his chair away from the table and wheeled himself out. He needed a cigarette and didn't care what the doctors said.

Matt stood up to follow him, but Polly put out her hand to stop him.

'Give him a moment, Matt. He's upset.'

Matt sat back down in his chair, his head in his hands, feeling like he had messed everything up. He couldn't leave without finding out what he had come for, so he finished his wine and apologised to Polly. 'Will you excuse me? I need another of your grandfather's cigarettes.'

Chapter Six

Matt picked up Fletcher's box of cigarettes. 'Do you mind?'

Fletcher shook his head. 'I thought you said you didn't smoke.'

'I gave up but screw it. I'll give up again after this.'

Fletcher stared towards the mountains, blue in the distance, annoyed at Matt's outward composure, when all he wanted to do was pace. Why come all this way to ask if he loved his mother? He read the letters, so he must know most of what happened. Although perhaps not. The only thing Matt would know was what Fletcher wrote to Celia, not what she wrote back to him. If Matt read her letters to him, he would have known who Cee was screwing. Except for that last letter, all the others were full of stories about Jake. But of course, Matt wouldn't know that. Cee's letters to Fletcher were locked in a drawer in his study, along with the official documents she stole. The question puzzling Fletcher was why Cee would have chucked Jake over to marry the Englishman George Reid. Fletcher didn't pretend to understand any of it then and had long ago decided it wasn't worth puzzling over. Now Matt had brought it all back.

Why did Celia defy her own father to keep seeing Jake, then just up-sticks and marry another man? Fletcher can't imagine Jake standing by and letting that happen. He remembered the fight when Cee's dad found out about her and Jake dating, and the lengths the two of them had gone to see each other.

It must have been late in the war when her parents found out she was dating Jake. Before that, they all played along with Celia's secret, pretending Fletcher was her boyfriend. She said it was because her dad didn't let her date soldiers. They had been on the veranda when Fletcher let it slip.

Harrison didn't say anything immediately, and Fletcher had been relieved. He had thought it would be all right and told Celia she was worrying over nothing. After all, Harrison liked Jake. But the next time he and Jake arrived at the house, it seemed everything had changed. Harrison ordered them off the property, calling Jake the scum of the earth, and the son of a traitor and a whore.

Jake kept his cool, just taking Celia's hand and leading her away. Harrison lost it, and charged, but Jake side stepped, leaving Cee's father sprawled in the garden bed next to the veranda. She had cried, torn between her loyalties to both men.

Jake had grabbed her hand and pulled her down the pathway to the car. Harrison was still shouting obscenities after them, threatening he'd have the Police arrest them both.

After that, Harrison banned Fletcher and Jake from the house and Cee wasn't allowed out. Somehow, she and Jake managed stolen moments. Then the war intensified, and Jake was seldom home, but still they clung to each other.

Fletcher blinked back the memories as his cigarette burned his fingers and brought him back to the present. He threw the butt in the ashtray, already wanting to light another one, and said, 'I need a drink. Want one?'

He glanced at Matt's brooding face, thinking he could see the glimpses of sadness that Polly had mentioned, but Matt turned. Any softness had vanished, masked by indifference.

Perhaps Fletcher had misjudged the man. Matt's demons might plague him, and he was just better at hiding the evidence.

He waited for Matt's reply. Seconds passed before he nodded. How hard was the question? Either he wanted a drink, or he didn't. What was there to think about?

Fletcher had little patience as he wheeled through the door, knocking the doorjamb, and denting the paintwork. He still couldn't control the damn contraption, and the doctor had said to use it for another week, just to be sure— it was bullshit.

He reached the booze cabinet, but his agitation required something more fortifying than wine or gin, and he wondered if Matt drank whisky. Of course, he did.

What person who had seen what he had seen didn't drink too much and anything that's offered. That's what they all do. Some lucky ones weren't haunted by what they had seen and done, but they were the exceptions.

Fletcher didn't believe any exist. Most of the old war correspondents he knows, drink too much, chain smoke and die young. Many take drugs, too, but Fletcher always stayed away from pills. Booze and cigarettes are his poison, and they helped with the ghosts even though the doctor told him he had to quit. He suggested counselling. What did he know, dumb arse? Fletcher preferred obliterating memories and he hadn't even killed anyone. Although, he had seen plenty of death, destruction and its executioners, a thing no one should see. He reached for the whisky bottle, just as Polly walked through from the kitchen.

'Oh, Poppa, not more alcohol as well.'

'As well as what?' Fletcher's voice was defiant.

'You know very well what I mean. The doctor told you that if you don't give up drinking and smoking, it'll kill you, and they won't operate again.'

'He's a quack. Don't nag Polly, not now. This is tricky. We'll just have the one.'

'Well, I'm not hanging around to watch you two obliterate yourselves. I've got work to do.'

'Ah, Poll'

'You're two of a kind. Go on, get drunk together and talk about old times while I clean up after you. It's just not on Poppa. I'm your granddaughter, not your servant.'

Polly stomped out, picking up her car keys and calling over her shoulder. 'Goodbye Mr Reid.'

Matt heard Polly's voice and stood up to go inside. He should have thanked her, helped clear away. It wasn't a good idea coming here. Nothing was going as planned, and Polly, despite her abruptness, didn't deserve poor manners. He'll go in and apologise, wash the dishes or whatever, and leave.

As he walked inside, he heard the front door slam.

Fletcher called out. 'Don't forget the albums.'

Matt strode down the hallway as the car backed out of the driveway. Too late.

Fletcher wheeled into the hallway with a bottle of whisky and two glasses.

Matt said, 'I should go. I'm sorry I shouldn't have come. Can you tell Polly goodbye, and I apologise for my poor behaviour. And thank you for lunch and for seeing me.'

'Bullshit.'

Matt frowned. 'Pardon?'

'I said bullshit. You're not going anywhere. You started this and you'll bloody well finish it. You can't come in here and tell me your mother's dead and ask me if I loved her and then bugger off. You'll finish it. I've got whisky, will that do?'

Matt nodded and then shook his head. 'I have to drive. I probably shouldn't drink anymore.'

'Bugger that,' Fletcher said. 'You'll have another drink with me and that's that.' He wheeled up to Matt. 'Back outside then. Polly won't let us smoke in the house. Carry those glasses, will you? If you want ice, you'll have to go to the kitchen for it or anything like a mixer—water or whatever you have in it.'

Matt shook his head and followed Fletcher.

Outside slate and purple clouds gathered on the horizon, giving the daylight an eerie intensity that made the green of the valley and blue of the hills pulsate. The sublime scenery reminded Matt of the Aberdare Mountains in the Kenyan highlands.

Fletcher twisted the cap off the bottle, handing it to Matt. 'Three fingers for me.'

Matt poured the whisky and handed a glass to Fletcher. Then he placed his glass on the table and took the offered cigarette. After a hit of nicotine, and a slug of whisky, he relaxed. He wouldn't say anything more. He had done enough damage for one day by speaking his mind, and he still didn't know if Fletcher was his real father.

Fletcher cleared his throat. 'What did she die from... your mother? She was young to die.'

Matt said nothing, and the silence lengthened. How could he tell him? The man would go nuts again.

'Well?' Fletcher demanded. 'What's so hard?'

Matt's vocal cords were strung like barbed wire, and he gulped his drink. When the words came, they squeezed out between his teeth, each one a regurgitated razor blade. 'She killed herself.'

After several minutes Fletcher asked, 'How—why?'

'Sleeping pills and booze.' Matt blinked and clenched his jaw.

'Sorry.' Fletcher trailed off.

Matt coughed. 'I don't know why she did it. She never left a note.' He got up, picked up Fletcher's pack and lighter, walked down the stairs and across the lawn to the azalea bushes. He took another cigarette from the pack, flicked the lighter and cupping the flame with his hands, he drew deeply. A man taking his last dying breath.

Fletcher was certain now he was Jake's son. The mannerisms are the same. Why didn't Celia tell him? What happened? Did Jake walk out? She couldn't have told him she was pregnant. It was too bizarre. Jake loved her to distraction. Even in the early days of their relationship, Jake took risks for her.

Fletcher remembered the first time he found Jake risking being caught AWOL just so he could see her. It was 1975 and Fletcher was heading back from Victoria Falls, where he had covered the peace talks between the Prime Minister and various African nationalist leaders. He stopped in Que Que. No, it was Gatooma, on his way to Salisbury. He pulled up at a hotel for lunch.

As he walked into the cool, dim interior of the hotel bar to order a beer, he saw a familiar figure standing hunched over the bar, chatting to his companion.

He walked up behind Jake and spoke to the barman. 'Castle and two of these.' He pointed at Jake and his companion's glasses, both of which were empty.

Jake glanced up to see who their benefactor was. 'Hey, Fletch my Shamwari, what are you doing here?' He turned to his companion and said, 'this is Mr Volker. He's been kind enough to give me a lift as far as Hartley. If you want perspective about the war from a farmer, he's your man.'

Then he said to Volker, 'Fletch here is an Aussie journo, but don't hold that against him.'

Fletcher was struck by the charm of Jake's lopsided smile even in the presence of the grizzled old farmer. No wonder Celia was love struck, and he glanced away as the barman lined up the beers. After that, Fletcher couldn't remember what they'd talked about, but it was most likely the broken-down peace talks he'd been covering.

'Where are you headed, Jake? Salisbury?'

'Ja man.'

'So am I. You can travel with me.'

Volker picked up his hat. 'I'll be going then. Thanks for the beer.' He put his hand on Jake's shoulder, 'keep your head down my china.' Then he left.

Fletcher ordered a counter lunch. Jake explained he had a twenty-four-hour pass after which he was to report to Cranbourne Barracks in Salisbury. He opted to hike rather than wait for transport because that way, he might have more time with Celia. He was worried he wouldn't make it in time, but now Fletcher had shown up. Things were working out fine.

'Does she know you're coming?' Fletcher asked.

Jake shifted. 'No man, I just got the pass this morning, and I was on the road as quick as I could before someone changed their minds. I'll chance it.'

Later, as they walked to the car, Fletcher noticed the sand-coloured beret tucked into Jake's kitbag. 'I thought you were Three Commando.'

'Ja, I was. I passed selection and well... But don't mention it. Even if you are a reporter, I'm trusting you, man.' He stuffed the beret down into his kitbag out of sight.

'So, that's where you were going when you came to the flat to see Celia?'

Jake shrugged but didn't answer.

Three hours later, driving down Jameson Avenue in Salisbury, Fletcher discovered Jake didn't know Celia had moved back home. He felt sorry for the bloke and, despite his misgivings, and offered Jake a bed for the night.

A man should know his father. 'Matt,' he called.

Matt turned around and walked back to the veranda. Fletcher said, 'Just wait here for a tick, will you? I have something you should see.'

Matt nodded. 'Tell me where the nearest shop is. I'll get you more fags. I seem to have smoked most of yours.'

Fletcher waved his hand. 'Tomorrow will do. I have a carton here.' He disappeared into the house. When he returned, he had an old photo album on his lap.

'Sit down, Matthew.'

Matt took the proffered album from Fletcher's outstretched hand.

'See the one, middle left,' Fletcher said.

'Old war photos.' Matt peered at the picture. 'Dead insurgents?' He held out the album.

Fletcher said 'Terrorists,' and waved his hand, rejecting the album that Matt was trying to give back. 'Check out the man on the left.'

He angled the album to catch the light.

The photo showed a man, head cocked to one side, hands cupping the lighter flame as he draws on a cigarette. Light glinted off the barrel of his rifle, a Belgium FN FAL. The soldier was in shorts and tee shirt and black canvas boots tied at the ankles.

Matt nodded. 'I've seen similar photos.'

'Don't you see it?' Fletcher stared at Matt, trying to read his expression.

'I'm not sure what I'm supposed to see.' Matt said, trying once more to hand back the album.

Fletcher pushed it back. 'Try again,' His voice was sharp. 'Who does that remind you of?'

Matt said, 'No sorry. He's vaguely familiar, but it's no one I know. This is old, I guess from the Rhodesian war.'

Fletcher pursed his lips. 'Pour another whisky.'

Matt poured a measure into Fletcher's glass.

'Have another yourself,' Fletcher said.

'Ah, no thanks. I should be going.' Matt rose from his chair.

'Sit down. You can't go yet. I have something to tell you. Sit down, pour yourself a whisky, and give me another of my cigarettes.'

'Alan, I should be going.' He glanced at his watch.

'Sit down.' Fletcher said again.

'No, really Alan, I have to go. I'm meeting someone and I'm late already.' Matt held out his hand. 'Thanks for everything. I'm sorry it turned out so badly. I didn't mean to shock you with my mother's death.' He paused. 'Are you all right, Alan?'

The pent-up words burst out of Fletcher in a whoosh of breath. 'That's your father in the picture. Or I think it is.'

Matt's face blanched. 'What? I mean, I beg your pardon. It's not possible. I thought you were.'

Fletcher stared. 'You thought I... you thought ... me... Oh Christ, what a muddle. No wonder... So that's why... ' Fletcher stopped speaking.

Matt picked up the whisky bottle. He poured himself a drink and helped himself to Fletcher's cigarettes. After a long slug from his drink and a deep draw of smoke, he picked up the album and re-examined the photo. 'There is a resemblance, if one can see such things from someone's back. We have similar builds. It's a coincidence, a vague similarity that's all.' A smile flashed across his face. 'Why did you think this bloke might be my father?'

'I don't know for certain. It's the likeness, that's all. You resemble him.'

'How can you see that from this photo? All I can see is his back.'

'I knew him well. I have other photos, but not here. Polly has them. I told her to bring them home because I wasn't sure. I can see why you came here. Your mother died, and you found my letters, but why think I was your father?'

Matt sucked on his smoke. 'I could tell you loved her from the letters, so I thought maybe you and she...'

'Yes, you wanted to know if we were lovers but even if we were, and we weren't, that doesn't lead to the conclusion I'm your father or that anyone else is besides your mother's husband. Why did you think it?'

'Blood type,' Matt said. 'I found out his blood type. It was on his dog tags that were amongst my mother's effects.'

'Blood type, what will that show?'

'I have blood type O and his was AB negative. A man with AB negative blood never has an O positive child. He will pass either A or B on to his offspring. My father was AB and I am O, so what other proof do I need?'

'Christ.'

'Yeah, I found the blood type, then I found your letters. It ate at me until I had to come and find out for myself. The PhD thing is true, but it wasn't the only reason.'

Chapter Seven

In an art studio in a row of industrial sheds, Polly stepped back to consider her work. The room was large, but light on furnishings. A wooden table hosted a clutter of CDs a player, cups, tubes of oil paint, jars filled with brushes, palette knives, charcoals, pastels, and pencils. Three wooden stools and a low step ladder stand on one side of the table. At the back of the room is a kitchenette with two longer step ladders leaning against the wall. A halogen lamp lit a canvas balanced on an easel. Stacked around the walls are dozens more assorted canvasses, some painted, some prepared, but otherwise still blank. The air is redolent with the smell of turpentine and filled with the sounds of Grieg.

The light in her painting wasn't right. She walked away, crossing to the other side of the room, and turned. The work showed a barren wasteland, bleak and forbidding, premised on the view from Fletcher's veranda, but the burned land was unrecognisable.

She glanced down at her watch and spoke aloud although there was no one to hear her. 'Crikey, it's after one already.' Time seemed to have vanish.

Painting consumed her, sometimes leaving her disoriented for a moment after she stopped. It could take her several minutes to refocus on the present, especially when jerked from deep concentration. Someone once told her it was her brain switching from left to right, from creativity to rational processing. She didn't know if that was right, but it was an explanation.

She would have to leave it for now. Tomorrow, she would figure out what was wrong with the light. She poured turpentine into a jar to soak her brushes and covered the oil paint on her palate with gladwrap. Then she picked up her bag, turned off the music, flicked off the lights as she left.

The other sheds on either side were in darkness. Their occupants had gone home hours ago. Jason next door used to pop in after work, usually with a bottle of wine, and they would sit and talk. She missed that, missed being his friend. He was still pleasant, but since her rejection of his ardour, he'd stopped coming. Now she worked later and later. At least she got stuff done without the interruption.

It was drizzling, and the streetlights flared as she drove home. She loved this time, the quiet night without traffic. It only took ten minutes to get home.

As she turned into the driveway, she saw Matt's car. Why had he left it? Maybe he was still here. The lights downstairs blazed as if Poppa was still awake. They must be still talking.

Indignation rose in her breast as she locked her car and walked into the house. They hadn't even bothered to lock the front door. Anyone could have walked in while they were out the back. A pulse in her neck thumped. She imagined finding them inebriated into idiocy.

It wouldn't be the first time. How many times had she come home to clean-up overflowing ashtrays, empty bottles, even vomit as she helped her drunken Poppa to bed, making up the spare room for his equally drunk companion?

She put down her bag and stalked through to the back veranda. It was empty and there was no mess. The ashtray was clean, the table cleared, the cushions plumped. There were no bottles or glasses left empty on the table or on the floor. Polly's adrenalin faded as the likelihood of confrontation receded.

Back inside, she checked each room as she passed. Poppa's study was empty, as was the sitting room and dining room. The kitchen too, but although it was as tidy as she had left it after lunch, a lingering smell of cooking remained.

She opened the fridge door. A plastic-wrapped bowl of Spaghetti Bolognese sat on the shelf next to the left-over quiche. The faint sound of the dishwasher penetrated her consciousness. She shut the fridge and examined the dishwasher dial. The cycle was nearly complete.

She had maligned her Poppa. But why was Matt's car in the driveway, and why did Poppa leave the lights on, and the door unlocked? Matt's car was still a mystery, although he probably took a taxi to his hotel.

Polly didn't know where he was staying, but if it was a local place, it would have been sensible not to drive home after the alcohol they had most likely consumed. That must be it. She locked the house and turned off the downstairs lights.

As she reached the upstairs landing, she diverted down the hallway to Poppa's bedroom, opening the door a crack to see if he was okay.

In the gloom she could make out his empty chair waiting by his bed, and a lump under the bedcovers snored loudly.

He would call her Cassandra. Dear Poppa, he had even cooked and left her supper and cleaned up after himself. Her barb about not being his servant may have pierced his conscience after all.

She tiptoed backwards from his room, pulling the door closed after her. Behind her, the bathroom door opened, and Polly swung around, a small shriek leaving her lips.

Matt stood in the doorway, a towel wrapped around his waist, his torso bare.

Before she could stop herself, she said, 'Oh, I wondered where you were.'

Her lip caught in her teeth, and she wished she had said nothing. Words always seemed to come out wrong when he was about. The blood rushed into her cheeks and her pulse thrummed in her throat. Then she noticed the livid scar that snaked its way over his left shoulder and sympathy replaced embarrassment.

Matt's smile faded, and his right hand crossed his chest to cover the scar. 'Sorry I startled you,' he said. 'I'm just going to bed. Your Grandfather offered me the guest room for the night. I think we stayed up a little late talking, and I've probably had too much to drink to drive back to Brisbane. Excuse me.' He turned and walked towards the spare room.

Polly stared after him before pulling herself together. 'Yes, of course. I'll find you sheets and make up a bed.'

He scanned her face for what seemed like long minutes. Polly wondered what was going on behind the impassive façade, but his eyes gave nothing away.

'I have sheets, thanks. Alan told me where to find them. I'll let you get to bed, and I'll be out of your hair in the morning. And Polly, thank you for lunch. I never thanked you earlier and I apologise for my rudeness.' He glanced at the floor and back to her. 'Good night.'

Polly gazed after his retreating figure. He was a lithe Apollo. She wanted to paint him. She could see his outline on the canvass, dark and light, shadowy and defined, a man of contrasts.

She scrabbled to find a reason to detain him, but she was too late. He closed the door to the guest room, shutting her out.

She stepped forward and stopped, hoping he might come out again, and then, chastising her own weakness, walked to her room. Did he do all the tidying downstairs? Did he cook the spag boll?

It was not like her Poppa to do it, especially if he'd been drinking. Most of the time he found cooking too hard, never mind while he was drunk, and in the wheelchair. The doctor said only another week. That would be such a relief. She could stop worrying about him once he was out of the chair.

The next morning, she skipped downstairs to make coffee, pulling her hair into an elastic band as she wandered into the kitchen to grind beans. She would be happy with instant, but Poppa was fussy about his coffee. She placed the coffeepot on the gas and walked down the hallway, wondering if Matt had left already.

The scarred shoulder must be something he'd got in the army. A bullet wound, probably. Flawed perfection, she would call the painting. She opened the front door to see if his car was gone.

Matt walked up the stairs and said, 'You live in a beautiful place?'

He was carrying a newspaper and a carton of cigarettes. 'Did you go to the newsagent?'

'Yes.'

'That's miles away. Did you walk?'

'I ran.'

'You ran! But you're not even sweating.' She stopped herself. 'Sorry.' Hot blood rushed to her cheeks.

She opened the door wider to let him pass, but he lingered, and she could feel the heat radiating from his body.

'Do you want coffee?'

'Desperate for some' He continued standing too close.

A bell sounded from upstairs. 'The pot is on the stove. I have to help Poppa.' She moved away.

Matt followed. 'I'll go.'

'No, he won't like it. He hates people thinking he's dependent.'

'He didn't mind last night.' Matt ran up the stairs and Polly returned to the kitchen. Poppa will be furious. He was probably too drunk to complain last night. He could manage most things now they had had the stair lifts installed, but he still needed help to get his trousers on.

She remained in the kitchen, tapping her teeth in indecision. Moments later, a jovial Fletcher wheeled himself in, with Matt following close behind.

'What, no hangover?' Polly asked.

Fletcher frowned. 'No, why should I have? We didn't drink that much and Matt cooked dinner, so we had something to soak it up. He's an excellent cook Polly; I might do a trade. At least he doesn't nag me.'

Matt interrupted. 'I should go. I have imposed on your hospitality long enough. Thanks for everything. If you point me to the laundry, I'll put my sheets on to wash.'

'No' Polly and Fletcher spoke together.

Polly laughed self-consciously.

Fletcher smiled and said, 'You can't go. We have to go through the other photos and compare.' He turned to Polly. 'Did you bring the albums home?'

She bit her lip. 'I forgot.' The coffee bubbled on the stove. 'Matt, have breakfast before you go.'

'Polly, I need those albums. I have to show Jake.'

She scowled at Fletcher. 'Jake, who's Jake?'

Fletcher shook his head. 'I mean Matt.' His voice became sullen. 'I'm going out to the veranda. Bring the coffee, there's a good girl. Come on, Matt.'

'I'll help Polly,' Matt said.

'No Matt, go on out with Poppa. I'll bring it in a minute.'

For a stuck-up Pom and an army lout, he was quite considerate, but it wouldn't do for her to be involved with someone like that, not at all. She had never been one for casual romances and will not repeat past mistakes.

After breakfast, Matt drove back to Brisbane. When he entered the hotel lobby, he was still thinking about Fletcher and Polly. Fletcher puzzled him, alternatively irascible and warm in the space of minutes. Insisting he stayed the night was a little unconventional, but putting up a complete stranger, especially one who arrived under false pretences, was downright odd.

An image of Polly in the hallway last night, with her enlarged pupils in those blue eyes, filled his mind. The confrontation had been electrifying, but she was Fletcher's granddaughter and was off-limits.

Fletcher had insisted he check out of his hotel and stay another night in the guest room, saying Polly could bring the albums back this afternoon. How Polly put up with the old man was anyone's guess.

Matt agreed to return later today as he was keen to see a photo of the bloke's face, although he didn't for a moment believe that was his biological father. Why had his mother never mentioned him? Maybe she had had a torrid affair and kept it hidden. Who said genetics didn't play a role in career choice? Although it was perhaps not that simple. Jake's country was engaged in civil war. Under those circumstances, he would have little choice but to fight. Or did Jake enjoy it as much as Matt had?

After all, Matt had stayed on for twelve years. When they had gone into Iraq, he didn't just go because he was a soldier. He volunteered. Then, after 9/11, he could wait to get a crack at Afghanistan. If he thought about the politics at all, he could not have justified the second Iraq invasion— never believed all that stuff about hidden weapons of mass destruction, but he volunteered anyway.

Hussein was a sadistic bastard, but if they had to fight every sadist running a country, they'd be spread pretty thin. There was no questioning it—politicians started wars, soldiers fought them, but for whom had he been fighting? It was a job, not something to analyse, just paid work.

The military was there to do the bidding of those in power. It was not there for the ordinary people, despite an illusion of democracy. He stopped himself, not wanting to go down that rabbit hole of circular logic again.

'You bastard!'

The woman confronting him jerked Matt from his musing. Her eyes were narrow and flashing with anger, and words shot from her mouth with the force of bullets.

Christ, he had forgotten about her. 'Hello um' Shit. He couldn't remember her name. 'Sorry about last night, but I got delayed. I've just got back.'

'Bullshit. You're a liar as well.'

'Have a coffee with me and I'll tell you about it.'

'Fuck off and die you pommy arsehole!'

She stalked back to the reception counter, stiff shouldered as she waited for the concierge to prepare her bill.

Matt let out a relieved sigh. She would be gone by the time he had showered and packed. He headed to the lift.

She was married. What did she expect? She shouldn't be running around behind her husband's back like that. Although she was right. He was a bastard in more ways than one, but surely she had realised that before she had dumped her conference and jumped into bed with him. He got into the lift and hoped the door would shut before she turned around. His wife's betrayal made him do stupid things, things he wasn't proud of.

He wished he had brought a pack of smokes with him, but that would have to wait. Right now, he needed to shower, pack, and change his airline ticket. This was supposed to be an in-out visit, ask, and then leave regardless of the answer. He hadn't bargain on staying this long and didn't want the emotional entanglement his visit had started. Never mind, it was only one day extra and maybe he would get the answers he'd come for.

Chapter Eight

Earlier that morning when Matt left to check out of his hotel, they had watched him reverse up the driveway.

Fletcher said, 'I wonder if we'll see him again.'

Polly shrugged. 'Who knows? The man is an enigma.'

He turned, and her wistful gaze gave him a shiver of apprehension.

A while later, after she had gone off to pick up the albums from her studio, Fletcher sat on the veranda, pondering the events of the past two days. He lit a cigarette and coughed as the acrid smoke curled into his morning lungs. Perhaps the doc was right. He'd been hammering it the past few days. The sun was warm on his face and his mind drifted to thoughts of Celia. What had caused her to take her own life? Why did she leave Jake to marry another man if she was carrying Jake's baby? It was odd that her father had taken such a dislike to Jake after he found out Cee and he were dating. Before that he had seemed to like the bloke.

It didn't deter Cee. After Fletcher had picked Jake up in Gatooma, Jake had asked Annie to ring her. When Fletcher pulled up outside the Harrison home, she was already skulking in the shadows of a clump of bushes. Fletcher stopped only long enough for her to get into the car before driving off again. She had climbed into the back seat and Jake, who was sitting in the front passenger seat, slid over to join her, leaving Fletcher to play chauffeur.

'Where am I going?' He asked.

There was no answer. So, he drove home, trying to avoid the rear-view mirror, trying not to imagine he was in the back seat with his mouth crushing Celia's soft lips, trying to contain the choking jealousy and unfairness of it all.

He parked outside the block of flats where he lived and stomped inside, leaving Celia and Jake in the car. When they came in a few moments later, her face was flushed, her eyes sparkling, her lipstick smudged all over her face.

At least Jake had the decency to seem contrite. 'If you give me your keys, I'll lock the car.'

When Jake left the room, he turned to Celia. 'Cee, are you sure you know what you're doing?' But her eyes were brimming with something; happiness, Fletcher surmised, as he jerked open the fridge door and took out a beer. 'Want one?'

She flopped down on the sofa, smiling secretly to herself, and it made Fletcher almost choke with jealousy.

After a few moments, Jake came back into the room and handed the keys to Fletcher. He helped himself to a beer from Fletcher's fridge and dropped onto the sofa next to Cee. He took his cigarette pack from his pocket, lit two, and handed one to Celia. Then he threw the pack to Fletcher, and stretched out his long legs, and slipped his arm around her shoulders, all as casually and comfortably as if he'd been doing it all his life.

No one spoke while they drank beer and smoked. Fletcher racked his brain to think of something to break the awkward silence. How had he become the third wheel? He should go out somewhere, but where? 'I think I'll get something to eat. Guido's anyone?' Fletcher jiggled his keys.

Celia glanced at Jake. He shook his head. 'Na man, I'm all right.'

She shook her head. 'I ate already.'

Fletcher picked up his keys and his wallet and walked out. 'If you get hungry, there might be something in the fridge other than beer, but I wouldn't guarantee it.'

He left them but didn't go to Guido's. How could he eat in his current mood and without company? He would feel a fool sitting in the Italian restaurant on his own. Instead, he drove to the Monomotapa Hotel.

It was where some of Two Commando hung out sometimes. Perhaps they would talk to him, although it wasn't so easy to gate-crash this mob. They were close knit and stuck with their mates, but he had once before got an introduction. All he needed was to recognise someone.

Fletcher glanced around the glittering lobby. A fez wearing waiter hurried past, carrying a tray of beers high above his shoulder, weaving in and out of patrons who lounged in armchairs around scattered coffee tables in the crowded room. The first table on his right hosted a group of men in civilian clothes, but there was no one he recognised.

He was just about to leave when he heard an Australian accent.

'Scuse mate.'

Fletcher turned to find a stocky, blond-haired man glaring at him. 'You're blocking the way.'

Smiling, but not budging, Fletcher saw his opportunity. 'Sorry mate, I recognised the accent. Made me homesick.'

The blond man grinned. 'Yeah, where from?'

'Perth,' Fletcher held out his hand. 'Alan Fletcher.'

'Me too. Greg... Greg Moore,' he said, shaking Fletcher's hand. 'Want a beer, mate?' He signalled to a fez-wearing waiter and turned back to Fletcher. 'Lion, Castle, or that other crap?'

'Castle, but it's my shout.' Fletcher nodded at the waiter. 'Bring a Castle and another round.' He indicated the men sitting around the table.

Greg introduced him. 'This here is me mate Alan, from back home.'

The men glanced up from their conversations, nodding quietly, and then resuming where they'd left off. It wasn't anything like Fletcher had expected, but at least he had broken into the group, and it had been as easy as that.

These men had a reputation for playing as hard as they fought, but their ferocity wasn't in evidence now for which he was grateful. They were polite, well dressed and mostly foreign as they engaged conversation in accents hailing from America, Australia, New Zealand, and England, and one from South America.

Fletcher settled in with his beer and his new friend, listening to the conversations ebbing and flowing around him. That was his entry into many meetings with Two Commando, and the beginning of a lifelong friendship with Greg.

The next morning, he had dropped Jake at Cranbourne Barracks and had taken Celia home. She invited him in, and he'd gone, curiosity about her family and home life motivating him against his better judgement.

Once inside, Celia left him in the entrance hall, dashing off down a passageway when she saw her father approaching. Fletcher was confronted by an angry Englishman in his late forties, dressed in the uniform of a ranking police officer.

Commissioner Harrison had drawn himself to his full six feet of height and spoken with chilled fury. 'Who are you and what are you doing with my daughter?'

Fletcher tried nonchalance. 'I'm a friend of Annie's sir. I just gave Celia a lift home.'

'Where was she last night?'

'She stayed at Annie's.' The lie made him redden. 'Annie lives upstairs from me.'

He was babbling, but the interrogation was unjust. He was merely the taxi driver, not the problem. Caution told him that perhaps it was better that Jake's name stayed out of the conversation.

'I rang Annie last night. She never saw Celia.' The man's eyes were like steel, cold and light grey, almost silver in their intensity. 'Where was she?'

Fletcher stood his ground, holding the other man's gaze, and said, 'You'll have to ask her that, sir.'

Harrison said, 'Don't lie to me. You think I was born yesterday? What are your intentions towards my daughter? If you take advantage of her, I'll have your tripe for my tea?'

Fletcher stumbled. 'You have it wrong sir. I respect her... but we are not dating.'

After a long, sceptical stare, Harrison seemed to relent. His brow lifted, and he said, 'You're not a conscientious objector or one of those homosexual chappies, are you?'

Fletcher was indignant, but he played along. 'No sir, I am an Australian journalist.'

Harrison punched his shoulder. 'Good, that's a fine profession. My daughter has taste. Come have a beer.'

It was eight o'clock in the morning, but what the hell?

Harrison said, 'Sorry to give you such a hard time, but my little girl's precious.' He stopped at a doorway and said to someone invisible to Fletcher, 'Miranda, bring two beers to the veranda.'

They walked out to a long terrace overlooking a manicured garden that sloped away from the house. The expanse of lawn merged into rockeries and shrubs at the far edge, bordered by towering conifers. Two gardeners toiled: one squatting on a rock, pulling weeds, another raking leaves.

A short, round black woman came out the house carrying a tray with two chilled glasses and beer bottles beading with condensation. She placed the tray on the table. Bobbing her scarf covered head, she curtseyed. Her broad bare feet slapped against the red polished concrete of the veranda as she walked back into the house.

Harrison took a pack of cigarettes from his top pocket and opening the lid, offering one to Fletcher. Cee's father was an unknown quantity, and Fletcher didn't want to set him off again, so he smoked, said nothing, and waited for the man to speak.

Eventually Harrison said, 'Tell me about yourself—Australian, aren't you?' He glanced at his watch. 'I don't have long. I have a meeting in half an hour, but that's long enough to down a heart-starter and get to know each other.' He paused, scrutinising Fletcher. 'So, you're a journalist, and if you're a foreign journalist, you won't be called up.' He smiled, but the smile didn't reach his eyes. This was a hard man, very English public school, and unyielding.

The phone shrilled, cutting through the quiet air, and bringing Fletcher back to the present. He flicked his cigarette into the ashtray and heaved himself out of the chair to answer it. The voice on the other end said, 'Fletcher my man, you left a message.'

'Bradley, mate, it's about bloody time you rang back.'

Brad and Fletcher once worked together in television. Now he had a successful publicity agency for film stars.

Once the preliminary chat was out of the way, Brad said, 'What's up?'

'You remember Polly?'

'Of course. How is she?'

'Good, yeah, she's fine. I need a favour.'

'What's the favour?'

'Polly needs an agent, someone to drum up a bit of publicity for her and who better than the man she's put to bed drunk umpteen '

'When you put it like that, I can hardly refuse. What's she up to then?'

'She's painting, an artist and she's got an exhibition coming up.'

'Any good, or will it ruin my reputation?'

'I think she's good. She did well at Uni, anyway. Her work might be a tad radical for my taste, but I think it's good enough. She wouldn't have this bloke at the local gallery interested if she weren't.'

'Okay, I'd like to see Polly again, and I'll check out her work. Email me the details. I'm coming up your way in a week or two. We should sink a beer or two.'

After hanging up the phone, Fletcher ruminated for a moment, eyes lingering on the desk. The bottom drawer still held her old letters and those documents she had sent him. He hadn't seen them for years. The documents had arrived in the mail without explanation or any covering letter. Celia handwriting was on the envelopes, but there was no explanation. The first one arrived years after her last letter in '79. When he opened the envelopes, he saw the documents were contraband with the hallmarks of Her Majesty's Government along with top-secret, stamped in red on their covers.

Perhaps he should have done something with them, leaked them to the media, but he worried the Australian federal police would track them back to her, and she'd be arrested for stealing them. Anyway, it was too late now to be of anything other than historical interest.

He could show them to Matt. Although he didn't know how he would handle knowing his grandfather, Commissioner Robin Harrison was MI6—a mole in the Rhodesian command, and a friend to Mugabe.

Among the documents was a top-secret letter, pinned to an envelope in which were several diaries. The letter claimed Mugabe wrote the diaries. When Fletcher eased them out of their envelope, he saw a pile of school exercise books, soiled with mud or blood. He was never sure which and didn't want to know.

He had read them once and found to his horror they were a kind of Mein Kampf or Red Book of Mao Tse-tung. They laid out Mugabe's strategy, not only for war, but also for his leadership of the country. In them, he had borrowed much from North Korea, from the Chinese people's revolution, and from the Nazis. They told Fletcher that Mugabe never intended to lead a democracy. The dictator believed now as he did then in absolute rule, and his own family dynasty. But Fletcher couldn't leak a classified document and anyway, it was too late. The man was already in power.

Other documents arrived from time to time, none of them verifiable, and all stamped top secret. Some of the information leaked out anyway, but some of it never had, like the assassination attempt and short-lived coup d'état that nearly put Nkomo into power. That never made the media, but Fletcher figured it had added some urgency to Mugabe's need to exterminate Nkomo's followers.

He took out Celia's last letter to him, dated 15th July 1979. It was an odd letter, not her usual blue scrawled aerogram. This one was stilted and typed on plain white paper. She had said she was marrying an English bloke and leaving Zimbabwe-Rhodesia. There was no mention of Jake, and she left no forwarding address.

Beneath the box, a corner of another envelope stuck out, and Fletcher hooked it with his fingernail. It contained a photo of Two Commando. Greg Moore had sent it to him after Greg returned home in 1980.

After that first meeting with Greg at the Monomotapa Hotel, they had become good friends. Then Greg met an American reporter, Pattie Stoughton and married her a few years They were still together, living in Perth. Most years they came out to the east coast for a visit.

It was through Pattie that Fletcher got an invitation to an American Crippled Eagles party one Saturday afternoon at a house the Avenues on the outskirts of the capital, Salisbury. The place belonged to the author Robin Moore. The party was in full swing when he got there. Bikini-clad girls mixed with the soldiers, mostly Americans, although like Fletcher, there were others, including Rhodesian soldiers. People sat around a swimming pool drinking beer, talking, or horsing around.

Two men in wheelchairs, victims of land mines, chased each other around in some kind of bizarre ball game, making spectators leap out of their way. That was where Fletcher got his first real insight into what motivated these men. Most of them were ex-Vietnam vets, vehement in their opposition to communism. They believed they had a sacred duty to fight on the side of anyone who was fighting the communist.

As Fletcher listened, he discerned an underlying thread. After fighting a war, how did men adjust to civilian life? They were misfits, missing the camaraderie, and bonds they had forged with men who thought as they did. They needed to carry on. Fighting gooks, killing communists, or terrorists, it was all the same, no matter the country.

Fletcher asked Greg if he felt the same.

'Yup,' Greg had answered. 'We were let down, and we caved in Vietnam. The bloody pollies just wanted us to disappear. We were an embarrassment,' he said bitterly. 'They wanted us to crawl away and pretend we never existed, but not here. Here we're needed, and they appreciate us.' He pulled on his beer and said, 'these people are fighting communism, and fuck man, they need all the help they can get. There are less than a quarter of a million white Rhodesians, and countless communists armed and trained by Cuba, Russia, North Korea, and China, waiting over the border with donated MIGs, tanks and weapons. They could sink this country just by their weight. Here, they barely have enough of anything to get by. They keep their planes in the air with chewing gum and sticky tape. You should see the bloody things. They were old when I was born. We have to be here.'

Fetcher asked, 'So you reckon this is a black versus white thing?'

'No, man, I don't see it that way. The Rhodesian blacks are fighting right alongside us. Three quarters of the Rhodesian security forces are black soldiers and policemen. It's not a racial thing or I wouldn't be here.'

Fletcher wondered how many people remember what it was like. Did people resent the whites who once governed the country, or were their memories filtered through Mugabe's propaganda? Perhaps they felt that at least now they had freedom from white oppression, regardless of the cost, merely the normal teething pains of a new country finding its feet.

If Celia's father hadn't interfered in '75 they might have had a decent settlement earlier with a moderate in charge, avoiding some of the needless slaughter. Christ. He put his head in his hands. Could he have done something about it— exposed them when he found out? By the time Celia sent him the evidence, it was too late. Mugabe's boot was firmly on the jugular.

He heard a vehicle. Perhaps Matt had returned as promised. How could he tell Matt that his grandfather aided the cause that had created so much misery and carnage, not to mention creating so many displaced people?

Chapter Nine

Fletcher and Matt sat companionably on the veranda, smoking and waiting for Polly to come home. A newly opened bottle of gin squatted between them, gleaming reflected emerald light as the glass caught the dying rays of the setting sun. But as night fell, Fletcher's irritation increased. Why couldn't she realise how important this was for him? Next to him, Matt appeared relaxed, but Fletcher didn't believe it. It was the relaxation of a jungle cat. Fletcher didn't like cats much because they preyed on native animals. A few years ago, a stray moved in uninvited. Initially he had tried chasing it, but it hung around, and eventually they became wary friends after he found Polly secretly feeding the blasted thing. He told Polly she'd regret it. They were killing machines.

She loved the cat and ignored him. One day they were sitting on the veranda, the cat asleep on the top step. Polly said, 'How can you say they are killing machines? He's so peaceful.'

Just at that moment, a dove flew overhead. The cat leapt two metres to snatch the passing bird from the air. They had rushed to rescue it, but too late. The dove had died.

An animal is as its nature commanded. Jake was like that. All muscle and sinew, a killing machine just like that cat. Matt is long and lean like Jake, but his arms and shoulders ripple with muscle at every movement, even lifting his glass to his mouth. They were both killer cats. Jake had to be his father, but how could a person prove that without a DNA test?

Was Jake still alive, and what about his family? He would be in his early sixties now. How would a person go about finding him? First, he would need to convince Matt, but for that, he needed the albums.

Where in the hell was Polly? 'She's forgotten!' He slapped his hand on the arm of his chair. 'Just like her. She paints, and the world disappears. If we wait, she'll turn up at midnight or beyond, and she'll have forgotten the bloody albums again. You'll have to go and fetch her home, Matt.'

Matt frowned. 'I don't think that's wise, do you?'

Fletcher said, 'I'll come with you.'

'I'm not sure your chair would fit in the hire car.'

'I don't need the chair for a few yards. The doctor said I can start walking a little every day, and you can help me.'

'What did you do?'

'I cracked my pelvis, fell off a ladder. Now I am supposed to keep off it for a few weeks to let it heal, but I'm sick of it.'

Matt nodded. 'Can't we ring her?'

'No, she'll have switched off her phone, and she doesn't have a landline at the shed. I keep telling her it's not a good idea. What if I need her urgently? She told me that's why she switches it off. Bloody cheek that girls got after all the years I've cared for her.'

'Okay. Tell me where she is, and I'll go.'

Twenty minutes later, Matt pulled up at a group of terraced industrial manufacturing sheds. All but one was in darkness. He switched off the engine, questioning the wisdom of disturbing her. He was humouring the old man, not actually believing that in those albums he would find evidence of his biological father. The prospect was far-fetched, a coincidence. The only interesting thing would be seeing an angle of the Rhodesian war he might not have contemplated.

He leaned against his car and lit a cigarette. He'd gone into battle less afraid than he was of barging into her workshop. At least in war he'd have an assault weapon and wouldn't see the surprise followed by disdain as she realised who was interrupting her work and for what reason.

The black terror in her eyes ambushed him as it still did, but not usually while he was awake. Behind her, children cowered in the corner. He froze. He had never killed a woman knowingly, and he couldn't now, even though she was pointing the ancient Kalashnikov at him. Then she pulled the trigger. Lucky for him, the rifled had jammed.

'Christ,' he shuddered and threw his cigarette to the ground, grinding it into the dirt with his heel. As he walked towards the building Fletcher had said was her studio, he rolled his neck to relieve the tension. The side door was closed, and he knocked. The sounds of Chopin's Nocturne drowned out the knock, and he opened the door.

Inside, a large cavern like room, pungent with the smell of oil paint and turpentine, was lit at the far end only. Canvasses lined the walls. Under a brightly lit arc lamp, she laboured over a canvas balanced on an easel. He cleared his throat, but she didn't turn around.

He moved closer, examining the painting and waiting for her to realise he was there. The canvas showed a wasteland, bathed in jaundiced light. There was nothing pretty about it. His skin prickled as he recognised the valley. What possessed her to paint something so beautiful in such a horrible way? The woman was crazy.

She was deep in concentration, stained jeans and an old tee shirt, hair pulled into an untidy ponytail. He wondered how long he could watch her before she realised he was there. As if by command, she stopped and wiped her brush against the rag held in her other hand before stepping back, eyes squinting to examine her work.

He cleared his throat again, and she leapt to face him with a shriek.

'Sorry,' He grinned. 'I knocked and called out.'

Her dilated pupils stared at him as if she didn't recognise him. The silence lengthened, and he became uncomfortable. 'Sorry to disturb your concentration, but your grandfather sent me.' He gestured at the painting. 'You're good, disturbing, but I am sure it's good.'

The air whooshed out of her as if she had released a dam's worth of energy. 'I forgot.'

Baffled by her behaviour, Matt asked, 'Are you all right?'

'Yes.' She put the brush and her rag down on a table. 'Sorry, I take a minute to switch.'

She walked over to the sink and filled a glass with water, which she downed in one hit and wiped her mouth. 'I didn't realise how thirsty I was.' She glanced at her watch. 'Oh, bugger, is Poppa furious?'

She packed up, filling a jar with turpentine to clean her brushes, splashing some of it on her clothing. Her forehead had a smear of dark paint, but he said nothing.

She walked over to a CD player and turned off the music. 'Okay, I'm ready.'

He followed her to the door, but at the last minute she swung back, almost colliding with him.

'I nearly forgot the blasted albums. Why does Poppa want them so badly?'

What could he say, but it didn't matter. The question appeared rhetorical? She picked up a box. It appeared heavy, and he made a move to help her.

'What, don't you think I'm strong enough to handle it.' Her voice pantomimed a whine.

He held up his hands in surrender. 'Sorry. Bad habit. I had a terrible upbringing.'

She relented. 'Okay, it's really heavy. You can help. Just this once mind, and only because I asked. Just don't make assumptions.'

'Never.'

She was so different from the women he had known, particularly his ex-wife, who used every trick in the feminine handbook to manipulate and get her own way. A viper in the soft downy mantle of a pretty but helpless chic. Polly's attitude was a shock in his lexicon of feminine wiles. She treated him... How... It wasn't as if she acted like a bloke, that's for sure. Blokes didn't behave like that. It was as though she wanted him at arm's length, didn't fully trust him, was not afraid, just saw him as an equal and didn't care enough about him. She reminded him of some of the more capable female officers he had met. He respected them. They were colleagues and in his book, you never flirted with colleagues. This was a novel experience for Matt. His fellow officers, his men, even the women officers, trusted him. He'd like Polly to see him as at least dependable. That was how he saw himself. Although the woman at the hotel this morning hadn't, but then she didn't have the full story. She obviously thought that episode was more than it was.

He followed Polly home. As he retrieved the box from the back seat, he heard her apologising to Fletcher. The old sod should be grateful to have her running around after him. He locked the car and walked into the house, and asked Fletcher, 'Where do you want it?'

'Take it to the back veranda.' Fletcher said. 'Polly will bring us some dinner out there while we go through the albums.'

Matt felt his pulse increase, strode down the hallway, out to the veranda, laid the box on the table, and returned to the kitchen.

Fletcher called after him. 'Hey, where are you off to? I want to take you through the albums.'

'I'll just help Polly prepare dinner, and I'll be out shortly.' Matt's reply was as much of a reprimand to Fletcher's highhandedness as it was to help Polly, and he was not sure why he was doing it. A memory flashed into his mind of his father telling his mother how useless she was. She hadn't ironed out the creases in his shirt and was crying. Matt was furious, wanting to ask why his dad didn't iron the fucking shirts himself. He wanted to ask Fletcher the same sort of question, but then he supposed the old man was in a wheelchair. It was none of his business, but at least this time his silence was not because he was afraid.

He walked into the kitchen. 'Tell me what to do Polly and I'll get the dinner. You take a drink and sit with your grandfather. You've been working all day.'

'No, it's okay,' Polly lowered her eyes. 'I'll get it. We can have a steak and salad. That's quick and easy.'

He opened the fridge. He could make a salad.

As he took the lettuce from the fridge drawer, she said. 'We should have a barbeque.' She raised her arms to encircle her ponytail in an elastic band. Only a thin film of tee-shirt covered her breast. 'I'll defrost the steak if you get the barbie ready,' she said.

Matt dragged his eyes away.

'Oh, and Matt, you can pour me a glass of wine if you don't mind.'

She smiled, and a warm wave of contentment rode up through Matt's chest to loosen his shoulders.

Fletcher barely staunched his impatience at the dinner preparations. The tear in the wheelchair's arm cracked under pressure from his picking, and a large coin of plastic came away. Bugger!

Watching Matt and Polly fuss about the barbeque reminded him of Celia's twenty first-birthday party. Jake had followed her around the garden with his eyes, at the same time joking and chatting with other guests. He never made his solicitude obvious, but he was always there when she needed him. Matt behaved the same way with Polly.

Fletcher tilted his head back and saw another world lit by small fires in tins set about the garden. Jake was talking with Cee's father as if they were old friends, but Cee's parents didn't know of their relationship then. Celia had forbidden any mention of it, saying her father wouldn't tolerate her seeing a soldier, even an officer. At that time, Robin Harrison was Special Branch, and Fletcher suspected he worked for the CIO, the Rhodesian Central Intelligence Organisation, but he never asked, and Harrison never mentioned it, not to him anyway.

Jake moved over and sat next to Cee's mum, Julia Harrison, Robin's wife.

She was a quiet woman of about thirty-nine or forty who seemed to disappear into the background, leaving the centre stage for her husband. Fletcher had never seen her laughing so much. Julia held her hand over her mouth to cover her mirth, her eyes gleeful as if she listened to something Jake said. He kept a straight face while he spoke, although his eyes never left off scrutinising the assembled guests, mostly checking on Cee's whereabouts. He had a way with people, friendly and charming, and everyone seemed to like him. How could Fletcher compete?

Polly called out, 'Dinner's ready.'

She sat next to Matt on the two-seater sofa while they ate dinner. As soon as dinner was done, Fletcher pushed his plate to the side and took an album from the box on the table. He flicked through it. 'Here.' He handed the open album to Matt.

Matt took it and stared at the photo of Jake.

Polly leaned over. 'Gosh Poppa is right. Same shaped face, see at the jawline, the squareness of this part and the way he holds his mouth. It's you.' She clapped her hands and peered into Matt's face. 'What colour eyes, Poppa?'

'I don't know. How would I remember something like that?'

Polly rose to poke about in the box of albums. 'Colour is what we need.' She took another album out and sat down again. 'Oh, pretty girl, who is she?'

Matt stared at the new photo in shock. It was his mother, but not the mother he knew. This was a young woman lying back in

Jake's arms, gazing into his eyes. He averted his gaze as if he was intruding on a moment of deep intimacy.

He took the album from Polly's hands and tilted it to the light. Rather than the short, highlighted hair he had always known her to have, this woman's hair fell in a dark sheet to her waist. Jake's hands were entangled in it

A strange sensation, anger, fear. He didn't know what rushed through him. This stranger, who until this week Matt didn't know existed, might be his father, and he didn't know how to handle it. Why had his mother never mentioned him?

Polly said, 'Is it your mother?'

He nodded, giving the album back, unwilling to speak. There seemed to be something blocking his throat. He got up from the cane sofa and walked down the steps. When he reached the azaleas, he took a cigarette from his pack and lit it, giving his brain a moment to absorb the shock.

If George Reid wasn't his biological father, why was he surprised to find this man was, or might be? He'd need a DNA analysis to know for sure. Why was he so disturbed that his mother was in a physical relationship with another man? What had happened to him? Why did she marry George?

The full moon cast Matt's shadow across the lawn as he lingered at the garden edge, gazing into the night until he had his emotions back under control. He ground out his cigarette and returned to the veranda, to where Polly and Fletcher remained silent and watchful.

'It's late; I might go to bed if that's all right. I'll leave tomorrow. Thanks for the information, Alan, and for your hospitality. Good night Polly and thanks for dinner. I'll be out of your way early to catch my flight.'

Chapter Ten

The next morning Polly heard the whirr of the washing machine. She checked the laundry just as the machine completed its spin, and the door clicked open. She pulled out the sheets he had slept in and stuffed them into the dryer.

After closing the dryer door, she walked down the hallway, knowing he was gone, but she wanted to be sure. How rude to disappear so early without saying goodbye, but at least he'd washed his sheets. No car in the driveway, definitely gone. She sighed and resumed making coffee. There was a note by the coffeepot.

Dear Polly

I couldn't sleep so I made an early start. I am flying back to London today and I wanted to say goodbye. You've been very kind. Please thank Alan for me and tell him I'm sorry for the false pretence. We might have sorted things out quicker if I'd been more honest, but I'm glad I came. I have my answer, even if it wasn't what I expected. I've left my sheets in the washing machine. Sorry I couldn't wait until you were up, but I wanted to get an early start to make the London flight.

Thanks again

Matt.

Annoyance faded to disappointment as Polly placed the letter back on the bench. If only he'd wakened her, she could have said goodbye. He was a much nicer man than she first thought. The note hadn't mentioned the photos. If he was still here, she could have scanned them for him. She still could, but she didn't have his address. Oh well, perhaps he didn't want reminding. She could appreciate that, understood avoidance.

Her parents' accident was still painful. Why court sadness when the memories go with you everywhere? No need for graphic details. When they died, she had gone crazy for a few years, lost friends, shirked school, hung out with undesirables, smoking dope until she met Richard. She shuddered at that memory. Had it been loneliness and loss that had driven her into his arms.

It was an episode she wanted to forget. Fifteen years old, and in love with her teacher, a married man with three children. Although at least she returned to school, even if it was just to arrange the next assignation. Had she really believed he had loved her? What an idiot. After Fletcher found out and reported him, it took her months and several counselling sessions to see him for the pervert he was.

She put the coffee on to percolate and ran upstairs.

'You awake Poppa?'

An indistinct grunt told her he was. She glanced along the hallway towards the bathroom, remembering Matt's naked torso, smooth and muscled, the scar over his shoulder. She spun around and walked towards the spare room. The place was tidy. The bedding folded in military precision, with each of the blanket's edges aligned.

Polly's throat constricted. If only she could have said goodbye. She picked up a pillow, raising it to her face, inhaling the scent of his after-shave. Realisation of what she was doing hit her and she replaced the pillow, smoothing it with her hands before skipping back to Fletcher's bedroom door.

'Need any help, Poppa?'

The door swung open, and Fletcher stood erect before her.

'Poppa the chair.'

'I'm sick of the blasted thing. I've been in it six weeks today. That's enough. I'm fine.'

'Wait for the doctor'

'I'm not sitting in that contraption anymore. Where's the coffee?'

They sat at the kitchen table, each with their own thoughts, until Fletcher broke the silence.

'I like the man.'

Polly said nothing.

'Well.' He demanded, 'what did you think?'

'About what, Poppa?'

'Matt.'

'Oh, he's all right, a bit rude to rush off like that, but I suppose he had to catch a plane. At least he had the courtesy to clean up after him. Good manners, his mother taught him well.' She sipped her coffee.

'Come on Polly, I know when you're prevaricating—spill it.'

'Well, he was nice. I thought at first he was arrogant, and he is a bit... I still think he was sad, damaged.'

'Why damaged?'

'Oh, I don't know. Stop bugging me. I have to go to work.'

'Just tell me one thing'

'What?'

'Should I have shown him the photos?'

'I don't know. It's too late now to change your mind. Just let it go.'

'But you saw his face, his reaction. I'm not sure I did the right thing. He thought it was me?'

'What?'

'Thought I was his father. That was why he came here.'

'You're kidding! Why?'

'I wrote letters to his mother.'

'What did you say?'

'It must have been in the one where I asked her to marry me.'

Polly gasped.

Fletcher forged on. 'It was after my first wife divorced me. I couldn't bear being apart from her, and I thought I would just take a chance. The war was over by then. I didn't know she was pregnant, though. Christ, it wouldn't have mattered.' Fletcher put his head in his hands. 'I would have married her on any terms.' Tears ran down his cheeks. He pulled out his hanky blew his nose.

Polly's voice lowered as she said gently, 'What did she say?'

'It was so strange. She said to leave her alone and not contact her again. She was marrying some other bloke, an Englishman. As soon as my divorce came through, I flew back to Zimbabwe, but she was gone.'

'Gone where?'

Fletcher shrugged.

'What about Jake? Did you talk to him?'

Fletcher shook his head. 'He'd disappeared. Anyway, I had to leave. I had a contract to cover the Russian invasion of Afghanistan. Then the Iran/Iraq war and when I came home, I found a parcel waiting for me from her. She sent me several after that but never anything personal, just classified documents. The first parcel contained a file on the Gukurahundi. At first I was afraid to even read the stuff. It had top-secret stamped all over it. In any case, I was too late to do anything to stop it. So, I locked it away, terrified I would be caught. In hindsight, I'm not sure what I could have done anyway without Celia being arrested, but I should have done something more. I let her down.'

'I don't know what you're talking about. What's Gukurahundi?'

'It's chiShona, meaning the first rains that wash away the spring chaff. Mugabe was cementing his dynasty, washing away his rivals, particularly his biggest threat and old enemy, the Ndebele. It was the first part of Mugabe's blueprint, his strategy to exterminate the Ndebele, and subdue all the tribes other than the Shona. In '82 he killed over twenty thousand of his rivals in the Gukurahundi, helped by the North Korea led fifth brigade. That was when I also found out that Celia's father was MI6. He fed the Brits and Mugabe information that helped Mugabe's cause over that of Nkomo. How can I tell anyone that? I only have circumstantial proof. Anything else is still classified and if anyone knew I had the files, I would be arrested.'

Fletcher put his head in his hands, pulling his sparse hair until it stood in upright strands. 'Mugabe will never allow democracy. There is no way he will lose the prize he won by manipulation and deceit. Sorry Polly, I shouldn't be going on. It all happened a long time ago.'

'But it's still happening. Mugabe's still president.'

'Yes. Now his blueprint's almost complete. He needs to consolidate his power. He'll do it and there's nothing I can do to stop it.'

'But they have a shared government arrangement now. Things are getting better with Morgan Tsvangirai sharing power. At least now, they are masters of their own destiny. It's better than colonialism and disenfranchisement. They still have the elections later this year. Surely, this time, they will vote Mugabe out of power and the country will heal itself.'

Fletcher shook his head. 'It won't happen—He'll have his dictatorship without interference. Ultimately, he wants the North Korea model. Mugabe and his henchmen won't allow shared power, and the Chinese will help him so long as he gives them the resources they wanted in exchange. Now of course it's diamonds and minerals. What they don't realise is the Chinese are exploiting Zimbabwe in the same way as any coloniser, but without the responsibility and rule of law that goes with it.'

He gazed at the ceiling, fighting back tears. 'I didn't understand how tragic it would all become, and I didn't know how to tell anyone, or even if I did, who would care? All those in power knew, anyway. All I could do was expose their dirty linen. They wouldn't thank me for that. Besides, I worried that Celia would be arrested for stealing classified documents.'

'You were right,' Polly said. 'Look what happens to whistle-blowers, Julian Assange, Edward Snowden, or that other person, Manning. You can't say anything. They will lock you up if you expose their secrets.'

'Yes, but they let it happen. They knew from 1975 when Smith tried to make a deal with Joshua Nkomo to transition to black rule. The CIA put paid to that and let the war carry on.

Not just carry on but actively helped by aiding recruitment of unsuspecting ex Vietnam vets, who volunteered willingly to help stop communism, not knowing they were being manipulated to prolong the war, to give the Americans time to ensure Nkomo wouldn't win. Even after Smith made a deal with Nkomo and Muzorewa to have full elections in 1978, Mugabe vetoed it, and the CIA and MI6 sided with him because they were worried Nkomo would bring the Russian tanks against Muzorewa. Nkomo was gearing for an all-out assault. For Christ's sake, he had MIGs waiting in Angola. All those dead and a country destroyed. What for— a deal made between secret services, the Brits, and the Americans to keep the Russian's out of Africa.' He glowered at his granddaughter and then softened. 'I'm sorry Polly, I shouldn't have unloaded on you.'

'What can you do?'

'Nothing, I'll do nothing.' Fletcher rose from the table. 'I'm going into my study. I need to think.'

Polly inspected her coffee cup. 'Poppa, you said he disappeared. What did you mean?'

'What? Who disappeared?'

'You said that Jake had disappeared?'

'Yes.'

'What happened to him?'

'I don't know. Someone said he took the gap.'

'What does that mean?'

'Oh, it was a saying. When Rhodesians fled the country, people called it taking the gap. The stalwarts frowned upon it, but who could blame them? The country was going to hell, and their sons were dying. I would have left if I were in that situation.'

'He wouldn't have left without Celia, surely.'

'I don't know. Leave it, will you? I can't cope with any more interrogation. I need to think. Ah, sorry, Poll. That was unfair.'

Polly got up. And took her cup to the sink. Her grandfather's crabbiness didn't bother her. He was often like that, and she was used to it, but she had a nagging feeling he was not telling her everything and that concerned her. But all she said was, 'I'm going to the studio. Will you be okay? Shall I bring anything home?'

Fletcher shook his head. 'I'm going to do some research. I'll see you when you come home. Don't be too late Polly.'

He kissed her forehead, surprising her. He was not usually affectionate. Her eyes prickled.

Fletcher limped into his study, exhausted from the unaccustomed walking. Perhaps he should have waited for the doctor's opinion before giving up on his chair. His thoughts reverted to Polly. She was all the family he had. There were his sister's twins, of course, but they lived in Perth. They hadn't kept in touch after his sister passed on and he hadn't tried to connect with them or her husband.

He had neglected his family being away, covering war anywhere it happened, and had never settled after losing Celia. He married again, had a child, but was seldom home. He had also never become involved in a country's plight again after Rhodesia. It had been a mistake to take sides when all he should have been doing was recording news for the world, as if none of it mattered to the individuals involved. Objectivity, they called it.

Had his life been worth it? He had thought so once, but was covering war and exposing the truth of any real value? It didn't change the terrible things that had happened. The adrenalin and excitement of war was what he'd lived for. Yet of all the wars he covered, it was the Rhodesians whose attitude struck him most, that last outpost of the great British Empire.

The Rhodesian determination was evident to Fletcher in the 1978 Zambian raid, after the first Vickers Viscount was shot down by Nkomo's military. Of all the shocks and horrors of war he'd encountered, that one made the most impact on him. To shoot down a civilian plane was an easy target. It was an act of terrorism. There was no doubt in his mind about that, especially when the people who shot down the plane slaughtered the remaining survivors.

When it happened, the BBC had contacted him. He was to get an interview with Joshua Nkomo. Apparently, they had already rung him, but all he said was his men had brought the plane down with stones.

Until that fateful moment, it seemed to Fletcher that the Rhodesian war was nearly over. Already Smith had an agreement with several black leaders to go to elections the following year. He had announced his deal with Nkomo a few days before, so the shooting down of the civilian Viscount was doubly shocking.

When it first occurred, Fletcher, like most others, was ignorant of the events that unfolded, until Celia turned up on his doorstep without Jake. She was crying and for a moment a surge of elation rushed through him with the hope they had quarrelled. He had led her inside, rummaged in his fridge for a chocolate egg left there from Easter five months before. Then he held her while she sobbed into his chest. Once she recovered, he heard the story.

They were at a movie matinee when a message flashed across the screen, recalling all military personnel. Jake caged a lift to barracks and Celia walked to Fletcher's flat, but by the time she got there she had worked herself into a state, believing she would never see Jake again.

Fletcher phoned a contact he had at *The Rhodesian Herald*.

'Mate, what's going on?' Fletcher asked Colin.

'No idea, Fletch, except there's a strong rumour a plane's been shot down. We're waiting for confirmation and details.'

More news trickled out across the rest of that day, and then the BBC called. Fletcher rang an old colleague, David Bromley, who lived in Lusaka, Zambia. Fletcher and Dave had been friends back in the early days of their careers in London. They had both done a cadetship with the Evening Standard. Dave went home to work for the Lusaka News Service. After independence, he reckoned his country needed every reporter they could get to keep the politicians on the straight and narrow, and it was his personal responsibility to hold them to account.

In the early days, while they were in London, Dave and Fletcher had stand-up rows about the Rhodesians. Dave was unsympathetic to their plight, saying they shouldn't have declared independence unilaterally, but surely even he could not countenance the shooting down of civilian airliners.

Dave set up the meeting, but when he and Fletcher arrived for the interview, nothing was as Fletcher had expected. Nkomo struck him as an incongruous contrast of smiling cheer and jovial callousness. His cherubic cheeks bulged above a beaming smile.

'Would you like tea?' Nkomo held up a hand to a man hovering near the door.

'No, thank you.' Dave and Fletcher said together.

Once seated, Fletcher opened his notebook and asked the first question.

'Mr. Nkomo, you have claimed ZIPRA shot down the Vickers Viscount Hunyani on the 3 September. Did you give that order?'

'Yes.' Nkomo's face remained impassive, relaxed, hands clasped around his stomach. His immense bulk filling the chair, his whitening hair giving the impression of an elder statesman.

'Can you tell me why you chose this plane?'

Nkomo's gaze rolled heavenward, then tracked left, and through the window. 'I had intelligence that the flight was picking up troops at Victoria Falls.'

'But it was a civilian plane, wasn't it, Mr. Nkomo? The people killed were all civilians.'

'That's what Smith's propaganda will have you believe, but it was a troop carrier. The Rhodesians use civilian planes to carry troops.'

Fletcher let the statement go. 'You say the flight took off with troops from Victoria Falls?'

'Yes.'

'I understand the Air Rhodesia Flight 825 was a scheduled passenger flight and was just taking off from Kariba when it was shot down. Its passengers were all holiday makers.'

'That is just Rhodesian propaganda.'

'With respect, I don't think that is true, Mr Nkomo. There were fourteen survivors, ten of whom were shot and bayoneted by ZIPRA soldiers at the scene of the crash, some of them children.'

'Pah, more Rhodesian propaganda. We have brought down at least thirty other Rhodesian planes, but they never admit that to you, do they? Now they are trying to make out we would act like terrorists.'

'What other planes have you brought down, Mr Nkomo?'

'Ask the Rhodesians.'

Again, Fletcher let that go. 'What surface-to-air missiles do you have?'

'We have rocks, nothing more.'

'But the plane was brought down by a Soviet-made Strela 2 infrared homing missile. Are the Russian supplying you with these weapons, Mr. Nkomo?'

That was when Nkomo got up, calling an end to the interview. Dave was furious at Fletcher for being belligerent, although Fletcher thought he was relatively mild in his approach. He felt much angrier inside.

As they were leaving, a man in uniform approached Nkomo, and Fletcher overheard the words 'British SIS' whispered in his ear. It appeared Nkomo had a phone call from the British intelligence service waiting for him to attend, and Fletcher wished he could stay to listen.

As they drove back to Dave's house in Lusaka, they stopped at a roadblock. A soldier stood by the window of the car until Dave rolled it down.

'Can you gentlemen tell me in which direction you are heading?'

'Home. What's up?'

Fletcher examined the white soldier with suspicion. He wore camouflage, but something wasn't right. There weren't many white men serving in the Zambian army at that stage, and the camouflage pattern and colour was all wrong. Not that he was a military uniform expert.

The soldier said, 'There are military exercise going on right now. No planes will be taking off or landing for the next half an hour. Please gentlemen, go home, and have a nice extended lunch. We'll be out of your hair in no time.'

He straightened and stepped back to let them turn around, cradling his rifle in his arms. That was when it dawned on Fletcher. The man was a Rhodesian soldier.

They arrived at Dave's home as the bombs began falling. The distant sounds of heavy artillery drowned out any further thoughts of trying to leave Zambia that day. That night Fletcher stayed with Dave, and they heard more fighting, more bombing, and gunfire. It wasn't until later they found out what happened.

In retaliation for the killing of innocent civilians, the Rhodesian's had taken over Zambian airspace, bombed ZIPRA camps, and raided Nkomo's house, but Nkomo had already fled. Warned by the British, Fletcher assumed. It wasn't until much later he discovered it was Celia's father, who had passed on that warning.

After the Nkomo interview, Fletcher filed his copy, but it wasn't published. The world ignored the atrocity, just like they disregarded the Gukurahundi. It wasn't until after he was back in Salisbury that he thought of something else Nkomo had said.

Nkomo and Mugabe would remain partners under the banner of the Patriotic Front until they had defeated Smith. They had never intended to agree to any settlement, no matter what Ian Smith believed. What did Nkomo think would happen? Certainly, Fletcher knew what Mugabe was planning. After taking the country, Mugabe planned a civil war to rid himself of Nkomo.

Mugabe had no intention of cooperating. Mugabe won the elections after paying off all the tribal chiefs and promising peace. It was all people wanted, and they would never get it while Mugabe was not in power. He had proved that when the black leader of the United African National

Council, Abel Muzorewa, was in power in the days of Zimbabwe-Rhodesia's transition to black independence. They were some of the bloodiest days of fighting in the war.

Somewhere in all that mess, there was some link with Jake's disappearance. If he could find out how Jake fitted in, he would know what had happened to him.

He picked up the phone and dialled a number in Western Australia.

'Greg, mate, I was thinking of coming out to Perth in the next month or two and wondered if you would put me up for a few days.' The last time Fletcher had seen Greg was a year ago, when he and Pattie came out to the Sunshine Coast for a holiday. Their son Hugo was in the Australian Federal Police.

They chatted for a while and then, after Fletcher hung up, he took the hidden box of secrets from his drawer.

Part Two

Chapter Eleven

Details of the Australian landscape diminished as the plane gathered height. The land below turning from grey green to a vague brown wash. The sky was an eggshell blue, without a cloud. Matt rested his forehead against the window, remembering the adrenalin rush before a jump.

He was feeling good about life and couldn't help the nostalgia even though his decision to leave the army was a good one. Probably not before time, as the Ministry of Defence was outsourcing more and more of British security to contractors. A mistake in his view, although he knew little about the machinations of politics.

The undercarriage grated, and the Captain welcomed passengers. A flight attendant doing the safety talk caught his eye and smiled, touching her blonde hair as she did. It's an invitation he ignores. He'll be home tomorrow, and he promised to ring Nikki the moment he got back. Nikki was good for him, and he makes a promise to himself that he will put more effort into their relationship.

'You've become institutionalised,' she once said, taking charge and organising his life. From their first meeting in their local pub, she took control. Matt was just back from Afghanistan, disoriented by the everyday humdrum of London. She walked into the pub with two men, her brother, and his boyfriend as it turned out. She was single, and pretty, an oasis to a man dying of thirst.

He pushed thoughts of Nikki aside, wondering about Jake. Did he abandon Celia or know she was pregnant? Polly persuaded him that Jake might be his father but believing wasn't proof. He needed verification. At least it wasn't Fletcher. If Jake Ryder was a candidate, he could ask his grandmother. She knew Jake, so she might know the truth.

He glanced at his watch. It was his 33rd birthday. It had almost slipped his mind. A third of a century had gone by in a blink, and he had nothing to show for it. No accumulated assets, or at least none he had earned. He had inherited the Chelsea house from his mother, who owned it courtesy of George Reid's family legacy. He owned a car, but other than that, he could count little other than failure. Failed marriage, a career less failed than ended, a quantity of bad habits, some pretty bad dreams, and only a vague idea of his plans for the future. If he undertook a mission as little prepared, it would fail.

He should sell the house and focus on building a new life with a different career in a place without memories. The house wouldn't bring in much although it was prime real estate, but the current economic climate had done negative things to house values. The place was old, and way too big.

like a mouldering old dear in a street of trendy renovated homes. His mate Brander's wife had been right when she had once observed a hut in the jungle might suit them all better.

She had been spitting mad when she said it. Matt didn't blame her. They were just back from Iraq when she came home from work to find her sitting room full of drunken soldiers. The place was a mess, beer bottles and overflowing ashtrays, clouds of cigarette smoke and stale body-odour mingling with left over curry.

He smiled at the memory, but selling his home was a daunting prospect, particularly having to do all the sorting and packing of his parent's belongings. He paid the bills, but otherwise he hadn't touched his mum's stuff since she had killed herself.

The old surge of anger hit him again. Why did she kill herself? The question consumed him. To hell with it. He signalled the flight attendant. Screw good intentions. He needed something to take the edge off.

'Whisky please.'

'Yes sir. Is there anything else I can do for you?' She smiled and touched her hair again.

He hesitated. 'No thanks, just the whisky.' Matt gazed out the window, trying not to think about the temptation on offer. An image of Celia in Jake's arms filled his mind. For as long as he could remember, her hair was blond with highlighted streaks and always kept short. It was never long and wild like the photo. He should have asked Fletcher for a copy of the photo. It was disturbing, but it told a story he wanted to hear. Damn it.

The woman in the seat next to him said, 'I beg your pardon?'

Did he speak aloud? 'Sorry.'

'Can you lower your window shade? The sun's blinding.'

'Yes, sure.'

She was fortyish, plain, with her hair scraped back from her face in a tight bun. A spinster dedicated to her career, judging by her bare wedding ring finger. She scrolled through a document on her laptop as he pulled down the shade. The plane's entertainment screen flickered. Perhaps they would show a movie worth watching.

The flight attendant brought the whisky and a glass of ice. What is it with these colonials and their ice? He asked for another glass to get rid of the ice, but she misunderstood and brought a glass of water with more ice. He sighed, drank it down and emptied both lots of ice into one glass, before pouring the whisky from the miniature bottle into the empty glass. Then, after all that, he threw the whisky down in one hit. Could have taken it straight from the bottle, but he needed to keep a veneer of civilisation.

Cheers, happy birthday boyo, he said to himself. He opened a book he'd bought at the airport. The whisky had stopped the looping thoughts, but the novel didn't hold his attention. He signalled the flight attendant to bring another whisky and plugged in the headphones, tuning into a classical station.

Beethoven's Moonlight Sonata was playing, immediately conjuring an image of Polly. Funny how this piece had once reminded him of his mother. Now it was Polly who flashed into his thoughts. The memory of her warmth unsettled him. Before being conscious of what he was doing, he got up. The new leaf would have to wait.

The flight attendant sat in the jump seat at the front of the plane flicking through a magazine, which she closed when he appeared.

'Hello sir, would you like another whisky?' She jumped up and smoothed her skirt.

He nodded. 'What about you? Can I buy you one?'

She giggled and twirled a strand of hair. 'We're not allowed to drink on duty.'

'Pity.'

Her nose was rather long for her face, and her ankles were pudgy. The imperfections made her vulnerable, and he wasn't proud of himself. 'Are you permitted to talk with the passengers while they have a drink?'

'Oh yes, of course.'

'Good. ' He sat down in the jump seat she had vacated.

She stepped into the galley and crouched to extract a miniature whisky bottle from a drawer. Her skirt rode up her legs, more than was possibly necessary.

He asked, 'Where are you from?'

Instead of replying, she said, 'I'll take the drink to your seat, sir.'

His gaze settled on her mouth. 'I'm Matt and you're Tiffany. Pretty name.' His smile widened, and he patted the seat next to him. 'Sit for a moment, Tiffany. It's my birthday. You wouldn't begrudge a little companionship for a lonely birthday boy.'

She sat down, back straight, knees together. He took her hand, playing with her fingers. 'Why are you nervous, Tiffany?'

'I'm on a break and will have to go back soon. Passengers aren't allowed to sit here.' Her eyes flashed back and forth like a trapped bird.

He smoothed the skin on her wrists with his thumb. 'We'll have to hurry then, won't we? You'll let me take you to dinner in London, won't you?'

She searched his eyes. 'Really?'

'Yes Tiffany, I'm serious.'

She laughed, relaxing a little, and glanced up from beneath thick sooty lashes. He placed the empty whisky glass on the galley shelf. Then, turning her wrist over, he rested his lips on the soft skin.

She giggled again. 'Not here.'

'Where then?'

Fifteen minutes later, he left the lavatory, while she straightened her uniform. He slouched back to his seat with his usual dose of regret and shame.

By the end of the flight, he had drunk too much whisky and woke up with a dead man's mouth and his head on Ms. Career woman's shoulder. He muttered a groggy, 'Sorry.'

She was a decent sort and said, 'It's okay.'

What he needed was a splash of cold water on his face, and coffee to wake him. He excused himself and slid from the seat to go in search of Tiffany.

Instead, he found the steward, Toby—Toby and Tiffany. How cute. Matt asked Toby for coffee.

Toby was regretful. 'We're coming to land, sir.'

Matt returned to his seat, and the career woman put on headphones. A not-so-subtle hint she didn't want to talk to him. He didn't blame her. If he were giving her advice, it would be not to speak to him either. He was a bastard in more ways than one.

A thought intruded. Did George Reid know he was raising someone else's bastard? It would explain a lot. Did he know Celia was pregnant when he married her? George wasn't home much when Matt was younger. That was a good thing. George must have known, or at least suspected, Matt wasn't his son. As a child, he had referred to him mostly as that little bastard.

A memory from childhood popped into his mind. He couldn't remember what he did, and being in trouble was nothing new, but now it held a special significance.

George was in one of his frequent rages and called Matt to him. Nine-years-old and defiant, Matt stood in front of his father, determined this time he wouldn't cry, knowing it gave George satisfaction when he did. The first open-handed slap connected with his ear, knocking him to the floor.

His mother raced into the room and stood between them while George took off his belt and wrapped the tongue around his hand. Then he waited for Celia to get out of the way. The buckle swung back and forth, mesmerising Matt. When she didn't move, George hit her, the belt wrapping around the flesh of her arm, the buckle biting into her breast. She fell to the floor, screaming. Matt leapt onto his father's back, his small fingers trying to gouge George's eyes, his fists beating against the man's head. George grabbed his hair and threw him to the floor, but Matt leaped up again, swinging wildly.

'So, you want to fight me, you little bastard? I'll show you what fighting's all about.'

He used a full fist and the skin across Matt's cheek split open, but he felt no pain. All he could hear was his mother sobbing. He staggered upright. Uncontrolled rage flowing through his veins, poisoning his nine-year-old reason. His fists bunched. He was past caring about the consequences. George moved so fast, Matt didn't see the boot heel until too late. It slammed into his stomach, and as he doubled over, retching, George hit him twice more in quick succession, catching Matt in the face as he fell.

Winded and gasping, he lay on the floor, helpless to defend himself. George moved around in deliberate consideration before landing another kick in his stomach. Foetus-like, he tried to protect his body and face. Then the attack came from behind. Agony shot through his kidneys and his vision dimmed. He opened his mouth, but like a fish out of water, he couldn't get a breath. Shards of pain stabbed through his body until everything became black.

In the hospital afterwards, they said there was blood in his urine. Just lying in bed hurt, his body covered with blue, red and purple marks that turned yellow and brown and black over the following weeks. He lied about falling from his bike, worried about what his father would do to his mother and not caring what the nurses believed. They wouldn't hurt him or his mum.

George could have killed him. The bastard was a sadist, enjoying the pain he inflicted, enjoying the control and fear he wielded.

After that episode, Matt's grandfather, Robin Harrison, decided he should go to boarding school, and he was grateful. The Duke of York's was where he had learned to fight. The school taught him indecisiveness was weakness. It was where he found that to make resolute snap decisions lead to winning. And it became good grounding for his subsequent career.

Sensei, as they instructed him to call his extracurricular karate teacher, taught him courtesy, respect, and self-control. He drilled into him that before he could learn to fight, he would have to develop inner peace and outward gentleness, where his moves were not about fighting, but about body mind coordination. Only then could he learn how to fight.

Form is emptiness, and emptiness is form, his mind chanted. That training changed him and he still practices, knowing he gets more from it than being able to fight. He recalled Sensei saying karate was not so much about fighting others, but more about fighting one's own internal demons. There was a psychological stillness the discipline gave him, better than any therapy.

After his father had put him in hospital, he avoided going home. During school holidays he stayed with friends or his grandparents, taking jobs on farms where he could get free board for work. Then, less than a year later, his father died in a freak vehicle accident in Germany. Matt didn't grieve for the man, and neither did his mother.

Perhaps Nikki was right about him being institutionalised, first boarding school, then the army. But life might have been much different. He'd be in gaol now, given the company he kept in those days. An angry, impulsive, and unhappy child was not one to leave roaming the streets. The martial arts he learned at boarding school gave him discipline to control anger. If it weren't for boarding school, he wouldn't have passed his A-levels. If it weren't for the army, he wouldn't have a degree or have gone to Sandhurst.

In a bizarre way, he owed George a debt of gratitude. No, the man was an arsehole. Matt didn't shed a tear at his death. Although growing up without a father is supposed to be hard for boys, it was better to go without than have a sadist like that for a father. He wished he could have another whisky. An announcement told the passengers to prepare for landing, and he tightened his seat belt,.

Three hours later, they took off again for Gatwick. Twenty-five hours after leaving sunlit Brisbane, a taxi dropped him in Chelsea. Snow, or rather, grey sludge, filled the gutter, running the length of the pavement. The house was dark, frigid breath from an alien shadow set back from the bright street lighting.

As he entered, he stepped over mail scattered over the mat, mostly junk, and a few bills. One was from his mother's solicitor. He left the bills on the hall table and walked to the kitchen, through the clamminess of neglect, to turn on the central heating. It sent a blast of stale air through the house. The whole place needed a good coat of paint.

The garden will be a rambling mess. He'll have to get stuck in, clean it up and then sell it. Let someone else renovate and turn the old mausoleum into one of the shiny new citadels that fill the neighbourhood.

A sudden longing for the warmth in Australian overtook him. The view, the sunshine, him dragging on a cigarette. Another instant craving possessed him. He had never smoked in his mother's house, and he can't now. The cupboard in the kitchen had a good store of whisky, but no fags. He took out a bottle. Perhaps he could exchange cigarette addiction with alcoholism. Tomorrow, he would visit his grandmother and find out what she knew about Jake.

Chapter Twelve

Matt slowed the car to the obligatory eight miles per hour as he negotiated the speed bumps threatening to take out the exhaust. The last time he visited his Gran was before heading off to Australia less than a fortnight ago. It seemed like a lifetime.

She was in the retirement's dayroom home, neat and groomed, a book on her lap. The smell of boiling beetroot reminded him of institutions, but the room was large and comfortable, and she liked it here.

'Hello darling. They told me you were coming this morning. I thought they must be mistaken.' She held her cheek, angled for his kiss.

'You look well Gran.'

He sat opposite Julia Harrison. Her blue eyes were darker and greyer than his mother's but there remained a resemblance, and she wore her eighty-two years well.

'I'm not as spritely as I was.' She tucked her blanket around her legs. 'I feel the cold, but at least the drugs help the rheumatism. Have you read this book?' She held up the cover. 'Fifty shades of absolute pornography, if you ask me.'

Matt smiled. 'Yet here you are, reading it.'

'I had to see what the fuss was about. How was your trip? Where did you say you were going this time?'

'Australia.'

'Don't tell me there's a war over there now.'

'No Gran, no war in Australia. I've retired.'

'I didn't know you could retire at such a young age.'

'All right, resigned my commission then. I'm a civilian.'

'You told me before, but what will you do?'

'Gran, I explained all this. I know you remember; your memory is as sharp as it ever was. You just don't approve, do you?'

'Well, it's too late to begin a new career, and going back to university at your age... I find it embarrassing when I have to tell people you threw away a promising career to go back to school. For goodness' sake Matthew, they were going to make you colonel. You should have stayed, accepted. Your father would have been so proud.'

Matt avoided engaging in her lament. He'd gone there before, and it would have been another few years before he made colonel, but that didn't stop her from insisting it was imminent. The discussion was pointless.

'That's what brings me here Gran.'

'What does? How was your trip? Tell me why you travelled to Australia again.'

'For research.'

'What research?'

'Gran, if you just hang on a minute, I'll tell you. It's about my father.'

Something flickered in her eyes. 'What about a cup of tea? See if you can find someone to bring us one. There's a good boy Matthew.'

He sighed, got up to find someone to ask for tea. When he returned, she was reading again. 'Tea's coming in a minute Gran.'

She seemed to have forgotten he was there. 'Oh, it's you Matthew.'

'Who else would it be?' She was playing a game, always vague when she tried to hide things, acting when it suited her. Her change in demeanour told him he was on the right track. 'Tell me about my father Gran.'

'Your father! What can I tell you that you don't already know?' She gazed longingly at her book. 'I'm tied Matthew darling. Perhaps you should come back another time.'

'Sorry Gran, but it's important. Don't send me away, not just yet.'

Her face creased into lines as she fidgeted with the page corners. 'What do you want from me, Matthew?'

'I want the truth, that's all. You don't have to be worried about my feelings. I just need the truth.'

'You're speaking in riddles—what truth?'

'You know what I'm talking about, Gran. I saw it in your face. You can't become coy with me now. I know George wasn't my biological father, and I know you know who is.'

She sucked air through her teeth.

'Gran, it's all right. It doesn't matter that George wasn't my dad. I'm glad in a way. I hated the bastard.'

'Matthew, you shouldn't speak of your father in that way.'

'He wasn't my father, though, was he? Was it Jake, the soldier in Rhodesia?'

Her faced blanched and there was a flicker in her eyes that told Matt she was afraid. Although why was a mystery?

In a whisper she said, 'Who told you?'

Her eyes scanned back and forth, seeking escape.

'What is it Gran? Who are you afraid of? It's just us. No one else can hear. It's all right. No one will judge you, or my mother. These things aren't as serious as they were back in the day.'

To Matt's horror, tears spilled from her pink lids and rolled down her lined cheeks, making runnels in the face powder. He rose, placing a hand on her shoulder. The angle was awkward, so he retreated to his seat.

A woman arrived with tea. She set the tray on the table. 'Will you be mother, dear, or would you like me to pour?'

Matt leaned over and picked up the teapot. 'Thanks.'.

He poured tea and handed her a cup while she regained her composure.

The woman who brought the tea retreated, oblivious to the drama playing out. Outside, a bus pulled up and off-loaded its passengers. The residents trooped into the dayroom, chatting and noisy from their outing.

Matt pressed his grandmother. 'Please tell me the truth.'

Tears welled in her eyes. 'I can't talk about it. Your grandfather will kill me.'

Matt frowned. 'Grandfather isn't here. Remember, he died.'

Julia seemed terrified, and Matt couldn't understand why.

Then she said, 'He said he would have me arrested. It would be a breach of the Official Secrets Act. I can't say anymore.'

Had his grandmother finally lost it? She didn't seem to see him at all, and her eyes had changed colour, becoming a light grey, like slate, shining with something he didn't recognise.

She held her hand in front of her face as if shielding herself from something, or someone. 'Please Jake, please go, and don't come back. Leave Celia alone. She doesn't want to see you again. She's in love with someone else. They're getting married—there's divorce papers—she's divorcing you. Just leave us in peace.'

Matt frowned. 'Gran?'

But Julia didn't hear him. She seemed to see some scene playing out before her, something Matt couldn't see. Her face changed from fearful to triumphant, and her fingers closed around something on her lap. Although Matt could see nothing there. Her breathing had become erratic. Then her hands shot out in front of her, fingers clasped. She shouted something incomprehensible.

Matthew stood up, wondering if he should call for help. 'Gran I'm Matt not Jake. Did Jake come to see you?' He took her hand, smoothing the wrinkled tissue-thin skin. The grey light in her eyes faded and she closed them, pressing her lips together. A minute later, she opened her eyes again and they had returned to the normal blue.

Matt said, 'Shall I call someone?'

She shook her head.

'Are you all right?'

'Why wouldn't I be?'

'Gran, look at me. No one will hurt you. Just tell me where to find Jake. Do you know where he lives?'

She whispered, 'There was a war' The fogginess lifted from her eyes. 'Please Matthew, if I tell you, will you let it go?'

'Yes.' He was concerned by his Gran's strange turn, but he had to know.

'And will you leave now? You can come back next month for a visit, but will you leave now?'

'All right, I'll go if you tell me.' Was he pressing too hard? 'I'm sorry Gran.'

She nodded. 'Your mother dated him for a while. He left her pregnant and abandoned, and it broke her heart. It was that bitch's fault. She made him desert her. There was such a row when they got married. Then he disappeared. They said he ran away. I don't know what happened, but I know he threatened me. Robin put him in gaol for stealing official secrets. It was the best place for him. I'm sorry dear, your father was not a nice man. It's better to remember George as your father. That's it. I know nothing else. There was a war. Who knew what happened in those last days as people fled the country? We assumed he left with them.'

Julia's eyes overflow with silent tears, but that weird eye change thing was happening again. He leaned forward, grasping her hand.

'Gran?'

'Was I wrong? Is that why my daughter killed herself? Matthew, I'm scared.'

He patted her hand. 'Mum was depressed. The doctors said it was a major depression. You're not to blame for any of it. You did what you had to do, and that's all we can ask of anyone.'

Tear had streaked her face powder, but her eye colour had returned to normal. 'I'm sorry, Matthew, so sorry. Will you take me to my room now? I think I need to lie down for a while.'

He held her arm as they walked out of the dayroom along the corridor and to her bedroom. 'Shall I call a nurse?'

'No dear. Kiss me goodbye. I can manage now. I'm sorry, my boy, so sorry.'

'Gran, who was the bitch?'

'What?'

'You said the bitch made him?'

'Did I?'

'Yes, Gran.'

'I don't know. It was such a long time ago. You should forget about it. I need to rest now, please, Matthew.'

As Matt closed the door, Julia sat on her bed, shoulders slumped. What was it all for? Her mind clouded. For a moment she had gone back, not just remembering but thinking it was real. Jake had stood before her, earnest and pleading like they did those men—just like Dennis at that age, and now Matt. Bitterness welled in her throat. Was she to be haunted by these men forever? But that bitch would not get her claws into this one, ever. She had made sure of that a long time ago.

As Matt drove home he replayed the conversation in his mind. None of it made sense. If Jake abandoned Celia, why did he search for her? The amazing part was that Gran had said they were divorced, so they must have married. Yet none of it tallied with Fletcher's account. Perhaps his Gran's mind was going. Who was the bitch, and what were the official secrets? His mind spun with unanswered questions. A fleeting thought took hold, and he discarded as quickly. His Gran wouldn't lie to him, but she might be confused. If Jake had gone to gaol, Fletcher would have mentioned it.

It surprised him no one told him his mother had married twice. If he was the child of a former marriage, why keep it secret? If she married George because she was pregnant, he could have understood her not wanting anyone to know, especially not back then. When did George and his mum marry? Was it before or after he was born? There must be records of the marriage and the divorce and if Jake was in prison, there would also be a record. He would just have to dig through the national archives.

It didn't turn out to be that simple. A few days after visiting his Gran, he paid for a copy of Celia's marriage certificate to George. The year was 1984. He would have been four, but he had no memory of the marriage. The General Register's Office in London didn't have a record of either a marriage or divorce for Celia and Jake Ryder, neither could he find a prison record for Jake. Not in Britain.

He tried the Zimbabwean Embassy. After seven weeks of paying out fees, waiting in queues, phoning every Zimbabwean agency he could find in the phone directory, he decided he needed to rethink his tactics. He visited his PhD supervisor to discuss his need to go to Zimbabwe for further research.

Matt sat in the cluttered university office watching his supervisor's ears moving up and down as he contemplated Matt's request. His face was stern, but a blob of mayonnaise at the corner of his mouth belied his authority. Tucked under a sheaf of papers, Matt saw its source. A sandwich. He had disturbed the man's lunch.

'What will you research over there that you can't get here?'

Matt hadn't prepared a lie. 'I'd like access to their records.'

'Tell me what records you need, and we'll order them for you.'

'I'm not sure it works like that over there. I've been trying and most of the time no one even answers the phone, let alone provides any help. They tell me I need to go through the archives for the files myself.'

'You should be able to find what you want through the Zimbabwean Embassy.'

'I've tried, but they said they have no records on the subjects I want. That was after I paid quite a sum of money and waited several weeks.'

'Well, if you must, but I'm not sure your grant will stretch that far.'

'That's all right. I'll pay my own way, like I did for my trip to Australia.'

'Why didn't you say so in the first place? How did Australia go, by the way? What was it you were researching again? Oh yes, that war correspondent fellow. Was he any help?'

'Ah... yes, in a way. He gave me a different perspective on things.'

'Good, write it up and let me have the draft.' He glanced down at his desk for a second, and then back at Matt. 'I can't see why you have to go to Zimbabwe now. The last draft I saw of your dissertation was nearly complete. Are you sure you need to go? Far be it from me to tell you what to do with your own money, but it might not be necessary to outlay such an expense when it's not warranted.'

Chapter Thirteen

A few weeks later, Matt arrived home after handing in the draft thesis to his supervisor. He placed his keys on the hall table while he took off his coat. He was in two minds. Should he still go to Zimbabwe?

Matt wanted the truth about Jake, but there were other things he needed to do. Self-discipline was required, and he resolved to finish his studies and sell the house before resuming his search. Julia Harrison was the key to the mystery, but he would need to wait until he visited her next month before deciding. In the meantime, he could ready the house for sale.

The back door was stiff with neglect, unused since his mother died. Outside, a small square of overgrown lawn sprouts weeds to his waist, and creepers crawled across an iron bench rusting under the Magnolia tree. The tree showed pink spring buds on bare branches. It wouldn't take long to get into shape.

Drops of rain spattered against the plate-glass window, and he closed the kitchen door. The light oak, yellow, and white décor of the kitchen needed little work. His mother loved this room, saying it was cheerful in the winter to have lots of yellow around, like sunshine.

Nostalgia swamped him. Perhaps the English weather made her so depressed. After growing up in sunlit Africa, she spent so many years hating gloomy days of drizzle, especially in winter. Each spring, as soon as the daffodils flowered, she would hurry to the markets and bring back armfuls, dragging Matt with her to carry them. She placed vases of the yellow flowers throughout the house with the largest arrangement taking pride of place on the entrance hall table. His father had come home early and complained the flowers made the whole house stink. One by one, he emptied each vase into a bucket and threw the lot into the garden.

Matt's throat constricted, and he headed for the cupboard to pour himself a drink. Then, taking the glass, he walked through to the sitting room. The furniture was Celia's choice, bought after George died. Cheerful floral linens, bright cushions and warm rugs made the room home. It was the one room that didn't remind him of George. He sat at the piano. The music for Beethoven's Moonlight Sonata should be here somewhere. He flicked through the sheets of music on top of the piano. When he found them, he sat at the piano to play. Thought of Polly and stopped. Then he launched into the Guns and Roses song, *November Rain*. It was his wife's favourite. He stopped playing. 'Screw it. The bitch was gone. Get over it.'

The doorbell chimed. He was not expecting company.

A pouting Nikki waited on the doorstep. 'You are back. I didn't believe it. Two months and you didn't call!'

'Sorry, it's been hectic.' He stood aside to let her in, guilt and annoyance at the intrusion jostling for supremacy.

She hugged him and walked down the hallway to the sitting room, her heels tapping out efficiency. 'Anyway, it wouldn't have mattered. I've only just returned home. I've been in France, buying for the store.'

A surge of relief let him off the guilt hook. She was a pretty woman, in her late twenties, full of confidence. Assertive in her high-heeled shoes and tight skirt. Her five feet two inches was all muscle and energy, and her blonde hair perfectly styled.

Matt followed her down the hallway with the realisation that she was another version of his wife. He felt he barely knew her, although they had been dating sporadically for nearly two and a half years. She had helped him sort out his mother's funeral and was so organised while he was a mess. He would always be grateful to her, but she shouldn't imagine their relationship was serious although perhaps he should make more of an effort.

She waited in the sitting room for him to kiss her. He put his arms around her and tried to put some passion into it, but she was like kissing plastic. There was no thrill. He looked down at her compact frame. 'You're so little.'

'Silly. Is everything all right, Matt darling?'

He said, 'Let's get out of here. The place is giving me claustrophobia. Let me take you out for a drink, dinner.'

They arrived at his local pub. Kevin was behind the bar. So, that's how she knew he was back. No secrets in this neighbourhood. Matt ordered and exchanged a few words with the regulars sitting at the bar. Then he carried his pint and her Babycham to a booth.

She smiled brightly. 'Well, tell me all about it.'

What could he tell her? He described Fletcher as an old colonial soak still living the glory days of his past. It made her laugh, but he recognised his treachery and stopped. Fletcher was a decent soul, and he didn't want him ridiculed, but he had to tell her something. If he told her the truth, he'd have to mention Polly. He settled for embellished anecdotes and changed the subject as soon as he could, asking about her latest trip.

Two young Sudanese men came into the bar and Nikki stiffened. 'Why does Kev allow them in here?' Her voice sounded strident.

Matt said, 'Keep your voice down. They'll hear you.'

'Let them.'

'Christ, Nikki, what's got into you? Their money's the same as yours or mine. They're not doing any harm.'

'I'm sick of it. Refugees are taking over. Soon England won't be England anymore. A family of them moved into my building?'

'A Sudanese family?'

'No—oh, I don't know, but they're dark.'

He laughed. 'Come on Nikki. They are probably as English as you and I. I can't imagine any refugee being able to afford to live in your building.'

'Don't laugh Matt, you don't know what it's like. The soon as they move in, property prices plummet.'

'Christ Nikki, you don't mean that, surely.' He got up, wanting her to shut up. 'Where do you want to eat?'

After dinner, they took a cab to her apartment. He wouldn't sleep with her in his mother's house, didn't seem right. For a start, his mother wouldn't have liked her. Funny, she didn't like his wife either. Perhaps Celia was wiser than the credit he gave her. He lifted his hands to cradle Nikki's head as he leaned in to kiss her.

'Matt my hair, you're messing my hair.'

For long seconds he stared in silence, seeing the real person for the first time. He dropped his hands and turned to pick up his shirt.

'What are you doing?' She moved in and ran her hands up his chest.

He removed her hands and buttoned his shirt. 'I can't do this anymore. I'm sorry Nikki.'

'What do you mean?' Her eyes were bright.

'I need more' He pulled on his sweater and took her hands. 'It's over Nikki. I'm sorry. You're a nice person, beautiful, but I don't love you.'

Nikki's face paled. 'You bastard, you absolute bastard. You've met someone else, haven't you? You unfaithful, unbelievable, inverted arsehole. Well, go, good riddance. You're all the same, you bastard!'

He let himself out, closing the front door softly behind him. Like his own guilt, her sobbing followed him down the hallway. Perhaps he should go back and apologise. He kept walking, taking the fire exit stairs two at a time, until he reached the fire exit door.

In the street outside, a taxi pulled up, but he waved it on. He needed the walk to clear his head. The evening was crisp and invigorating, as he sauntered toward the Strand.

A noisy pub had Australian flags flying along its façade and he pushed his way through the crowds to order a whisky. Most of the patrons were young Australians, although Matt could also make out New Zealanders, British and South African accents. A girl slid into the small space between Matt and the next bloke. She leaned into him, tiptoeing to speak into his ear. 'Buy me a beer, soldier.'

When the drinks arrived, she took his hand and led him through the crowd to a table with a dozen others in their early twenties. Matt felt like granddad.

It was quieter away from the bar and the woman said. 'I'm Kimberly and these are my friends Lydia and Ray. We're from Cape Town.' She ignored the other people at the table.

Matt scanned the group, wondering what the hell he was doing there. Although Kimberly was already three sheets gone, her friends were relatively sober.

Kimberly said, 'I have to go. Come with me, Lyd.'

Lydia got up and the two women wandered off towards the ladies.

Ray leaned forward. 'Kim says you're in the army.'

'No mate, not anymore. I used to be, but now I'm a student.'

'Ag, sorry man, she's army crazy—thinks there's something special about British soldiers.' He shrugged. 'Buggered if I know why.'

Matt smiled and the two men lapsed into silence.

After a minute or two, Ray said, 'We have just finished. I mean Cape Town varsity. Business Commerce. What are you doing?'

'History.'

'That's interesting, man. I think history is awesome. What are you reading?'

'Guerrilla warfare in British Colonial Africa.'

'No shit. Like the independence wars and things. Like the Rhodesian war.'

'Yes.' Matt tilted his head. This bloke had heard about the Rhodesian war. Even if it took place in the country next door to him, it happened before he was born.

'No shit.' Ray shook his head. 'You should talk to my old man. He fought in that war. Bitter as all hell over coming second. He rants at the T.V. whenever they mention Mugabe.'

By the time the women returned, Matt had ordered another round of drinks and was in deep discussion with Ray.

After listening for a while, Kimberly wandered off, but Lydia said, 'Ray, doesn't your dad belong to some old Rhodesian club?'

'Ja, that's right, hey. It's online.'

Matt swallowed his whisky. He should have thought of that. What was he doing in here? Chasing shadows... Searching for evidence of his father had become a compulsion, although it was unlikely he'd find anyone who knew Jake in an Australian bar, so what the hell drew him in?

He got up. 'Thanks for the information. Have a good holiday.' He shook Ray's hand and nodded at Lydia. Kimberly had disappeared. As he left, the bar seemed noisier and more crowded than when he arrived.

Chapter Fourteen

Polly contemplated the canvass leaning against the wall. She had never completed a painting so quickly. It was her best work. It was not what she should have painted; not part of the global warming theme for her exhibition, and the Gallery was becoming impatient.

Instead, she had painted him out of her system. Now she had completed the portrait, she could forget him.

She walked back to the painting of her valley wasteland, determined to put Matt from her mind. The painting rested on its easel, neglected because she couldn't figure out what was wrong with it. Perhaps coffee would help focus her mind.

As she filled the jug with water, she stared out of the window at the lightening eastern horizon. An Allegro by Mozart played on her CD player. Her stomach rumbled. She should have eaten breakfast before leaving the house.

Once the kettle boiled, she poured hot water over the coffee granules in her mug and walked back to stare at the valley painting, but before long her gaze strayed back to a newly finished painting leaning against the wall.

The portrait showed a man walking uphill from the valley below the house. It was done in a style new to her, of contrasts, dark and light within an abstract tangle of foliage. Every brush stroke was a familiar note, every angle, even the way he held his head and the colours of his eyes, all crafted from memory.

She turned back to the valley wasteland, remembering the aversion in his expression. 'Why did you hate it Matt? What did you see?' Then it dawned on her.

She placed her coffee cup on the ground and selected a newly prepared canvas, tossing the other aside. It clattered across the room. She chose a palette knife to block in colour. The painting took shape in the new style, great slabs of colour for the tempestuous sky, the same colour palette she had used for his eyes. In the foreground, wind flattened sparse yellow grass and tore through bent and ragged trees, their stunted misshapen limbs clinging to the last vestiges of life. The dark landscape became a barren wasteland in the stormy light.

Finally, she stepped back. Her foot touched the cold coffee cup. Darkness had fallen. Her mouth was sticky. She had been painting all day without a break and yet it seemed like minutes, except for the ache in her arm. The painting was right. She packed up, let herself out of the shed and headed for home.

When she reached home, Fletcher opened the front door. He was so much better tempered since he had got out of the chair, and she no longer had to worry about taking care of him. He opened the car door, even before she pulled on the handbrake. A sure sign he had something to get off his chest.

'I've made dinner.'

That's a first. 'Thanks Poppa, I hope I'm not too late. I had an amazing day.'

'Me too. I had an epiphany.'

'Must be a day for it.'

'What?'

Polly was at the front door. 'Never mind. I need a drink.'

She headed into the kitchen for a drink of water. A chicken roasted in the oven. Crikey, he had made dinner and not just vegemite sandwiches.

Fletcher poured her a glass of wine. 'How would you like to go to Africa with me?'

'Are you serious?' But clearly he was. Hope made him seem younger, more invigorated.

'I'm serious. I've been thinking, remembering, and I want to see it, at least once more before I die. It won't be the same, but I want to go, Poll.'

'I've got the exhibition'

'Yes, I know, but afterwards. You'll have time then and it'll take a while to get things organised, visas and stuff.'

'What's this about Poppa? Is it Jake and Celia? You won't do anything stupid like point-out Mugabe's flaws to the world, will you?' She chewed her lip. 'Is Zimbabwe safe to visit?'

'I think it'll be fine. We'll be a couple of tourists taking in the sights. Oh Poll, just wait until you see Vic Falls. They're incredible and he can't have ruined that, at least.'

'Can I think about it? Let me get the exhibition out of the way and then I'll see.' She saw his face crumple and added, 'only a few weeks, okay? Anyway, you will have to wait until they take the pins from your pelvis.'

Fletcher sighed. 'That's sensible and anyway, the weather now won't be good. The place will be rife with cholera and malaria. In the meantime, I can help with the exhibition if you want me to.'

'I'd love you too.' She could use all the exposure she could get, and Fletcher had the networks. But what if she wasn't good enough? Rather than being a blessing, she'd be crucified. Mates or not, they wouldn't promote rubbish.

Fletcher smiled. 'Don't panic, Poll. You'll be fine. Brad said you were good, and he should know.'

'Brad was just being nice because he's your friend.'

'He wouldn't say it if it wasn't true, but if you like, I can come to the studio tomorrow and see what you've done. Have you completed the work yet?'

'Nearly. Oh, Poppa, I am nervous. Until a moment ago, all I thought of was getting it done. Now... well, what if it's rubbish, and no one likes it?'

'C'est la vie. You start again. Nobody makes it straight away. These things take time. This is the first step on your journey. Just don't get too wrapped up in the whole thing. What happens if they don't like it—so what? You love painting. Thanks to your parents, you don't have to earn a living, so enjoy your art. There are few as lucky as you.'

'You'll give me your honest opinion, won't you, Poppa?'

Fletcher gazed at her for a moment. 'I've seen your paintings before. They are still hanging in the sitting room wall.'

'Those are old.'

'I don't know what makes a painting good. I just know what I like. Some of your paintings might be a bit controversial for everyone's comfort, but they make a statement.' He patted her arm. 'But of course, Polly. I'll give you the benefit of my enormous wisdom. Now set the table. Dinner's ready.'

The next morning, Fletcher drove to Polly's studio. As he got out of the car one, another tenant arrived in a Ute laden with sawn timber.

'Jason, my boy, how are you?'

Jason gave a thumb up and switched off his ignition. 'Lo Fletch, how are you doing?' He climbed out of the pickup and shook Fletcher's hand. 'How's Polly?'

'She's fine; getting ready for her exhibition, the first one since her graduation. It's a big deal for her.'

Jason looked at his feet. 'I'll be there. She banned me from the studio until she finished painting so I've seen nothing, but I'll be at the exhibition, so will the others. We're all backing her.'

'How's the furniture business going?'

'Slow. No one's got any money at the moment and if they have, they buy cheap and nasty from the retail outlets. I think I'm in the wrong business. The Indonesian's can make stuff for a fraction of what I charge. I'm thinking of chucking it in and going to the mines. That's where the money is.'

'That'd be a shame.' Fletcher meant it. Jason was an excellent cabinetmaker, designing and producing exquisitely crafted furniture.

'Well, best get this lot unpacked and into the shop. Give Polly my love, Fletch, and tell her I'll be there.'

Fletcher watched him go. He had thought there was a romance blooming there at one stage, but it seemed to have fizzled. Jason was a handsome fellow, and Polly seemed to like him. But Polly wouldn't talk about her love life and when Fletcher asked, she told him to mind his own business, or words to that effect. It was clear Jason was still keen, so Polly must be the reluctant one.

As he pushed open the door, the sound of Wagner filled his senses. Something from Tristan and Isolde. Polly was painting, and oblivious to her grandfather's presence. He stood quietly, watching, not wanting to disturb her concentration.

The work astonished him. It's the valley behind the house, but nothing like the valley he saw every day. This was apocalyptic, its beauty terrifying. He could almost hear the howling wind. Nothing lived there easily. He didn't realise she was that good. There was maturity in her work that wasn't there previously.

Pride surged in his breast, and he stepped forward to speak, but stopped when he saw the other painting against the wall. Its dark tones showed a shadowy figure walking uphill. It could be the valley behind Fletcher's house, but it had an abstract foreignness. Perhaps it was the colours she had used for the foliage.

He moved closer. The figure could be Jake, but Polly had never met Jake so, it must be Matt. Not an illustration of the man, but a portrait of his essence; a primordial masculinity shrouded in formidable light. The raw passion left Fletcher feeling as if he had invaded something private. Reluctant to be caught prying, he retraced his steps to the door.

Just as he reached it, Polly sighed and straightened, stretching her back. The music ended, and she turned around to see him apparently coming in the door.

'Oh, Poppa, perfect timing, I've finished. What do you think?'

Fletcher closed the door and walked toward Polly. He stood in front of the painting, hand to his cheek. 'It's amazing.' '

'I think it's the best of the lot. I'll call it Desert Valley. Not my usual style, but I'm pleased with the way it turned out. The others aren't as good, but hopefully this one will make up for them. I learned something through this exercise, Poppa.' She was smiling up at him. 'Can I make you a coffee? Only instant I'm afraid.'

'I'll have a fag while you make it. If I have to suffer instant I'll need the nicotine hit. Jason's out there.'

Polly shrugged. 'Yeah.'

In that moment, Fletcher understood or thought he did. There was one more test. He walked out, leaving the door open, leaning against the wall outside smoking, and chatting to Jason as he unpacked. He returned when he had finished his cigarette.

Polly said, 'Coffee's ready.'

The portrait of Matt faced the wall. Now why would she hide it? Polly would never cover such an exquisite piece of art, unless she found the emotion too raw, too intense to expose to scrutiny.

That night Fletcher scanned through his emails until he found the thank you note. He hadn't shown it to her, and he should have. It was not something he bothered about, and both his wives had criticised him for it. Now he contemplated the consequences of interfering.

The email arrived weeks ago, and what does he know about the man, or his life in England? All he had was an irresistible urge to act foolishly, and he was not sure why. He hadn't wanted to be a matchmaker before, but he was anyway. This was different. What if he interfered, and Matt broke Polly's heart? He tried once to interfere in Celia and Jake's relationship. He was not proud of himself, but he gave it his best shot. Celia didn't even notice. Nothing took her mind off Jake.

It was New Year's Eve. They had gone to First Street in Salisbury, which was awash with cheerful, drunken revellers waiting for the countdown to midnight. Celia was forlorn because Jake hadn't made it. She stood in the crook of Fletcher's arm, while he pretended his aching arm was there for her protection.

'To keep randy opportunists at bay,' he said.

Celia laughed but let his arm stay.

That year, every party in Salisbury had paused to allow their revellers to head into the city. The police were everywhere, and young women saw it as their mission to garner illicit kisses. It amused Fletcher to watch the poor sods valiantly fending off amorous women. In the British tradition, the police officers were under strict instructions to keep the peace while they maintained their feeble pretence at refusal. Most were kissed anyway.

The impromptu street parties stopped traffic. People swirled in a wave of coming together and parting as they milled along the street, meeting friends, picking up strangers. Fletcher was in no hurry to move from Celia's side. He could feel her breast rise and fall against his chest as they waited.

Jake had promised to meet them on the corner, but Fletcher was convinced he wouldn't show. It was obvious he couldn't get leave.

As they waited, a man dressed as a clown stood arguing with one of the police officers. Fletcher assumed he was drunk until he ducked away and in his big shoes clambered up the traffic lights. Two police officers ran to head him off. Robots, as traffic lights were called, arched high above the crossroads where they joined in the centre. The clown climbed across the road via the robot structure, swinging baboon-like and playing the fool while police and pedestrians watched on. The cross beams were high and dangerous, but the clown was a skilled performer, and Fletcher wished he had brought his camera with him.

Celia's face, illuminated by the glow of the red traffic lights, enchanted him, and he watched her instead of the clown. Her teeth gleamed, her eyes sparkled with merriment, and Fletcher wanted to kill Jake for not showing up. Her long hair caught the breeze and fluttered across his face, and she turned, her pink tongue poking out to touch her top lip.

'Sorry.' She dragged her hair away, tucking it behind her ears, and flicking the rest down her back.

Fletcher thought his heart would break with tenderness for her and rage at Jake. He bent his head to her ear. 'He's not coming, Cee. Let's get a drink somewhere.'

She shook her head. 'He'll come.'

'How can you be so sure? We've been waiting nearly an hour.'

She turned to him fully then. His arm had dropped from her shoulder. The air felt cold along his side in the space she had vacated. He wanted her back close to him, wishing he'd said nothing.

'Fletch, you go. I'm ruining your New Year. Have fun. I'll wait. I'll be fine by myself. If anyone accosts me, I've got policemen to call.' She grinned. 'That's if they have time to defend damsels in distress instead of chasing robot monkeys.'

He wanted to tell her then. He wanted to say leave him, he's not worth it. Come with me. I'll protect you. Forget him Celia, but he couldn't find the words. Instead, he just shook his head. 'I'll wait with you.'

Chapter Fifteen

Matt walked down the stairs as the post dropped through the letter slot. His head thumped with each footfall. Once again, most of the mail was junk, except for one official envelope: his mother's solicitors. He presumed they were demanding payment for their bill. With a flick of his wrist, he tossed it on the table with the other one, unable to cope with paperwork.

He drank too much last night, but at least it had given him the courage to dump Nikki. Dutch courage, his mother would have called it.

The kettle boiled, and he made coffee, carrying the mug to the sitting room, where he opened his laptop and typed Dutch courage into the search bar. In the 17th century, English soldiers went into battle against Dutch soldiers full of gin. Hence the phrase, coined by alarmed British soldiers.

An email from Fletcher dropped into his inbox. He had been disappointed when Fletcher hadn't responded to his last email and had assumed there would be no further contact.

Matt,

Sorry I took so long to respond. Hell, I wasn't even going to but never mind that now. Here I am, with a proposition for you. I'm hankering to go back to Zim, just as a tourist to see how it fares. A bit of a lark.

I'll be there next month after Polly's exhibition. We may as well do the sights and stop at Cape Town before heading to Harare, then on to Vic Falls. My proposition is this. Come too. I'll show you some of the old hangouts and places your mother frequented, and we might find out if Jake still lives there. I can't find a record of him anywhere else. If you're not interested, I'll understand completely, but let me know.

Cheers Fletcher.

Matt re read the email, a tingling charge running through his veins. He thrummed his fingers on the table and took a gulp of coffee. He was trying to delay his immediate response to fire back an email saying, Yes. He stood up to pace. Why did the proposition excite him? He was thinking of going anyway, so why get excited because Fletcher asked him. Did he want to spend time on a trip down memory lane with Fletcher? The bloke could become a millstone around his neck, especially in a wheelchair.

He sat down and picked up the laptop, re-reading the second paragraph. Fletcher says we. Is Polly going? His stomach contracted, and he gulped down the last of the coffee. The hangover was making him jittery.

Matt reasoned if Polly was there, she could care for Fletcher. Problem solved. He stretched out his hands to type and then hesitated. It might be helpful to go there with someone who was familiar with the country. He leaned forward to type.

Funny you should ask. I was planning to make the trip myself, so the answer is yes. Let me know about logistics. Matt.

He pressed send and leaned back on the sofa, staring at the laptop as though it might provide some answers to questions as yet unformulated. It'll be afternoon in Brisbane. Polly's image filled Matt's vison. But Polly was just a friend. 'Bullshit!' The word cracked in the quiet room. He wanted to see Polly, liked her, but she deserved better. Anyway, Fletcher would never forgive him if he mucked about with his granddaughter. Still, it would be good to see her again.

He typed *Zimbabwe visas* into the search bar and learned he could buy a visa on entry. That was a relief. He couldn't face the queue at the Embassy again.

One after another, he read the British, American, Australian and New Zealand Government's travel advisories. They said similar things; the country was no picnic. It was a pity they couldn't go now, but he would wait to hear from Fletcher again.

Besides, he had the house to sort out. He walked upstairs to his mother's room, opening the door and scanning the room. It was six months since the cleaners... He didn't want to think about it. The room smelled musty, and the surfaces were dusty. He opened the window to let air in.

Again, the question arose. Why? Why did you do it? She never left a note, and that made the police suspicious. It took the coroner ages before he declared suicide. At one point, Matt was a person of interest until his ex-commanding officer intervened. He had gone to Pakistan with the American JSOCs under contract for six weeks. He wasn't able to tell the police and that had caused the furore. Eventually, Nikki had contacted Dog, who contacted his old CO, who spoke to someone, and suddenly they let him go. Nikki had been great. He hitched back the curtains, and sunlight poured in showing the dust on every surface.

The suitcase where he had found Fletcher's letters was still on the top shelf of the wardrobe. He pulled everything out, piling it on her bed. Five minutes later, the wardrobe was bare, and the room was a mess. Now what? He headed to the kitchen in search of plastic bin bags.

He stuffed the first three dresses into the bin bag before he realised he should fold them. He emptied the bag to begin again. When he finished, piles of clothing run in militarily straight lines. The coat is trickier to fold. As he shook it out, something clattered to the floor. He picked up a key. He hadn't thought to check pockets.

As he searched through each item of clothing, memories crowded into his mind. Celia pushing toddler Matt on a swing.

'Higher,' he demanded.

'No, baby, it's too dangerous.'

'Higher,' he insisted. Even then, he was an adrenalin junkie.

She was a lonely woman, an alien in the country. All their family friends were George's friends. When George died, they had all drifted away. Was that why she killed herself? He refolded all the clothes, and then continued on to the next lot, unpinning broaches, searching for pockets and pocket contents.

An hour later, he had folded and packed all the clothes into bin bags that now stood sentry along a wall. He should have done it months ago. On his mother's dresser was a growing pile of broaches, coins, small squares of lacy hankies, two folded receipts, keys, and other pocket paraphernalia.

His stomach rumbled, and he picked up several bags to take downstairs. He needed some lunch, but the fridge contained only beer, stale bread, hard cheese and a wrinkled apple. Situation normal, he should do some shopping. An image of Fletcher's fridge, full of fresh food and Polly's quiche, made his mouth water. He groaned, but he can get something to eat at the local pub.

Matt let himself out of the front door and walked to the pub, his head down, lost in thought. When he reached it he went inside and sat at the bar. There were only a smattering of other customers.

Kevin greeted him. The place wouldn't be the same without Kev. He had been there for as long as Matt could remember. Gave Matt his first pint.

Kevin slid a pint across the bar and resumed drying glasses. He had resisted all modernisation and Matt was glad. This wasn't a tied pub.

'How's the study coming along?'

Matt swallowed a draught of beer. 'Yeah good, finished my draft and handed it in, but no doubt there'll be more I need to add or correct. I'll have your special too, Kev, when you've got a minute.'

Kevin called to his wife, Sally. She came out, drying her hands. Sally was a Vietnamese immigrant and sometimes the plain English menu got an odd mixture of flavours, but the food was always fresh and edible, if not always recognisable.

Sally walked around the bar, hands on hips, and said, 'So, what d'you get rid of that lovely girl for then, Matt?'

'Sally!' Kevin scolded.

Sally shrugged. 'Everyone's asking.' She grinned, her crooked teeth crowding her mouth.

The news had leaked quickly. 'She dumped me Sal, reckons I'm a bastard, and she's probably right.'

Sally cackled and patted him on the knee. 'One lunch special coming up.'

Kevin put down his cloth and pulled over a stool to sit opposite Matt. 'So how was Australia then?'

Matt searched for something to change the subject. 'It was fine, warm, lots of sunshine. I've been sorting out my mum's things, and I need to know where to take them. Is there a charity that'll have them?'

Kevin gave him a sympathetic nod. 'Are you coping okay?'

'I'm fine. I'm contemplating going to Zimbabwe, and I'd like to have it all squared away before I go.'

'Zimbabwe, you say. There's a fellow who comes in here, says he's from Zimbabwe. You should have a chat.'

Matt said, 'I'd like that.'

'I'll call if I see him again.'

After lunch, Matt arrived home with a belly full of beer and shepherd's pie, liberally garnished with Vietnamese mint, and the phone number for Oxfam in his pocket. He sat on his mother's bed, staring at the handbags. Another memory flashed into his mind.

He was three or four years old, sitting on the carpet in the sitting room, taking things from her handbag and examining each one for its usefulness. A few of the objects were familiar, but some he couldn't work out, so he set off to ask.

'Mummy, what's this?'

She said, 'Where did you get that?'

He retreated out of the kitchen doorway, ready to bolt, but she caught his arm. She marched him back to the sitting room.

They stood by the door, his arm still clutched in her hand, and the tampon clutched in his fist. His mother's face was stony when she saw the contents of her handbag piled on the floor.

She turned to him and said, 'Matthew, sit down. I need to talk to you. This is very serious.'

Matt sat on the sofa, Celia facing him. He knew he'd done something wrong by her tone and the seriousness in her face.

She examined him for what seemed like minutes, and then had said, 'It is very rude to go into a woman's handbag without her permission. Never do it again. Do you understand?'

'Yes,' he whispered. He wasn't sure what he'd done. At least she hadn't punished him.

Now here he was again, about to violate the sanctity of her handbag, and not just one bag, but five of the damn things. He wished he had a cigarette.

With a deep breath, he took the bags off their hooks and opened each one, shaking them so the contents would fall out onto the bed. He made sure they were empty by peering into each one but without putting in his hands. Then he dropped them into the plastic bin bag.

As he picked up the last one, something rattled. He opened the bag as wide as it would go, peering in to see what remained. It was empty. He stuck his hand into the bag and felt the lining. Beneath it was hard and round.

His mother had always kept her sewing basket in the hall cupboard. There was a little unpicking tool in it. He didn't want to destroy the bag by ripping out the lining, so he found the tool to unpick a small section. A silver chain fell through the opened seam, and he tugged it. Out popped a silver locket. It was one of those lockets girls wore around their necks. He remembered, when he was a teenager, Susan, the girl from down the road, made him stand still while she cut a small piece of his hair to put into her locket. It scared the pants off him, and afterwards he avoided her, ducking out of her way whenever he saw her. Funny, he'd forgotten that.

This small silver oval was unfamiliar, and he turned it over in his palm, seeing a tiny inscription on the back. He took it to the window to catch the light. *Always, Jake.* His heart pounded. He pressed the catch with his thumb. The locket sprung open, and a tiny, folded piece of paper fell out. At least there was no hair in the locket.

Inside were two miniature black and white photos. One was his mother and facing her, Jake in full dress uniform. It was a mirror image of an old photo he had of himself. Matt searched for the folded paper and found it under the bed. On it, in his mother's writing, was a number along with letters and a hyphen. Not a phone number anyway. He placed it on the dresser while he examined the photos in the locket. He couldn't deny it any longer. He was Jake's child. He needed a drink.

The next morning, he awoke in a cold sweat. He had had the dream again. He had hoped it would go away, but it hadn't. They told him this might happen, but he hoped he was one of the lucky ones. Her dying eyes haunted him, and he recognised it was guilt. His head pounded. His mouth tasted like he'd licked a public lavatory. He had been smoking again. Damn. What the hell did he get up to last night? 'Fucking eegit,' he muttered and rubbed his temples.

Someone stirred next to him. Christ, there was someone in bed with him. The top of a tousled blond head stuck out from the duvet, and he scrambled for a name, but there was nothing.

She turned. 'What time is it?' Her accent was Australian.

A memory of calling Dog and Brander came back to him. They hadn't gone on a bender for a long time, and Matt was out of practice.

'It's the middle of the night. Go back to sleep.' He got up to go to the bathroom. He was a fool hankering after the Australian connection. So much for his vow that he wouldn't bring casual dates into his mother's home.

He heard her voice, *Matthew. When are you going to get over this Barbie fixation?* He was not proud of it. He filled a glass with water, and drank down one, then another. Then he scratched about in the vanity for Berocca and Nurofen and swallowed those too.

He walked downstairs to make coffee. It was four in the morning, almost time to rise anyway. There were several bodies littering the sitting room floor, along with overflowing ashtrays, empty liquor bottles, glasses, and pizza boxes. The bodies belonged to Dog and Brander, with two semi naked and unfamiliar women tangled between them.

Dog was married, and he was certain Brander was also, although she was threatening to leave him last time Matt and Brander spoke. He had met their wives and these women aren't them. He contemplated waking them. Half-heartedly, he kicked Dog's foot. He stirred and mumbled. They were big boys and could take care of themselves.

Matt made coffee, leaning against the kitchen bench waiting for the kettle to boil, remembering the coffee Polly made. Matt heard the front door slam. Dog and Brander must have left. He hoped they had taken the girls with them.

He walked back to the sitting room to make sure. The only evidence of occupation, a lone black lacy thong lying abandoned under the piano. Now all he had to do was get rid of the woman upstairs.

Chapter Sixteen

Polly waited for the gallery curator to pass judgement; her lip caught between her teeth. Fletcher smiled at her and then turned back to watch the curator, a tall, thin man with a shaved head. The man's demeanour and dress gave Fletcher confidence, although his name, Taffy Bottomley, was a temptation, twice as tricky depending on one's sexual orientation. He might be gay, but Fletcher thought every inner-city trendy seemed gay nowadays. Polly said it was a metrosexual thing, whatever that meant.

Taffy stepped back, casting a glance about the room. 'There's something missing from the space here.' He pointed to a gap in the paintings that Polly had spent two days arranging and re-arranging. He turned to Polly. 'Don't you think?'

Polly's lip was red and puffy from all the chewing, and the pallor of her face made the freckles across her nose more noticeable.

She gazed around the room, screwing her eyes into slits, before sighing. 'You're right, but I have nothing else to hang. Please don't say I must re hang everything.'

Taffy turned a calculating gaze toward her, then back to Fletcher. 'What do you think, Mr Fletcher?'

'I think you're right and I know just the piece to hang.'

Polly said, 'What piece? There's nothing.'

'Yes, there is Poll. I saw it when I was at the studio the other day, and it's good.'

'Polly's face took on the hue of a tomato. 'It doesn't fit the theme.'

Fletcher said, 'Why don't we ask Mr Bottomley for his opinion?'

'No!' Polly twisted one leg around the other. 'It... It's not ready.'

'The painting's finished though, isn't it Polly?' He pressed her further. 'It seemed finished to me.' Fletcher turned to include Taffy in the conversation. 'Mr Bottomley, I think you should see it. I think it's one of Polly's best works. The figure is very masculine and dark, on a background of abstract jungle, but it might fit that space perfectly.'

'I would like to see it,' Taffy said.

They waited as Polly tried to turn herself inside out. 'I am not sure it's any good. Poppa was talking about an old friend, and it conjured such imagery. I thought I should try to get it onto canvass. The man was a soldier.' Her cheeks flamed again.

'I'm interested. Go on. It could work. When can I see it?'

Fletcher intervened. 'I can take Polly to pick it up now, and we can have it hung this afternoon, if you approve.'

Fletcher had trapped her. He would cop it when she got him alone, but she shouldn't hide such work away in the dark shadows. Works like the Valley Desert and the portrait of Matt will make Polly's name. The other paintings are technically excellent, but they lacked the passion of these two.

'Come on, Poll, what do you think?'

Polly ducked her head in acquiescence.

Taffy clapped his hands together and wrung them as if washing away a dilemma. 'Good, I'll expect you back this afternoon. We don't have much time, and we can't delay the opening again. I'm expecting a sizeable crowd. There's been a lot of publicity. The venue is hot property, which is wonderful for you Polly. I suppose that was your influence, Mr Fletcher.'

Fletcher smiled at Bottomley. That was cleverly done. Polly owed him and Taffy was reminding her. He walked towards the door.

'Come on Polly, let's get to it. We'll grab lunch on the way.'

By the time they arrived back at the gallery, Polly was in a state.

'It'll be your fault if Taffy doesn't like it. The entire journey was a waste of time. It doesn't go with the theme of global warming and it's too corny and too big.'

'It'll be fine, Poll. It's a good painting.' That was the wrong thing to say.

'You're a sneak Poppa, ferreting through my private things.'

'I didn't ferret through anything. It was on display when I walked in. Polly, you're being unreasonable.'

Polly was silent for a moment. 'I shouldn't have asked you to help. I should have known you would just interfere. You ruin everything!' Polly blinked back tears and scrabbled in the glove box for a tissue before settling for wiping her sleeve across her face.

Fletcher drove, letting her vent before handing her his hanky. When she calmed down, she would apologise for her temper. That was his Polly. He wondered if Matt was man enough to handle his granddaughter.

Taffy loved the painting. When hung, it dominated the room with its hard masculinity. The yang to the landscapes yin.

Fletcher reckoned it would be the focus of the exhibition. Pride in his granddaughter's talent made him place his arm around her shoulder and kiss her temple.

'Sorry Poppa, I was a witch, and you are right, again.'

Taffy interrupted. 'Goodness, that's perfect. What is the title?'

Polly shrugged. 'It doesn't have a title.'

Taffy scowled. 'We need a title—something that will bind it with the theme.'

Fletcher said, 'What about *Everyman: destruction and salvation.*'

'Why?' Taffy asked.

Fletcher walked up to the painting. 'Well, the theme of the exhibition is about climate change, and science agrees that humans have caused the radical changes. So, if humans can destroy the earth, they should be the ones to save it. This painting is of an Everyman, representing the anthropomorphic cause of climate change. He is the destroyer, but he is also bold enough to save the world.'

Taffy clapped his hands again. 'Perfect.' Then he hurried out the door in search of someone to get the name printed.

Fletcher said, 'You happy with that, Poll?'

'I'm not happy about any of it, but it's fine.' She slid her hand into Fletcher's. 'I'm just glad it's done. Let's go home and rest before the onslaught tomorrow.'

At the opening the next evening, Polly loitered in shadows, hoping no one would notice her. The room buzzed with conversation. Art students wound between the crowds with trays of canapés and wine. The smell of sausage rolls made her nauseous, and her nerves shriek with fear. She gulped vinegary Sauvignon Blanc, pretending to be engrossed in the programme. Her hair hung over her shoulders and down her back, ready to fall forward and hide her face at a moment's notice.

She wished she had half Fletcher's confidence and his effortless ability to find common ground with people. A crowd of half a dozen people collect in a semi-circle around him as he talked with authority about the painting, *Everyman*.

Polly sidled closer to listen. The familiarity of his words coalesced into meaning as she began to recognise what he was doing. He was an old hack, but brilliant and what a memory.

Fletcher was in full flight. 'This young patriot, idol of our hearts, represents those dead in their prime. Those who will never laugh nor love again, despite that, we neglect to act. The future holds a climate of smoking frontiers, crimson skies and dimming mist, leaving souls in despair because we lack leaders—heroes that shine as rare as the morning-star.'

He paused, giving his words time to soak into memory, and for the journalists to scribble quotes. Then, dropping his voice, he said, 'We are betrayed by politicians who dismiss our needs in seeking their own. Never in our history have we needed leaders as we do now.' His voice firmed. 'We need defenders of daring, courage, and honesty. *Everyman* is a metaphor for a new saviour. For as our climate calamity draws near, he will rise, facing darkness to stare straight into the moonlight of terror as a dazed nation races toward the eve of destruction. Who can stand? When the souls of the oppressed fight in the troubled air that rages, who can stand? When the whirlwind of fury comes from the throne of God, when the frown of His countenance drives the nations together, who can stand?'

Polly could not understand why no one recognised William Blake's words. Poppa was an old fraud. How could they not realise he was using snatches of other people's poetry? Words not about climate change, but war. She conceded not every child was brought up on a diet of war poetry, but she would have expected someone to notice. They didn't, and she was just grateful that he was keeping them entertained.

Fletcher was talking again, this time from his heart. 'Politicians give way to expediency, taking the path of least resistance despite their own misgivings because they listen to those with vested interests who warp the truth—the liars and the deceivers. How many people must die at the hands of politicians who give up, claiming pragmatism as their motivation? When all they seek is their own continuing power at the expense of honourable action.'

He paused. The crowd of people around him grew. 'We must always question such claims because often the ends do not justify the means. Instead, their actions cause misery and destruction. Is this the world's future where, because of pragmatic expediency, our leaders will allow continuing neglect of a growing problem? Will we continue to fiddle while Rome burns?'

He waited for people to digest his words and then said, 'This man of bold courage and purpose is symbolic of what we need in our politicians today. It is a painting modelled on a courageous man from history; one whom we betrayed and yet now we need. For this man is the embodiment of our world, a masculine Gaia, and a representative of a new leadership of intelligence, of courage, of daring, skill, and honesty. We need real leadership, not pragmatism, to lead us into this new battle.'

Fletcher had once scoffed at climate change now he was preaching as if converted. She felt faint. The lights were too bright and the room too warm. The wine made her woozy. She stepped into the street and sat on a bench, listening to the noise spilling from the opened gallery door. All she wanted was to go home and sleep.

The next morning Polly slept in. But the urgency was over. She had no attachment to the rest of the exhibition. The sun streamed into her bedroom. She rolled over to go back to sleep, but her sleep was fitful and full of dreams she couldn't grasp. Eventually, she got up and mooched into the bathroom, tying not to think about last night.

Coffee, that's what she needed, and so will Poppa. He would have a hangover for sure. He drank nothing at the opening because he said he'd drive, but when they got home, he took the whisky bottle to his study.

On the way home, he kept chuckling. 'Half the paintings sold, and there's a bidding war on Everyman.'

'It's not for sale.'

'Taffy will be furious. You should have made that clear earlier.'

'I did, and he was. But I don't want to talk about it.'

'You can't blame the bloke. He would have seen big dollars and big publicity for his gallery slipping away.'

This morning, she hadn't changed her mind. The painting was not for sale. It was too personal and should have stayed buried in her studio.

Fletcher had beaten Polly to it. The coffee pot was still hot, and she poured a cup before heading to the sitting room and her tablet. She should go into the studio, but she didn't have the energy right now. Out of habit, she switched on the tablet and the television at the same time. Nothing on T.V. grabbed her attention, and she turned to the tablet. Will there be any reviews of her exhibition? It was probably too early. She touched the news icon, afraid but determined to face whatever they said.

The headlines screamed.

Everyman: Daring, Courage, and Honesty: Are our leaders the politicians we deserve or are they liars and deceivers? Is it our choice?

Next to the article, there is a large colour photo of the painting and next to that, an interactive quiz.

Polly's breathing became erratic. A voice in her head chanted, oh no, oh no, oh no, oh no.

She checked other news services. The story and photo were everywhere. He'll see it. What will she do? The phone ringing interrupted her panic.

It stopped.

She could say it was a painting of Jake, not him, but he won't believe her. You can make out the scars. The telephone rang again, and she got up to find Poppa. He was in his study; the phone pressed to his ear. She plonked herself in an old armchair and tucked her legs under her bottom.

Fletcher said, 'Hold on, I'll put you on speaker. Polly's here with me.' There was a pause and Fletcher said, 'Hello, can you hear me?'

A voice from the speaker said, 'Hello Polly. I see you've made it as an artist with a bang.' Brad sniggered.

Tears sprang into Polly's eyes. 'But it's not about my art.'

'Sorry, can't hear you Polly. You'll need to get closer to the phone.'

She didn't move. Fletcher repeated, 'She said the hype is not about her art.'

'Publicity is publicity, and that's what you said you wanted, Fletch old boy. Provoking debate, isn't that what art is about? Isn't that why you chose climate change as a subject, Polly? Now you have it and you're complaining. I must admit, I didn't do it all by myself. Take some of the credit, Fletch. That little impromptu speech you made about the politicians we deserve captured the imagination. Brilliant touch if I may say. People are so weary of politics and politicians that to have a romantic hero of courage, honesty, and imagination... Well, it's what people want, isn't it? The press knows that, and it sells copy. And the painting is good. A work worthy of celebration. It doesn't hurt to have such an aura of romance, handsomeness, and strength. Your model is an Adonis. Every woman is in love and many men, too. If they're not in love, they're jealous. The masculinity, compassion, and sexuality are palpable.' He paused and then added, 'the fact that you have people bidding and then tell them it's not for sale has added to its desirability. Everyone wants to know who he is. They smell romance. There's nothing more compelling in the human condition than love.'

'What do you suggest, then?' Fletcher shrugged at Polly.

'I wouldn't worry. It's a flash in the pan. It'll be over in twenty-four hours. Something else will have taken its place. I must admit I hadn't expected this kind of hype, but there you go. Give the press a slow news day, a beautiful man, a young and may I say, attractive artist and an old hack, tugging people's heartstrings, then add that to my brilliance at PR, and you have a cocktail that's effervescently refreshing but drunk down like lolly-water, disappearing just as fast. You've made your name now Polly, so as your agent, I suggest you sit-tight and enjoy it. Plan your next exhibition. It'll be a sell out.'

Polly walked over to the phone. 'Brad, if you want to continue being my agent, make it known that I modelled this portrait from old photos of various men, long dead. It's an idealised image. There is no flesh and blood person for them to find. If you can get that across, then we've got a deal.'

'Polly darling, we need one man, not an idealised image. Give me one man please, even one who's dead. People need to know that such an existence is possible, and not just in imagination or they'll label you a phoney. All the good work will go up in smoke. It had pariah potential. You don't want that, do you?'

But this was different, a dilemma tossing between her reputation as an artist and her fear of how the portrait would impact Matt's view of her.

Fletcher intervened. 'There was a person, Brad. Hold on while I have a chat to Polly.' He pushed the mute button on the phone. 'Poll, Jake is most probably dead and won't care, anyway. If he is still alive somewhere, it will help us find him.'

Polly remained silent, searching Fletcher's face. She nodded and slumped back into her chair.

Fletcher released the mute button. 'Okay Brad. The man's name is Jake Ryder. He was an SAS soldier in the Rhodesian war. We think he's dead, but we are not sure. I have several photos of him in my albums from when I was a war correspondent in the 70s. We don't have his permission, and as far as I know his parents are dead, although what other family he has I don't know, possibly a brother. The likelihood of family is our biggest concern.'

Polly let herself breathe. It would be okay. Matt would think the painting was of his father, and she can apologise. A flash of resentment surged through her. She blamed Fletcher for pushing her into exhibiting the damn painting. Yet, if it weren't for them, few people would have attended her exhibition.

This is what people dream of, and it almost never happens. She should feel lucky. After all, Fletcher was helping as she asked. She shook her head. Matt had gone, and while he might see something on-line it was unlikely. It certainly wouldn't make the British news.

'Poppa, do you have an address or email for Matt? I would like to send him an explanation and apologise for not consulting him prior to the exhibition.'

Fletcher nodded. 'I'll send it to you.'

While Polly prepared a salad for lunch, she composed the email in her head. The doorbell rang, interrupting her thoughts.

Jason was standing on the porch. He hovered, grinning, with his camera held out towards her.

'Hey Poll, sorry to come crashing in on you, but I have a great photo. I also wanted to say congratulations, mate. You have made the big time. It's everywhere. We're all proud of you; me at the others at the sheds. Just wanted to tell you.' He trailed off.

Polly tried to disguise her surprise at seeing him. 'Jason, I thought you were the bloody press. Come in. Sorry, I didn't get to talk with you and the others last night. It was kind of mad and this thing... well, it's nuts.'

Jason wiped his feet on the mat with more vigour than what removal of dirt might have required. 'You deserve it, Poll. You're good, you know that?'

'Hm. Sure—sure.' She laughed. 'I'm making salad for me and Poppa. Do you want to join us?'

Chapter Seventeen

Matt took in the disarray with distaste. At least the bodies had gone. He pried the laptop from under a pizza box. There was an email from Fletcher.

Good news Matt, we can leave for Zim in June. That gives us six weeks to get things organised. BTW, Polly's exhibition opening was tonight. It was a success as I expected. You may want to find it online. One of Polly's friends took the photo attached. Jason is a cabinetmaker who works in the shed next door to her. He's been sweet on Polly for a while.

Matt opened the attachment. A photo showed Polly sitting on a bench in a city street. Her eyes were closed, and her pale face tilted to the sky. Dark strands of hair fell over her breast and back over her shoulder. He never thought of Polly having a boyfriend, although he was not sure why.

A wave of nausea brought him back to reality. He could read Fletcher's email another time. The woman upstairs was still asleep, and he hoped she would stay that way until he got back. He didn't want her roaming his house, but he had to run to cure the hangover and the restlessness.

Outside the morning was grey and chilly. Low clouds skulked across the sky, blocking the light from a pale rising sun. There was a stale smell in the air, like congealed porridge. Boarding school all over. He jogged along Horseferry Road, crossing Lambeth Bridge and ran as far as the university before turning back.

When he returned home, Matt found the woman in the sitting room in her underpants watching the television. He sat next to her. 'Do you want breakfast? There's nothing in the house, but we can go out.'

She glanced at him, and then back to the television. 'Did you see this?' The sound on the telly was low.

'No, I haven't had time to watch the news yet.'

She ignored him, her gaze fixed on the screen. 'Fuck man, it's you!' She peered at him.

He could see the blood veins in her sclera. She drank as much as he did last night, and he wondered if she remembered his name. She must have a good constitution to cope with all that booze, but then she was young with a decade advantage over him.

'Check it out!' Her hand pushed against his cheek to make him face the T.V.

It annoyed him, but all he said was, 'What am I looking at?'

'Wait, it'll come back in a moment. Wait, wait... there! See, what did I tell you? It's you.'

A painting came into focus, taking up the whole screen. 'Christ!' He could see it was him, even make out faint scars running across the shoulder. He reached for the remote. The reporter talked about an unknown Australian artist and her first exhibition.

His mouth became dry, and he couldn't take a proper breath. Nausea rose in his throat and his heart hammered. He rushed to the bathroom and splashed his face with cold water. Jesus, he stank. He took off his clothes and got into the shower.

The girl followed him, calling from the other side of the door. 'You all right in there? Want the hair of the dog? Can I smoke in here or do I have to go outside and freeze my backside off?'

He opened the door, and she held out a pack of cigarettes. He took one, saying silently, sorry Mum. Then he headed to the kitchen for a bottle of whisky. They would have one for its medicinal purposes, get breakfast, and then he had to get rid of her. The shot of whisky helped, and he dragged at the cigarette, drawing smoke deep into his lungs. The woman was still talking, but he ignored her.

'Hey, what's with you?' She said.

'Nothing.' He dropped the cigarette into the sink. 'I'm going to shower, and you have to go.' He walked to the bathroom, no longer caring about offending her.

The phone rang.

'Shall I get it?' She called through the bathroom door.

'No, leave it. It'll go to message.'

Ten minutes later, he came out of the shower.

She sprawled on his bed, still in her underpants. 'What the frigging hell's going on?'

'Nothing, just leave it, but you'll have to go.'

She pouted. 'What about breakfast? You said.'

'It's off, sorry. I've got something urgent.'

'It's that painting.'

'No, yes. Fuck, it doesn't matter. It's not me. It's someone else.'

'You could have fooled me. Will I see you again?'

Matt smiled. 'Do you even know my name?'

She blushed. 'I can't remember. It was wild last night.'

'Where are you staying? I'll call a cab. I'll see you tonight at the bar. My name's Pete, by the way. What's yours?'

Her face lifted. 'Christina.'

'Great, um Christina, and thanks. It was a good night. So, I might see you later.'

He was a bastard, but he was never going near that bar again. She dressed while he called a cab. At least she wouldn't make a scene.

The taxi pulled away, and he lifted his hand in farewell before turning back inside to make another call. He waited while someone connected him. The line crackled and the familiar tone of his ex-commanding officer said, 'Reid. Missing us already? Want to come crawling back, eh?'

Matt explained the news story while his CO listened.

'Wait.' He said when Matt had finished.

Five minutes passed before his CO came back. 'You're in the clear. The painting is of an old Rhodesian soldier. C Squadron in the 70s, I believe. Anyway, the bloke's been dead and gone for a while. So why did you think it was you? Are you posing for artists now? You have sunk to an all-time low, my boy.'

His cackling rang in Matt's head as he hung up the phone, relief washing through him in waves. Then he realised he would never live it down. His mates would hear that he model in the nude for an Australian artist. The old boy will make sure of that. He sighed. Better than having the press knowing the painting is him. Bad things can come from that, even though he had left the squadron.

He opened his laptop searching for the Australian news. Christ, it was everywhere. He realised she was pretty good, capturing his likeness in an abstract way. There was something else also, something he couldn't put his finger on. The torso in the painting was naked, but the closer he zoomed in, the less detail he could see. The scars were only visible from a distance, suggestive rather than obvious. Perhaps it was Jake. He sat back, gazing at the picture, wanting to see her, wanting to ask why she painted it.

That night Matt turned on the news, and saw Christina, being interviewed by a journalist.

She said, 'The Australian painting is of Pete, and he lives in London.'

The reporter raised an eyebrow. 'The artist said it was an image from an old photo of a Rhodesian soldier from the seventies'.

'It's not,' Christina said vehemently. 'I stayed with him last night. I'm telling you it's him.'

'Where does he live then—this man you're talking about? What's his name? Pete—Pete who?'

But to Matt's intense relief, she didn't know his surname or where he lived. She said she was new in London, and she couldn't remember. She started crying. Matt felt sorry for, but he was also relieved.

The phone rang. His CO on the other end. 'Christ, Reid, you've made a muck-up of this one. Whatever possessed you? You need to go away for a while. Got anywhere quiet to hang out until this thing blows over? Who the hell is the woman blabbing on the T.V. now?'

Matt ignored the last part about Christina. It was probably rhetorical anyway. Instead, he said, 'I was planning on going to Zimbabwe. I have some research.'

'Zimbabwe, for Christ' sake! Oh, hang on, Mugabe doesn't like reporters, does he? You might be all right there but keep your head down and don't do any more posing.'

'Sir, not that I want to ruin a good story, but I would like it on the record that I actually didn't pose for that painting. She, the artist that is, did it from memory.'

'Well, blow me. What, is she in love with you or something?'

Matt remained silent.

'Lucky beggar, let me know when you're leaving. I'll give the press something to take their mind off things.'

'Yes, sir.'

Matt hung up the phone. He would call the travel agent in the morning. He wouldn't feel safe from the press until he was in the air.

The phone rang again. Matt contemplated ignoring it but reluctantly returned to pick it up.

Half expecting his CO Matt said, 'Reid here.'

'Dickhead, what the fuck are you up to?'

'Nice of you to call, Dog. How's the wife?'

'Fuck off, dip stick—what's with the news story? Pete, hey, who the hell is Pete?'

'Christ! Matt couldn't believe it. Even Dog had seen the news. He never watched the news.'

Dog said, 'I just saw that woman from last night talking to the press. I assume Pete is you?'

'It's complicated.' Matt rubbed his neck.

'Gen dit boyo. I saw the painting, pretty boy, what you bin hiding?'

'It's not like that. It's someone else, just with a slight resemblance.'

'No shit—at least we know how you spent your time in Australia. Good painting though. Who's the pash?'

'No one. Just a friend. Look, I'm getting out, lying low for a while. Do me a favour, keep me out of this?'

'Just saying... we can decommission it pretty easily.'

Matt shook his head. 'No, it's good art. Fuck, I wouldn't mind owning it myself, so leave it, don't do anything to destroy it. You got that Dog? The press will tire of it soon.'

'Okay boyo, I get the picture and if we see the gobshyte from last night, we'll tell her Pete's got a wife and five kiddies, and the wife's out to flay her alive.'

'Dog, I'm sweating neaters with this shit. Don't do anything stupid, okay? I have to go. Got a plane to catch.'

Chapter Eighteen

Polly sat at Fletcher's desk staring at the phone, horrified. Moments ago, bolstered by bravado, she dialled Matt's number, and a woman's voice said no one was home. She hung up, terrified of leaving a message on a phone owned by a woman's voice.

'Pull yourself together,' she scolded.

She's an artist. She doesn't need permission to paint people. Ringing him was a courtesy. She'll write instead. What will she say? On the phone, you can leave silences for the other person to interpret, you can't do that in an email.

She dithered. Perhaps he wouldn't see the media articles. If she writes to him, she will only draw attention to the story. Perhaps she was catastrophising. What are the odds of him seeing the painting? The hype will be over before the pictures of the exhibition will reach the U.K.

The press was driving this frenzy, not the public, and the media had a short concentration span. She walked out of the room feeling lighter than she had all day. The phone rang, summonsing her back to the study. For a moment she thought it might be him, and nerves tightened her throat. She cleared her voice and lifted the phone. 'Hello.'

Brad said, 'Polly, is that you?'

'Hello Brad. I'll call Poppa.'

'No, Polly, it's you I need to speak to.'

'Oh, what is it? Not something else about the painting. I couldn't bear it.'

'Well, yes. It's a bit of a concern, but something you were expecting, I imagine. The news has unearthed family.'

Polly's legs buckled and she pulled up Fletcher's chair.

'What family?' Did the voice on the message bank belong to his wife?

Brad continued, 'There was a call from Zimbabwe. It was a man, Mr Ryder, asking who was in the portrait. I've fielded several of those inquiries already, so I gave the story Fletcher gave me about the old Rhodesian soldier.'

Brad paused and Polly almost choked on the pulse beating in her throat.

His voice cracked. 'Polly, it may be this man's son. It was horrible. He broke down on the phone begging me to tell him where Jake was.'

Polly couldn't breathe.

Brad spoke again. 'I said you would ring him. I have his number and email. The phones don't work that well over there, apparently. Do you have a pen? Polly, are you still there?'

She coughed. 'Yes Brad, I'm here.' She coughed again, but the lump remained wedged. 'I'm just shocked. The poor man, but who would have thought it would make the Zimbabwe news?' She blinked tears away, and then, when that failed, wiped her eyes with the back of her hand. 'How horrible. What have I done?'

'Mr Ryder said he saw it on BBC on-line. It is shocking. How awful not knowing where you son is. Are you sure this Jake fellow is dead, Polly?'

'I thought so. It never occurred to me he might be alive. Poppa thinks he's dead. Ah, Brad, what will I do?'

'Ring them and explain. Tell them what you told me. It'll be all right. He seemed like a decent sort, very down to earth and practical.'

'Okay, give me the number. I'll ring him now.'

After she hung up, Polly stared out the window, trying to collect her scattered thoughts. What could she say to these people? Should she tell them about Matt? Perhaps she should call Poppa and tell him.

Instead, she lifted the phone, pressing the international numbers. Alien seashell waves and whistles sounded in her ear for the second time in the space of an hour, and then the phone rang. A man answered.

'Dennis Ryder speaking.'

Words refused to form, and Polly coughed to clear her throat.

'Hello. Hello, is someone there?'

'Yes sorry, I'm Polly. Polly Fletcher. I painted the portrait. You spoke to Brad. Um, you said you think your son is in the picture.' Polly took a breath.

'Yes, yes. Thank you for calling. We're so grateful for anything you can tell us. You are the artist, is that right?'

'Yes.'

'Do you know where my son is? Please tell me. His mother's distraught. We haven't seen him for thirty-four years. If he's still alive... Please... anything you can tell us.'

Tears filled her eyes and her voice choked as she said, 'I'm so sorry.' She wiped her face on her sleeve. 'This is not your son. Well... I know who your son is. My father knew him. He has photos, but they're old from the Rhodesian war. I don't know where he is. I'm so, so sorry. I didn't think.'

Fletcher walked into the room and saw Polly crying into the phone. Concern flitted across his face. 'Poll, what's wrong?'

Polly sniffed. 'My grandfather is here. Please hold on—he'll tell you.' She held out the phone to Fletcher. 'It's Jake's father, Dennis Ryder, on the phone. Oh, Poppa Jake's parents are alive, and want to know where he is. They haven't seen him for thirty-four years.' A fresh flood of tears filled Polly's eyes and spilled over her cheeks. 'Please talk to them. I don't know what to say.'

Fletcher took the phone. 'Hello Dennis. I'm not sure if you remember me, but I came to your farm once with Jake in '77... Yes, the Australian journalist.'

When Fletcher hung up, Polly said, 'What did he say, Poppa?'

'How did that happen? How did you get hold of Jake's parents?'

'Brad, they rang Brad, and he gave me their number. They saw the painting on the BBC news and think thought that their son was still alive. Oh, Poppa, how sad for them. What have I done? What did Mr Ryder say to you?'

'I told him you're coming to Zimbabwe, straight away. How can it be possible that they don't know what happened to Jake? If anyone knew anything, you'd think it would be them.'

'Zimbabwe. Now? What about the rest of the exhibition? What about your operation? You were going to do that first.'

'I said you're going. I'll join you when they've taken the pins out of my pelvis. It'll be fine. They've invited you to stay with them, and said they'll pick you up at the airport. You'll be safe enough with them. The exhibition will get along fine without you, and when you come back, the furore will have died down.'

Anxiety crawled up her neck. 'Who will take you to the hospital and bring you home? Who will take care of you, Poppa?'

'I've managed for seventy years, Poll. I can do it now.'

'But what about visas and things?'

'You can buy a visa at the airport. Dennis said bring lots of U.S. currency in small bills. Stop panicking, they're just details.' Fletcher stopped writing and walked over to her, putting his arms around her and pulling her close. 'You'll be fine, my girl; Dennis is a good bloke. Zimbabwe isn't as wild as it appears on T.V. Since Tsvangirai's been sharing power, things have improved. At least there's food in the shops now.'

'What about Matt, Poppa?'

'What about him?'

'Did you tell Jake's father about him?'

'Ah no. One shock at a time, eh? Besides, we will need Matt's permission before we charge into that territory.'

'Are you going to tell Matt, then?'

'Yes, of course. I'll ring him now unless you want to.'

But again, Matt didn't answer the phone.

Chapter Nineteen

The plane circled to land at Harare airport. Dark green trees dotted the ground below and in the distance there was a suburb of khaki-coloured housing. The eastern sky, Wedgewood blue at the edges, had great bruised mushroom caps of rain clouds. Raindrops radiated across his window. Water lay in lakes across the flat landscape. They taxied along the runway, passed the airport tower, an astonishing snow cone of confectionary. Matt hadn't expected such dazzling architecture. His stomach churned in unexpected excitement. This was the land of his parents, most likely where he was conceived, its history ingrained into his DNA. Why did he feel nostalgia for a country he'd never seen? Is it the connection to the possibility of what might have been?

For a moment he let his imagination construct an alternative existence until he realised if he had stayed in this land with Jake and his mother he would be a different person. Would he trade his experiences and opportunities? Wishing for an alternative life was a funny thing. It meant you couldn't keep the one you had. Matt felt attached to this one, even if it wasn't perfect. Life's experience made him who he was, and he could live with that. Although it would be good to meet his biological father if he was still alive. Now he was in the country, he would find him.

The plane emptied, and he retrieved his laptop from the locker above his head. Once he passed through customs and immigration, he collected his luggage, just his old Bergen, and walked out of the building in search of a taxi.

The taxi took him to Meikles Hotel, a place recommended by the travel agent. Matt could see why. As he entered the hotel, he admired the two bronze lions either side of an obsidian entrance. An effusive doorman took his Bergen. Matt held onto his laptop.

The doorman grinned. 'British, sah?'

Matt was not sure if it was all right to be British given the whole colonial thing but nodded anyway. 'English actually.' He sounded more uppity than he intended.

The hotel's faded splendour showed the colonial bones of its heritage. He realised now why his mother complained that the service in Britain was so awful.

The hotel was closed, in part, for refurbishment, but Matt had stayed in worse places. The chintzy décor was clean and comfortable, although in need of renewal. His room overlooked a park, backed by modern skyscrapers. A massive glass structure loomed larger than the others. In the foreground, a traditional cathedral stood sentry to the park entrance, busy with hawkers and pedestrians. A circular fountain in the centre of the park pulsed water jets. It was so different from the African capitals Matt had seen in the continent's north. Here there did not seem to be overt oppression and terror, but then he was in premium accommodation.

The internet connection worked, and Matt shook his head in wonderment. He thought the country was a basket case. He checked the news on his laptop, searching for the diversion his CO promised to take the press's mind off him and the portrait. An earthquake in China... Not even his CO could arrange earthquakes. He soon found it, an article where the Ministry of Defence confirmed U.K. was using Reaper drones in Afghanistan.

Matt smiled. That would have people frothing, and yes, a protest march. That will get the painting off the front page. But another article showed the portrait.

Everyman Stolen:

In news just at hand, a bold raid on an Art Gallery in Brisbane last night resulted in the theft of a painting that made sensational news at its debut four days ago.

Thieves broke a window to access the Gallery, setting off an alarm, but by the time police arrived they had long gone. Police are appealing to any witnesses that may have seen anything unusual in the Gallery's vicinity. The thief or thieves have left no trace of their calling except for the broken glass and the missing painting. Police are trying to contact the artist for questioning.

In a bizarre twist, she has left the country, travelling to Zimbabwe to meet with the parents of the man in the painting. They have not seen their son since his disappearance in 1980, shortly before Zimbabwean Independence. The mystery of Everyman deepens.

In his haste to reach the phone, Matt tripped over the laptop cord, saving himself with his hands as he fell but still cracking his knee on the floor. Rubbing the hurt knee, he picked up the phone, and asked reception to put him through to Australia.

He scanned his emails for Fletcher's number to give to the operator and saw an email from Fletcher asking him to call as soon as he could. The operator placed the call, and Matt waited for what seemed an interminable time before he heard Fletcher's voice.

'Fletcher, it's Matt, what's happening?'

'Matt, thank goodness you rang. I'm scheduled to have my op on Monday, and I thought I might miss you. Where have you been? I've left a dozen messages.'

'I'm in Zimbabwe. It's a long story.'

'Zimbabwe!'

'Yes, I'll tell you another time. What's with the burglary and where is Polly? Who are these people she's going to see?'

'Okay, Matt, take it easy. The people she's seeing are Jake's parents, your grandparents, if you want them to be. The strange thing is, they're still living in Zimbabwe. It never occurred to me they would still be there, let alone still alive. Polly painted a portrait.'

'Yeah, I saw it.'

'Well, they did too. They tracked Polly down through her agent. Matt, are you still there?'

'Yeah, I'm here. I guess I'm shocked. Where is Polly now?'

'I put her on the plane this morning. She'll be in Harare the day after tomorrow. She has a stopover in Perth, then Johannesburg, and then a connection to Harare.'

'Who are these people—my grandparents?' Even as Matt said the words, they confused him. 'Do they know about me?'

'No, we didn't want to tell them without talking to you first.'

Fletcher fell silent, waiting for Matt, but Matt said nothing. He was staring out the window at a bird circling above the park across the road, asking himself how he felt about this new twist in his life?

'Matt, say something. What do you think? Will you tell them?'

'They're in Harare, you say.'

'Yes, actually no, I don't know. They're in Zimbabwe, but I don't know where they live. When I met them, they lived on a farm in the southeast. I don't suppose they're still there, but I wouldn't know. I have their phone number, and an email address, if that helps. I'll email it to you along with Polly's flight details.'

After Matt hung up, he continued staring out the window. Should he contact these people and say, *hi I'm your grandson but I didn't know that until recently*? It seemed like a worse dilemma than flying to Australia to ask a complete stranger if he was his father. Did he want this? Is Jake his biological father? Could he say that with certainty, without a DNA test? What about the burglary? He picked up the phone and asked to be reconnected to Australia. Fletcher answered again, but when Matt asked about the theft of the painting, he had little more to tell Matt other than what he had read on the news.

'What did the police think happened?'

Fletcher chuckled. 'They think Polly stole it and whisked it off to Zimbabwe with her, or at least that's what I reckon, but when they found out the thing is not insured, they couldn't figure out a motive. Personally, I think they haven't a clue. There was not a print in the place, and hardly any signs of thieves having broken in. Anyway, Polly doesn't know yet, but I rang Dennis and told him. I've left a message on Polly's phone. She'll get it when they land in Perth.'

'Who's Dennis?'

'Your grandfather. His name's Dennis Ryder and his wife. Your grandmother is Dolly. Jake also had an older brother, Tom, who lives in Zim. Sorry to dump all this on you. I know it must be a bit to absorb all at once.'

Christ, you're not wrong there. All Matt said was, 'It's fine, Fletch, and thanks.'

He lay back on the bed. This was his father's family. It was too much to comprehend. Instead, he dealt with the immediate issue of the burglary. That was weird, and he hoped it was not something Dog and Brander dreamed up. How would Polly react? Why did she paint the blasted thing?

Perhaps it was narcissistic to think the painting was of him, not Jake. Maybe he just hoped Polly painted him. It meant she felt something. No. He was in enough of a tangle without that. Matt smelled cigarette smoke and sat up like a dog waiting for dinner.

He headed for the bar downstairs. It was his solution to most things. Why change a habit of a lifetime? He needed something to calm his raging mind so he could think straight. Besides, he might meet people who could tell him about this place. How he should behave, whom he should see, where it was safe to go.

Aside from hiding from the press, he was here to find his mother's marriage certificate, and to find his father. Uncovering new grandparents and an uncle wasn't part of his mission. He needed a new plan.

He ordered a whisky from a friendly barman. Matt asked the barman his name.

'Tadeous, sir.'

'I'm Matt, call me Matt will you? This sir business makes me sound like my grandfather.' He grinned, realising what he just said. The word hadn't meant much to him before, just an old saying unrelated to his grandfather. Now everything had added significance.

Tadeous asked if Matt would like ice in his whisky. Matt shook his head. 'Where are you from, Tadeous?'

'Chiadzwa.'

'Sorry mate. I don't know where Chiadzwa is.'

'Ah, it is about 90 kilometres southwest of Mutare. A very beautiful place.'

'Where is Mutare?'

'In the eastern highlands. Also very beautiful, but it is in the mountains. My home is in the Lowveld.'

'Should I visit Chiadzwa? Is it a good place for tourists?'

'Ah myweh, you cannot go there, sah.' Tadeous's fine English diction lapsed as his eyes scanned the room.

'Why not?' Matt asked.

'Sah, it is a no-go zone, where there are the Marange diamond fields. If you go there, sah, they will kill you. The army patrol this area with helicopters.'

'But it's your home Tadeous, can't you go there?'

'Ah, no sah.' Nervous beads of sweat stood out on his forehead. He said, 'Excuse me. It's my busy time now, happy hour, Saturday evening sundowner time.'

Tadeous hurried to attend to an order at the other end of the bar.

Matt slid onto one of the swivel top cane bar stools and turned his back to the bar to survey the room. He imagined a colonial clubroom from Rider Haggard's time, airy and inviting, with wood panelling and papered walls. Old elephant tusks displayed their indignity on the wall, along with the mounted horns of an antelope. The tight basket weave armchairs clustered close to small tables, each with a large ashtray in the centre. Potted palms punctuated the furniture, and brass lamps hung from the ceiling. Conscientious waiters glided effortlessly between the tables, serving drinks and snacks to well-heeled locals and a few international businessmen. He wondered what he would find outside this rarefied atmosphere.

A woman sashayed up to him and leaned against the bar. 'How are you?' She said, clicking her fingers at Tadeous.

Tadeous hurried over, his manner obsequious, while placing a drink in front of her. A cola with a confection of fruit cocktail and paper umbrella. Obviously not a prostitute. She must be someone important the way the barman kowtowed. A warning flashed into Matt's mind, and he wondered if she might be the undercover police.

'Fine, thanks.' He responded before swallowing his drink and signalling Tadeous for another.

When Tadeous brought the drink, Matt noticed the whites of his eyes showed above dark irises. He was terrified.

The woman shifted her weight, her English precise, but with a strong accent. 'Are you visiting on business or for pleasure?'

'How did you know I was a visitor?'

He wasn't intending to engage in small talk with her but at least he'd try to be polite.

'You are new. Business or pleasure?'

'Pleasure.' If she was soliciting, he would soon know. 'I'm here to see the sights.' His gaze travelled along her body. 'And they seem pretty good from where I'm sitting.' Jesus, that sounded sleazy, even to him. But he wanted to be sure of her game.

The coke disappeared in one hit. Her hair was straight and oiled, so it shone like inky black plastic, and she was wearing a midnight blue dress covered with sequins. Her high heels were obviously uncomfortable, and she shifted from foot to foot.

'Have a seat.' Matt tried more sleaze tactics. If she was an official, and he could help her out of her torture, she might return the favour sometime. 'Can I buy you a drink?'

He signalled Tadeous, who came running with another drink for her. Another coke, although it might have had something alcoholic in it.

'Thank you. My feet are killing me.'

'I can imagine. They designed those heels for torture.' He wondered if he had gone too far, but she laughed.

'I like you, Englishman.'

'Matt, call me Matt, please. Englishman is so formal, don't you think?'

She ignored him. 'I recognise you.'

'You do? I haven't been here before. Have you been to London?'

'Please, Mr Reid, you can stop playing games now. I want to know what you're doing here. One minute, your portrait is all over the news as a so-called Rhodesian SAS soldier. The next minute you are sitting here in my country, in my favourite bar. You must admit this is a little odd, is it not?'

'Christ.' Matt stared at her in amazement. 'Everywhere I go, the bloody thing follows me. You're right. I'm here trying to hide from the blasted British press. I was planning to come on holiday anyway, but I came earlier to get away from them. Are you a journalist?' He was sure she wasn't, but he wanted to appear naïve.

She ignored him again. 'Are you an old Rhodesian, Mr Reid?'

'I was born in London. This is my first visit to your country.' He calculated how much she might know and stuck close to the truth. 'My mother was born here.'

'Yes, you are too young. I think to have been here much before Independence. So, is your mother driving this?'

'Driving what?' He was becoming exasperated. 'My mother is dead. She died a few months ago.' He had an idea. 'Actually, that's why I am here on a kind of pilgrimage. I want to know more about her life.'

At this, the woman's forehead crinkled. 'Why did you not ask her when she was alive?' She quickly pulled back to focus on the task. 'It is a terrible thing to lose a mother,' she said. 'I'm sorry for your loss.'

'Thank you. I am very sad without her.' He realised the admission was true. He felt sad. This was the first time he noticed the sadness. Until now, he was just angry.

She was silent for a moment, and Matt hoped the interrogation was over, but he wasn't going to be that lucky.

'Mr Reid'

He interrupted. 'Call me Matt, please. What's your name?' He was trying the charm offensive again, but she wouldn't meet his gaze.

'My name is of no concern to you, Mr Reid.'

'Okay. Well, if you want to hear my story, have dinner with me, and I'll tell you. It'll take a while, and I'm hungry. I hear the food in the restaurant here is pretty good.'

It seemed to work. He watched indecision cross her face, but clearly the idea of eating in this establishment provided the temptation he needed. The last thing he wanted to do was have dinner with the woman, but he couldn't see an alternative. If he didn't placate her, she wouldn't let him out of her sight, and he didn't want to be followed everywhere.

'The Grill is closed for renovations, but we can eat on the terrace.' She seemed to decide. 'You must tell me the whole truth for me to do that, and I must take notes. No funny business.'

'On my honour.' He held his hand to his heart. 'But I can't eat dinner with you if I don't know your name.'

She frowned for a moment. 'My name is Gracie.'

'Okay, Gracie.' He got to his feet, holding out his arm in old-fashioned courtesy.

She giggled but didn't take it. Instead, she turned her might on poor Tadeous, speaking in a language that Matt didn't understand. Tadeous ducked his head in acquiescence. She walked off, wobbling across the room in the high-heeled shoes.

Matt followed, noticing her shoes were a size too small for her feet. Her heels overhang, oozing sole-pink flesh between the sling back strap and heel of the shoe. No wonder she was in pain.

They sat at a table on the rooftop terrace overlooking the park. A waiter attended to Gracie, then unfolded a white linen napkin for Matt's lap and handed him a menu.

Matt didn't look at the menu. 'So, what's the food like here?'

Reluctantly, she took her eyes off the menu to focus on him. 'I have never eaten here before.'

'Really? Why not? I thought you'd be a regular, sophisticated woman like you.'

'Eiish! Too expensive.' She buried her head in the menu again.

A waiter handed him the drinks menu. 'Would you like another drink Gracie, a bottle of wine perhaps to go with our meal?'

'I don't drink alcohol.' She looked at the waiter and spoke in her language. Matt assumed the language was chiShona. He didn't understand any of it until she said the word, *coke*. That he recognised, and he wondered what her teeth were like, and if they were any worse than his liver. Once she chose her meal, the waiter turned to

Matt said, 'Steak, rare.'

Gracie took a notebook out from her handbag, and with elaborate care folded it back to a clean page. She looked at the end of her pencil to see if it had a point, then wet the tip with her mouth. Then, holding the pencil poised above the paper, she said,. 'Now we can begin.'

He played the game, telling her about finding out about his blood type differing from his father's. He figured the truth was his best defence. It wasn't easy because at every step of the story, Gracie seemed confused.

'Blood type, why is that—how does it mean he is not your father?'

Matt sighed. He could see the night stretching out endlessly and signalled the waiter for another whisky.

The waiter served his steak after a spectacular flambé. The night sky was clear, with the occasional stars bright enough to be visible against the city blaze. He would bring Polly here when she arrived. Then he remembered the Ryder's would meet her.

Should he tell Gracie about the Ryder's being relatives? He decided against it. He didn't yet know the lay of the land, and he didn't want to bring grief to people who had presumably suffered enough in their lives.

In the end, the story he told Gracie left out all the bits about Jake and Rhodesia, and he claimed he modelled for the portrait in England. He asked if Gracie recognised the artist and she shook her head, so he explained it was an Englishman whose father was a journalist here at Independence. He left out so much from the story; it became incomprehensible, full of holes and inconsistencies.

Gracie dutifully wrote it all down in her spiral-bound notebook. So long as she doesn't try to check the details. He should leave Harare for a few days. He heard Victoria Falls was a good place to go.

'Mr. Reid, what can you tell me about diamonds?'

'Diamonds! Nothing. Why?' The left-field question flummoxed him.

'Are you here to smuggle diamonds, Mr. Reid?'

'The first time I heard about diamonds was from Tadeous.'

'Tadeous?'

'Yeah, apparently that's where he comes from, and he just told me no one can travel there. Not that I'm interested in diamonds.'

'Are you planning a coup d'état Mr. Reid, with the old Rhodesians SAS.'

Now, Matt became seriously worried. 'What? You're nuts. Any bloke who was in C Squadron would be a granddad by now.'

'Yes, this is true, but perhaps you are a recruit.'

Did she know his background? How could she? It was impossible. 'I'm too old for that kind of thing, and no, I'm not here for anything like that. I don't know anyone here, and I'm just on holiday, not for diamonds or for coups or anything else. I have heard nothing so crazy in my life.'

'Are you accusing me of being crazy, Mr. Reid?'

'No, Christ.' He ran his hands through his hair. 'The things you are accusing me of are crazy, not you. Look I'm a student.' He fished out his wallet and showed his student card. 'I am a mature age student on holiday, that's all.'

Eventually Gracie lay down her pencil, stretching cramped fingers. She ate, although the questions kept coming, eating with her right hand, while writing with her left. Her interrogation method was direct and amateurish, but unsettling.

Watching her laborious concentration, Matt wondered what was behind this and why him. Did they do this with every tourist that arrived in the place, just to let them know whose was boss. He needed another whisky and a cigarette if he was to endure the interrogation further.

Everyone here seemed to smoke, without restriction. The smell surrounded him.

She sat back in her chair. A small burp escaped as she packed away the notebook and pencil. 'That will be all for now, Mr. Reid, but you should be available for further questioning if we need you.'

'I was planning to go to Victoria Falls.'

'We will find you, Mr. Reid. Rest assured; we will know where you are at all times.'

She pushed back her chair to leave, and Matt rose, relieved the ordeal was over.

'Good evening Mr. Reid.'

He watched her totter off and then sat down again. 'Bugger, what a disaster. Waiter, can I get a pack of cigarette?'

'Certainly Sah, what brand?'

The waiter came back with the pack, and when Matt put the cigarette to his mouth, the waiter was there to light it for him. Matt smiled. 'You'd better get me some matches too, unless I can take you along with me.'

The waiter grinned. 'I cost extra.'

Smoke filled Matt's lungs, and instantly he felt the calming hit of nicotine. He leaned back in his chair, taking another slug of whisky and relaxed. If only Polly was there. He would remain in Harare until she arrived, then head out to Victoria Falls. The bizarre questioning about diamonds and coups had left him unsettled, but he needed to decide what to do about Jake's family. What could he say to these people? *Hi, I'm the long-lost grandson you didn't know you had.* Maybe not. Screw it, he would need to get a DNA test to be sure Jake was his father. Besides the Ryder's might not want to know him. He tried to put himself in their shoes, but there were so many possibilities it was doing his head in.

Part Three

Chapter Twenty

In a leafy street in Borrowdale, an elegant Harare suburb, four men stood around an open barbeque in a private back garden. Along a pathway, behind trellises covered in fruiting grapevines, a swimming pool glinted through the leaves. Around the side of the house, the early construction of a fort was taking shape, made from various items purloined by two young boys.

A tennis court showed casual neglect, with a sagging net ripped at one end, causing it to drag on the ground. Occasional weeds broke through the baked clay surface where they survived unattended. The gardeners realised the task was low on their priority list.

The rambling house, with its wide, white-pillared verandas, and grey-tiled roof, reclined in graceful command of its green acres. High walls, topped with razor wire, stood guard over domestic peace.

Each of the four men stood arms folded, a beer tucked into his chest while he watched steaks and boerewors sizzling on a cast iron plate. Twenty metres away, sitting in garden chairs under a spreading Poinciana tree, a group of women and a young man lounged. The man looked to be in his thirties. He stroked a glossy dark moustache between thumb and forefinger as he listened to an elderly woman. She appeared to be in her seventies, tall and elegant, her hair iron grey, her face a legacy of life lived in sun and wind, fissured, and cracked but cheerful.

She sipped a gin and tonic and resumed telling the young man a story with the air of a woman used to commanding men's attention. Every once in a while she threw up her hands in a gesture of emphasis, always careful not to spill her drink. Between the outstretched index and middle fingers of her liver-spotted left hand, she held an unlit cigarette.

She said something which caused her companions to shake their heads, and then she called to the men at the barbeque. The oldest man in the group of four was also in his late seventies, or perhaps eighties. Tall and gaunt, his shoulders stooped as he walked over to stand in front of the old woman, blocking her from view.

She got up and the other women follow her to the veranda, leaving the men in the garden. Affectionately, she scolded the two large Rhodesian ridgebacks as they leaped up from their shady positions and followed her in-doors.

Two children, boys aged eight and six, spilled out of the French doors as she made her way towards them. Dolly reached out to touch them, but they dodged her and tore around the corner of the house towards the fort.

Most of the women disappeared into the cool gloom of the interior, but one followed the boys. Their grandmother Jessica tiptoed with exaggerated stealth as she pretended to hunt, her eyes alight with mischief. She loved being in Harare with her grandchildren.

The three men at the barbeque walked over to join the elderly man, Dennis. He took the chair Dolly had vacated and sat down next to the young man with the moustache.

The young man, Chris, said, 'My turn I guess.' He got up and went over to tend to the barbeque.

One of the other men, a man called Dop, said, 'I like my nyama, still bloody inside young Christopher. Don't overcook the bastard, hey?'

Chris grinned. 'You'll get it how it comes, Dop unless you want to braai it yourself.'

'Bloody cheeky kids these days, hey Dennis? Tom, sort your kid out.' Dop sucked in his belly and pulled up his long trousers.

The other man, Graham, said, 'Who's for another chibuli?' Then he walked towards the house in search of more beer.

Dennis called, 'Graham, tell Dolly not to forget that wine Tom brought back from South Africa.'

Dop said, 'Not for me. I'll stick to beer.'

Graham came back out. 'Dolly said she's keeping the wine for when that Australian bird arrives.'

Dennis made a noise that sounded like a snort. 'Well, did you bring me a beer then?'

Graham turned to go back to the house to fetch another beer.

Tom, Dennis's son, said, 'Do you reckon the Petersons will be here just now? They're late.'

'They said they can't come today.' Dennis looked at his watch. 'They go to Church on Sundays so they can't make it.

We should have done this yesterday. Next time we'll make a better plan.'

'What d'you reckon Dennis, will Morgan win this?' Dop offered his pack of cigarettes around the assembly.

Tom and Chris both took one, but Dennis shook his head, saying, 'Doubt it. The bastards won't allow it. They're already offering money and promises to the N'angas. Livingston told me that his Dad and his Uncle both got an enormous flat screen T.V. delivered the other day—they are trying to make sure his father does the right thing, but at least we're not seeing the violence of last election, not yet anyway.'

'Best investment you ever made, sending that boy to boarding school with Tom and Jake.'

A young woman, her feet bare, her blonde hair swinging about her shoulders, walked down the steps from the veranda carrying a bowl of salad. 'Are Livingston and Bridie coming today?' She put the bowl on the table and looked from Dennis to Tom expectantly.

Tom shook his head. 'No Meg, he can't. He promised to take Bridie to visit her Aunty in the hospital. He says he'll come for dinner when what's her name gets here.'

Dennis said, 'Her name is Polly, Tom, and you be nice to her.'

'The boys will be disappointed. I said I thought we'd see them today. They were looking forward to seeing Blake and Simon.' Meg walked over to Chris and slipped her hand through his arm. 'How long before the steaks are ready?'

He squeezed her arm to his side with his elbow and dropped a kiss on the top of her head. 'Just now. Get me a clean plate, will you Meggie? I think the meat is done.'

'Mom says she wants her steak well-done, none of this raw shit that Dop likes.'

Chris sighed, 'Christ, what am I, the bloody cook '

Meg laughed and ran into the house to fetch a plate. The phone in the hallway rang. 'I'll get it,' she called.

'Hello Ryder residence, Meg here... Yes, he's here. Who shall I say is calling... Okay Mr Reid, hang on a tic, I'll get him.' She put down the phone and walked back outside. 'Granddad, phone.'

Dennis pushed down on his hands to leaver himself off the chair, his arms straightening before his legs did. He walked toward Meg. 'Who is it?'

'Someone called Matt Reid. Very British.' She pushed up the tip of her nose with the back of her index finger and disappeared into the house.

Chris called after her, 'Where's my plate?'

In the kitchen, Dolly told Meg to take the other plates, knives, and forks and a platter for the meat. The women, including Dop's wife Sheila, and Graham's wife Gloria, picked up bowls of food and condiments and trooped out after Meg.

As they passed the phone in the hallway, Dennis told them to hush. 'Can't hear a thing with your racket.'

Dolly pulled a face, and the other women giggled. In exaggerated stealth, they tiptoed outside into the brilliant Borrowdale sunshine.

A few minutes later, Dennis came out, ashen faced.

Dolly inhaled. 'What's wrong Dennis? Who was that on the phone?'

Dennis fell into a chair at the table. 'Give me one of those bloody cigarettes of yours, Dop.'

Dolly frowned. 'You've given up. The doctor said'

'I don't care what the doctor said. I need to get my head straight. Good grief, I can't believe it.'

Dop leaned over to give him a light, his jowly face creased with concern for his old mate. He glanced at Sheila, but she merely shrugged. None of them understood what was bothering Dennis.

'That person... The bloke on the phone' He stopped and drew on the cigarette, coughed, and stubbed it out in the ashtray on the table. 'That bloke... Christ... He said he thinks he might be Jake's son.'

There was silence around the table for what seemed like minutes as the others stared at him. Disbelief, incomprehension, and horror flitted across their faces.

Dennis said, 'I didn't know what to say. He says he's here. He's only just found out we exist. That Journo told him. The one whose granddaughter painted the picture. We met him once when Jake brought him home. He says he didn't know about Jake until Fletcher told him. Christ!'

Eyes reddening, he sniffed before turning to his wife, 'Dolly I think it might be true, he sounded genuine. He might be Jake's son.' His expression beseeched his wife for understanding. 'I have to see him' His voice cracked. He rose to his feet, hands trembling, and turned to Tom. 'Son, you'll have to drive. I'm not in a fit state. He's at Meikles.'

Dolly burst out. 'What son? Jake never had a son. It's a trick, Dennis. Who's doing this?' Tears spilled over her lids, and she hurried into the house.

Meg got up, but Sheila put out her hand. 'I'll go.' She had known Dolly for a long time.

Just at that moment, Jessica came back from around the side of the house with her grandsons. 'Look what your sons have been up to Meg, they're filthy'. She stopped when she saw the sombre faces. 'What's wrong?' She looked at her husband. 'What is it Tom?'

He put his arm around her but remained mute.

Graham explained. 'Someone rang—Meg. What was his name?'

'Matt Reid.'

'He told Dennis that he's Jake's son.'

Jessica plopped onto a chair and took a cigarette from the pack on the table. 'Christ, do you believe him, Dad?' The nurse in Jessica was gauging Dennis's visible vital signs carefully. A jolt like this could do bad things to people.

The two muddy boys waited a moment before inching away out of the adults' line of sight.

Tom looked at his feet. 'I believe him.'

Everyone turned to him.

'Tom, what do you know?' Jessica got up again and took Tom's hand, trying to look into his eyes, but his glance slid away, avoiding her, looking instead at Dennis.

Tom took a deep breath. 'I'm sorry, Dad. I didn't tell anyone. I couldn't.'

'Tell what?' Prompted Jess?

'Jake was in love with someone. He planned to marry her. Jake told me—fuck.'

'Who was she?' Jess glanced from Tom to Dennis.

'Celia someone.' He walked a couple of steps away, his head bowed, hiding the tears that filled his eyes. 'I'll get the car keys, Dad.'

Jess walked over to Chris, putting her arm through her son's. They stood staring at the meat congealing on the plate, before she said, 'No one will eat now, not for a while. 'I'll put some foil over it. It'll keep for a bit, hey darling.' She stroked his arm affectionately. Her beautiful son, she couldn't bear to lose him the way Dolly lost Jake. It would kill her.

'Thanks Mum.' Then it dawned on him. If this bloke was his Uncle Jake's kid, then he was his cousin. 'Shit,' he said under his breath.

'I'll come with you hey china.' Graham put his arm around Tom's shoulders.

'Ah thanks Gray, but I think it's better Dad and I go alone. We don't want to overwhelm the bloke. You stay and have lunch with the girls and Chris. Keep some for us when we get back, '

Dennis drew himself upright. 'I'll just see if Dolly's all right.' He shambled towards the house; his shoulders stooped further, as if he had aged ten years.

Chapter Twenty-One

Dennis Ryder's reaction wasn't what Matt had been expecting. Now, although curious, he was dreading the meeting. What would they be like? He had made it clear to the old man, the claim to any relationship was tentative and they would need a DNA test to be sure. The wait for Mr Ryder to arrive seemed interminable. He stubbed out his fag and began tidying his room, folding his things into his Bergin. It struck him, he was making ready to escape, although it had always been his practice to have his things contained so he could make a move with a moment's notice. Besides, tidying the room filled a few minutes with mundane occupation.

Eventually, there was nothing left to put away except his laptop. He opened it to check his emails. One from his mother's solicitor asking Matt to get in touch. He responded that he was away and would contact them on his return in a few weeks. There was also one from Dog. Here was another surprise. Dog was a committed technophobe.

Dear Matt

This is the first letter I have written since school and that was with pen and paper. I hope you realise how much this sacrifice has cost me. I have had to beg my kid sister's help, and you know what that'll cost. I have been calling you and leaving messages, but I guess you are still not home. Let me know me when you will be back. I need to speak to you urgently about two things. One must be a face-to-face conversation because it's about something very close to you. The other is the letter attached. I received it out of the blue. A lot of us got one, and I wondered if you did too. Brander and I are considering it, so are some of the others.

Yours sincerely,

Wilfred Barker (Dog).

Matt chuckled at the formality of the email, imagining Dog pecking out letters with one finger, his tongue poking out between his teeth as he concentrated. He opened the attached letter and scanned its contents. Someone was recruiting for a private army, but there were no details of whom or where. He checked his watch. He was now a minute late. No time now to respond. He picked up his key, wallet, and phone and left the room.

The lounge downstairs was packed. How would he recognise these people? At that moment, two men walked into the lounge from the door opposite. One was old, tall, and stooped with white, wispy hair. The other was a fit, barrel-chested man in his early sixties, tall and broad shouldered. He looked as if he'd spent his life in the sun. Both men stopped and stared across the room. Matt guessed the old bloke might be Dennis Ryder but was not sure about the other man.

He moved towards them and as he got closer, the older man staggered, taking a step back, and putting his hand to his throat. The other man placed his arm around him in support, but neither make any advance, just stared. Matt stopped and looked behind him. Perhaps this was the wrong old bloke. The action broke the spell, and both men rushed forward.

'Hello, you must be Matthew. I'm Tom Ryder. Jake's brother. This is my father. Sorry about the reaction, but Dad thought you were Jake when we came in. You nearly gave him a heart attack. Welcome to the family.'

'Matt, call me Matt. Ah... hem... Please to meet you.' Matt shook hands with Tom and then turned to Dennis.

The old man's eyes were red rimmed and watery, and to Matt's dismay, he ignored the outstretched hand and pulled Matt into a hug. His voice croaked, 'I feel a bit overwhelmed, like I have known you all your life. You look so much like him. No one can doubt who your father was. Come on, we're taking you home, son. Dolly will be impatient to see you. I'll wait until you've packed, and Tom will bring the car around.'

Matt frowned. 'Packed? I didn't realise I was going anywhere.'

Tom grinned, 'Neither did he until he saw you. Now there is no way on God's earth you are not coming home, even if we have to kidnap you. I'd better warn Mum. She just could have a heart attack if she sees you without a heads-up. She didn't believe your story.' His face lit with humour. 'Wait until she lays her eyes on you.' He chuckled as he made his way through the tables and chairs to the exit.

Matt turned to go back to his room for his Bergin and laptop. Packing must have been a premonition. Dennis followed.

Once they reached Matt's room, Dennis said,. 'I see you were ready to check out.'

'I was tidying up, to fill in the time while I waited for you.'

Dennis nodded. 'Yes. A daunting situation.'

They fell silent while Matt unplugged his laptop and retrieved his toiletries from the bathroom. He was ready to go.

Tom had already paid Matt's bill, but there was nothing he could do except tell Dennis he would prefer to pay his own way.

Dennis muttered. 'Looks like him and as stubborn.' Then he beamed at the concierge. 'My grandson.'

The car was a Mercedes four by four, and Tom drove it northeast, out of central Harare. Dennis sat the passenger seat and Matt sat in the back, his arm resting on his Bergen. He leaned into the middle of the seat to see through the headrests to note the route. There was a police roadblock ahead, and he glanced at Tom's face to see if he should be worried.

Tom slowed to a stop and lowered the window before turning off the ignition.

A police officer stooped to look through the window. 'Driver's licence please, sir.' Then he requested Tom pop the hood.

Tom sighed and got out, pulled out his licence from his wallet along with a banknote, and walked around the car with the police officer speaking the staccato chiShona.

After a few minutes, he got back into the car, and the police officer waved him on.

'Bloody idiots.'

'How much this time?' Dennis asked.

'Ten bucks.'

'A twenty dollar round trip, not too bad.' Dennis turned to grin at Matt.

Matt asked, 'What was that about?'

Tom said, 'Daylight robbery, and to add insult to injury, we end up paying ZANU's booze bill.'

Dennis explained. 'They claim to be looking for car defects and roadworthiness, but even if your car's brand new and you don't give them the money, you'll be in for a long wait to get away. That's if your car's not impounded. Everyone knows it's just another fund-raising exercise for ZANU coffers. The bastards are broke.'

Tom laughed. 'Not all broke, only the hoi polloi. The inner cabal has plenty, but it's not used to run the country. Thieving bastards.'

After twenty minutes driving, they pulled up at a formidable-looking gate between stone walls topped with rolls of razor wire. The electronic gates swung open.

Matt said, 'There must be a steady supply of electricity in Harare.'

Both men laughed.

Dennis said, 'The electricity supply is dreadful. We have our own generator. It kicks in automatically when the power goes down, which is often enough. Luckily, we have our own bore too. Services like electricity, water and sanitation are a joke. The saying goes we used to have four seasons here. Now Mugabe, in his generosity, has created an extra season. The fifth is the cholera season. It starts just after the rains. Is this your first visit to Zim my boy? You're in for a treat. One warning, though. Never get out of the car to open the gate if the electric supply is cut, particularly at dusk or night. Skebangers—thugs looking to steal cars—have killed people.'

At the end of the driveway, a cluster of people stood as if waiting. He hadn't been expecting a reception committee. As he climbed out of the car, there was a collective gasp. The oldest woman clutched a hankie to her mouth, her eyes rimmed pink with crying. Fresh tears filled her eyes, and she sniffed, wiping her nose with the hankie. The woman next to her tightened her arm protectively around her shoulders.

Matt stood next to the car, not sure what he should do.

Then Dennis came around the car and took Matt's arm. 'Dolly, come and meet your grandson and stop blubbering. You'll frighten the poor boy off.' Dennis's caring tone belied his harsh words. 'Matt, my son, this is Dolly, my wife, and your grandmother.'

It was a long time since anyone called Matt, son, and a surge of panic rose in his chest. Did he shake her hand or kiss her? He hadn't a clue what might be appropriate.

Dolly placed her hands on his forearms and looked into his eyes. She was a tall woman whose graceful movements show evidence of faded beauty, with a classically symmetrical bone structure, silvery grey hair, and lined and leathery skin showing years of weathering from sun and wind. Her dark green eyes were swimming behind the tears. His throat choked, so he couldn't speak. He didn't need to.

She said, 'I'm so glad you've found us. We have so many years to catch up on.' Her voice faltered, and she kissed his cheek. 'Have you eaten? We have lunch.' She tucked her hand under his arm. 'It's congealed now, but I am sure we can rescue it. Anyway, if we drink enough, none of us will care. Will you have a drink, Matt? I know I need one. Come'

'Mum, don't you think we should introduce Matt to the others first?' Tom seemed amused at his mother's pretence at being in control.

'What? Oh yes, I suppose so.' She flicked her hand around the group, and then, as if it was all too hard, she said, 'You do it Tom.'

Tom stepped forward. 'Matt, this is my wife Jessica and your aunt. My son Chris and his wife Meg. Friends, Dop and Sheila. Dop is short for pisshead. His real name is Vivian, which is why everyone calls him Dop.'

Dop puffed out his skinny chest. 'Bloody cheek. Don't listen to him, my boy. Good to meet you. I suppose it's superfluous telling you, you're the spit of your old man.' He shook Matt's hand.

Chris stepped forward to shake Matt's hand. 'It's bloody good to have a cousin. I always wanted one. I don't suppose you can fly a plane, can you?'

Matt grinned, a little envious of the moustache. 'I've only jumped out of them, but I'm willing to learn.'

Chris raised his eyebrows and ushered Meg forward. She tiptoed on bare feet to kiss Matt on his cheek, smelling of warm sunshine. Sheila hugged him, her bony old arms encircling his waist as she held him close for a moment.

Tom said, 'And this Graham, and Gloria, his better half. Gray and I go back to the war. He and I were in PATU together.'

Graham said, 'Neighbouring farms. We patrolled together in the early days before they pulled Tom into the police air wing. You see Matt, the farmers used to... hem, not anymore though, hey. Not since Mugabe's thugs... Well, anyway we lost the farm.' Graham stopped and cleared his throat.

Matt nodded. 'I've read about it.'

Zimbabwe's land distribution policy had become violent land grabs by the ZANU soldiers and younger thugs posing as veterans. The British had funded the Zimbabwe government to pay the farmers. They had never received a penny. There was no goodness or honour coming from Mugabe winning the election in 1980, no truth or reconciliation unless one belonged to Mugabe's inner sanctum.

Gloria said, 'The bloke won't know what PATU is, Gray. Give him a break.'

Matt smiled at her. 'I've read about the Police Anti-Terrorist Unit, and it was impressive, like all the Rhodesian security forces.'

Graham's face lit up at Matt's approval.

Gloria said, 'Not just a pretty face, then.' She kissed him, hugging him close to her cushiony bosom.

'Leave the man alone, Gloria. We don't want to scare him away,' Graham said.

'Oh, you.' She swatted at her husband, who laughed and dodged out of her way.

Dolly took his hand again. 'Come on in Matt.'

The two young boys sidled up to Dolly. 'Goodness we almost forgot you two! These urchins are Chris and Meg's boys, Alex, and Jay. My great grandchildren, she added, her eyes tender as she gazed at them.'

The boys held out their hands to shake Matt's hand, their small grubby faces serious in formality. Matt nodded, taking the eldest boy's hand and then the younger boy's hand.

The younger one said, 'We're building a fort.'

Matt put on an impressed expression. 'I'd like to see it.'

'Later,' Dolly said. 'Let's get lunch first. Go and wash boys.'

'We did already.' Their chorus was indignant.

'You didn't do a very good job. Take Matt's bags to the blue guest bedroom and wash your faces again.'

The boys grabbed the Bergen and laptop bag and raced indoors. The adults followed. After the heat outside, the interior of the house was cool under high ceilings. As they walk through the entrance hall and on through other living rooms, Matt's eyes adjusted to the shadows. There was an old world feel, decades of colonial privilege, along with the smell of beeswax and lilies emanating from an enormous flower arrangement.

The soft furniture was old, mismatched, and comfortable with roomy sofas and deep armchairs. European antiques were scattered throughout. The carved tables had Indian and African designs. Cabinets displayed family paraphernalia, sporting trophies, and mementos. Threadbare silk Persian carpets and Indian cotton rugs provided a sense of luxury despite their wear. Their age a defiant continuity of family inheritance from a long line of families who have survived British foreign policy before and will again.

Highly polished wooden furniture and parquetry flooring, along with the crisp linens, spoke of servants, although Matt hadn't come across any.

Generations of collections hung on the white walls, war shields, assegais, paintings and photos, masks, animal hides and tusks. Celia would have loved this place. A lump formed in his throat as he followed Dolly out to the back veranda.

On the lawn outside, a long outdoor table was set for lunch. Intricate bead-edged netting covered the food bowls, and he realised they had held back lunch. He shouldn't have called at lunchtime, didn't think.

Chris said 'Beer Matt?' Then laughed. 'Beermat - get it.'

Matt's wry smile accepted Chris's corny humour, and he took the beer. He was overwhelmed by the family's easy acceptance of him.

Crystal sunlight bathed his face and the smell of mown grass and damp African dirt from a sprinkler tsitzing across the far side of the lawn filled his senses. Weaverbirds squabbled in the trees, and the coo-ra-coo of doves gave the place a tranquillity belying its razor wire surrounds.

Graham offered him a cigarette, and while he lit it the family waited, watching his every movement, until Tom said, 'Give the bloke some air. Take a pew, all of you. The steaks are ruined so no complaining yours isn't rare enough, okay Dop.'

Matt said, 'Where do you want me?'

Chris grinned. 'You, my Shamwari, can sit anywhere you like. You are the guest of honour. It's the others who need organising.'

Dolly patted a chair. 'Sit here, next to me, Matthew.'

Matt doesn't know what to do with his half-smoked cigarette and looked around for an ashtray, but the others sat at the table smoking so he joined them, sitting next to Dolly, and wondering what to call her.

Dolly said, 'Have a steak, Matthew. They're home grown, overdone and congealed, but still the best steak in the world. Help yourself to salads. Do you want a bread roll? Meg baked them fresh this morning.'

The two boys stood at Meg's shoulder, watching Matt. 'Sit down, boys. You can sit at the end of the table. Alex, you'll have to bring out another chair.'

Alex headed back to the veranda and Jay slid into a vacant seat. He said, 'Alex says that Matt's in the army because of his ber... ber... his suitcase.'

Everyone stopped what they were doing to look at Matt.

Matt gazed at the kid. There was nothing on his Bergen to mark his former career. The battered bag was olive green without camouflage, standard army equipment, the kind you can get in any army surplus store, but the child can't know that. 'I was, but I'm not anymore. How did you know?'

Alex came back lugging a chair. 'What regiment?'

'Para's.' Matt said.

'Bet you were in the SAS.'

'Whatever gave you that idea?'

'Your secrecy. Your bag is military, but there are no badges or markings.'

Jay piped up. 'Alex knows all about the SAS.'

Matt nodded. 'The Para's are the best.' He wanted to change the subject without hurting the boys' feelings.

'I'll look up the Para's after lunch, but I'm going to join the British SAS when I'm big, If they'll let me.' Alex announced.

'Me too—C Squadron.' Jay looked pleased with himself.

Alex punched him, frowning. 'Shush stupid.' He turned to Matt. 'Uncle Jake was in C Squadron, but there is no C Squadron anymore. My brother's just little and he doesn't know we don't talk about that. You look like the pictures of him on Grammy's table.'

Chris intervened, 'Enough now—eat boys. Let the man get a breath before interrogating him further.'

'Okay,' they choroused, turning their attention to the food.

Dolly put her hand on Matt's arm and squeezed. 'Eat,' she said, 'before the next onslaught.'

A surge of empathy for her loss engulfed him. He had an urge to hug and reassure her that he wouldn't disappear as her son did. He asked in a low voice, 'What shall I call you?'

Dolly looked surprised. 'What's easiest for you?'

'Dolly, I like your name. It suits you.'

'Okay Dolly,' she beamed.

They both picked up knives and forks to eat. For a while, the people at the table concentrated on their food. No one spoke until the silence became restraint.

Gloria put her knife and fork down with a clatter. 'We all want to know. It's pointless pretending.'

'Just leave it, babe.' Graham placed his hand on her arm, shaking his head.

Matt put down his cutlery and swallowed the mouthful of food. 'Yes, I imagine you do, sorry. It's all a bit bewildering. I didn't know you existed until yesterday, but you didn't know I existed until today. You'll be as curious as I am.'

Dolly's hand crept onto his leg, patting his thigh in moral support, but her eyes were as eager as the rest of them.

'Okay, I'll do my best. What do you want to know?'

'Everything,' Tom said. 'Start from when you were born.'

'Christ! Sorry,' he looked at Dolly, apologising for his language.

She shook her head. 'It's all right, dear, go on.'

He ran his hand through his hair and took a breath. 'I was born in London in 1980'

'Year after me,' Chris said.

'I always thought my father was George Reid. My mother was Celia Reid. Harrison was her maiden name.'

There was a collective intake of breath, and Dennis and Dolly glanced at each other.

'Did you know her?' Matt asked.

Dennis and Dolly both stared at the tablecloth. Then Dolly said, 'We knew a Harrison, but he was in the police force.' She avoided looking at him.

What were they hiding? 'I think my grandfather was in the police at some point, but later he worked at the British Treasury. It sounds like you might have known him?'

Dennis fiddled with his knife. 'If it's the same bloke, we met in the fifties. Anyway, keep going with your story. Everyone knows everyone in this joint.'

Something was amiss, but Matt shrugged the information aside. This would take forever with all the questions and interruptions. He cut the story short, going straight to his mother's death. 'When my mother died'

There was another collective intake of breath.

'Had you met my mother, too?' Matt asked.

Heads shook around the table. Dolly took his hand and held it. The thin membrane of her skin, her fingers' knobbly joints, her hard wedding rings, comfort him. 'Anyway, I found some of my father's things. Sorry stepfather. He died when I was about eleven.' There were more sounds of pity. Matt sighed. It was difficult enough without everyone staring at him, sympathy and secrets written across their faces. 'Look. it's fine. That's just the background. My mother had kept his dog tags and a few months ago I came across them. That was when I discovered that the man I always thought was my father wasn't.'

'How?' Tom asked, leaning forward.

'His blood type. He was AB and I'm O, so I realised it was unlikely.'

Dennis nodded. 'Jake was O like me.'

'So am I.' Tom and Chris spoke together, then laughed.

Chris said, 'We'll have no problem sourcing blood donors.'

Dennis said, 'Not that I needed it, but this is more confirmation. You are family.

Gloria asked, 'What happened when you found out?'

'I found some old letters from Alan Fletcher. He and my mother had been friends in the seventies. At first, I thought he was my father and travelled to Australia to confront him. That was when I found out about Jake. He and Fletcher were friends. In fact, Fletcher introduced my mum to Jake.'

Tom nodded. 'Yes, that's right, Jake told me about it. He was crazy about your mother.'

'Why didn't you tell us this, son?' Dennis's face furrowed.

Tom shook his head. 'It was Jake's story to tell and afterwards, well, I didn't want to distress you any further. I didn't know then how significant it was.'

Dolly's voice was sad as she said, 'Why didn't Jake tell us?'

Tom looked uncomfortable. 'It was a pretty whirlwind romance, and he was out bush through most of it. Then Dad and I were busy transporting... ahem... anyway, he told me when he first met her. That time he brought Fletcher home, she was supposed to come and meet you, but at the last minute, she pulled out. Her father wouldn't let her date soldiers, apparently. Odd given we were all in the Forces one way or another, even if only as Territorials. She swore Jake to secrecy.'

Matt said, 'I think they might have got married.' All eyes swivelled to look at him.

'No. I would have known that! He would have told me,' Tom said.

'And divorced.' Matt added.

Tom shook his head, worried eyes reassessing Matt.

'Why do you think they got married, Matthew?' Dolly asked.

'My grandmother told me. My mother's mother, I mean.'

'Is she still alive? Perhaps she can tell us more. What did she say?' Dennis was on the edge of his chair.

Matt explained his visit to his grandmother. How evasive she'd been. 'She knew something, but she was terrified of telling me. I couldn't get anything more out of her, except that Jake had visited her. She became confused and thought I was

Jake, but when I pressed her, she clammed up. Sorry, that's all I know.'

There was more to this story, and these people were hiding something. Matt said, 'I came to Zimbabwe to find out. I thought here, I could get a copy of her marriage certificate. If they were married and didn't get divorced, it means my mother wasn't actually married to her second husband, unless she was widowed—Oh Christ... sorry.'

Matt looked down at his plate. Jake was an unreal abstract to him, and he forgot, the man was these people's son. He had to be more diplomatic. 'Anyway, I couldn't get anything from the Zimbabwe Embassy in London, so I came here. That was when Fletcher told me you had rung Polly.'

Matt skipped the bit about having to get away from media attention regarding the portrait. There was too much to explain, and he didn't know these people. Even if they might be family, he was not sure how much he could trust them.

They were all silent for a moment. Dolly let go of his hand and said, 'Finish your lunch, dear.'

Tom said, 'We'll go down tomorrow.'

'Go where?' Jess asked.

'The Registrations office—if they were married, there'll be a record.'

'Don't forget Polly's coming tomorrow,' Jess said. 'That's why we're here—to pick her up.'

'Ja, bugger, I forgot. There's so much happening. We'll pick up Polly and go the next day.'

'Can't we do both?' Matt asked.

They all laughed, and it eased the tension. 'Be prepared to wait all day in that joint, probably more than one day.'

Matt asked, 'What about Jake's friends?'

Tom looked thoughtful. 'I don't know if there are any of them still left in Zim aside from Livingston. I think most took the gap.'

Dop chuckled. 'None of the SAS or Selous Scouts hung around after Mugabe took power. There was that story about them removing everything from their barracks. Everything gone, not a stick of furniture, weapon, sign, or person left in the place... even a couple of planes.'

Matt asked. 'Where did it go?'

'No one knows. It simply vanished along with them, like ghosts in the night.'

'That's not possible,' Gloria said.

Chris intervened. 'It's just a legend. Bullshit, most probably.'

'I don't think it is bullshit,' Dop said. 'I know a lot of the stuff ended up in South Africa along with a few helicopters and a couple of planes'.

'Yeah, drop it Dop.' Dennis frowned at him.

Matt knew what the SAS could do if they had a mind and the spiriting away of an entire barracks along with weaponry and machines wouldn't be a problem.

Tom said, 'He had other friends from school and the RLI, but once he left the RLI to join the SAS they kind of lost touch. Jake's life was hectic in those days--Mozambique, Zambia, Tanzania, and even Angola and Nigeria. He was all over the place. I think he once even travelled to Portugal.'

Matt said nothing, remembering the same thing happening to him. How easily he lost touch with people. You can't talk about your work. There are too many questions you can't answer. It became too difficult. In the end, you stuck with the people who do what you do, eating and sleeping and breathing with people who get it and don't ask questions. That's why Dog and Brander are still his best mates. But the prevarication and fleeting glances flashing across the table told him these people, or at least some of them, knew more than they were letting on. They're hiding a secret and he wanted to know what it was.

Chapter Twenty-Two

Polly walked through customs, the unfamiliar sights, sounds, and smells overwhelming her jet lagged brain. How would she recognise Dennis? With any luck, he will have seen her photo in the media and recognise her. Although she had avoided the press, they managed to get a few shots.

Two white men were waiting near the cordon. It must be them. One looked just like Matt or Jake. This family must all look alike. The Matt look-alike grinned and raised his hand. It was him.

Her stomach flipped over, and her face became a pale shade of crimson. 'Matt, I didn't expect you to be here.'

'Hello Polly.' He took her bag and turned to the other man. 'Tom, this is Polly, Alan Fletcher's granddaughter, the woman who made all this possible.'

Tom held out his hand. 'Good to meet you Polly. How is Fletcher?'

'He's fine. He's recovering from an op, or he'd be here himself.' Polly focused on Tom, internally praying, please, please don't let anyone ask why she painted the portrait. 'I had two stopovers to recover, but thanks.'

Her artist eye took in every detail. She could see a resemblance to Matt, but Tom's hair was darker, although streaked with grey. He was also stockier. His eyes were hazel and didn't have the deep bluey green of Matt's eyes, the colour that made her go all squidgy. Tom's nose was not as finely sculpted, nor was his jaw.

Tom replied with clumsy gallantry. 'I'm grateful we have you here. I think we got the better deal.' He hurriedly added, 'Not that Fletcher's not welcome, but it's just... well, you're much prettier.' Tom was blushing under his tan. 'Sorry, I sound like a dirty old man.'

Matt changed the subject. 'Did you know your painting was stolen? Fletcher told me about it when I spoke to him on the phone the other day.'

'Yes, I found out in Perth.' She found it hard to meet his gaze and looked at his feet instead. 'The cops paid me a visit. Silly beggars think I stole it. Why would I do something like that?'

'What's this?' Tom asked.

Matt said, 'Let's get out of here. Polly can fill you in on the way, Tom.'

At the car, he opened the front passenger door for Polly. She said, 'I'll sit in the back.'

Matt shook his head. 'You've never been to Africa. It's interesting to see the sights.'

She smiled and dropped her gaze.

'How's Fletcher?' He asked.

'He's fine. He's out of hospital and says he's like a new man.' She climbed into the front seat and put on her seat belt.

As they pull out of the parking area, Polly pulled a camera from her hand luggage and took off the lens cap.

Tom said, 'I'd put that away quickly if I were you. Hell, in fact, even if I wasn't. You'll get us all arrested.'

She fumbled in her haste to get the camera back inside its case. 'Sorry I didn't know.'

'Don't worry, you'll get the hang of things, and we'll leave for the farm soon, where you can relax.'

What farm? Polly didn't know about a farm. 'I thought all the white-owned farms were seized.'

Tom nodded. 'Most were, but thanks to a bit of chicanery, we still have ours, or some of them. The farms are a game ranch now and cater to tourists. There are two adjoining farms and they're both in our partner's name. We had another couple of farms near Harare and two more southwest of Birchenough Bridge on the Save River, but... well we can't go anywhere near them now.'

'Confiscated?'

'Ja, the two near Harare first. Later they found diamonds on the others, and well, we aren't allowed anywhere near those. But never mind that. All these land seizures have done nothing for the poor. Grace Mugabe owns the ones near Harare, and still the people are starving. Our business partner, Livingston, did something about it. He's a paid-up member of ZANU, not by conviction but by pragmatism. He knows it's the only way he or his family will stay safe. His father is Chief of the district near the game farms, and his uncle is the local N'anga, or witch doctor. Both of them tell hair-raising stories of Mugabe's bribery, beating, or bullet diplomacy. Take your pick. Anyway, when Mugabe's thugs turned up at the game farms, Livingston met them along with his uncle, all dressed in his witch doctor regalia. He told them he owned the farms, and the thugs left quickly. Black Zimbabweans are a superstitious lot.' Tom grinned. 'After that, we bulldozed all roads leading into the place and left the bush to grow back. Now the only way in is on foot or via air. Dad and I both fly, but Chris is our company pilot and flies tourist in and out. Dad's getting a bit long in the tooth to fly. I don't know how long he will be able to pass the medical to keep his licence. He still does short hops to the local town for shopping, but otherwise he doesn't go far now. We've been breeding up the wild herds. The greater numbers mean an increase in the cat population. Lions and leopards keep foot traffic to a minimum. We border the game reserve with the Chiredzi River, and other rivers run through our place, so there's plenty of water. The game trails criss-cross the country from Mozambique, Kruger, Gonarezhou Reserve, and our place. We use the locals as rangers to keep poaching at bay. It works because if they weren't employed by us, they would be the poachers.' He chuckled.

Polly said, 'Doesn't it bother you that you had to give it all away for nothing, even if it is to someone you respect?'

Tom turned to her. 'We haven't given it all away. We have a business arrangement. Livingston pretends to own the game farms. None of the veterans who seized the other white farms own title deeds, and although Livingston pretends ownership, the title deeds are still ours for the moment. I'd happily pass them on if it means the game survives, and we can keep our business interests going. The land ownership is not the issue here. All I want is the safety of the animals and good land management. That's a rarity with Mugabe's lot. The bastard couldn't give tuppence for the people here. He's not seizing land for them. It keeps the thugs who support him onside and happy, so he can stay in power. Mugabe and his personal henchmen own most of the old commercial farms now. There's not much land distribution among the ordinary people. One day when sanity, law, and order prevail, we'll sort it out. In the meantime, thank God for Livingston. He pretends to employ us and for his protection, we make sure he gets half the profits from the two places. You'll meet Livingston and his wife Bridie tonight. Mum's invited them to dinner to meet you both. They're good people. Your father,' Tom turned his head towards Matt, 'and I grew up with Livingston, even attend boarding school together. Livingston was your dad's best friend.'

Polly glanced back at Matt, but he was looking out the window.

Tom resumed his story. 'Our situation was unusual in those days, and Jake spent most of his time fighting to defend Livingston and his right to hang out with us. He and Jake were inseparable as kids. We spent a good deal of our school holidays with his family. That's where Jake and I learned to track. His uncle could track a phantom from the trail it left. Tracking's a sixth sense with him. He taught us most of our bushcraft. That's what made Jake so valuable to the SAS. He could have tracked a man through water, and he never needed to come in from the bush. I reckon he could have managed the rest of his life without going near civilisation.'

The sound of sirens interrupted Tom's story. 'Damn it.' He pulled over to the side of the road. The drop off was steep, and he bumped and rolled across to a tree copse and turned off the engine. 'If it's Mugabe and his goons, and they decide we haven't shown enough respect, they'll stop and donner us, or worse, arrest us. It's best to give them a wide birth. Never give the bastards any excuse, hey.'

A few moments later, a cavalcade passed by with a woman in the back seat of a Mercedes Benz.

Tom said, 'That's Joyce Mujuru. She owns many of the seized farms and is a favourite to take over from Mugabe when he dies, but it won't happen. There'll be a bloodbath when he goes with all the factions vying for the role. We'll have civil war again.' He sighed and manoeuvred his way back to the road. 'I just hope that come the elections, Mugabe, and his cronies are ousted, but that's unlikely.'

Polly said, 'Won't the MDC win? The Australian news said it's probable, after the last elections.'

Tom laughed. 'Sorry, I'm not laughing at you. Really, I laugh in despair. We have high hopes, but Mugabe is already promising his supporters new spoils. He's planning the next stage of his strategy, promising the indigenisation of business enterprises. He'll take away businesses from legitimate owners and give them to his thugs, just as he did with the farms. Livingston will tell you how he operates, but the outside world doesn't seem to care. It beggars belief that they just ignore what he does. There's a rumour that an Israeli company is doctoring the electoral roll, and then there are the bribes and intimidation. Mugabe won't let anyone else win. This is a one-party State. The rest is just candy floss.'

Matt broke into the conversation. 'What will you do if there's another civil war?'

'We're taking precautions, and like we did before, we'll survive. At least now we are paid in U.S. dollars, we can squirrel something away outside the country, and it doesn't lose its value on the way to the bank like the Zim dollar did. There is no way on this earth I'll ever be able to pry Mum and Dad from this place. Dad's great grandfather carved the farms out of raw bush. He won't leave, and if Dad doesn't leave, neither will Mum. If they don't leave, I can't. If I don't leave, Chris won't and so on. Bloody stupid if you ask me, but there you have it. Our roots are too deep here, and where else can we go? We hope and pray for democracy to be returned?'

Polly said, 'You could come to Australia.'

Tom glanced at her. 'It's not that easy, believe me. Jess looked into it once before, and we have friends over there. They spend their days in safe nostalgia wishing they were here, homesick and alien and never quite fitting-in. No, we'll stay here. One day, sense and justice will prevail, hopefully not too far into the future.'

Tom put the car into gear and took off, driving in silence until they arrived at the Ryder's home.

'Here we are.' Tom slowed and pointed the remote control to open the gates.

Polly stared at the razor wire but said nothing. Two men worked in the garden beyond the gate. They straightened as the car passed; their hands held in greeting. Tom stopped, rolled down the window, and spoke in their language. Both men laughed. He introduced Matt and Polly and then continued along the driveway.

Tom had an easy leadership style, with a quality most men would willingly follow, and she wondered if Jake had been the same. This was everything she had learned to abhor, the last vestiges of colonialism. Even so, she could see the appeal of this sort of gracious living, so out of date and foreign in Australia.

They pulled up outside the house and Matt opened Polly's door. He'd been infected by this life already. She wanted to shout that she was quite capable of opening her own door.

'Amahli, Bongani,' Tom addressed a man and woman waiting for them at the door. He was formal and courteous as he said, 'Miss Fletcher and Mr Reid are our guests.' He turned to Polly, 'Amahli is in-charge of the house and Bongani looks after the cleaning women and manages the kids.'

'Aiyee!' Bongani lifted her apron to cover her face, and Amahli was staring at Matt.

Polly said, 'Haven't you met '

Matt shook his head. 'They weren't here yesterday when I arrived.'

Tom said something in their language and Bongani dropped her apron.

Amahli beamed and stepped forward to shake Matt's hand. 'Sir, your father was my brother.'

Polly watched the confusion cross Matt's face and turned to Tom.

Tom said, 'For a minute, Bongani thought Matt was Jake's ghost.' He grinned. 'Amahli and Bongani have been with our family for as long as I remember and before that, their parents and their parents. The men in the garden are their sons. They're Ndebele from the west but live here with Meg and my parents when Jess and I are away.'

Bongani smiled shyly at Matt, touching his arm. Polly felt a kinship between them. She also wanted to touch him to find out if he was real, but she suspected he would not appreciate it coming from her.

Amahli said, 'Mr and Mrs Ryder and Miss Jess say they will be back for lunch. They've gone to Harare. Miss Meg has gone into Borrowdale and will be back soon.' He turned to Polly. 'Welcome Miss.' He spoke to Bongani, who smiled and bobbed a curtsey to Polly.

'Come Madam, I will show you to your room.' Bongani took Polly's bags and walked into the house.

Polly followed her.

Amahli said, 'I will bring tea to the veranda, sir.'

Minutes later, she walked out to the veranda to join Tom and Matt. 'You have a beautiful home, Tom.'

'It's my parents' home. We all live here when we are in Harare, but. Jess and I spend most of our time at the farm. Chris and Meg are here a lot. Well, Meg anyway. Chris flies back and forth ferrying visitors and supplies, so having a base here is essential. Meg would be lonely on the farm, and her boys go to school here.'

Amahli came out with a tea tray laden with dainty china and small cakes. He placed it on the table and disappeared back into the house.

'Do you want to play mum Polly?' Tom asked.

Polly shook her head. 'No, it's okay, you do it.' The cups and saucers were old, their porcelain fragile, the decorative roses finely crafted, with gold filigree worn with age. She would hate to drop one. They are probably as old as the Ryder family in these parts.

Tom offered Polly a cigarette.

She shook her head.

Matt took one. 'Thanks. I had given these things up, but everyone smokes here. I'll have to try again when I get back to London.'

'Ja,' Tom said, 'the national product, tobacco, or used to be. It's patriotic to smoke even if it kills us. The trouble is now the Chinese are into it. They pay big money, and all the small landholders are growing it. It gives them cash, but the curing takes heat. They can't afford heat, so they cut down the native forests to build their drying fires. Zimbabwe will be a desert one day. I should give up smoking in protest, but I guess it'll kill me first.' Tom lit his and Matt's cigarettes before he said, 'Chris has gone to the farm this morning to resupply. He's flying to Vic Falls the day after tomorrow to pick up six guests to take to the farm. Jess and I will fly down the same morning to be there when they arrive. Tourism is picking up again, so we want them to feel welcome. Mum suggested we make a plan, and instead of going straight to the farm, you two might want to go to Vic Falls. It'll be a chance to visit the Falls and Chris can pick you up again in a few days and bring you to the farm.'

Polly sipped her tea and waited for Matt's response. She would take her lead from him. She wanted to see Victoria Falls. Of course, who wouldn't, but the problem was going with Matt, spending time alone with him. She would make a fool of herself.

Matt sounded enthusiastic. 'That's great. I was planning to go there, anyway. It'll be good to have Chris to point out the landmarks.'

No mention of her, but she followed his lead and nodded. 'Yes, thanks, that will be lovely.'

'Good, it's settled. I'll ring later and book you into the hotel there. Polly, you look tired. Are you okay?'

'I think I am a bit jet lagged.'

'Why don't you rest. We'll call you for lunch. Matt, if you want we'll do a run into town this afternoon and see how things are with the Registrations office. You never know your luck.'

Chapter Twenty-Three

The evening of Polly's arrival, Livingston and Bridie came to dinner. Polly was in the garden when they arrived, and she walked up to the car as they pulled up. The car's back door was flung open, and two boys raced into the house. A woman alighted from the front seat.

Polly said, 'Hello I'm Polly Fletcher, and you must be Bridie.' She held out her hand to a young woman who dripped diamonds from her ears, from around her neck and from her fingers.

Bridie dropped her gaze and took the tips of Polly's outstretched fingers in her limp but brief clasp. This must be an African handshake. She would have to learn about their culture.

Jess came out the front door. 'Hello Bridie. Good. I see you've already met Polly. Come along in then, all of you. Where are the boys?'

A man, Livingston, Polly assumed, came around from the other side of the car and gave a small bow towards Polly. 'Jess, we haven't been introduced yet.'.

Jess said, 'Polly meet Livingston Moyo, best friend, brother, and business partner, and his wife Bridie, the world's best bride for putting up with Livingston.'

Unlike his wife, Livingston's handshake was firm. 'G'day mate.'

The greeting sounded ridiculous with the phoney Australian accent, but she smiled anyway. She tried not to stare but wondered if she could ask him to sit for a portrait. His skin was like sculptured mahogany, his features regal, his nose aquiline, his hair just beginning to grey into salt and pepper curls. Livingstone was a handsome man, well-built and commanding, with something of the younger Mandela about him, supreme confidence. This man carried himself like a prince.

They walked through the house to the veranda, where the others were already sipping the obligatory gin and tonics. Chairs scraped on the red polished concrete floor as the men stood. Polly couldn't accustom herself to the manners and envied the way the other women took curtesy in their stride.

Livingston walked in. Where is he then? He stopped short and for a moment, no one moved. He walked over to Matt and placed both hands on his shoulders. 'You are your father's son.' He paused before saying, 'Your father was my brother. In his absence, you are my son.'

The greeting was like some weird initiation ceremony that Polly didn't understand. Meg took Matt's arm and pulled him away from the crowd.

Dolly stood next to Polly and said, 'Livingston is of the Kalanga, of the Rozwi people. Their custom is to take responsibility for the children of their deceased brothers. Come, you need a drink. Gin and tonic all right?'

Polly nodded. 'Thank you.' She followed Dolly to the drinks tray. Meg was still whispering to Matt, holding his arm as he stooped, head bent to listen. Resentment at the perfect-blonde woman's easy familiarity left her feeling gauche and unattractive, and Meg was nearer Matt's age. She took the gin and tonic and walked back to sit at the table. Meg was Chris's wife and had no designs on Matt, surely. Polly forced herself to stop imagining what wasn't there.

Livingston said, 'Come Matthew, walk in the garden with me. I will tell you about your father. I hear you knew nothing of him until recently. Perhaps through my eyes you will see him as I did.'

Matt took a cigarette and followed Livingston down the steps to the pool, where the boys were diving for something on the bottom. For a moment, they sat in companionable silence.

Livingston sighed. 'These boys remind me of my childhood. It could be me, Tom, and Jake in that pool. This is how we were.'

Matt waited. There was more.

'I am the chief's son, so my position is privileged, but in reality, without Dennis, my family would be poor and uneducated.'

Matt hesitated, then said, 'Without the whites you would own the land, surely.'

Livingston nodded. 'Perhaps, but perhaps not. The British colonisers did terrible things to my people, but no worse than MaShona and Amandebele before them. They took away our land and our culture and our language. Before they came, my people ruled this plateau for a thousand years. Now the country lies devastated because we are wrong now, just as they, the British and the Rhodesians, were wrong. It has taken me many years to see this. In history there are many wrongs and few moments of righteousness, but if we Africans, white or black, do not move beyond tribalism, we are doomed.'

For a moment they smoked in silence, Matt aware that Livingston would tell him whatever he had to say in his own time.

'Being an African is not merely being born in this place,' Livingston continued. 'Africa is within one's soul. It is a part of you, and you are a part of it. Our place in this, is very important, for to belong to Africa is to belong to the land. Only once you understand this can you appreciate Africans. One cannot exploit the land, for in exploitation is ruin. We are one with the land, and if we do not respect it, this land will not respect us. Already, this has come about, and we will live to regret our actions. You have heard of Gaia, Matthew, the symbiosis of all natural systems of earth?'

Matt nodded.

'Africans have a symbiotic relationship also with the land and with the heavens,' Livingston pointed upwards but stared at the pool, 'with the animals, with everything on God's earth. If we interrupt this symbiosis, Africa will die.' He turned to look at Matt. 'Do you understand this, Matthew?'

'I think so, sort of. I will need to think about it, but it sounds reasonable.'

Livingston said, 'It is good to think about this. You must keep it in your mind while you are here. This understanding will keep you here, otherwise you are only a visitor who will leave when things are not right for you.'

'I wasn't born here. I'm British, one of the colonising people who did this to your people. You must resent my kind coming here.'

'I used to think so. There were bad things done by the colonisers, but so too by my people. Now I realise we need the whites. They created a great country from the bush, and we are destroying it through greed. We need people like the Ryder's, or our country is lost. If we lose symbiosis, we are lost. I didn't agree with the civil war. I wanted to bring about equality through education, negotiating for equal voting rights for all. That is why I studied to appreciate the white man's law. I wanted change through progressive means, and Jake fought to keep the status quo through violent means. Mugabe and Nkomo and Smith—brutality against brutality. Jake and I argued over this. I tried to see his point of view, but I do not think war solves anything—ever, or I didn't. But now.' Livingston laughed, 'Not even you, Matthew, can condone the way my government treats the white farmers.'

'No, but I understand their resentment.'

'Yes. It is a tragedy. I grieve, not for the individuals, although I weep for their grief and loss, for they too love this country. It is the country's loss for which I am concerned. The people who benefit most from the land seizures are Mugabe's inner sanctum. For the rest, they are peasants who try to scratch a living by subsistence farming. They have no skills; no tools and the banks will not lend them money, for they have no legal tenure to the land. Subsistence farming cannot feed the country. Land that was once productive is now laid waste.

'You are with Mugabe, aren't you? You are a member of his party.'

'Yes, I am. I do it because the party needs sanity, even if it does not yet prevail. I am a lawyer, Matthew, and I try to uphold the law, but it becomes increasingly difficult. Tsvangirai was the same, but he broke from the party to form the MDC. I have not joined him for I am more use within, as the voice of conscience, and now the MDC, or some of them at least, seems to become like many ZANU Ministers. They glory in the trappings of office without the hard work or restoration of our country. I sometimes feel we are doomed but I will continue to fight for change.'

Matt ventured the question that had been burning in his mind since his arrival here. 'What about all this?' He waved his hand around, indicating the lavish lifestyle the Ryder's led.

Livingston chuckled. 'You think I begrudge wealth, Matthew? I am not a communist. As a liberal I respect individual wealth. The Ryder's have wealth because they work hard for it. Yes, they had privilege to begin with, but they also took the responsibility seriously. You must understand the Ryder's, Matthew. They are Africans in their hearts. When the times get tough, they stay and fight. They love this land. It is in their hearts as in mine, even though this land has seen dark days. The Ryder's appreciate symbiosis and they are good people.'

'You don't think of the Ryder's sense of responsibility as paternalism?'

'Call it what you will. Moral responsibly by some, for the good of all, is necessary. Some must become the stewards of the land; some merely pass through. My people came to Zimbabwe more than a thousand years ago. We shared the land with a nomadic people and traded with many who plied their trade up and down the east coast. We built the Great Zimbabwe.'

Matt nodded. 'What about the other tribes living here?'

'Ah, you mean MaShona, Mugabe's crowd? They are not from here, but sub-tribes from Tanzania. From my point of view, they are invaders and colonisers who stole our country. One day we will take it back, soon I hope.'

He paused, and Matt remained silent. The British descendants of colonisers were okay, but not the MaShona descendants. That didn't make any sense.

As if he read Matt's mind, he said, 'Yes they are from that stock of colonisers, as I am of the stock of my people, and you are of the stock of your people. You British should understand this best. Conquerors come and go, but the legacy they leave is all that's important. Think of the Gaul's, the Romans, the Angles, and the Saxons, the Vikings—shall I go on? The British and their Rhodesian offspring left a fine country. Mugabe has ruined it.'

Matt hesitated and then decided it was time to throw away caution. 'What about the land? Who owns the Ryder's farms if you own them publicly, and they own the title deeds?'

'You speak of their land, which I hold in trust. You do not speak of the farm they handed over to my family in payment for land stolen from us, or the land seized by the government because of the diamonds, or the farms in the high veldt that are now owned by the wife of our fearless leader.'

Matt had no idea what he meant.

Livingston gave a low chuckle. 'I can see you are confused. I will try to explain. The Ryder's once had many farms. Now they have two, side by side near Chiredzi. Many years ago, Dennis's father understood our loss, for we had nothing among the invaders British or Shangaan or MaShona. To re-establish our dignity, he gave my grandfather title deeds for a farm on which our village still prospers. He gave this with the understanding it was to become our tribal village and not sold for profit by one family. With the land redistribution in 2000, war veterans seized the Ryder's farms in the high veldt. They seized the farms in Manicaland for diamond mining. The Ryder's still hold title deeds but cannot access that land. Their remaining farms in the southeast make money from tourism, and I have no quarrel with that. They have made my family rich with their business savvy. They will continue to hold title deeds until this country grows from an anguished teenager into responsible adult. Then they promise to gift the game farms to the State. It will extend Gonarezhou game reserve. Once rule of law is re-established they should return to farm, for the people need food and jobs, but I fear we have lost them for this purpose. They are too old or, like Chris, do not have the experience in farming, even if they regained the farms to which they hold title deeds. Now it is not farming that holds them, but for Tom it is the animals and for Dennis, the people.'

Matt, astonished by the revelation, said, 'How...?'

Livingston interrupted, clapping his hands. The boys looked up from their games and swam to the sides of the pool. Livingston had not said a word, but the boys obeyed his signal without argument. When they were out the pool, Livingston turned once more to Matt. 'Now I want to tell you about your father.'

Matt didn't move. Livingston watched the boys troop to the house before turning to Matt.

'You must understand what I owe the Ryder's Matt, and not just because Jake was my friend. Our families are one in spirit if not in blood. Dennis is my father, as my father is his brother. Tom was my big brother and Jake's. He and I were the same age. We played together since we were little boys, and when Dennis saw I had aptitude, he sent us both to join Tom at boarding school. It is for this reason I am now a lawyer. The school we attended was a catholic school and multicultural but exclusive. There were a few African boys and some Indians or mixed race, but mostly whites. It was not colour that was a barrier, but exorbitant fees that excluded most Africans. The ones who could afford it were city boys, sophisticated and used to the ways of white society. I was not. I was neither fish nor fowl and I could not understand the black city boys. The whites, coloureds, and Indians rejected me.'

Livingston paused for a minute, and Matt waited, holding his breath.

'It was Jake who made sure they did not bully me. He was a fighter, your father, and spent many hours in detention because of me, but he never lost a fight. The boys respected him and left me alone. At first, they accepted me because Jake said they must. Once we got to know each other, we learned to get on, and they accorded me respect for who I am, not the colour of my skin. I have Jake to thank for allowing me to grow-up without a bullied-boy's consciousness. I have seen the results of bullied boys, and I am grateful this never happened.'

'What happened to him?' Matt's voice wavered as he asked the question? It was rhetorical. If this man knew then so would the Ryder's, but he had to ask.

'He is dead.'

Matt watched the emotions play across Livingston's sorrowful face, waiting for more information. Eventually, he prompted. 'Why do you think he is dead?'

'If he were not dead, he would be here. He loved his family above all things. Your mother to him was the light of the sun. He would never have abandoned her. He would have fought with death itself to remain by your side. I told you; Jake never lost a fight.'

A lump grew in Matt's throat.

Livingston said, 'My uncle—his mhondoro, his spirit, consulted the ancestors, and they told him your father's bones lie beneath dark waters in a place far from here.'

The hairs on the back of Matt's neck quivered. 'What water?'

Livingston shrugged. 'It is a stranger's place to which my ancestors have no access.'

'Have you told the Ryder's, Dennis, and Dolly?'

'They are aware, but like all parents, they hold on to hope where there is none. Your father is dead. I am your father now. This is how Jake would want it.' He patted Matt's knee and got up. 'We must go in; the light has gone.'

A warm glow spilling from the veranda in the distance was the only light left in the darkened garden. Where had the past hour gone? Matt tried to absorb all Livingston had told him. 'I'll be with you in a minute.' Perhaps there was something more to all of this than he understood.

At dinner that night, he pressed Livingstone for more.

'You must learn it from my father,' Livingston said. 'It is proper to learn from my father and my uncle rather than from me. You will do this when you come to Mwenezi for initiation.'

Matt looked mystified and Dolly whispered, 'Have you been circumcised, Matthew?'

Matt felt his neck turning red.

'At least then, they won't have to cut off your foreskin.' She giggled at his shock, and he realised she was teasing him.

Chapter Twenty-Four

After dinner Polly yawned, unable to keep her eyes open, excusing herself as the rest of the party adjourn to the veranda for a nightcap and a smoke. Lulled by muted voices floating in through her window, she fell into a deep sleep.

Several hours later, she awoke to a sharp noise. The night's inky darkness pressed against her eyes as she strained to recall the sound. Perhaps it was her imagination. She fumbled for the bedside lamp switch. Hot breath washed across her face. She screamed and lamplight flooded the room. Liquid brown eyes rested above a long brown nose on the edge of her bed. In whispered relief, she said, 'What are you doing in here?' The dog licked her face. 'Pooh,' she said, 'who gave you a licker licence?' She wiped her face on the sheet.

Padding paws click on the parquet floor, and a second dog arrived. It examined her for a moment, and then, with a sigh, flopped onto the rug at the foot of the bed. The other joined its mate. They scratched, licked, and settled as Polly's anxiety dissolve. The dogs must have woken her.

The strangeness of the place, the subtle but pervasive threat of danger, its wild foreign beauty, contrasted with the old-fashioned hospitality and welcome she had received. It left her confused and unable to know what emotions she could trust. Everything she was enjoying here, back home in Australia, would have gone against the grain. That, coupled with anxiety over her feelings for Matt, was exhausting. She lay back in bed, but she was wide awake. There was another noise, and she sat again, but it was just the click of a car door shutting in the driveway. It was an odd time for car doors to close. She got up and peaked out the window, but it faced onto the lawn out the back and she couldn't see the driveway. She was thirsty.

The hallway light was dim, so she trailed her fingers along the wall for reassurance, trying not to bump into anything, trying to be silent so she didn't wake the household. The dogs followed behind her, their nails clicking reassuringly on the parquet floor. The lights were still on in the kitchen. The dogs continued along the passage ahead of her, heading towards the dining room, as she turned into the kitchen. She filled a glass from the tap and was about to turn back to her room when she heard another noise. Without the dogs for company, fear returned. She crept across the kitchen to the far door and peeked through the gap. A light shone from the open study door, and she could make out three men. Two were black Africans, the third a white man. All of them were in military gear, equipped with side arms and rifles. Her hand flew to her mouth and then Tom came into view, closing the study door.

She backed away, mortified that she was spying on her host. For a moment she thought they might be intruders, but they must be security, although it was an odd time for a meeting. It was none of her business. She tiptoed back to her bedroom, climbed into bed, and switched off the lamp. A while later, she heard a car backing down the driveway. And breathed a sigh. Security or not, she didn't like armed men in the same house.

The sound of voices woke her, morning sunlight pouring in through her bedroom window. It was eight o'clock, and she had slept in. The dogs were back on the mat at the foot of her bed. She got up and dressed hurriedly, going out to the veranda, dogs padding after her. Dennis and Matt were alone, drinking coffee at the table. They both rose from their chairs as she joined them.

Dennis said, 'Good morning Polly, I hope you slept well. I see the dogs have taken to you. They weren't a nuisance; I hope.'

'I enjoyed their company, actually. They're beautiful dogs. Ridgebacks, aren't they?'

'You like dogs?'

'I like any animals. '

'Can I pour you coffee?'

'Yes, please.' Polly folded herself into a chair. She was becoming accustomed to this gentlemanly behaviour, although she should be offended.

Dennis handed her a cup of coffee. 'I'll leave you to include sugar and milk.' He indicated the jug and bowl. 'I've just suggested that Matt might use the car today, seeing he never got to go to town yesterday. You might like to go with him into the city and look around while Matt's at the registry office.'

'Is it safe?' Polly asked.

'Oh yes, you'll be fine if you stick to the centre. Just don't walk alone through the Park or down dark alleyways and don't leave your things unattended. It's usually safe enough if you take care, but it's not wise to pick up unofficial taxis or hang around the less salubrious places, especially after dark, but you'll be home before then.'

An hour later, they drove towards the city. Matt checked the sat nav. and set it for a destination, and they move off down the driveway. He waved to the gardeners as they pass and then he clicked the remote. The gates opened, and they were on the road.

Polly racked her brains for a conversation starter but couldn't think of anything. The silence dragged on, and she glanced at him. He looked lost in thought, so she gave up any notion of conversation, and rested her forehead against the window, watching the passing sights.

When they arrive at their destination, Matt parked on the side of the road. 'This doesn't exactly look like the city centre. Perhaps it's not a good idea walking around alone. You better take the car if you want to go into the city.'

The streets were wide and busy with occasional vehicle traffic and lots of pedestrians walking along the gravelled verges. Trees lined the roads, behind which were buildings and gardens in various stages of upkeep. Some looked residential, but some were clearly office buildings. It was the city fringe, not the centre. Across the road is a park. She recalled what Dennis said about not walking through parks, but it looked inviting, enormous trees and flowering gardens beautifully kept.

Matt said, 'We can arrange somewhere to meet later if you like?'

Polly shook her head. 'I don't know my way around.' Their eyes meet, and for the first time since she arrived, she didn't drop her gaze. His expression didn't change as he waited for her to speak. She felt like a child. 'Can I come with you?'

'It'll be boring I imagine.'

'It's all right,' she said. 'I'll feel safer with you.'

'Is that a compliment.' He grinned. 'Come on then. Let's get it over, and then we'll explore. I think the City proper is on the other side of that Park.'

She followed Matt into the building, wishing she could relax. He thought she was crazy, and that painting had caused so much trouble. If only she could be as casually friendly as Meg.

The office they entered was empty. That augured well, no queues, but there was no one behind the reception desk either.

Matt pinged the desk bell. Eventually a woman came through a door, wiping her mouth as if she had been eating. She looked surprised to see them. Polly could hear her shoes slopping against the linoleum as she moved towards the counter. 'Yes.'.

Matt said, 'I'm looking for an old marriage certificate. My mother's actually.'

The woman said, 'You must fill in a form and pay the fee. Then I can look for it.'

'Okay, I can do that.'

She stared at the counter, her tongue pushing against closed lips as it ran around her teeth.

Matt asked, 'Can I have a form?'

She pursed her lips. 'No, we don't have.'

'Sorry—you don't have? You don't have what?'

She sighed, as if dealing with someone simple. 'We don't have forms.'

'But you said I need to fill out a form and then pay money, and you will look.'

Another heavy sigh. 'We don't have forms.' Her voice was slow and deliberate with exaggerated forbearance, as if she was speaking to someone who didn't understand English.

Another woman came through and walked past the counter and in through another door.

Polly watched hope fade from Matt's face. He repeated. 'You don't have forms?'

'No.'

'No forms?' He said again.

'No forms,' she confirmed.

Polly couldn't bear it. She took charge. 'Okay, where can we get a form?'

The woman shrugged.

Polly said, 'Why are there no forms?'

The woman sucked her teeth. 'Nothing has come from the printer yet.'

Matt asked, 'When will they come from the printer?'

'Next week,' she replied.

Polly asked, 'Is there anywhere else we might get a form?'

The woman shrugged and walked away, not bothering to answer Polly.

Matt said, 'Come on Polly, let's get out of here.'

There is clearly some sort of cross-cultural issue at play. Polly said, 'Perhaps Livingston can help.'

Yeah, I'll ask him.

They walked out the building into sunshine, and Polly started giggling.

Matt smiled. 'It would be tough to live here. What do you say we walk across that park to the city?'

'But Dennis said it's dangerous.'

'Just at night. Come on, Polly, I'll protect you.'

He was teasing, referencing her earlier declaration, and she felt almost carefree

He said, 'At least if we leave the car here we have a parking place. I'm not sure how easy parking is in the centre.'

They crossed the road and headed to the park. Branches overhung the pathways, casting cool shade, a tranquil refuge in the middle of the city. They meandered along winding walkways until they came across a miniature waterfall minus water, a small replica of Victoria Falls, full of rubbish. A neglected band stand on the left spoke of past glory, and a little further on a restaurant served patron's morning coffee. They walked on through formal gardens until they reach the other side where open lawns, show people taking their leisure, reading newspapers, or just soaking up the sun. Children chased each other, dodging in and out of bushes, keeping out of the adult's way. On their right was a large entrance to a municipal swimming pool and in front of them a busy dual carriageway, with a towering, building on the corner.

'The Monomatapa Hotel.' Polly said, 'I know that name. That's where Poppa used to come in the seventies to meet with foreign soldiers. It was where he met his friend Greg. Let's go in.'

The reception area was modern opulence like a Hollywood depiction of Africa. It didn't have the colonial sumptuousness of the Meikles Hotel, but there was the same effusive service. A service that clearly didn't extend to government offices. Perhaps the woman hadn't been paid in a while. Apparently, going months without pay was common in Zimbabwe, at least for civil servants.

'Shall we have lunch here?' Matt asked, glancing at his watch.

'It's early for lunch's keep going and see what else we find.'

They strolled out into the sunshine again. Polly tilted her face to the sky and held out her arms. 'The weather's divine. I love it here.'

Matt was acutely aware of Polly's change of mood as they ambled along a broad main street. Wedged between modern skyscrapers are older, slightly shabby buildings that looked in need of paint and maintenance, but the ultra-modern glass-building Matt had seen from his hotel room when he first arrived towered above the other side of the dual carriageway. He oriented their position from the glass edifice and steered Polly towards the grand old hotel he stayed in the first night he arrived. After passing a pavement café, they turned right into another street, walking past shops and banks.

Polly ducked through the door of Barbour's department store. They walked through it and out the other side. A block away, Matt spotted the little park opposite Meikles.

It was called Unity Square, and they walk under avenues of trees that cast a hint of autumn cool in the shadows. People sat about idling away time. The place was teaming, unhurried, relaxed, friendly, and curious.

Matt noticed a group gathered around a speaker and wondered if it was like Hyde Park Corner in London, where anyone could pull up a soapbox. A sixth sense warned of a possibly more dangerous situation. He quickened his pace, taking Polly's arm to hurry her along. 'I don't like the look of that group. Let's pass it quickly, shall we?'

Fear flashed across her face and Matt wished he hadn't said anything, but she walked faster. He dropped her arm, alert now, taking in their surroundings, noticing the flower sellers had gathered to watch. MDC placards were everywhere.

He shouldn't have brought Polly here. Perhaps they should turn back. He heard sirens behind them and grabbed Polly's hand. They walked faster, and Polly tripped on uneven flagstones. Matt put his arm around her waist. They passed the group, and walked towards a park exit, opposite Meikles Hotel.

Behind them, tires screeched as vehicles pulled up on the far side of the Square. Doors slammed. Then the sound of gunfire, broke up the crowd. People surged past them. Matt quickened his pace, searching for the best way out. He tasted tear gas and pulled his hankie from his pocket to cover his nose and mouth.

'Cover your face with your tee shirt Polly, I'll guide you.'

He ran with Polly at his side. They dashed past the flower sellers' stalls, from where the hawkers had all disappeared, and ran across the road to Meikles Hotel. By the time they reached the entrance, Polly was coughing, eyes streaming and Matt almost carried her up the steps into the lobby.

Inside, people turned to stare, startled, and shocked. He examined her face and looked around for a ladies' toilet. Then, arm around her waist, he guided her to the door and said, 'Splash your face with water, lots of water. We didn't get much of it, luckily.'

Polly slipped into the ladies, and Matt waited outside, berating himself. He shouldn't have left the car. He should have driven her around, instead of exposing her to risk by walking the streets.

When she came out, her eyes were pink rimmed and her face blotchy.

At least she was smiling.

She said, 'That was exciting. Not.' She slipped her hand into his. 'Thank you for saving me.' She tiptoed to kiss his cheek, and then just as abruptly dropped his hand. 'I'm starving. Now, I'm ready for lunch'.

Matt thought of the rooftop garden, but perhaps not given the tear gas floating around. In any case, the rooftop was now also closed for renovations. A waiter showed them to a table in the Explorers Bar.

The pinched look of anxiety Polly had worn since arriving had gone, and for once she looked him in the eye. 'I think we should have a glass of wine with our lunch. It's not every day you can say you've been involved in a riot like that.'

'Some riot,' Matt said drily. 'The poor bastards.' It's a strange place. On the surface, it seemed normal. Then out of left field, something like that happens. 'Do you mind if I smoke Polly?'

She shook her head. 'No, but you should give up.'

'I will when I get out of this country.'

He held her gaze. Polly's eyelids looked bruised from the aftereffects of tear gas. Her freckles stood out against her pale face. An urge to protect her consumed him and he looked away.

After lunch Matt suggested they take a taxi back to the car, but Polly wanted to walk. He stalked off to find the concierge while Polly took the opportunity to pop into the ladies and wash her eyes again.

The concierge assured him that the police action was just a brief intervention to move on the protesters. It was now safe to walk through the city, but they should avoid protesters and any large gatherings. Great.

He lit a cigarette and watched people come and go in the lobby, wondering what it might be like to live in a place like this, never knowing for sure what would happen next. At least he wasn't bored.

Polly walked towards him, and a prickling sensation ran up his neck. He recognised the adrenalin surge. Women didn't usually have such a dramatic effect on him, but she was smiling, swinging her handbag, as if without a care in the world. He turned to walk out ahead of her.

Outside he said, 'Right ready for the dash for freedom.' His voice was gruff.

They crossed the road to Unity Square. Canna lilies blazed. People sprawled across the green shaggy lawn. Matt leaned down to pick up a 303 shell. It seemed almost impossible that two hours ago there had been such a brutal crackdown on a peaceful demonstration.

Polly lingered at the flower stall. 'Let's get some for Mrs Ryder.'

They bought flowers and walked back the way they had come, through a mall now littered with dropped lunch wrappers. Everything looked peaceful as they continued on past the restaurant, past the waterless miniature Victoria Falls and along the path towards the exit.

They were alone on a pathway under enormous trees that cast their branches cathedral like above them. Without thinking Matt stopped and took her hand. She looked at him uncertainly. He placed the flowers on a nearby bench before pulling her into his chest. She came into his arms, silently but stiffly, as if reluctant. He kissed her.

After a moment's hesitation, she kissed him back with passion. He hadn't planned this, not consciously anyway. It had just happened.

A small sound brought him back to earth.

She pulled away and turned to retrieve the flowers. 'They've gone.'

He scanned the bushes for signs of the fleeing thief, but there was nothing to see.

Polly took his hand. 'It doesn't matter, Matt.'

'No, it doesn't.'

But it did, and if he catches the bastard, he's dead. The lapsed judgement was a lesson he would not repeat. He strode off along the path. She let her hand slide out from his but kept pace until they reached the car.

Later that day, as they relaxed on the veranda sipping gin and tonic and chatting, Polly was acutely aware of Matt but tried to avoid looking at him. What was that episode in the park? One minute passionate, the next, cold as ice. She ignored him and regaled Tom, Dolly, Chris, and Dennis with the story about the forms and the woman in the registry office.

Dolly said, 'It's pretty typical. That's probably why there were no queues. People know it's pointless.'

Meg came out to the veranda, diminutive and neat with her dainty feet bare, and toenails painted with a light pink blush. Blunt ended blonde hair swung around her shoulders, and her slender bronzed limbs protruded from crisp white shorts and a pink scoop necked tee shirt. The ensemble gave her a fresh femininity that made Polly feel gauche again. She pulled her long legs, clad in ripped jeans and old runners, under the table, and smoothed her untidy long hair.

Meg was unaware of the effect she was having, and slipped onto the bench next to Polly, sitting too close. She said, 'At last the boys are clean, fed and watching a video.' Then she smiled. 'What am I missing?'

She slid her hand under Polly's linking arms. 'What have you two been up to all day?' She brought up one knee up, heel on the bench, and placed her chin in her hand, elbow resting on her knee, leaning companionably against Polly.

The intimacy seemed strange but harmless, and Polly didn't react, although she wasn't comfortable. Without thinking, she blurted out, 'We were caught in a riot and were tear gassed.'

'With these blasted elections coming up, the intimidation is just beginning.' Leaning forward, elbows on the table, Tom asked, 'Where were you?'

Matt said, 'Unity Park.'

Polly said, 'It was nothing really, just a little demonstration, and when we came out from lunch, it was all over. We walked back and there was no sign of any problems. The flower sellers were even back among their flowers.'

Meg squeezed her arm. 'You must be careful. We can't let anything happen to you.'

Polly chastised herself for being jealous of Meg. She was such a sweet person. 'Talking about flowers, we bought some beautiful roses and carnations for you Dolly.' Her hand flew to her mouth, attempting to stop her second faux pas of the evening from leaving her mouth.

Matt lit a cigarette.

Dolly glanced at him, then turned to Polly. 'That's lovely, thank you dear. Where are they?'

Matt covered. 'I put them down in the park and someone nicked them.'

Tom chortled, spilling gin down his chest. 'Bugger.' He mopped the mess with his hankie.

Dennis said, 'I warned you. Nothing's safe in that place.'

Dolly asked, 'Which park, Harare Gardens?'

Matt nodded.

She smiled and got up. 'I'd better see how dinner's getting along.' She turned to Polly. 'Come and help me, dear.'

Meg jumped to her feet. 'I'll help.'

Dolly shook her head. 'You stay and have your drink. You've been busy with the boys. Polly will help, won't you Polly?'

Christ, the wily old woman, could read him like a book. Matt watched the two women go indoors. Now she will winkle the entire story out of Polly. He didn't know what to do. He didn't like things to be out of his control. The shrink's voice sounded in his head. *Matt, you have to let go. You can't control everything. You particularly can't control women or love.*

Fat lot she knew. If he didn't control everything, he'd be dead, or his men would be dead. You can't leave things to chance in a battle. You had to plan for every contingency. Although that wasn't what happened today, was it?

The Shrink responded. *Love isn't a battle, and you couldn't control your wife, could you?*

That was true, or she wouldn't have done what she did.

The Shrink said, *trust in love. Don't try to control it. It's about trust and commitment for the long haul. It's about what you give, not what the other person does. Without trust, you have no love.*

What the hell was he thinking? He realised if he wanted to be with Polly, he couldn't control her. Did he even want to? It would be so easy to sit back and let it slip out of his control, or would it? He couldn't think about that now. He took a long swig of his gin and turned his attention to what Dennis was saying.

'We have to buy grain from Zambia now, and guess who's growing that grain?'

'Who?' Matt asked.

'The ex-commercial farmers, the ones that Mugabe kicked out. A lot of them moved to Zambia and Mozambique when they were chucked off their farms. The Zambian and Mozambique governments invited them in, to revive their disastrous farming sector, and now look at those countries' flourishing. Yet, Zimbabwe has no food and must buy it in or get aid from the UN. Mugabe, the fool, says the Europeans are to blame for the food shortages. Poetic justice, but little compensation for losing your life's work or for people starving. Still, it goes to show you, things will turn around here too. One day, justice might come.'

Chapter Twenty-Five

Matt awoke with a start and sat up in bed. The dream was vivid, its horror real, and the guilt choking. He lay back and stared into the dark void, trying to rid himself of lingering fragments. He can't understand why the incident still gives him so much trouble. It was not the worst thing that ever happened. Not by a long shot, but it's the one for which he suffered most remorse. Is that it? Was remorse triggering the posttraumatic dreams? He tried out the shrink's words. My job, my duty, not my fault. It didn't work and the image of her dying eyes remains.

He would see Livingston in the morning and ask if he could help retrieve his mum's marriage certificate. Then he remembered Chris was flying them to Vic Falls this morning. He would sort out his kit. An image of Polly's laughing face flashed through his mind. What confidences did Dolly wring from her? He hoped she hadn't mentioned that kiss. He already regretted it. She was too young and vulnerable, and he was a fool to get himself entangled. He should have controlled his desire. She was off limits. He had known that in Australia. Why had he forgotten? This country was doing strange things to his head. What the hell was he going to do, alone with her at Vic Falls? Perhaps he could call it off, and go straight to the farm, see Vic Falls another time, but how would he explain his change of heart? It would look odd.

He turned on the bedside light, his watch telling him it was 04:20 hours. He ran his hand through his hair, determined to stop thinking of her. He picked up the book on the bedside table and flicked to chapter 1. Ten minutes later, he had read the same paragraph several times and still couldn't absorb the context. He got out of bed to retrieve his laptop and connected it to his mobile. There was another email from his mother's lawyers asking him to call when he got home. They were a persistent bunch.

A few minutes later, he pulled on a pair of shorts and let himself out the room to go in search of a cigarette. His bare feet made no sound as he walked along the dark hallway past Polly's bedroom. Her door was ajar, and the dog put its head out. He hurried past, and the dogs followed him to the veranda. There was a pack of cigarettes and a lighter on the table. The morning air felt cool and damp on his naked torso as he stepped out onto the lawn. Above, the stars were brilliant in the clear night, and the lawn was damp with dew. He paced as he smoked, remembering his mother's place in London with its pocket size lawn out the back and its single tree. Despite the situation in Zimbabwe, he'd rather have a life like this. It would be better than the one he had in London. Perhaps living in Australia would be as good, he conceded.

The haunting sound of an owl sounded in a tree nearby. Frogs croaked in a bulrush infested pond. Despite the underlying threat of tyranny there was a sense of freedom in the wide-open spaces that he never felt in London. He couldn't imagine his life once his PhD was finished, commuting to and from some office, returning home to his mother's house each evening to mark papers. He couldn't do it, why on earth did he ever think that was an option. What made him think he could commute to a nine to five in London? He would go mad and shoot himself. Is that why his mother was depressed? Was it London after the freedom of Africa that depressed her, or something else?

A sound came from the direction of the driveway. The dogs seemed unperturbed as they waited for him on the steps of the veranda. An owl flapped out from the tree and swooped away. It would be dawn soon and the Weaverbirds would begin squabbling and swooping about the garden, collecting grass to build their elaborate nests. He supposed he should get some sleep, or he would drop off in the plane on the way to Vic Falls and see nothing.

As he returned indoors, he bent to pat the dogs. They followed him as he put his cigarette out in an ashtray, wiped his damp feet on the mat, and headed back to his room.

There was that noise again, but it was coming from a different place, like someone was moving about the house. The dogs parked themselves outside Polly's closed door.

Polly was awake, holding her breath as she hid behind her door, feeling foolish. She heard him get up and walk down the hallway, watched him through semi-closed lids as he stopped when the dogs opened her door, and then got up to watch him in the garden, crouching at her window. He caught her unawares, returning inside so suddenly. She scrambled to close her door so he wouldn't know she was awake, and too late, recognised her stupidity. Why didn't she just get back into bed and pretend to be asleep? Now he would know she was up because her door was closed. She couldn't believe she was such an idiot. But why shouldn't she get up? If he could wander about the house at night, why couldn't she? It was not that straightforward. She was spying, hiding behind the curtains, sneakily peeking into the starlit garden from her dark room, weak with desire.

Now hugging her pillow, she imagined him kissing her, remembering the feel of his mouth on hers, remembering his fierce passion. Then his mood changed, and his face looked angry as he scanned the park for the flower thief. It frightened her and she felt rejected as he strode back to the car.

In the kitchen earlier, Dolly knew something had happened between them. Her gnarled old fingers had reached out to tuck a stray tendril of hair behind Polly's ears. The delicate brush of soft papery hands on her cheek was so intimate Polly took a step back, but Dolly clasped Polly's hand and led her through the house to her and Dennis's bedroom. She picked up a framed photo of Jake from the bedside table and handed it to Polly.

Dolly said, 'Can you see it's the same?'

Jake was in an olive-green tee shirt, but Polly realised Dolly was referring to the composition. 'The pose is a classic.'

Dolly shook her head. 'How did you know?'

Polly hastened to reassure. 'No, I didn't know. It was a coincidence, that's all.'

Searching Polly's eyes for the truth, Dolly said, 'There's more to heaven and earth than we mortals know, my dear, but this was not a coincidence. To me it's a sign.' Putting her arms around Polly, she pulled her close, hugging her and kissing her cheek. 'Whatever happens in the future, you have brought his son to us, and I am forever in your debt.'

Dolly's stood in silence for so long Polly wondered if she should say something, but she remained still, waiting while the old woman mused. Eventually she said, 'Dolly, are you okay?'

Dolly laughed. 'I'm an old woman, dear. At the most inconvenient times, I am transported back in time. I was just thinking about how I met Dennis. Oh, the splendour of Government House on the night of the federation ball, the women's gowns, the men in uniform. Dennis was so handsome; I couldn't take my eyes off him. These Ryder men are all like that, aren't they? They steal a woman's soul, making her do things she would otherwise never dream of doing. I remember that night I wore a cocktail dress. I didn't realise then how inappropriate it was, but it was the only evening dress I had.' She shook her head. 'Come, dear, let's go back and join the others before they send in a search party.'

Chapter Twenty-Seven

The plane took off from Charles Prince airport near Mt. Hampden, heading Northwest towards Victoria Falls. Chris levelled off and grinned at Matt, then glanced back at Polly. 'You okay in the back?

She smiled and nodded. No point ruining everyone's day with her bad mood.

She leaned her forehead against the window and concentrated on the patchwork green and brown land below. The scenery and romance of Africa was a mirage. She had read a little about Zimbabwe's history. Cecil Rhodes started the colonial trouble with his dreams of a world map covered by the red ink of British dominion. The warrior nation of the Ndebele in the West of the country made the lives of the peasant farmers in the East a misery with their raids on cattle and women. Rhodes exploited that old enmity between the Ndebele and Shona, which eventually led to the power struggle between the

Russian backed Nkomo and the Chinese backed Mugabe. The Gukurahundi campaign wiped out Mugabe's rival claimants to the land and brought Mugabe one step closer to achieving total control of power in Zimbabwe.

She crouched forward to lean over the front seat. 'What was the chief's name who sold the land to Rhodes?' She asked Chris.

'Lobengula Khumalo.'

'Thanks.' Polly returned to her seat.

In the distance, smoke rose from the bush. 'Is that a bush fire?'

Chris shook his head. 'You'll see.'

Banking the plane towards the smoke, they were soon flying over a great gash in the world's crust, into which the mighty Zambesi River plunged—sunlit, wide, and terrifying, to the rocky base of the gorge. The spray filled the air with smoke-like mist.

Chris shouted, 'Mosi-oa-Tunya—the smoke that thunders.'

Polly gasped. Glancing at Matt, she saw he was also gazing in fixed concentration at the spectacle. She wanted to share the moment but turned back to look out her window.

They flew along the Falls and then circled the gorge. Awe made Mat immobile, and he strained to commit the geographical details to memory, but the plane moved too fast. All he had was an impression of immense power, dwarfing his problems into insignificance.

Chris said, 'It's the right time of the year to see them. In the rains there's too much water, and the spray obscures the view. A bit of useless knowledge... The Falls are 1708 metres wide and drop 108 metres. At the height of the rains, 500 million litres of water per minute go over the edge.'

'Jesus.' Matt breathed out, craning to get a last glimpse before they were too far away.

Minutes later, they circled the airport and descended to land. Another small plane sat on the apron.

Chris nodded in its direction. 'My new passengers, they're early. If it's okay with you, I'll leave you to your own devices. There should be a car and driver waiting to take you to the hotel. Sorry I can't come with you, but I'll need to refuel and head back to the farm. I'll be back with another lot in three days. Then the car will bring you back, and we'll fly home. Vic Falls is good, but you'll love the farm. It's much better.' He laughed, almost self-consciously. 'At least, that's my biased opinion.'

As they walked to the building, Matt counted five men standing next to the other plane. There was something familiar about them, the way they walked and moved, unloading the kit. It was methodical, a practiced drill, like an operation. That was fanciful. They were probably hunters. He walked into the cool interior of the building where a man stood holding a card with their names.

Twenty minutes later, they pulled in through the archway leading to the hotel. It's a palace of white colonial elegance, in sprawling and immaculately manicured grounds. The veranda's dark red polished concrete floors, the cool and fresh interior all spoke of old wealth. He walked to the reception and gave their names, acutely aware Polly was standing a little behind him, leaving him to carry out the formalities.

The porter showed them to their respective rooms, which adjoin on the first floor of the gracious colonial building. The porter opened the door to the first bedroom.

Matt nodded at her. 'You have this one. I'll have the next.'

Matt waited in the corridor while the porter showed Polly around her room. He heard her cries of delight and turned his back to look out across the gardens, frowning, but unseeing.

The room was old-fashioned colonialism at its best and Polly imagined herself with a bustle, frilly umbrella, and a hat with yards of lace. She exclaimed at the four-poster with its white mosquito netting draped over the bed like a bridal veil. Out of Africa, the Great British Raj, or Hemmingway's *Kilimanjaro,* all popped into her mind. After the porter left, she walked out to the balcony, squinting against the bright light. In the distance, a suspension bridge spanned a gorge, so perfectly framed it was almost a chocolate box cliché. She wanted to explore. Bugger Matt. She was not hanging around, waiting for him to notice she was alive, and was quite capable of entertaining herself. A quick peek out her door showed a deserted corridor, and she skipped back down the stairs to reception.

Minutes later, map in hand, Polly strolled along a pathway. Guinea fowls fled at her approach. A family of warthogs ran across the lawn, their tails erect, their legs stiff and straight kneed. The earth smelled damp, and newly mowed lawn glistened with the jewelled droplets from a sprinkler. Leaving the manicured vicinity of the hotel, she walked along a pathway, across vacant land, and in through the gates to the Falls. Then she continued towards the trees in the distance. After the hotel, the place felt wild, dust underfoot, and in her nose. The boundless washed-out sky shimmered, dazzling light that domed across the vast continent.

Still following a pathway, she entered under sentinel trees. The rainforest was shadowy and appeared deserted. Was it wise to have come here alone? Was it dangerous? Would there be wild animals? The people she had met seemed friendly enough, but what about animals, or even criminals? Screw all of them. She couldn't turn back now, not with the din of falling water drawing her on.

The surrounding bush became dense and every one of her nerves was vibrating with hyper-vigilance. The roar of the water grew, battering her ears drums, its mist condensing about her, dripping from ghostly trees and hanging lichen.

At her feet, the fecund growth of ferns gave feathery enchantment to the rainforest, but nothing deadened the deafening sounds of falling water. Polly quickened her step as glimpses of the falls came into view.

An animal moved further along the path. Polly froze. It was a small ginger and white spotted creature, with white trimmed ears, flicking back and forth. The chocolate doe eyed her warily. She held her breath in enchantment, but the timid antelope bounded away into the undergrowth.

Polly kept a sharp lookout, hoping to see more of the fey creature, until rounding a bend in the pathway the glory of Victoria Falls, Mosi-oa-Tunya, or Shungu Namutitima, spread before her. The view was framed by a tangle of trees leaning across the pathway, and her breath caught at the beauty.

She put her hands over her ears, and stepping with care on the slick pathway, she walked out into a grassy area beyond the trees. From there she could see along the length of the Falls, across the deep gorge that separated her from the plummeting Zambezi River. The grass plateau on which she stood ran along the gorge's cliff face, opposite from the escarpment over which the river plunged down to the rocky gorge below. Spellbound by its might, Polly blinked back the mist condensing on her face and stared with rapt exhilaration.

The spray soaked her clothing and seeped into the core of her being. No painting could ever do this justice. The map in her hand was a soggy rag, but she could make out that to her left was the Devil's Cataract, creating its own breathtaking off shoot of churning waters. Time seemed to stand still, confronted by such supreme power, and she didn't notice Matt's arrival.

Matt had seen her leaving from his balcony, saw her disappearing along a pathway, and feared she might step into some unknown danger. He caught up as she entered the rainforest, but he hung back, not wanting to intrude. She stopped when the antelope crossed the path. It saw him and skittered away to seek refuge in dank undergrowth. Following her was like stalking innocent prey. Her thin tee-shirt was damp and clinging, her linen trousers translucent with spray. A primeval surge tingled though in his blood, but she wouldn't thank him for this covert surveillance. He remained out of her sight as she stepped onto an open grassy area.

Mist made rivulets down his brow, and he wiped the water from his eyes. Her scream sounded above the roar of the water, and adrenalin surged, demanding instant action, but he couldn't see what was amiss. She remained in the same place as a minute ago. He edged through the trees, leaf litter masking his footfalls. Then he saw the elephant. He backed away, but the animal was engrossed in stuffing green morsels of sunlight into its mouth. The elephant stopped feeding and raised its trunk into the air. It's great ears waved back and forward, and Matt decided it was time to move.

He called. 'Polly, step back and walk towards me slowly.'

Matt was not sure if the colossal creature was any danger to them, but he was taking no chances. He stepped over to an immobile Polly, grabbed her hand and walked backward, dragging her with him, his eyes fixed on the elephant. He didn't speak until they left the rainforest. Then he stopped and, dropping her hand, he asked, 'Are you all right?'

She nodded. 'I was terrified.' She lifted the neck of her tee-shirt to wipe her face.

He said, 'They're serving tea on the terrace. What do you say we pretend we're English colonials a hundred years ago?'

'I'll have to change first. I'm soaking. Matt?'

He turned back to look at her.

'Thank you for saving me. It's becoming a habit.'

Matt's forehead furrowed.

She said, 'The tear gas'

He nodded and walked on.

She walked after him, chattering about the beauty of the Falls, and her terror of the elephant. 'It was so huge.'

A family of baboons crossed their path, and she ducked behind Matt, using him as her shield. 'Do you think they're dangerous?' She peered around his shoulders until the baboons had moved far enough away.

They drank tea on the terrace. The sound of a piano floated in the air, and there was a fresh sweet smell of damp lawn. The atmosphere was old-worldly and romantic and there were few other guests. Such a shame for the country, but not for Matt.

'You smoke too much,' Polly said.

'Hell, I'm on holiday. I'll give up when I get home.'

'Will you live in Zimbabwe, now you have family here, or will you go back to England?' Polly asked.

Matt gazed at her for a long second before he answered. 'I have family back in England, too.'

She held her breath.

'My grandmother is still there, my mother's mother. She lives in a residential nursing home, but I'm the only family she has. She's quite frail.'

'Do you have any other family, a wife, children, a girlfriend?' She coloured at the transparency, but she had to know.

He shook his head. Then he surprised her by saying, 'Do you?'

'What? I'm not married.'

'But you have a boyfriend, don't you? That bloke who makes furniture. What's his name? He took that photo of you.'

She stared at him. 'What photo?'

'The one of you on a street bench outside the gallery.'

'How do you know about that?'

'Fletcher.'

Polly's blood rushed to her head. That interfering old meddler. She picked up her teacup and swallowed the last of the tea. 'Yuk. It's cold.'

Matt said, 'Well?'

'Well, what?' Polly snapped.

'What's your boyfriend's name? Fletcher mentioned he had been sweet on you for ages.' He was grinning at her.

'I don't have a boyfriend. Well, he's a friend. His name's Jason. He works in the shed next to mine.' Polly realised Matt was teasing her, and she suspected it was to move the subject away from his family life.

She decided he would not get away with it. 'How come you haven't got a wife or a girlfriend? You're thirty-two'

'Three,' He said.

'Pardon?'

'I'm thirty-three.'

'But you said'

'Yes, but that was before my birthday. Now I'm thirty-three.'

'Okay, well how come a man of thirty-three can avoid marriage or girlfriends unless... You're not gay, are you?'

No gay man would have kissed her like he had, but she was enjoying teasing him for a change. His reaction surprised her.

'Would it matter to you if I were?'

He was so serious she couldn't tell if he was joking or not.

Stumbling over her words, she said, 'But you, the other day... you kissed' Her face flamed.

He was grinning again but still hadn't said if he had a girlfriend.

She changed the subject. 'What will you do when you get home?' Too late, she realised she had asked the wrong question.

His eyes darkened. 'I don't know. It's a question I have been asking myself, and I can't come up with the answer.'

This time, he was not just avoiding the question.

'What about you?' He asked.

Polly wrinkled her nose. 'I don't know. Go back to the same old, I suppose. Begin painting for another exhibition. But I thought you were doing a PhD?'

He nodded. 'It's almost done, and my next task is selling my mother's house, but I can't see beyond that.'

'That sounds bleak.'

'I feel bleak about it, I must admit.'

'I thought you wanted to teach military history.'

'When I left the army, they offered me career counselling. That's where I got the idea, but lately I have thought about commuting to and from work in London. It's a depressing thought to be honest.—Anyway enough of this gloomy talk. How about I buy you dinner at that thatched roofed restaurant we saw coming in? We can walk into town first and then head for the bar to watch the sunset. Then when we get hungry, we'll go there and eat.'

They walked along the road to town and wondered among little shops selling souvenirs. A man took Matt aside, telling him he had special muti to make a baby for his wife.

Matt laughed. 'No thanks mate, I don't think I need that just yet.'

He explained what the man had said when he returned to Polly. 'I guess muti is a word like juju or medicine.'

Polly blushed to her roots and hurried ahead of Matt.

A couple of hours later, over dinner under the starry magic of an African sky, with a hint of wood smoke in the air, Polly realised she was drinking too much. How many more such nights would she ever experience such romance?

After dinner, they walked back to the hotel, a palpable connection to Matt making her euphoric. She never wanted the night to end and racked her brain to think of a way to prolong the evening without actually throwing herself at him.

They arrived at her bedroom door, and Matt moved a few meters away, waiting for her to retrieve the key from her bag and open the door.

Then he said, 'Good night Polly,' and turned away, walking towards his room.

It was her last chance, and with the alcohol providing courage, she said, 'Matt.'

He stopped and turned back to face her.

'Will you come in?' She twisted her fingers in fear of rejection.

'I don't think that's a good idea, do you Polly? If I come in, I won't be responsible for my actions.'

Her gaze flew up to look into his eyes. Was he serious? She didn't want him to be responsible... she wanted him to... She dropped her gaze. 'Matt, I want you, not your goddamn responsibility.'

'I'm too old for you, Polly, and no good. I have nothing to offer you.'

'What century are you in? I'm not asking you to marry me, just fuck me.'

The next morning Polly awoke alone and sat up. Her head spun, and she groaned and lay back against the pillows, wishing he hadn't left like a thief in the night.

A few minutes later, the door opened, and he came in cheerful but sweating. 'You're awake, sleepyhead.' He leaned over her and planted a kiss on her head.

She snuggled down into the bed. 'Pooh, you're all sweaty.'

'I am.' He wrapped his arms around her.

She leaned into him.

He pulled back. 'I thought you were rejecting me for being sweaty.'

'Later, when my head's clearer.'

He laughed 'I'd better shower. Now I've made you all sweaty, do you want to join me? It'll clear your head.'

They were late down to breakfast and Polly couldn't keep the smile off her face. She was in love, knowing it was foolish knowing she would have to enjoy the moment. Matt had made it clear that a moment was all it could be, but she would worry about the future when it came.

It came sooner than expected via a phone call. A waiter arrived at their table. 'Mr Reid, there's an urgent phone call for you. Will you take it at reception?'

Polly sipped her coffee until Matt returned. He looked drawn.

'What is it?'

'My Grandmother. That was the British Embassy. They've been trying to contact me for a couple of days. My grandmother's had a stroke.'

'Matt, I'm so sorry.'

'I have to go Polly.'

She nodded. 'Is there anything I can do?'

He shook his head and left.

She would never see him again and her heart was breaking. They never even got a chance. The waiter placed her breakfast before her, but the food had lost its appeal. She retreated to her room, where she stood immobile, staring out the balcony door.

There was a knock on her door.

Matt was outside with his bag. 'Polly, I have a flight to Johannesburg, and a connection to London, but I have to go now, or I'll miss it. I rang Dolly, and Chris is coming to fetch you. Polly.'

He took her in his arms and kissed her, then stood back, gazing at her for a minute before he picked up his bag and walked down the corridor. He didn't look back.

Tears pressed at the back of Polly's eyes, but they refused to spill. She threw herself onto the bed, willing herself to cry to relieve the ache in her chest, but the pain was an endless dry and jagged wound.

She rang Fletcher's mobile. A sleepy voice answered.

'Poppa?'

'Polly, it's the middle of the night. What's wrong?'

The dam broke, and she howled into the phone.

'Poll, what is it? Are you okay? Speak to me Polly.'

'Poppa,' she sniffed, trying to pull herself together. 'Poppa, I want to come home.'

'What's happened? Take a breath and tell me.'

'Nothing. I'm just so unhappy.'

'Polly, tell me. I'm going crazy here imagining things. What's happened? Are you hurt?'

In a voice barely a whisper she said, 'Matt had to go home Poppa, his grandmother had a stroke.' Even to her distraught ears, it sounded ridiculous that she could cry over a stranger.

'Ah... Poll. I'm nearly halfway there. I'm staying a few days with Greg in Perth, and then I'll fly on to Joburg. I'll be with you in a couple of weeks, sooner if I can change my flight. Hang in there, my girl.'

She dabbed her eyes with the edge of the sheet. 'Are you well enough to gallivant all over the country?'

'Never been better, and I'm just doing a little research. It's hardly gallivanting.'

'What are you up to, Poppa?'

'It's a long story. I'll tell you when I see you. Take care of yourself and sit tight, my girl. I'm on my way.'

Chapter Twenty-Eight

The next morning, Fletcher sat on the veranda with his friend Greg, looking out over a swimming pool, while he explained the 3 am phone call.

Greg handed Fletcher a cup of coffee. 'Is she all right?'

'She's gone and got herself involved with a bloke, but it doesn't sound like it's working out very well. Apparently he's left her, although I'm not sure the circumstances don't warrant it. His grandmother had a stroke.'

'Christ. It's easier to have sons, Fletcher, and even grandsons in preference to granddaughters. Women are too bloody complicated.'

'Hm. This bloke is complicated too. He's the one I was telling you about. The Pom in the painting who came here looking for his father, thinking it was me. That was a shock, I can tell you.'

'You must have sown a few seeds in your younger days, mate. It wouldn't be that much of a stretch, would it?'

'Piss off Greg. I was never like you lot of randy buggers.' He got up from his chair. 'Lovers, huh!'

'No, that was never us. You're thinking of three Commando, although bananas was more appropriate.'

'That's right. You guys thought you were a cut above, didn't'

'Only in the air mate, the rest of the time we were just the cutting edge... just saying.'

'To quote my granddaughter–what_eva!' Fletcher rolled his eyes.

Greg glanced at the sky. 'It's a nice morning but I reckon it's going to be a hot one later.'

Birds dipped and dived, flicking water over their wings, the droplets sparkling in the early morning sun. Fletcher got up. 'I'd better see if I can book an earlier flight to Africa.'

'Why the rush?'

'I want to go over there to see what Zimbabwe's like now, before Polly gets on the first plane and comes home. If that happens, I'll never get there.'

Greg stroked his chin. 'Are you sure you want to go back after all this time? Some friends of Pattie's visited last year and wished they hadn't. They would have preferred to keep their memories of the old days.'

Fletcher shrugged. 'I'd like to take you and Pattie out tonight before I leave. We could go to Freemantle for dinner again, just for old time's sake. What do you reckon?'

'Pattie won't come. She has pottery classes tonight, but I'll give Barney a ring and see if he's free. He lives in Freo. Don't say I told you, but he used to work for ASIS. He's retired now, but he might know a thing or two. Oh, and like you asked, I rang my son Hugo to see what he could find out. Nothing official, you understand. He won't tell us anything like that, but if the cops have any lead on who stole the painting, he might find something. He said he doesn't think he can get any guff about what happened to this bloke Jake. It's out of his jurisdiction.' Greg ran his palms down his jowls, feeling the morning stubble. 'I remember meeting Jake once with that hot little blond number you fancied. There was another girl, dark-haired woman, his girlfriend I think. Geez, that's straining my memory, Selous Scouts wasn't he?'

'The blonde was Annie, just a friend, and he was SAS. His girlfriend was this bloke's mother, the bloke in the painting.' Fletcher didn't mention it wasn't Annie he fancied. Greg need not know about that sorry saga. 'Perhaps Hugo could find out where Annie was now? The Feds can do that, can't they? If you wouldn't mind asking him for anything that will shed some light, I would be grateful. I haven't seen her in thirty-five years. I don't even know if she's still alive. Her family came from Cape Town, so she most likely returned there.'

At dinner that night in a Freemantle restaurant, Fletcher wished they had chosen a quieter venue. The place was full of tourists and young people, playing hard and drinking harder. He could barely hear Greg as he introduced Barney.

When they finished their meal, Fletcher told Barney the story of Jake's disappearance, Matt's visit, and the stolen painting.

Barney listened, his jowly cheeks moving as if he was still chewing on a piece of steak. 'I can't shed any light on any of it.' He paused, twiddling with the stem of his wineglass. 'I've been out of the game a few years now.'

Fletcher felt absurdly disappointed, although he never expected this bloke to have any information.

'There is something I can tell you that you never heard from me, okay?' Barney said.

'I guess.'

'If you are going out to Zimbabwe, just take care. There's something going on over there that's causing my erstwhile employers a few sleepless nights.'

'What? Fletcher leaned forward sensing a story, his antennae on high alert.'

'Don't know, except... do you remember an article in the paper last year about Australia having spies in Africa?'

'I remember.'

'Well, of course it's not true, and Australia would never spy on another sovereign nation.' He grinned at Fletcher. 'But some, shall we call them miscellaneous types who have nothing to do with us, were reporting rumours about someone planning a coup in Zim. It was only a rumour, mind, but no one seemed to pinpoint where it was coming from.'

'Shit!' He should tell Polly to come home.

Barney glanced about the room as if bored with the conversation, looking for something more entertaining to occupy him.

Fletcher suspected the gesture was a ruse, scanning the room for people who might be eves dropping. It must be a habit. He weighed up the risk of asking Barney about some events referenced in the stolen documents Celia had sent him. 'Tell me, was there an attempted coup in Zim in '82 that didn't make the news... after the Gukurahundi?'

'How did you hear about that?' Barney's eyebrows met across his nose.

'Rumour and gossip, mainly from miscellaneous types.' Fletcher enjoyed the look of consternation on Barney's face.

Barney laughed. 'Touché.'

'Thanks,' Fletcher chuckled. 'Reporters will give a spy a run for his money any day, don't you think?'

'Hm, but that information is still classified. Just as well I'm retired, or I would have to dob you in.'

'It was a lucky guess.' Fletcher was contrite over his foolish jousting. He had overstepped the mark, all for the sake of winning.

'Seriously, though, I know nothing, but if I were still operative, I would be interested. The '82 episode had the hallmarks of seriously dangerous politics. I assume you think this bloke Jake was tied up with it?'

'I don't know. All I have is a lot of unrelated bits of information, and I can't join them up in any coherent way. What I know is that a bloke I once knew disappeared. His son turned up, looking for him. My granddaughter painted a picture of him that was immediately stolen, and you're talking about coups being planned in Zimbabwe?'

Barney frowned. 'Keep your voice down, mate.'

Fletcher dropped his tone and leaned closer to Barney. 'Years ago, I heard a rumour there was a coup in Zim. I also heard it was foiled by MI6, but I don't know how accurate my source was.'

Barney looked pensive and concentrated on twiddling his wineglass, holding the stem, and twisting it in circles. After a few seconds, he said, 'I'll tell you one thing for sure. Twice in the history of Zimbabwe, the community, our community that is, were notified of coups in Zimbabwe. The one in 2007 we know was just a setup. It was about one faction blaming the other and that sort of internal politics taken to the extreme. The other one in '82 has never come out in the press. All we know is what we learned on the wire, and through rumour. Don't know who or what was behind it. Frankly, I always thought there was something suspect about the story. I wasn't assigned to the case, so I didn't follow up. Not sure anyone did. There's never much interest if it's foiled before it starts. Leave me your email, and if I find out anything I can tell you, I'll let you know.'

Chapter Twenty-Nine

At the Victoria Falls airport, Matt grabbed his Bergen and laptop from the car and paid the taxi. He was lucky to get a flight out so quickly. He hurried into the building and joined the check-in queue. Guilt at abandoning Polly weighed on him. He saw the hurt in her face but was at a loss to know what to do about it. When he rang the Ryder's home, Meg said Chris would be back as soon as he could fuel up and return.

Matt hated leaving Polly, but what choice did he have? In any case what future was there in a relationship with a woman nine years his junior who lived on the other side of the world. This unexpected separation was probably the kindest way to severe any expectations.

Two men in plain clothes approached. Thugs, with bulges under the armpits, perhaps security. One had the blood-shot eyes of a heavy marijuana user. The other looked more alert and spoke to him.

'Mr. Reid?'

They knew his name. Matt wondered if they were from the Embassy, or the hotel.

'Yes?'

'You must come with us.' The spokesman was polite, but it was an order, not an invitation.

'What's this about?'.

'My superior will explain. It will only take a few minutes.'

'I have a flight to catch. Can this wait until I've checked in? Then I'll have plenty of time to chat.'

'No, Mr. Reid, this cannot wait. You must follow me now.'

He took Matt's arm, the dope smoker fell in behind, and Matt was in trouble. The people in the queue shuffled away, watching but saying nothing. If he bolted, he would not get far. The men would shoot first. Playing along like a tourist seemed his best bet.

He complained. 'My bags. I left them in the queue.'

The man clutching his arm spoke rapidly to the other man, and then said, 'My colleague will take care of them.'

'Let go my arm. I can walk unaided. I want to call the British Embassy.'

He ignored his demand and escorted him to a room, where the spokesman frisked him, and took away his phone. The dope smoker dumped his bags on the floor. The two men left, locking the door behind them.

Matt checked out the room. It was windowless, about four-by-four metres, and contained a wooden table and four chairs: an interrogation room.

'Shit.' What was the problem and what did they think he was doing? Perhaps it was a mistaken identity, but he doubted it. Those thugs knew his name. They were looking out for him, and he, the fool that he was, was so lost in thoughts about Polly that he walked straight into their trap.

Was the call from the British Embassy faked, a ploy to get him here? No, that was genuine. Otherwise, how would they know about his Gran?

He sat down at the table, head in hands. Mosquitoes whined in his ear, and he slapped at them distractedly. There must be a rational reason for his being here. After ten minutes the door was unbolted, and Gracie walked in. She balanced a cup and saucer in her hand, treading carefully so as not to slop the tea.

She was vulnerable in her concentration, and he contemplated taking her out, but caution prevailed. He stood up. 'I'm very glad to see you again, Gracie. I think someone has mistaken me for someone else, but you know who I am.'

She placed the tea, along with a tea-soaked biscuit, on the table in front of him. 'I hope you take sugar, Mr Reid. I didn't know, so I only put in one spoon.'

'What's going on, Gracie? I'm a tourist. I told you the other day that I intended to visit Victoria Falls.'

'Yes, Mr. Reid, I know who you are.'

'Look Gracie. I'm desperate. The British Embassy phoned and told me my grandmother has had a stroke and is dying. I can't afford to miss the flight. I might not get back in time.' His voice choked, and he didn't try to hide the emotion from her.

A look of concern flitted across her face. 'That is something we can verify, but first, Mr. Reid, I must ask you why, the day after I spoke to you at your hotel, you disappeared. We searched for you for several days. You were not at any hotel, nor had you taken any public transport or hired a car. For days, Mr. Reid, you go missing in my country and then turn up at the Victoria Falls Hotel. I asked you to make yourself available, but you disappeared, so what am I supposed to think?'

'Christ, is that what this is about? Is it because I didn't stay under your surveillance at the hotel?'

'Where did you go, Mr. Reid, and what are you up to?'

'This is crazy'

'Are you smuggling diamonds, Mr. Reid?'

'For fuck's sake.' He saw the shock register on her face. 'Excuse me, but I haven't seen a diamond since I've been here.' Not quite true. He recalled Bridie's jewellery. 'A friend arrived from Australia, and I've been with her and some other friends, staying at their house in Borrowdale. We flew up here yesterday on a private plane.'

'Hm,' she looked sceptical. 'We can verify this. You will give me your friend's address, but before I do that, Mr. Reid, I must ask you. Have you been for any interviews since you have been in my country?'

'What? Interviews... What for? Is it illegal to have an interview?' This new line of questioning baffled him.

She ignored him. 'Mr. Reid, do you belong to any old Rhodesian Societies?'

Christ. Now he was in trouble. What could he say? She was probably spying on his social media as well.

'I joined a Facebook site called Rhodesian's Worldwide or something like that, but it was only to see if my father was a member. You remember I told you I was looking for him.'

'Yes, Mr Reid, the Rhodesian SAS soldier whose portrait has mysteriously disappeared and cannot be found even on the internet. But I am not concerned about public websites or social media. It is other more clandestine organisations I am asking about.'

'I'm just a tourist. I don't know what you're getting at, but I stayed with friends until I flew up here yesterday. I know nothing about clandestine organisations or diamonds.' Matt's concern was giving way to anger. He didn't understand where this was leading or what she thought he was doing here, but whatever it was, she was wrong. Although being wrong had never stopped secret police forces, anywhere or anytime in the history of world, not if it didn't suit their agenda.

'Who are these friends?'

Matt didn't want to bring the Ryder's to the attention of these people, who were obviously from the Central Intelligence Organisation. He gambled. At least Livingstone was a black man, and a member of Mugabe's party. He called himself Matt's father, although if he denied Matt was staying with him... What did he know about any of these people, anyway? He should have been more cautious.

'I stayed with Livingston and Bridie Moyo.'

A flash of fear flitted through her eyes, and she got up and opened the door. 'Just a moment please, Mr. Reid. I shall verify your story and get back to you in a short time. Meantime, I do not want to prevent you from seeing your grandmother, so we will hurry the process and ensure the plane does not leave without you.'

Part Four

Chapter Thirty

Julia Harrison lay in a bed in the intensive care unit. The gentle rise and fall of her breathing was almost imperceptible. Tubes ran from her nose and disappeared into the neckline of her nightgown to reappear from her sleeve once again. They looped across to hook up to a machine that made little peeps and lines on a screen.

She hadn't regained consciousness since the nursing home staff found her five days ago. Her pulse was weak under the fragile wrist bones Matt held in his palm. Her fingers were dry twigs, wrapped in veined tissue. The pale mask of skin on her face fell away to reveal a beaked nose and sharp cheekbones, with sunken and grey eye sockets.

He pulled his chair closer to her bed, hoping she would open her eyes. He squeezed her fingers and waited for some response, but there was nothing. The nurse told him to hold her hand, hug her, talk to her, but she wouldn't appreciate hugging. She had always considered such displays of affection undignified.

'I met someone Gran, someone you'll like. She's Australian and an artist, a painter.' He searched for something else to say. 'I met her in Australia.' It sounded so lame.

He lapsed into silence, but she couldn't hear him, so what was the harm in verbalising his thoughts? Eventually he said, 'We visited the Victoria Falls together. You would have been to Vic Falls when you lived in Rhodesia. It is the most amazing place, and Mugabe hasn't ruined it yet. I didn't get to see much because I had to come home to see you.' That sounded like a criticism, and he added, 'so, I intend to go back again one day when you're better. Perhaps we can go together. Would you like to see Victoria Falls again, Gran?'

For some bizarre reason, he had become a person of interest to a paranoid secret service. It didn't sound real, but he can't tell his Gran that.

'I saw an elephant.' He put his head in his hands. He was tired and grubby and not thinking straight. All he wanted was his Gran to wake up so he could go home, put his bags down, and have a shower. He saw her eyelids flicker like someone having a dream and leaned forward. His voice might be having an effect.

'Can you hear me Gran? We stayed in this magnificent old hotel, like something out of the Victorian Era. You would have loved it.' Jesus, this was hard work. I think it was even better than the Meikles Hotel. You would remember that in Harare. You once lived in Harare, or Salisbury, didn't you Gran? I saw that photo of you in a ball grown at some posh do.

Deep in the fog of Julia Harrison's mind, synapses flashed. Electrical pulses shot through blood, seeping into the cavities of her brain. Julia was transported back to her youth, sitting at a table of society's dignitaries, next to the Governor General's table.

Her mother had ordered her dress from London, and she outshone all the other debutantes in the room. The ballroom glittered and her diamond necklace responded. Her father had some misgivings about federating the three countries, Southern and Northern Rhodesia and Nyasaland, but it was going ahead anyway.

Dennis smiled at her and held out his hand. His dark greenie/blue eyes alight with mischief as he led her to the dance floor. He was the most handsome man in the place, and he was all hers. She straightened her young shoulders, and held her head higher, filled with the pride of knowing she had captured society's most eligible bachelor.

All the other girls in the room glanced enviously at her handsome airman. He stood head and shoulders above the throng, medals glinting on his chest. It wouldn't be long before he popped the question. Her father had hinted at it. The marriage would make their families the biggest landholders in the country, and all Daddy's financial woes would be fixed.

She relaxed into Dennis's arms as he foxtrotted to the popular *You Belong to Me*. She tiptoed to whisper in his ear. 'This will be our song, Dennis.'

He stopped dancing and threw back his head laughing. Then he gave her arm a little squeeze, confirmation, and she was thrilled. They headed back to their table. Robin Harrison, the handsome new Police Inspector from England, was talking to Daddy. He introduced his new fiancée. She looked like a tramp, but then Julia had heard she was working class. What could one expect? That dress, totally wrong for the occasion. It made her look cheap, which no doubt she was.

Then the tart thrust her hand at Dennis, like a man for goodness sake. She left him holding it for far too long, her witchery green eyes lingering on his face as if she was about to devour him with that wide red mouth.

Julia pushed in front of Dennis, taking the woman's arm. 'Dorothée what a lovely name. French isn't it.'

The witch actually had the gall to correct her, saying she preferred Dolly. Looked like a doll and had the brain of a doll.

In her sweetest voice, Julia asked, 'What does your father do, Dolly? I haven't heard your family's name mentioned before.'

Julia already knew her father worked for the Wankie colliery and was dismayed by the pride in the woman's voice when she spoke of him. Good lord, did she have no shame? How dare she have the temerity to move into these social circles?

It had taken a lifetime, but she had exacted her revenge. Julia took one last triumphant look into that upstart bitch's face and a surge of rage pounded through her weakened arteries, bursting more vessels in her brain. The image of her face morphed into his, as blood filled cavities and blocked any further communication signals. Shuddering with a lifetime of hurt and bitterness, Julia Harrison exhaled one last time.

Matt saw a flat line creep across the monitor's screen. People rushed into the room. A nurse took his arm and said something he didn't catch. He remained staring at Julia, willing her to open her eyes.

They left him to wait in a waiting room, watching the clock on the wall ticking its loud jerky seconds, one by one. That line on the monitor hadn't look good. He should not have used those precious seconds to indulge his own fantasies. What else could he have talked to her about? But she wouldn't have heard him. It dawned on him, that she had gone, and he had no one in his family left, unless he could count the Ryders. Although he was still not sure about that connection.

He had never been close to his grandmother. She wasn't that kind of person, and even to the last, he had struggled to find common ground with her. Their relationship had always been more about duty than intimacy. Her death was not gut wrenching like when his mother died, but still he would like to have talked to her again, asked her questions about her youth, found out more about his mother and perhaps even Jake.

He'll never know now what happened or why she was so terrified of revealing anything to him. He shouldn't have spent her last few moments indulging in talk about Polly. Although if his Gran had lived, she would have been interested, if only to make sure he made a suitable match. In her eyes that would have to be someone of higher social standing. Perhaps it's just as well she never met Polly. Her Australian frankness would not have gone down well.

A man in a white coat came through the door. He looked like an adolescent, and Matt saw the task was making him nervous.

The doctor fiddled with his stethoscope. 'I'm afraid your grandmother couldn't be revived.'

'Okay, thank you. Is there anything I need to do?'

'You might wish to say goodbye.'

Matt stood at her bedside. 'Thanks for waiting for me Gran.' The guilt would have been overwhelming if he hadn't been here. He kissed her dry cheek and left the hospital, heading home for the first time since landing in England.

When he opened the front door, mail spilled across the mat. He sorted through the junk and found another envelope from his mother's solicitors. He had almost forgotten about them. Their bill would have to take priority tomorrow. He placed the envelope with the other two, still lying where he left them before going to Zimbabwe.

Over the next few days, Matt busied himself with arrangements for his grandmother's funeral. He drove to the residential home to collect her things and put them with his mother's belongings, still sitting in black bin bags in the hall outside her bedroom. He made an appointment with his PhD supervisor, and one with the solicitors, and then got stuck into the garden. It felt good to get his life back under control.

The next morning, he took the two suitcases and five boxes of his gran's belongings into the sitting room. It was almost time for the solicitor's appointment. He closed the last two boxes, full of papers and photo albums. He would look through them later. Then he picked up the bags, placing them with his mother's clothing and ran upstairs to change.

He arrived at the solicitor's office ten minutes late. A disapproving woman with blue hair showed him through to an office. The man behind the desk stood when Matt entered. He was in his mid-forties, dapper with a thin moustache, dark hair, and suit pants with turn-ups held up with braces. The office was cluttered with papers and files.

Matt walked across to the desk to shake hands, easing back on his grip as he felt the effeminate grasp. 'How the hell can you find anything in all this?' Matt indicated the desk clutter with a small sweep of his hand.

The lawyer ignored his comment. 'Mr. Reid, good of you to make time for us.'

Smarmy bastard. ' I've been abroad.'

'So, we hear. I am Peabody. Richard Peabody. I am your late mother's solicitor, but of course you are aware of that. Please take a seat. Would you like some tea?'

'No thanks.'

'May I offer our commiserations? We understand you are recently bereaved again?' Peabody said it as though Matt had been careless.

'Thanks.'

'Is there any service in that regard we can undertake for you, Mr. Reid?'

'I don't think so. It's pretty straightforward. I'll just settle your bill and get out of your hair.'

'Our bill? There is no bill, Mr. Reid. Your mother was very careful to settle all of that before...' Peabody lapsed into silence and shuffled about his desk as if looking for papers.

'What is this about then?' Their repeated requests to see him mystified Matt. Particularly if there was no money outstanding. They had settled the will months ago.

'It's the bank,' Peabody said. 'Apparently there is a safe deposit box. They requested the box be retrieved or the annual invoice paid. Ah, here it is.' He picked up a single sheet of paper from under the clutter and waved. 'It was most unfortunate that we were unaware of the deposit box when the will was finalised, but you may wish to go to the bank and deal with them yourself. You can access it directly. Your mother did not include it in her will specifically, but as she has no other remaining relatives, now your grandmother has passed on, you may as well circumvent the legal red tape and collect it yourself.'

Matt held out his hand for the paper, but Peabody ignored him. Instead, he took a pair of reading glasses from his jacket pocket and placed them on his nose to read the bank letter.

'It requires you to attend the bank in person along with a key, and a particular number.' Peabody placed the letter on the table. Then methodically he took off his glasses, folded them with exaggerated care and tucked them back in their case, which he returned to his inside pocket. He looked at Matt. 'Do you have the key, and the number, Mr. Reid?'

Matt shook his head. 'I don't think so.' Then he remembered the key that fell from his mother's coat. 'I don't know.'

'It would make it much easier for you, Mr Reid, if you could find them. Otherwise, we will need to make a submission to the courts to retrieve it as part of your inheritance. We, of course, can handle the court order if you require.'

'Okay, look thanks. Can I have the bank letter?'

'I shall have a copy made for you on your way out, Mr. Reid. If you have any difficulty in retrieving the contents of the safe deposit box, please feel free to call on our services.'

Ten minutes later, Matt drove home, dwelling on the conversation. They could have told him in a letter rather than insisting on an appointment. But what could his mother have left in a bank safety deposit? It didn't seem in character with his mother's meticulous planning. She left nothing to chance before killing herself, squaring away papers, wills, paying the solicitor's bill in advance, but not this bank box.

When he got home, he searched for the key. He got as far as the landing outside his mother's room when the doorbell sounded.

He opened the front door, and Dog stood scowling at him. 'So, arsehole, when were you going to let on, you were back in Blighty?' Dog pushed past Matt into the hallway.

'Hello Dog, nice to see you.' He followed him to the kitchen.

Dog walked straight to the cupboard where he unearthed the whisky bottle, and taking two glasses poured and handed one to Matt. 'I'm still waiting for a response to my email arsehole. Do you know how much it took to overcome my vow, to write that bloody thing... and then you fookin ignore me!'

'Shit.' Matt ran his hand through his hair. 'Sorry, I forgot man.'

'Sorry, what good's sorry?'

'A lot happened. Come out back and I'll tell you.'

They took their drinks out to the bench in the garden. Dog took out a cigarette, offering one to Matt.

Matt shook his head. 'No mate, I've given up.'

'Bullshit.'

'Gen dit.'

'Bullshit.'

Dog inhaled and Matt wished he could have one. Succumbing is easy, and he said, 'Screw it.'

For a moment, the two men sat side by side sipping their whisky, and smoking cigarettes.

Then Dog said, 'So, I'm waiting.'

'Fuck man, I don't know where to start.'

'At the beginning, arsehole.'

Matt told him about finding his father and his family, but he said nothing about Polly. He ended with his return from Africa to see his grandmother before she died.

'Sorry to hear that mate,' Dog offered Matt another cigarette and returned to the kitchen, for the whisky bottle. While he poured, he asked, 'So what's her name then?'

'Who?'

'The shag.'

'Come on Dog. That's not nice.'

'Well, who is she?'

'What says there is *a she* in all this?'

'Maaate.' Dog dragged out the word and looked at Matt pityingly.

'Okay, Polly—her name's Polly.'

'The artist? Nice. I've seen her picture on the telly. She's the one that did the painting of you. It's a bloody good painting. So, when do we meet her?'

'You don't.'

'Come on Reid.'

'It's finished.'

Dog took a long drag of his cigarette.

Matt shook his head. 'So, what did you want then?'

'What?'

'You emailed.'

'Oh yeah. Well, it's about the artist.'

'Polly?'

'Yes, indirectly. How upset was she about the theft of the painting?'

All Matt's suspicions came to the fore. 'Why?' He was not sure he wanted to hear what Dog had to say.

'It wasn't us.' Dog hastened to assure Matt. He took another suck on his smoke.

'Who then?'

'The cousins.'

'Fuck.'

'Yeah.'

'Where's the painting?'

'It's safe--at the head shed over there, some island, I hear. Duck, no Swan Island or something along those lines.'

'Fuck. What am I going to tell her?' Matt drank his whisky and poured another. 'Fucking gobshytes. What did they do that for?'

'Settle down mate.' Dog looked at Matt with concern. 'It's not that bad. No one knows who did it or where it is, and they never need to. I just thought you might want it. You said you would like to own it, but mate, you can't go getting your dial all over the media like that. It's just not helpful for anyone, and well they owed us a favour so... '

'So, you called in the bloody favour, okay. But to steal the frigging thing, well... fucking idiots, they could have just asked her to take it down, or I could have. Anyway, it didn't help. The photos are already all over the media.'

'Not anymore. CO's taken care of that, and there is a media suppression order.'

Matt had a flash back to Gracie's comments about the painting's disappearance. He had thought she was speaking about the physical theft. No wonder she was so suspicious.

'It is not possible to suppress the internet. Something will be out there, but it doesn't matter. All that shit's behind me now, so it's not much of a disaster, not as much as if I was still operative. The cops thought she had taken it, accused her?'

'We heard. It's okay though, we would have come clean, even returned it if there'd been a problem. How did she take it, the theft, I mean?'

Matt hesitated. How did she feel? He should have asked. 'I really don't know how she feels about anything.' He put his head in his hands. She would think he was a complete idiot.

'Sounds like you got it bad, mate.'

'Fuck off, Dog.' Matt tried to change the subject. 'What about the letter you attached to your email? What's that about?'

'Oh yeah, a few of us got one. Didn't you?'

'Na, but I'm not interested. I've had that game and I'm not getting involved with the circuit. I already told a few of them that when they tried a couple of years ago and I'm serious mate. They probably know that, so it's not surprising I didn't get a letter. What's it about?'

'It's not the circuit, but that's the mystery. None of us know anything—just that they want to interview us if we were interested in signing on to some private peace keeping outfit in a training capacity for six months.'

'Peace keeping! That's a new one. Where?' Matt laughed and flicked his cigarette away.

'Don't know, very hush-hush, it seems. No one will tell us anything just—are we interested? Then they'll do an interview, and only once they think we're suitable will they tell us more.'

'Jesus. So how do you know if you want to do it?'

'I don't, but I'm tempted and so is Brander. Thing is. The contractors are taking over the world and there's no place left in this government's mind for government employed soldiers. I reckon it's a matter of time and the MOD will outsource our jobs.'

'You should get out, Dog.'

'Yeah, and do what? I can't get a PhD like you, mate, not clever enough and I would just end up on the circuit, anyway.' Dog held up the empty whisky bottle. 'We'd better adjourn to the pub.'

Chapter Thirty-One

The dream was intense, and this time he saw it all before waking; saw the woman's eyes as the Kalashnikov jammed. Miraculously he was alive. Dog's muzzle flashed, and the women crumpled. Matt watched her fall in slow motion. Then the boy leapt on him from behind, sinking the rusty bayonet deep into his deltoid muscle. There was a grating sensation as the blade scraped bone.

The boy ran and Dog fired again. The boy's head disintegrated, tiny flakes of bone and flesh splattering across Matt in a bloody mosaic. A bullet ricocheted, hitting his bayoneted shoulder, and spinning him around before throwing him to the ground. He lay helpless and staring into her dying eyes as their light faded.

Matt awoke with his legs on fire. The sheets were tangled as if he had a restless sleep. He dropped back into torpor, wishing the pain would go. Polly arrived and stood by his bed. Surprised and pleased, he reached out to grab her hand. 'Thank you for coming, but I can't get up. My legs hurt.'

Polly vanished, and he fell into a deep sleep. Hours later, he awoke again, freezing cold. He pulled up the blankets, but he couldn't get warm. The shivering was exhausting. Somewhere, a ringing mobile confused him. Then he recognised the phone next to his bed and answered it.

It was Dolly. She was cross with him for not ringing.

He said, 'Dolly, Dolly I'm sorry.' He laughed at the rhyme. 'My legs are sore. Polly was here, but she disappeared, and the woman died. I killed her Dolly... I'm so sorry.'

He fell back into a deep sleep, and his phone fell to the floor.

When he awoke again, Polly was standing at the doorway. She refused to come in, and he couldn't get up to go to her. She faded as he fell down a dark tunnel.

Sweat saturated the bed. It was dark and he smelled bad. He needed a drink. The pain had moved from his legs to his head, blinding him. Thirst drove him up, and he rested on the side of the bed, waiting for the strength to stand and walk to the bathroom. He clutched at the furniture for balance and drank straight from the tap before staggering back to bed, pulling the limp blankets to his neck, but he couldn't get warm.

It was morning, and Dog stood in his room telling him to lie still. 'You're bleeding everywhere, mate.'

'I need water. I'm hot Dog, so hot... hotdog, hotdog, hotdog.'

Dog was gone, and he was in a dark room. The blackness pressed on his eyeballs, and he couldn't see. He was blind. Panic rose. The darkness lifted, and it was light again. He heard a doorbell. Someone was hammering on the door. The hammering merged with the thumping in his head. Pain was everywhere now, flashing like a beacon. Then he was flying. He had left his body with the pain behind and was flying through the brilliant blue of Polly's eyes.

Someone shook his shoulder. Don't they know there's a bayonet with a bullet in that shoulder, but he couldn't feel the pain anymore?

He heard his name. 'Matthew, Matthew.' He struggled towards consciousness, opening his eyes against the intense blue light.

'Matthew.' A strange woman stood over him, her brow furrowed with deep vertical lines between her eyebrows. 'Good, you're awake,' she said.

Of course, I'm awake. You woke me. But he didn't say anything because he had drifted off.

The next time he awoke, he did so by himself. Outside, dawn was breaking, and he could see the light creeping up the wall opposite. He didn't know where he was, didn't recognise anything. He sat up and his head swam. A sharp tug caused him to turn his head. A tube ran from his arm up to a bag on a pole. He closed his eyes.

Someone walked toward his bed. 'Matt, Matt darling, are you awake?' Jess sat on his bed.

How could it be Jess? He closed his eyes, but the hallucination leaned across the bed, and a gentle brush of a warm hand on his brow smoothed his hair. This dream was so tender and kind.

'Matt, how are you feeling? Are you in pain?'

She was real. He tried to speak. 'Jess,' but it came out as a croak.

She lifted his head and gave him a drink. He was so thirsty; water spilt out of the sides of his mouth and ran down his neck.

She said, 'Enough.' Then rested his head back on the pillow.
She took his hand. 'You had us all worried, Matt.'

'Jess.' He cleared his throat and tried again. 'Jess, what are
you doing here? Where am I?'

She laughed. 'You're in hospital. St Thomas's. You have
malaria, darling. You've been out for the count for days.'

'How did you..?' It was too much, and Matt lapsed into
silence.

Jess patted his hand. 'You were a naughty boy. You
promised to phone, and Dolly was beside herself. She rang, but
all she got was you talking gibberish. She rang a friend in
London, who tried to get hold of you. Your door was locked, so
he called the police. That's when they found you. It was just as
well. You were in a terrible state.'

'But you.... what are you doing...?'

'You don't think we would leave you on your own when you
were sick, do you? The soon as Dolly hung up she rang Tom and
told us to come over. We'll take you home to recuperate. Tom's
gone back to the hotel to change. We've been doing bedside
shifts.'

'You flew all the way from Zimbabwe for me?'

'No dear. We were in Amsterdam, so Tom cut our business
short. We'll go back when we know you're all right. Don't worry
about it. Just get better.'

He was weak, but recovered quickly, plaguing the nurses to
bring him boiled eggs, which he craved. Two days later they let
him out of the hospital. After getting assurance he would finish
the course of pills.

Matt insisted Tom and Jess use his home as a base. He
wished he had cleaned it. It occurred to him that if he has
malaria, perhaps Polly had it too. They slept in the same bed
and didn't use the mosquito net. Then he remembered the

mossies in the interrogation room at the airport. 'Have you heard from Polly? Is she okay?'

'Yes, of course. She's at the farm. She was anxious about you.'

'At the farm. I thought she was going back to Australia?'

'She was, but after Fletcher got out of hospital, he asked if he could come out. He's been hankering to come back to Africa. They are planning a trip down memory lane. Oh, and Livingston wanted to know when you will be back. His father wants to meet you.'

Chapter Thirty-Two

The bedroom needed cleaning. There was a film of dust coating the once glossy wooden surfaces of the dresser and bedside tables. A pile of assorted items from Matt's mother's handbags and coats remained where he had left them. The lawyer said he needed a key and a number for the deposit box. If this was the key, where was the number? The screwed ball of paper caught his eye. Was that it? The locket, the paper had fallen from, lay next to it. He opened it, touching the tiny photo of his mother's face, and then looking at Jake's picture. 'What have you left behind, Mum?'

There was a knock on the door, and Matt turned to see Jess. 'Are you all right, Matt? You're very pale? Are you up to this now?'

'Yes Jess, I'm fine.' He concealed his emotions.

'Can I come in?'

'Of course.'

'This is your mother's room.'

Matt was not sure if it was a question but answered, 'Yes.'

He saw the room through Jess's eyes and shame at not cleaning it surged into his neck. Her calm appraisal was a reprimand.

'Is that her locket? May I see?'

He held out the locket, swinging at the end of its silver chain. Jess took it and looked at the photos, her eyes glistening with unshed tears.

'I loved Jake, too. Oh, not romantically, but we were about the same age and attended the same junior school. It was always his older brother I was interested in, but Jake was a nice boy, nice to the girls anyway. Most of the boys were mean to us, but Tom and Jake were always polite. I never met your mother. It's such a pity. She would have been my sister-in-law. How strange.'

Matt never thought of that. He put his arm around Jess's shoulder. 'Mum would have liked you a lot.'

Wiping her eyes with the back of her hand, she laughed. 'Look at us, a pair of sentimental old sillies. Well, not you, but me. I'd like to clean the room if that's all right with you, Matt.'

'You've done enough, Jess. I should do it. I've been meaning to.' He glanced around the room, realising it was a poor excuse and a sudden prickling pushed against the back of his eyes. 'I was angry with her. I thought she didn't deserve any sympathy for what she did. Jess, it was so hard. I didn't realise how I felt about her going, not really, not until now. I miss her.'

Matt fought to regain control, and sat on her bed, his head in his hands. Jess sat down next to him, patient and silent, with her arm around his waist.

The minutes ticked by before he stood up. 'I'm all right. I have an appointment with the bank, so I'll be out for the morning, and back at about lunchtime. Can I get you anything while I'm out?'

She shook her head. 'No, I don't need a thing, but if you're all right now, Tom and I will head back to Amsterdam in the morning to finish our business and then go home. You will come back home again once you've sorted out everything here? At least, finish your holiday with us. It's Dennis's eighty-fifth soon and he'll want you there.'

Matt pocketed the key and the scrap of paper. He wasn't sure what his response should be. He had already decided he wouldn't go back to Zimbabwe. 'I don't know Jess; I'll think about it.' He headed out the door.

Half an hour later, he was in a private room in the bank, a box open in front of him. Inside the box were two shoeboxes. Marked clearly on each box is a number one, and two. It was his mother's handwriting and Matt's apprehension grew. He wanted to close the box and run.

Such elaborate planning, such secrecy, could only mean that what was in the boxes is something he doesn't want to know about. She was sending him a message from beyond death, something she couldn't say to him when she was alive. How could he possibly want to hear it now?

The woman who opened the box for him left the room. 'Ring the bell when you have finished, Mr. Reid, and I'll show you out.' She closed the door.

Matt was alone, staring at the boxes, but seeing his mother's face across the table. He was ten and going to boarding school for the first time, leaving home. Celia was telling him how to behave. 'The most important thing in life is to live honestly. I don't mean like not stealing or lying, Matthew, although that's important. I mean, being true to yourself, to whom you are and what you believe in. To do that, you must know who you are. An unexamined life is worse than a prison. Understand who you are and why you do things and then stand up for yourself.'

Tears seeped into his eyes, and he brushed them away. Then, taking a deep breath, he lifted the box marked, one. There was an envelope at the top. His name, written in his mother's characteristic script, was on the envelope. He squeezed the top of his nose near the tear ducts to stop the leakage.

The envelope was unsealed. Folded papers bulge from the open flap. The envelope ripped a little as he eased out the papers. Contrite, he took more care, winkling the wad loose, not knowing why it mattered if he tore the envelope, it just does.

Once out, he lay the papers on the table, unfolding and smoothing the white photocopying paper with its typed lines. At the top of the paper, is a date. 2 November 2012. Matt's throat choked as he realised this was her planning stage for death. This was the suicide note he had never found.

By the time he finished reading the letter, Matt's eyes were red, and his nose was running. He searched for his handkerchief. The door opened and the same woman poked in her head.

'How are you getting along, sir? Do you need more time?'

He turned his face away from her. 'Yes, please. I won't be long. I will remove the box today, but first I need to sort a few things.'

'Certainly, Mr Reid, I will prepare the release forms.'

She closed the door behind her, and Matt folded his mother's letter back into its envelope. He cannot make it fit. Placing it to one side, he lifted the next envelope from the box. It was a large brown manila envelope. Inside, he found Celia and Jake's marriage certificate dated 26th April 1979. He replaced the certificate carefully.

Then he picked up a small box. Inside, lying on black velvet, is a plain gold wedding band, with a set of stamped dog tags lying alongside the ring. A leather thong joined ring and tags. Matt picked up the dog tags and turned them over.

Jake's name and blood type were stamped into the metal, as was his religion. The blood type O stood out clearly.

The small narrow wedding band was plain and without inscription. He assumed it was his mother's but not the one she wore while George was alive. That was an elaborate set still in the jewellery box on her dresser.

He closed his hand around the ring. It must have meant so much more to her than the expensive, jewel-encrusted rings George gave her. A fresh surge of grief reached his eyes, and he blinked swiping his thumb across to catch the escaping offenders.

Beneath the box was another envelope. The documents within, letters and notes between George Reid, and Robin Harrison, his stepfather and grandfather. They were cryptic, written in a kind of guarded code. In one there was a discussion of some package, and in his grandfather's writing, *the package must be removed, and all traces eliminated.*

A note from George to Robin dated a week later said, *Mission accomplished, package jettisoned.*

He picked up another note, and a chill ran across his shoulders. *Dispatch successful, evidence contained.* There was just the note, minus any contained evidence. Matt felt the growing horror that his mother had read these notes and saw their treachery unfolding.

The woman knocked and opened the door. 'Here are the forms, sir. Can I leave them with you to sign? We are closing in a few minutes.'

He had been in the room for three hours.

He arrived home and retrieved the boxes from the back seat of his car before walking into the house. As he opened the door, the smell of baking bread assailed him. The house was fresh with flowers, and his throat tightened. It was almost as if his mother was home. There was no sign of anyone about so, placing the boxes on the hall table, he walked through to the sitting room.

Jess and Tom were leaning over the coffee table; a slim black box opened in front of them. The box rested on top of Matt's laptop bag. Unable to believe what he thought he was seeing, Matt stopped short, watching them through the crack in the door, indecisive over what he should do.

Jess looked up, saw him, and touched Tom's arm to alert him.

Tom followed her gaze. 'Ah bugger! Sorry you had to see this, son. We were hoping to keep it from you for a while longer.'

'What the fuck?'

'Look... ,' Tom said.

Matt interrupted. 'What the fuck is going on? D'you know they nearly caught me with that shit.' It was a wonder

Gracie hadn't found it. 'The bastards interrogated me, and I had no idea what they were talking about.'

'What?' Tom looked perplexed.

Jess's face swung back and forth, looking from one to the other and frowning. Slowly, her brow cleared. 'Hang on Matt. Tom, I think there is some misunderstanding going on here. Matt, tell us what you think happened?'

'I can see what happened. You hid that case in my laptop bag so I could smuggle the stuff back for you. No wonder you came running as soon as you could. It was just fortuitous that I got sick, and you could pretend to care for me. The bloody secret police stopped me. I'm just lucky they didn't find it.' Anger surged through him. First the letter from his mother, now this betrayal.

Jess was smiling.

'What, you think this is funny?'

'No, darling, but you have the wrong end of the stick. Do you think you smuggled these out of Zim for us?'

'Well, what else?'

'No Matt, we are selling them, but we brought them out ourselves, which was why we were in Amsterdam.' She turned to Tom. 'We'll have to tell him.'

'Tell me what? What the fuck is going on here?'

'First, tell us what happened with your interrogation. You said nothing about that before.'

Tom was looking at him with mistrust and scepticism, as if it was up to Matt to explain, and not the other way around. Matt felt the hot fury rising again and fought to control it. The emotional rollercoaster of the day's events made losing it to rage a beguiling thought.

'Tell us what happened? Who interrogated you... where and why? How do we know you're not MI6 rather than army? How do we know the whole elaborate meeting with us was not some scheme concocted to expose us to ensure Mugabe stays in power?'

Things couldn't get any weirder. Matt said, 'If I tell you about it, will you be honest with me about these?' He pointed to the coffee table.

'I can't tell you everything, Matt. It's too risky at the moment okay, trust me.'

'What? Trust you—I hardly know you. You have a box full of what I presume are uncut diamonds in my sitting room, and you're telling me to trust you. You must be frigging crazy if you think I'll buy that.'

'Ja. I see your point, but that's the deal.' Tom shrugged. 'I need a drink and a smoke. What about you Matt?'

But Matt was not buying into the nice guy shit. 'Tell me where you got those bloody diamonds first.'

'Ag. That part is simple. These are the spoils taken off several ministers' in Mugabe's government.'

'You stole them?'

'Not yet, but we will. These stones belong to the people of Zimbabwe, and the members of Mugabe's elite are syphoning them off and putting them in their own Swiss bank accounts. They are stealing the people blind and leaving the poor bastards to starve in a country they are busy destroying. We are just making sure that the people get what's due.'

'How?'

'Through Livingston, we have a system. For a fee, certain Zim government ministers entrust their spoils to Livingston to have them smuggled out of the country. We deposit the diamonds in nominated Swiss banks. If the CIO stopped you, they may suspect you are the courier.' He paused, 'But that bit doesn't fit very well, unless a rival faction wanted in on the deal.' He shook his head. 'Anyway, we are the couriers and take care of the deposits. What they are unaware of is that on the journey from Zim to Switzerland we swap the real for fake. The fake diamonds go into their safe deposits. We sell the genuine diamonds and then deposit the money into a bank account to benefit the people of Zim. Livingston takes care of the certificates, the bank accounts and the services run to support the people, supplying food, housing, jobs and shelter.'

'How do you get them out?'

'Come on, Matt. We have our own planes and fly all over the place, ferrying tourists. During the war, Dad and I worked for the Smith government as sanctions busters, so we know all the tricks. Anyway, as I was saying, Mugabe will die soon. The man's eighty-nine and supposedly has cancer. What will happen when he goes? There are at least three factions vying to take power, and that's just within his own party, never mind the Ndebele or any others in the country. We will have another civil war. Preventing these diamonds falling into the wrong hands will stop the factions finding the financial means. Instead, their money will enable us to defend democracy, free and fair elections, and the rule of law.'

Tom paused. 'Look Matt, I can't tell you anymore, not yet. I'm sorry, but I have to be careful. I hardly know who you are even if you are Jake's kid, and of that I'm sure. You are family, and we love you, son, but I have to know if we can trust you.'

Jess disappeared and came back with gin and tonics. He took one from her and then told Tom and Jess about Gracie and the two occasions she had interrogated him. 'She accused me of being party to some plot by old Rhodesians but backed off when I mentioned Livingstone.'

'Christ, we'd better warn Livingstone. You should know our very own CIO spymaster, Happyton Bonyongwe is an influential supporter of Joice Mujuru, the vice President. She is the head of the faction vying to take over from Mugabe. Look Matt, we need you on our side. We could do with your help if you can trust us. At least I know why they think you might be a diamond smuggler.'

Matt asked, 'Was there an attempted coup in Zimbabwe after the Gukurahundi?'

'What?' Tom looked up from his drink.

'A coup against Mugabe to instate Nkomo?'

'No, who told you that? That's just crap. There's never been a coup, attempted or otherwise, in Zim. There was a supposed coup in 2007, but that was bullshit, just Solomon Mujuru's faction, trying to discredit Emmerson Mnangagwa. What's this about Matt?'

'I don't know. I'm not sure of anything anymore.' Matt said. 'But before we go on, there is something else you should know. My mother's letter said Jake was killed in a coup, foiled by the British in 1982. Apparently, my grandfather, Robin Harrison, was MI6, a spy who had infiltrated the Rhodesian command structure. After he returned to Britain, he maintained responsibility for the Zimbabwe desk. That was when he uncovered the plot. It was through his intervention that the CIO, and the Zimbabwean army foiled the coup. They killed the plotters, including their leader. Grandfather Harrison told Mum Jake was the coup leader and gave her Jake's dog tags to prove it. So, in a way, my grandfather was responsible for Jake's death.' He stopped, assessing the horrified faces in front of him.

'Bullshit!' Tom said.

'It's in my mum's letter. The evidence is in a box in the hallway, including Jake's dog tags. They were in my mother's safe deposit box. It is also full of top-secret documents, but I'll trust you not to hand me into the authorities. I could go to gaol if I'm caught with these. We can go through them and then destroy them, but at least your family will get some closure.'

'That's bullshit, Either someone is trying to trick you or you're lying.' Tom got up. 'Let's have a look at this box, shall we? I'm intrigued, but I can tell you now Jake disappeared long before '82, and there was no attempted coup. That's just a load of rubbish.'

Matt was fed-up with the whole thing. He collected the boxes and placed them on the table next to the bottle of gin. He said, 'It's all in there, the entire contents of my mother's safe deposit. She found the evidence in my grandfather's safe after he died, a little over a year ago. It was why she killed herself.' Matt felt his eyes burning again and picked up Tom's pack of cigarettes. 'You mind Tom?'

Tom shook his head, still staring at the boxes.

Matt lit a cigarette and picked up his gin. 'Read the letter in the box marked one first.'

He couldn't bear to watch them read it and headed out to the garden. The magnolia tree was green with glossy summer foliage and cast long shadows. He sat on the bench and smoked, then swallowed the gin. The evening sky deepened into twilight as the sun sank into the horizon, where clouds gather into a brooding storm. Raindrops spat on his neck as he hunched over the empty glass, taking a last drag on the cigarette.

He retraced his steps through the kitchen door. The smell of burning coiled in the air. He turned off the oven and took out the bread, only a little singed about the edges. He walked back to the sitting room and hung by the door.

Tears ran down Jess's face. Tom blew his nose and then spotted Matt at the door.

'This is not your fault. You and your mother are as much victims of these bastards' treachery as we are.'

Matt would like to believe him, but guilt remained. He turned to Jess. 'I took the bread out of the oven. It was burning.'

'God, I forgot.' Her hand hit her forehead, and she hurried from the room.

'Sit down, son. I have to tell you something else. I swear I never knew until I read your mum's letter, but we have some responsibility here too. Your grandfather seems to have had all of us dancing to his tune.'

'How?' Matt searched Tom's face.

Tom said, 'My mum and dad go way back with your grandparents. It's really a story Dolly and Dennis should tell you. The bit in your mum's letter about Jake and the documents he found was true. Jake was in Mozambique on a mission. They had hit Mugabe's headquarters in Mozambique. In the mop-up, they found hundreds of documents along with arms and other equipment. Among the documents were diaries, belonging to Mugabe.

I didn't know what was in them until I read your mum's letter. I did not know your grandfather was in league with the jackal. It was true, Jake found Mugabe's blueprint for the country he was planning to smash, but Jake handed it in to his Commanding Officer. The CO passed them on to the Central Intelligence Organisation. Anyway, the documents disappeared around mid1979.

You have to understand in April 1979, the UANC led by Bishop Muzorewa, won government. They took office in June. It didn't end the war because Mugabe wouldn't stop until he was in power. The new black government needed the documents to expose Mugabe's treachery.

When they couldn't find them, they accused Jake of stealing them and chucked him into Chikurubi prison. Let me tell you, it's not a very nice place. My father moved heaven and earth to get him out, but he was there for months awaiting trial. When the Brits took over temporarily in December '79 to prepare for elections in 1980, Dad made a deal. He got Jake out of prison, but it came at a cost.'

Tom put his head in his hands as he struggled to get his emotions under control. Matt lit up two cigarettes and handed one to Tom. He wanted to believe the man. Instinct told him he could trust him, but he remained cautious.

Tom cleared his throat and continued. 'The only person who would touch the case was someone who hated my dad. Your grandfather, Robin Harrison, struck a deal with Dennis and Jake walked free. All charges were dropped, which told me he hadn't stolen the documents. We were just relieved that he was out and carried out our part of the deal. When we came back, Jake was gone. We never found out what happened to him, and your grandfather had left the country.'

Tom paused again, grief creasing his face. 'It seems now it was your grandfather who stole the documents, if what your mum says is right, but that's not all Matt. It seems Dad, and I handled your mum's forced transportation to England. I swear, son, we didn't know who it was, except that our passenger was unwilling. The deal to get Jake out of prison was our priority.'

'Sorry, I'm not with you. How did you kidnap my mother?' Matt sat forward, shocked by this revelation.

'We didn't do the kidnapping, just the transport. Throughout the war, Dad and I were sanctions busters. That was our role, and we were pretty good at it, flying to many places, country hopping, and getting supplies vital to the war, including planes. We had contacts and fake Zambian,

Portuguese, and South African passports, and we had the networks.

Robin Harrison, your grandfather, knew all about it. He was in the Special Branch of the Police. Although no one suspected he was MI6. He said he would get Jake out if we took a package to the U.K. for him clandestinely. Hell, Dad agreed immediately, although at the time he hadn't known the package was human. That must have been what your mum meant when she said Robin kidnapped her. I'm sorry, Matt, we had no idea.'

Matt couldn't deal with this new turn of events. He needed quiet to work out what it meant, but for now, he just needed facts.

'You said when you came back Jake was gone. Gone where?'

'Well, that was the bizarre thing. There were reports Jake boarded a flight for the U.K. Rumour claimed he took the gap. That was a believable story, as it was just a matter of time before the SAS would become persona non grata. Certainly, Mugabe would never have kept them on, despite British reassurances. Anyway, the story was he'd taken the gap, although we didn't believe he would go without telling us.

Dad and I flew to England again looking for him, but it was like looking for a needle in a haystack. We made an appointment to see Harrison, but he swore he hadn't seen Jake. Hell, he even promised to make inquiries. Remember, we never knew about your mum and Jake. I had an inkling he had met someone, but I didn't know she was Harrison's daughter. Jake hadn't a clue about Harrison's and Dennis's past connection. Anyway, I suspect that when Jake found Celia gone, he followed her.'

Matt recalled grandmother saying, Jake came to see her, so it sounded likely. A growing fear that his grandfather or his stepfather had something to do with Jake's disappearance, other than foiling a coup, was troubling Matt. The question was, why? What conceivable motive could either of them have for wanting Jake dead?

It couldn't be to silence Jake. The incriminating evidence of his grandfather's complicity with Mugabe would make Robin a hero in the British and Zimbabwean eyes. In her letter, his mum accused Robin of helping to rig the elections so Mugabe could win. That wouldn't have been easy, and he would need proof, but it wasn't a motive either. Perhaps there would be something more in the other boxes to shed light on it.

'What was the issue that cause the feud between Dennis and my grandfather?' Matt asked.

'Ah, it's better left for Dolly and Dennis to tell you, Matt. I don't really know the details.'

Jess walked back into the room and said, 'We all need to go home. Matt, you're better now. You can come home with us, and we can talk with Dolly and Dennis. We'll go to Amsterdam to finish our business and meet you in Zim. Contrary to what you said, Matt, we came over here when we heard you were sick, to help because like it or not, you are family.'

'I can't go back,' Matt said.

'Why?' they both asked together.

'The CIO will not leave me alone, and I don't fancy being locked up in one of their prisons. I've heard they don't feed their prisoners and most die from starvation.' Matt gave a lopsided smile to show he was joking, but it was only a half joke. He didn't want to be mixed up in this sordid business even if it was playing Robin Hood, stealing from the rich to give to the poor. Only some of the rich, he thought. An image of Bridie's diamond jewellery popped into his mind.

How was he going to find the truth? Could he live with the idea that his grandfather was involved in Jake's death? What was the feud between grandfather and Dennis? Was it enough to cause murder?

Jess said, 'Matt you have to come home with us, even if it's just to tell Mum and Dad what Celia said in her letter. It's only fair they know what happened to their son. Fly into Johannesburg and Chris will come down and pick you up. He can bring you through customs and immigration the way we bring in tourists. Livingston will make sure no one gives you a hard time. They're all his people on the customs and immigration at the Zimbabwe/Botswana crossing. Ms Gracie and Happyton Bonyongwe won't even know your back. He'll make sure of that.'

Chapter Thirty-Three

'Annie, it's good to see you again. You don't look a day older than you did the last time I saw you.'

'Fletch, you old dog, you haven't worn so well. Look at the state of you. I bet you're still smoking like a chimney, and a boozer too.'

'Yep, you hit the nail on the head, and I might add it's charming of you to say so.' Fletcher grinned, thrilled to see Annie again after all this time.

It was funny how comfortable old friends were. He stepped through her pillar box red front door and took her by the shoulders, kissing her cheek. Then on impulse he pulled her into an embrace, feeling her frail bones beneath his large, gnarled hands. A little embarrassed by his display of emotion, he released her and stepped back.

She was laughing up at him, her eyes bright, her face a little battered by time. Her hair was short now, but still blonde, although he could see white streaks forming. Not dyed anyway.

'Oh Fletch, if only you'd done that years ago, you could have had your evil way with me, but I'm a bit long in the tooth for romance now.' Her eyes scanned his face. 'I can't believe you're blushing. Well, well, well. Come into the kitchen. I'll make you a cup of tea. You've had a long drive.'

'It's nothing. Don't forget I come from Australia. Three and a half hours from Joburg to Nelspruit is nothing.'

He stood watching her make tea, feeling too large for her tiny modern, red, and white kitchen under an eave-less roof of a one storey townhouse, within a gated community. He wondered what her life had been like through the intervening years.

'What brought you to Nelspruit, Annie? I thought your family was from Cape Town.'

'Love, Fletch. Love is the only motivator that drives people. Hm, along with fear, hunger and...'

'Safety, work opportunities' He finished for her.

'Ja, even so, it was love for me. Cedrick's family farmed here in the old days, citrus orchards, and he set up a bottling and canning factory. I met him in Cape Town when he was there on holiday. That was after I left Zim in '82. After that bastard Mugabe killed all those innocent people in Bulawayo. It was just a matter of time for the rest of us.'

'Where's Cedrick now?' A stab of jealousy surprised Fletcher. After all, he had his shot with Annie and rejected it.

'Dead, he passed seven years ago, massive coronary. It was terrible, but there you go. It happens to the best of, us doesn't it.' Shadows flitted across her face, but she smiled at him. 'It was all a long time ago now. What about you, Fletch?'

'Divorced twice. I wasn't a good husband. You're lucky I didn't catch you, Annie. Your life would have been a misery.'

'You never wanted me. It was always Celia. Did you keep in touch with her? It's funny, once she left the country I never heard from her again. I was so mad at her for not telling me she was going. I still can't believe she just dumped Jake for that bloke, just ran off with him behind Jake's back. Less than six months after they were married and she just up and dumped him, while he was in gaol and couldn't do anything about it. I wasn't happy with her; I can tell you. When I told him he looked devastated, but what else could I do?'

She shuddered at the memory and broke off. 'Didn't you know?'

'No Annie, this is all news. Why was Jake in gaol? I didn't even know she and Jake got married. How did you know she dumped Jake and ran off with someone else? Who was he, this other bloke?' Fletcher remembered the letter he got from Celia saying she had met someone else but waited for Annie to tell him more.

'Come, we'll have our tea in the lounge, and we can catch-up.'

Fletcher took the tea tray from her, following her into her sitting room, cosy and ultra-feminine, with its ornaments, frills, chintz, and cushions. A Siamese cat sprawled across the sofa and Annie scooped it into her arms.

'Meet Cleopatra.' She hugged the cat, and it protested with a harsh meow. Laughing, she put it down, and it rubbed against Fletcher's legs, before wandering out the open French doors to a courtyard.

'I'd like to smoke if I may Annie, can we sit outside, or do you object to smoking now? I remember you didn't smoke much.'

'Except for a bit of dagga, hey? Those were the days, but no, I don't mind. Ced, my husband, smoked like a chimney. Hence the coronary. You should give up Fletcher. But I'll get you an ashtray. It's a lovely day to sit outdoors. You carry the tray.'

Fletcher followed the cat out into the sunshine. A table and chairs sat in the middle of a courtyard crowded at its borders with plants and creepers. A tree in the corner spread shade across the yard and dripped nectar-filled flowers from horizontal branches. Tiny honey sippers flitted from flower to flower.

Fletcher plonked the tray down. Annie tripped from the house with an ashtray in hand and a photo album under her arm. She was still an attractive woman; her figure trim in three quarter length trousers and a tight tee-shirt. She looked younger than her years. Fletcher figured she must be late fifties, heading into sixty.

She said, 'So, you didn't know they got married, hey? It was sudden. I assumed Cee was pregos, but she couldn't have been, otherwise she wouldn't have taken off with the other oke from England.'

Fletcher lit a cigarette and sat back, watching Annie fuss over the tea. So, Jake and Cee got married. It didn't surprise him given the way they obviously felt about each other, but if they got married, that letter she sent didn't make sense.

'When did they get married Annie, can you remember the date?'

'It was in 1979, April because it was around the election that put Muzorewa in charge. I was pissed off with them for rushing things, but Jake only had a twenty-four-hour pass. I got a call from him saying it was a surprise, and I should get Cee's friends together, but no family. It was a debacle. The bloody District Commissioner's office was full of soldiers in uniform, and just a handful of us girls. Celia didn't even have a proper dress to wear, just a fancy black cocktail outfit. It was bizarre, and no reception, no family, nothing arranged. I'm surprised Jake arranged the Banns. You know what he was like. That little boy smile of his, so sorry, please forgive me. He said it wasn't Cee's fault, because she was in the dark until the last minute. They were a strange couple. Anyway, we had a whip round and bought them the honeymoon suite at the Monomotapa Hotel for the night. The next day, Jake returned to the war. Cee was supposed to stay with me until he got a longer pass and they could find digs, but she returned home. I visited my folks in Cape Town. When I came back, she had run off with a British soldier.'

'How did you know she ran off with him?'

'I rang her and spoke to her mom.' Annie lapsed into silence, reflecting on the moment. 'Mrs. Harrison told me all about it in lurid detail. She was glad she was divorcing Jake. I was just so hurt and angry at Cee for not telling me I didn't contact her again. You remember how she made us swear we wouldn't tell her folks about Jake? I thought it was because he was a soldier, but the bloke she ran off with was a soldier too. There must have been some other reason because her mom was gleeful.' Annie shook her head. 'It was a long time ago, and I've probably forgotten. I've got photos.'

She opened the album and turned over a few pages. There's you and Cee at her twenty-first, remember that? March '75 I think.

Fletcher took the photo and saw himself as a young man. Celia was laughing up at him. God, she was lovely. In the background two men were talking. The younger man was Jake, the other Celia's father.

There was another photo of Celia in a dark dress standing next to Jake in a dress uniform. She was holding a bouquet. They look like flowers picked from the garden, bunched together hastily. Behind them, Fletcher recognised the Salisbury Gardens and Les Brown swimming pool.

'This must be Jake and Celia's wedding photo.'

'Ja, that was taken after they got married. Here's another one.'

Celia and Jake were kissing under a tree in the same park in the same clothing. Fletcher sucked on his cigarette, trying to keep the emotion from his face, but Annie had sharp eyes.

'Geez Fletch, you're not still smitten, are you?'

He cast around for something to change the subject and asked, 'What became of Jake, Annie?'

She shrugged. 'I only heard rumours. The last time I saw him was when he got out of gaol.'

'You said before he was in gaol. When... why?'

'Didn't you hear? Apparently, he stole top-secret documents. She frowned. It was just after they were married. Jake had to go back to the war, and when he came back from the bush, they locked him up. It was in all the papers. When they were married, they only had one night together, so Celia was beside herself with excitement that he was coming home. She asked me if they could come and stay at my place again. You must have been in U.K.'

Fletcher nodded.

'Anyway, it never happened because he was arrested. Then, by the time he got out, she was gone. She was a cow, Fletch. She was running about behind Jake's back with an

English soldier who was there for the transition, while poor Jake was in gaol. When they released him, wrongly accused it seems, he came looking for her. He was skin and bone, poor bloke and devastated when I told him she'd gone. That's right. I remember he said he'd been to her folk's house, but they'd sold up and left. I told him Celia had run off with a British bloke. I thought after all the poor bastard had gone through, he should know the truth about her no matter how awful, but I wasn't prepared for his reaction. First he acted hurt, then angry, and then he decided he didn't believe me. I wasn't sure if he was going to cry or kill me. It was scary, but he buggered off and I never saw him again. I heard later he took the gap, immigrated to the U.K. That's what everyone said.'

Later that day, Fletcher drove back to catch his flight, promising to come back and spend longer with Annie after he had been to Zimbabwe. He doubted what Annie had told him was true. It didn't fit Celia's character; she would never have done it. Although she did marry a British soldier, Matt's stepfather. He thought of the letter he had received. That was also out of character, so perhaps it was true.

Chapter Thirty-Four

Polly sat on the Ryder's farmhouse veranda; the water colour propped on a chair before her. Her gaze flicked between the painting and the horizon. The low veldt colours were different, even the sky was a different blue from the Australian sky. Polly screwed her eyes against the glare. The distant khaki greys, browns, blues, and sand colours eluded her. She was so used to the colours of Australia she had probably brought the wrong palette. The green lawns around the house were similar, but the distant horizon were all wrong. She picked up her palette and began mixing colours. She would have to start again.

Since arriving in Africa, it was the first painting she had time to do although her sketchbook was full of drawings. Now she was finally alone, she worked contentedly, glad to be painting once more. Cooing doves and insects created white-noise, rhythmically punctuating the place's incredible stillness. The air was redolent with warm sunshine on damp lawn, and dry dust competed with the mouth-watering smells of lunch cooking.

Tom had gone off with Jess and Dolly to pick up Fletcher from Chiredzi airport and do some shopping for Dennis' birthday party. She had elected to stay behind with Dennis.

The place had seemed so peaceful, although she was looking forward to seeing her grandfather again. They had planned to stay with the Ryder's until Dennis's eighty-fifth birthday party next week and then head out on a tour of the country. Apparently, the entire district was expected to turn out for Dennis's party along with many others who would fly in. The place had been a hive of activity for days, preparing to cater for everyone, sort out sleeping arrangements, and transport requirements.

Aside from Dennis, who was somewhere about the place, she was alone with only the staff for company. She relished the tranquillity; glad she hadn't gone home after Vic Falls. She had grown fond of the people, and this place with its enormous, thatched roof, soaring vault-like above her. The high spaces kept the house cool in the heat of the day.

She was also looking forward to Meg and Chris's arrival. Although she cringed at recalling her initial jealousy of Meg. After Matt left, she was so depressed she moped around the Borrowdale house all week. Meg had been so patient and gentle, even though Polly wouldn't say what was wrong. Then Chris flew her down here, and Polly put Matt from her mind. Chalk it up to a holiday romance, brief, intense, and delicious but dead. The dull ache would heal in time, but she was sick and tired of being heartbroken. It was probably her own fault. After all, she threw herself at the man, even after he said no.

She gazed at the watercolour and then at the horizon, watching the light bounce off the river in the distance. Like the colours of the landscape, the shapes here were different. The trees along the river spread out like horizontal brush strokes against the sky. In Australia, eucalypt branches seemed to reach for the heavens.

A small girl sidled from around the house. Polly smiled. 'Hello.'

In a flash, the child was gone. Polly concentrated on sketching a quick colour wheel to work out the right palate for the landscape. From the corner of her eye, she saw the girl edging around a bush. This time, she ignored her.

The girl moved closer. Inch by inch, she crept up to the veranda, watching every move Polly made. Without looking up, Polly took a brush and slid it with another sketch pad towards the girl. The girl remained motionless. Minutes passed. The girl spoke in a language Polly didn't understand, but her pointing hand was enough. Polly followed the direction and saw a shape move. She shaded her eyes, trying to make out what had emerged from the shadows.

Elephants, five of them and one baby. They walked towards the house. Polly was on the veranda, surely that was safe enough. She glanced at the girl who seemed unperturbed.

Polly grabbed a stick of charcoal, turning the page and sketching furiously, getting down the negative spaces as quickly as she could to capture movement. The elephants veered to the left and continued on, giving a wide berth to the homestead. The one in the lead faced her, lifted its trunk, and moved away.

Another movement by the river caught her eye. The shapes were human, difficult to make out in the shadows. Perhaps they startled the elephants.

'That's remarkable,' Dennis said.

Polly cried out in surprise. The young girl had vanished.

'How long have you been there?' Her cheeks glowed with embarrassment.

Dennis chuckled. 'Long enough to watch you getting the elephants onto that page.' He bent to look at the drawing. 'You're very talented. You have captured them perfectly and so quickly.'

'I can't get the colours right here.' Polly sighed. 'I think I'm using the wrong yellow and I haven't brought another.'

'Can't say I can see the problem, but in any case, the others are back. They found some decent wine in the store, a miracle in this neck of the woods. We can try a sample in a minute. Julius has lunch ready.'

'I saw people down at the river, or at least I think I did, just after those elephants walked past.'

Dennis shrugged. 'I expect they're the group of tourists we have over at the lodge. There are a dozen of them staying there now, and they're all fitness nuts. I wouldn't worry about them, although I will let them know we have some big cats out there. I'm not sure they'd take a human, but you never know.'

Dolly and Jess came out to the veranda.

Jess said, 'Polly dear, your grandfather is in his room. He said he would only be a minute.'

Dolly said, 'Chris rang. He, Meg, and the boys are arriving early. We'll have a full house tonight. Oh, my goodness, look at that.' She pointed at Polly's painting. 'You are so talented.'

Jess peered at the elephant sketches. 'These are brilliant.'

'Thanks.' Polly's face was burning with all the compliments.

Dolly, said, 'You could paint Dennis's portrait, for his birthday.'

'I would be happy to, if he accepts.' She packed away her things, forgetting about the tourists wandering along the river, eager to get indoors and see her poppa.

Chapter Thirty-Five

Alighting from the plane at Johannesburg International Airport, Matt experienced the effects of high altitude and glanced up at the sky. It's winter blue wash lifted his spirits although the wind was cold, dry, and cutting. He was glad to be back in Africa despite his earlier misgivings.

Chris greeted him as he cleared customs. 'Howsit Matt, my shamwari. It's good you're back. We missed you, man.' He clasped Matt's hand and hugged him.

Matt was still tense from bringing the boxes through customs. 'I didn't understand a word of what you just said, but I assume it was hello.'

Chris grinned and took the loaded luggage trolley from Matt. 'Are you all ready to head out to the farm? It means more sitting on a plane. Sorry, last-minute change of plan. Some blokes arrived yesterday. There're on a hunting safari and will stay at the lodge for a few days. I hope that's okay, man. We'll tell them you are my co-pilot.'

'That's fine, and I wouldn't mind being a co-pilot—so happy to play the part.'

'I can teach you if you stick around for a while. If you get up your hours, you can get your licence, but you have to keep it up, fly regularly.'

'Don't know I'll have that much opportunity in the U.K., but I'd like to have a go.'

'Stay in Zim with us boet. Dad could use another pilot, and if you get a licence, it's keeping it in the family, hey?'

'You don't know how tempting that sounds.'

'I mean it. Oh, the car's over here. We're taking off from Lanseria Airport, about an hour north across the city.'

At Lanseria they clear customs again to leave the country before walking out to the apron. Three men stood next to the plane talking to a fourth man, who waved when he saw Chris. He was a burly, khaki shirted man with curly black hair, about Matt's age.

He hurried towards them, leaving the men at the plane. 'Meneer Ryder, your tourists are all ready to go. If you just sign this,' He held out a clipboard, 'you're set to take off.'

'Thanks Gert. Hey, meet my cousin Matt. He wants to learn to fly so you might see him here instead of me one of these days. Matt, Gert's our man in Joburg. He's invaluable and does everything, knows everyone, a good all round oke.'

'Ag, man, you'll have me blushing like a girl in a minute. Good to meet you Matt. Anyway, I'll let you get on. Your tourists have been here a while and are getting jumpy.'

Matt looked toward the plane. *Wild Tours* was written in bold letters down its fuselage. The three men, standing with their baggage around their feet, watched them approach.

There was something familiar about them.

As they came got closer, one man grinned and walked toward them. 'Holy she-ite, you changed your mind, you jammy bugger. Glad you made it. Like old times, mate.' Brander walked up to Matt, his sun-bronzed face beaming his delight. 'Dog said you wouldn't be in it.' He turned. 'Wrong again, hey Dog. Just as well, you're not a betting man.'

Brander pumped Matt's hand and Dog followed. 'Shit mate, you could have told us, instead of that bloody poker face. *Oh no, I'm not getting involved with that shit again.* You had me fooled.'

'Damn!' Chris looked at Matt. 'What are the odds of you lot knowing each other.'

Matt tried to keep his shock from showing. 'What are you two doing here?'

Dog and Brander laughed. 'That's good, fantastic. We're tourists just like you, mate, and this here is Steve, from the States.'

Steve, a stocky, dour looking man, stepped forward to shake Matt's hand.

Chris ran his hand through his hair. 'Ja and I'm Chris. Let's get this show on the road, shall we? We need to load the plane. Gert, over this way. Matt, we'll talk when we're airborne, okay?'

Matt remained pensive as they loaded the plane. He tried to put the pieces of the puzzle together, wondering what the letter Dog showed him, had to do with Chris. Of course, Chris might be ferrying them somewhere, without being part of a recruitment drive. But he was certain Dog and Brander were not here on a safari.

They took off, and it wasn't until they cleared the Lanseria airspace, Chris said, 'Okay, let's talk. You weren't supposed to be implicated in this.'

'In what?' Matt straightened in his seat, glancing back at the passengers in the back of the plane.

'In the recruitment.'

'What's going on Chris?'

'Can it wait until we're home and Dad can fill you in?'

'No, frankly, I'm tired of being ambushed by this family.' First the diamonds and now this, this... whatever this is, a private peacekeeping outfit, the letter said.

'It's a long story.' Chris' face screwed into worry lines.

'Yeah and we have a long flight ahead so I'm listening. ' Matt's face was placid, but inside he was seething.

'Well, it is a kind of protection for the game ranch, an anti-poaching squad.'

'Bullshit. You don't recruit special forces to carry out anti-poaching patrols.'

'How do you know they are Special Forces? '

'Matt pressed his lips together.'

'Sorry boet, but we will have to wait for Tom, okay?'

Less than an hour later, they landed at the border crossing near Plumtree, on the Zimbabwe side, to clear customs and immigration, and then headed onto the farm. Three hours after leaving Johannesburg, they circled over a large oval thatched house. Several outbuildings were scattered to one side, and a circular driveway led up to the house.

In the distance, a wide, sluggish brown river meandered across country, flat land on one side and bordered by hills on the other. Beyond the row of hills in the distance, Matt could make out another clearing with a large, thatched building surrounded by thatched rondavels, green lawns, and a swimming pool.

Chris pointed. 'That's *Wild Lodge* in the distance. It's the tourist part of the operations and that down there is home.'

As they came into land on a dirt airstrip, a Land Cruiser waited at the airstrip. In the distance, another Land Cruiser kicked up a trail of dust as it bowled along the road towards the airstrip. The Land Cruiser at the airstrip had the same bold writing on its side, *Wild Tours*.

Matt had his anger under simmering control. He would wait for a full explanation, but he felt cheated. But what does it matter? If these people want to build-up a private army, why should he care? Except now he knows they're family, and they've conned his mates into joining them. He suspected that the whole Robin Hood story about stealing diamonds for the people of Zimbabwe was all bullshit. What was Tom keeping from him? Of course, it wasn't hard to guess. Fuck. He wanted no part of it.

A tall African man claimed out of the *Wild Tours* Land Cruiser. He was wearing a smart khaki uniform with *Wild Tours* written on his breast pocket. Chris introduced him as Simon Moyo. Then he said, 'Matt's not going along with you guys. We have some business to conduct.'

For want of knowing what else to do, Matt played along, shaking his mates' hands. 'We'll catch up later.' Although that wasn't likely.

All he wanted was to give Dolly and Dennis the boxes with the information about their son, along with Jake's dog tags. Then he would leave this benighted country, putting his father and his crazy family in a box labelled the past. He watched the blokes leave in the *Wild Tours* Land Cruiser, while Chris fussed about the plane.

A few hours ago, Matt would have been interested in learning everything he could from Chris, but not any longer. The offer to teach him to fly was something Matt no longer expected would be forthcoming, given he wouldn't be there long enough. An unmarked Land Cruiser arrived at the plane, kicking up another cloud of chalky dust.

Tom got out. 'Welcome home, my sons. I see you brought another load of tourists home with you, Chris.'

'Ja, Dad, good to see you, but Matt knows they're not tourist, hey.'

'What?' Tom's face creased into a scowl.

'He knew two of the okes, okay? Who would have thought?'

'Aw shit, son.' Tom walked over to Matt. 'We're not doing a very good job with you, are we? You must be fed-up to the back teeth with us, and our secrets. I'll explain on the way to the house. When you hear, you'll understand why the secrecy is required.'

'I can guess.' Matt spoke drily, slightly mollified by Tom's obvious concern and regret, but he was still cautious and untrusting.

'Tell us.'

'It was in your recruitment letter.'

'You saw that?'

'Of course. Don't you think I talk to my mates?' He brushed their exchanged looks aside. 'I guess with the diamonds, and the build-up of the army, you're planning a coup of sorts. I'm not having anything to do with it. I'll just stay until you can take me back Chris, and we'll call it quits. Nice knowing you, but it's not a game with which I want any involvement, got it?' He glared at Tom.

A grin spread across Tom's face. 'You're a good lad, son. Jake would be proud of you, but you have it wrong.' He drew a breath as if making up his mind. 'I told you part of it in London. That stuff about the diamonds was true, but in addition, we are preparing for civil war between the political factions. Once Mugabe dies, all hell will break loose, and someone's got to protect the people and the animals.'

'Spare me the Robin Hood tearjerker, please.'

'I'm getting there. Already were skimming off the best Zim soldiers. We pay and the Zim government doesn't. Poor bastards haven't been paid for months, so they're loyal to us. All we are doing is hedging. It's an insurance policy against the Zimbabwe National Liberation War Veterans' Association or ZNLWVA, the so-called war vets led by Jabulani Sibanda. They are a bunch of murderous, drugged-up thugs who, although they are called war vets, are too young to have been in the war. These are Sibanda's private army. They are the ones who create intimidation at the polling booths, killing and terrorising people who might vote for someone other than Mugabe and his thugs. They are the ones who drove the farmers from their farms, killing and looting indiscriminately, killing farmers, their families, and their workers.'

'So, you recruit Special Forces soldiers to go up against drug addled thugs?'

Tom shrugged. 'No, not to fight them, to train our soldiers properly. It's not just thugs, there's also what's left of the army and air force. Special Forces can train, indoctrinate with rules of engagement, teach ethical standards, and keep order. We need to keep corruption out of the equation, driving values through the force.

There are some excellent Zim officers, but they don't have enough experience of the way others do things, like the British. We need to drive a culture of service to the country and rule of law.

If we don't do something, there'll be a bloodbath, and we'll never get this country on the road to a democratic, peaceful, and prosperous future. It's all we have left, Matt, and we'd like you to be with us on this, but I understand if you don't want to know. This country isn't everyone's cup of tea.

If you like, I can take you down to the camp to have a look and talk to some of the Zimbabwean soldiers, we have there. If you don't believe me, you might believe them. You can also talk to your mates. Then if you still want to leave, Chris will fly you back to Joburg, although Dad would like you to stay for his birthday party on Saturday.'

Tom drew a breath. 'Look son, others would have left the country by now, but what about those who can't? Who will look after their interests? This is not taking a white stance against a black government; this is trying to install democracy for all, beginning with the military, who will have the major say if there is civil war.

Once the dictator dies, we can give people a real chance to exercise their democratic right to have a government of their choosing. We can't stop thugs from gaining power through a fair election, but we can stop wholesale slaughter. We can stop rigged elections, and the bullying and intimidation that goes with it. People are dying at unprecedented rates from malnutrition, cholera, malaria, AIDS, thuggery, and murder. We can help. But come on, let's get to the house instead of standing out here in the sun and dust.'

They drove along a dirt road, with Matt deep in thought. It sounded plausible and less ominous than the coup he envisioned, although private individuals making such decision was an ethical minefield. If it was a peacekeeping force, it didn't sound so extreme. He understood their need for secrecy, but he didn't enjoy being on the receiving end. Bugger this family. Why did he ever get involved with them? They were turning his life upside down.

Tom said, 'By the way, it would be better if you don't mention this to Fletcher... or Polly, or anyone else. Just don't talk about it at home in their hearing, all right?'

Astounded by this new revelation, Matt said, 'Are Fletcher and Polly here?'

'Didn't you know?'

'I thought Polly returned to Australia. She was supposed to leave a couple of weeks ago.'

'She stayed to wait for her grandfather. Fletcher came out after he detoured to South Africa to see an old friend. Actually, he has some interesting news to tell. The friend was a friend of your mother's, but that can wait. Fletcher knows nothing about the diamonds or the operations and he's a reporter—or was. I would like it to stay that way, if that's all right with you, Matt?'

'Christ.' Matt lapsed into silence. He thought that lapse of judgement was behind him, certain Polly would have gone back to Australia and forgotten about him by now.

Chris leaned forward, interrupting Matt's introspection. 'How is it you know those blokes? Were you Special Air Service?'

Matt remained silent. This was not something one told people lightly, but these people were family. 'It's not something I want bandied about. You're family, so it's okay, but no one else. I wasn't regular, not with SAS. I only did two, three-year stints. As I said, I was in the Para's.'

'So, my boys were right,' Chris laughed. 'Cunning beggars. Same as Jake, hey.'

They arrived at the house. Matt was too nervous of coming face to face with Polly to appreciate the building with its soaring ceilings. It was furnished, similarly to the house in Borrowdale with an enormous vase of flowers, reeds and other foliage dominating the entrance hall table. Matt followed Chris and Tom to his room.

The men dumped Matt's boxes and the bags in his room, and Tom said. 'Cold chibuli on the veranda unless you want to change or shower or something.'

'No, I'm fine,' but Matt procrastinated, fiddling with his bag, rearranging the boxes.

Chris hovered. 'Come on boet. I'll show you the way.'

Matt followed him through the house, and out on to the veranda. Polly slumped in a chair, her bare feet propped against a stool, a sketchpad balanced on her lap, sketching Dennis, who stood leaning against a veranda pillar.

Dolly, Jess, Tom, Meg, and Fletcher sat around a low table chatting, gin and tonics in hand. Three dogs, alerted by their arrival, thump their tails at seeing Chris. They walked stiff legged towards Matt, to sniff his hand. The dying rays of afternoon light cast long shadows across the open savannah, the sky was awash with broad strokes of yellows, pinks, green, and purple.

Fletcher said, 'Matt, good to see you, lad. I didn't know you were joining us.'

Polly spun around, dropping her charcoal.

Matt rubbed his sweating hands along his jeans and avoided looking at her.

Dennis walked over to shake his hand. 'Matt, my boy, we weren't sure you'd come. Jess said you would, but hell, I wasn't sure. I'm glad you made it, son.'

Dolly leapt up and hugged Matt, kissing him, and running her hand down his cheek. 'Welcome home, son.' She kissed Chris. 'I'll get you boys a beer. I bet you're gasping.'

Jess and Meg followed, kissing Chris, then kissing Matt. Chris slid his arm around Meg, and Jess said. 'See, told you he'd come, Dad. He wouldn't miss something as important as your birthday, would you, Matt?'

Matt shook Fletcher's hand, and then having greeted everyone, he had no alternative but to turn to Polly. 'Hello Polly.' His voice caught on his larynx, and he coughed.

'Lo Matt.' Her lashes dropped to veil her eyes, and she bent to pick up the broken charcoal from the floor, her long hair swinging forward like a curtain.

Chapter Thirty-Six

At dinner that night, sitting around the dining table, Fletcher waited until the servants were out of the room before clearing his throat to make an announcement. 'I want to tell you all about something I have uncovered, about Jake.'

'What is it, Fletch?' Tom asked.

'I've done a bit of scouting around and learned some odd things about Jake. You might verify the truth of the stories. But there are a few questions that need answers.'

'What do you need to know?' Dennis sat forward.

'Was Jake locked up for stealing classified documents around mid '79?'

Dennis nodded.

'Is it also possible that he was involved in an attempted coup in '82, which was thwarted by Mugabe with the aid of MI6?'

Matt picked up the bowl of vegetables to occupy his hands, hoping someone would say something. They should take Fletcher into their confidence. He was sure the man was trustworthy, but it was not his call.

Tom said, 'I think we have the answers you want. We were going to tell you, man, but we only just learned about it.'

'How?' Fletcher asked.

Matt said quietly, 'Celia left a note explaining what happened.'

Fletcher put down his knife and fork.

Matt ran his hand across the back of his neck. 'The note was a bit garbled and some of it doesn't seem possible, but she explained that her father, Robin Harrison was an MI6 officer, posted to Rhodesia at Federation and stayed on after Smith's government declared their unilateral independence from Britain in the early sixties.

At the time of the black independence, he returned home but continued working with Zimbabwe. She said he uncovered an attempted coup against Mugabe. He helped coordinate an ambush against the plotters. It seems he had Jake pegged as the coup's ringleader. Mum thought it was because of that, he died, or that's what she said in her letter. She also said it was her father and my stepfather who arranged it.'

Tom intervened. 'But we know there was no coup, so that bit isn't true, although I don't for a moment imagine Celia was making it up. I suspect Robin, her father, wanted her to believe that for his own nefarious ends.'

Fletcher wiped his mouth. 'You must have known about his imprisonment, though?'

'Ja, everyone knew about that. It was in all the papers, but their claims he stole the documents was rubbish. Why steal documents that you originally found and brought back from Mozambique? It didn't make sense, and Jake said it wasn't true.

What did he have to gain? The only person who was worried was Harrison because the documents showed him and Mugabe, in cahoots throughout, like Siamese twins. Harrison would have been strung up if it was found out that he was a spy. It turned out it was Harrison and Mugabe who buggered the deal for peace with Smith in '71 and again in '75 because he wasn't going to chance Nkomo or someone else winning. Celia also said he helped rig the elections. I assume she meant the 1980 ballot, but perhaps it was later.'

Matt hadn't considered that. Surely his grandfather's involvement ended at Independence, but perhaps it hadn't. He had also assumed Celia was talking about the 1980 election, but her letter wasn't clear.

Fletcher nodded. 'So, we are back to where we started. I visited Annie, Celia's old friend. She said Jake had contacted her when he was released from gaol before he disappeared.'

'Really? What did she say?' Dennis leaned forward, excited by the prospect of new information.

Fletcher said, 'Annie told Jake what Celia's mother had said about Cee marrying a British soldier. Apparently, Annie hadn't seen Celia for a while because she was visiting her folks in Cape Town. When she came back, she rang Cee's mother. Julia Harrison told her that her daughter had taken up with a British soldier and had gone to England with him.'

Matt interjected, 'But Jake and Celia were married. I found their marriage certificate dated 26th April that year.'

Fletcher said, 'Matt we don't know what's true. I'm just repeating what Annie told me. Anyway, she said she was pissed off with Cee because she had only been married to Jake for a couple of months. The date you found on the marriage certificate would fit. When was Jake in prison, Dennis?'

Dolly said, 'Definitely June to December '79. He was home by Christmas. After Christmas, he drove to Salisbury to meet you and Tom coming back from your trip to the U.K.'

Tom said, 'That's right, we left in November '79, and had a bit of business to conduct, clearing away our sanctions busting evidence, mostly. We didn't get back until 2 January 1980. I remember because it was the only Christmas we ever missed at the Farm. I remember Jake was here with you because that made Dad and me feel better about not getting back.'

Matt said, 'If you flew my mum to England, she was here until November '79, is that right? Is that when you took her?'

'Sorry, who took her?' Fletcher frowned.

Tom explained the deal to get Jake out of prison, and how they hadn't known the package for delivery was human until the night they left.

'We might have been instrumental in Celia's abduction and transportation to the U.K. I can't be sure it was her because we never got a good look at our passenger. I am sure the passenger was a prisoner, and Harrison probably drugged her.'

Matt ran his hand across the back of his neck, horrified at his grandfather's treatment of his mother. 'None of this can be right either.'

'What do you mean, son?' Tom placed his elbows on the table.

'Well, if the last time Celia and Jake were together was at their wedding in April '79, and I was born in January '80, then in November Celia would have been almost eight months pregnant. It's unlikely that she would have been running around with another bloke at seven or eight months pregnant. And even if Annie hadn't seen her for a month, she would surely have known her friend was pregnant by that time.'

'You're right. Crikey!' Fletcher picked up his wine and sipped it thoughtfully. 'I'm pretty sure Annie said it was just after Jake was imprisoned. Celia started running around with the other bloke. Before that, she said Celia was excited that Jake was coming back from the bush. She asked Annie if they could stay at her place. Annie said that was less than two months after they got married. That would have been June. Annie might not have known Cee was pregnant at that stage.

I'll have to ask her when she came back from her holiday with her folks in Cape Town. If it was June or July, where was Celia until she left for the U.K. in November? If it was in June or July, why did Celia's mother tell Annie she had run off with a British soldier, and gone to England? According to your story Tom, she was your reluctant passenger in November?' He rested his forehead against two fingers. 'I got a letter from Cee. I can't swear to it, but I think it was dated early July '79.'

'What did it say, Fletch?' Tom's face creased with confusion.

'It was a weird letter, not her usual style, and it was typed, but basically it was a reply to my letter. She told me she had met someone else.' Fletcher stopped, looking sheepish. Only Matt and Polly were aware of his feelings for Celia. 'Oh hell, I might as well come clean. I asked her to marry me. My wife had applied for a divorce, and I thought I'd have a shot with Cee, especially as Rhodesia was going down the gurgler. I asked her to come to Australia and marry me. I knew she had been dating Jake, but I knew nothing about a wedding. I guess I was trying to steal her away from him.'

A smile spread across Tom's face. 'You sly old dog, but really, who was this woman, Mata Hari, that she had every man in love with her? Sorry Matt.'

Matt recalled the photos. She was quite a woman, his mother, and full of secrets.

Fletcher took a breath. 'So, let me get this right. The entire story about her running around with this English soldier was rubbish. Is that how you see it?' Fletcher watched the nods around the table. 'Okay, if its rubbish, what happened to Celia between June, when Jake was imprisoned, and November when Tom and Dennis transported her to England?'

Matt said, 'She said in her letter she was kidnapped and held hostage. How long or in which country she didn't say? Like Annie I also assumed she had an affair with George Reid. He was a British soldier over in Zimbabwe Rhodesia for the transition. I assumed Celia married him because she was pregnant. Yet I found out that too was wrong. She didn't marry my stepfather until I was nearly four.'

Fletcher pressed his lips together. 'So, lets recap. She's kept hostage in Rhodesia from June or July to November. Julia knows because she tells Annie some fable in July about Cee running off with another man. The letter I received was also a deception, devised by her mother. She would have opened my letter to Celia and concocted the story. I was a journalist, so they didn't want me sniffing out the truth.'

Dennis said, 'Back up a bit, Fletcher. You were telling us what Annie told Jake.'

'Ah yes. That bit was awful. Annie was so mad with Celia that she told Jake the whole sorry tale of Celia betraying him and running around with another man, running off with him to the U.K. Poor Jake. Christ! There has been one bit of misinformation after another. I also found out...'

Tom interrupted Fletcher, 'Dennis and Dolly must tell you about'

'Hang on Tom. Let me say this before we move on. Annie also said she heard Jake took off to England, and the rumour mill had it he'd taken the gap. Considering he knew Celia had gone to England, he might have followed her to get her back. Anyway, the idea intrigued me. If he entered the U.K., there would be an immigration record. I asked a friend to find out, and he came back with a date. Jake arrived in the U.K. via Heathrow Airport in January 1980, and there is no record of him ever leaving.'

'Jesus.' Matt breathed. He should have thought of that. It made sense. 'My grandmother, Julia Harrison,' he looked at Dolly apologetically, 'said Jake, came to see her. I didn't know that was in England. I assumed it was in Rhodesia before my grandparents moved to the U.K. But if Jake was released in December, and she was already in the U.K., the only place Jake could have seen her was England.'

'What else did she say, Matt?'

'She wasn't clear. At one point she became so muddled she thought I was Jake, and said Celia was divorcing him.'

'Yes, she told Annie that too,' Fletcher said.

Matt rubbed his forehead. 'When her mind cleared, she said Jake had abandoned Celia and broken her heart. She also said something about some bitch forcing him to abandon her, someone who forbade the marriage. Gran also accused Jake of threatening her in some way although she didn't say how.' His voice caught, and he paused a moment to regain control. 'When Jake called to see her, she said Robin had put him in gaol, but he wasn't in goal in the UK, I check, so it must have been when he was here. You must understand her recall of events was pretty garbled, and I didn't place much store in it. And by the time he went to see Julia in the UK., he had been released him from gaol.

Then there was only a marriage certificate and no divorce papers in the deposit box. There is no record of a divorce in England. I checked. So, either the divorce occurred here, or my mother was a bigamist. Unless Jake was dead. So, when she married my stepfather in 1984, Robin must have told her Jake had been killed in the coup in 1982. A coup we know now never happened.'

'Who was the bitch she talked about?' Dolly leaned forward, clasping Matt's hand.

'I don't know. I asked her, but she pretended she couldn't remember saying it. She got all vague, like she always did when she didn't want to talk about something. I couldn't get anything else from her.'

'It was me.' Dolly said, squeezing Matt's hand.

'You, why you?'

'She hated me. They both hated me and Dennis.'

'Why?'

Dennis sighed and got up to get another bottle of wine. They waited as he uncorked it and topped up glasses. When he sat down, he said. 'I dated Julia for a while. I had just come back from Korea, and there was this big bash to celebrate the Federation of Northern and Southern Rhodesia and Nyasaland. My folks wanted me to escort Julia. We were old family friends, and I had taken her out a few times. She was keen, and I had no one else on the horizon, so I was happy to do it. My folks wanted us to get married, but there was no way I was going to marry her just because they wanted it. Then I met Dolly, and it was lust at first sight.'

'Dennis!'

'Sorry Doll, lust first, then love, hook line and sinker type of love. I wanted to marry her straight away, but she was too chicken.'

Dennis smiled and grasped her other hand. Dolly let go of Matt's hand and turned to her husband. They exchange a look that told Matt how much strength they derived from each other.

Turning back to Matt, Dolly said, 'I was engaged to your grandfather, Robin Harrison. When I met Dennis, I fell head over heels, crazy for him. We had an affair. I was too scared to tell Robin, but he found out. You must remember things were different in those days. An engagement was almost as binding as marriage. Anyway, he and Julia walked in on us, caught us red-handed if you like.' She shuddered. 'After that, the scandal was bitter, and the recriminations carried on for months. They ostracised us from our social set. Julia's family made sure of that, and Robin made Dennis's life hell for years, every opportunity he could. Julia and Robin eventually found solace in each other's arms, but still they never forgave us. Then a few years later, Julia's father got into financial trouble, and Dennis's father bought two of his farms in the high veldt. That seemed to have been the last straw. Julia never got over it. But her accusing me of interfering and forbidding Jake anything to do with Celia is rubbish. I didn't even know about Celia, and Jake didn't know about Robin and me. Not even Tom knew. We only told him about our relationship with your grandparents after we met you.'

'Christ, what a mess.' Fletcher said.

Matt ran his hands through his hair leaving it standing on end. 'So, it seems, my grandfather, Robin Harrison, either killed Jake or arranged for Jake to be killed. Whether he did it in the U.K. or in Zimbabwe in a coup, it doesn't matter. He was responsible, and I'm sorry Dolly and Dennis.'

Dolly grabbed his hand again. 'It's not your fault, Matt, none of it. I'm just grateful we've found you, and we don't know anything, not really.' Her eyes were red rimmed and starry with tears.

He shook his head. 'But Dolly, just think about it. The last known place anyone saw Jake was at my Gran's... at Julia's place in England. Julia said Robin got rid of Jake. My mother's effects include Jake's dog tags, which apparently Robin gave her. Mum believed Jake died in the abortive coup. A coup fabricated by my grandfa... by Robin in his capacity as an MI6 officer. It's pretty clear. You don't get a man's dog tags because he leaves them in the bathroom. Then there are the cryptic notes between my stepfather and Robin, about a package and proof, dated January 1980. At first, I thought it related to my mum's forcible transport to U.K. but that happened two months before.

Now I suspect the package was Jake, or his corpse. I'm certain Robin and George between them killed Jake and did away with his body. My mum married George four years later not knowing he killed her husband. So, after all those years, she uncovered the lies. It was too much for her. She found out Jake had come looking for her. That he loved her, and she discovered her father or her husband or both, killed the man she loved. That's why she killed herself.'

'Then I am to blame for my son's death.' Tears rolled down Dolly's face. I started this by falling in love with Dennis, and taking my son was Robin's revenge.

'Unless it was Julia who killed him, and George and Robin hid the evidence.' Polly said the words quietly.

All eyes swivel to stare at her.

'Christ, why?' Matt said. 'Why would she kill him?'

Polly said, 'If she hated Dolly, she might have wanted revenge, or perhaps she was afraid of losing her family. Maybe she was terrified Jake would steal Celia, and the baby she was caring, away from her. It would mean Julia would have lost Dennis, her family's farms, her daughter Celia, and her grandchild to the Ryders. It might have been the final straw. She may not have been able to face losing you, Matt.'

Aghast at the suggestion, Matt realised he was staring and put his head in his hands. This was too much. These were his grandparents they were talking about. He had trusted them. Surely they couldn't be that... that... he didn't know what word to use. He pushed his chair back from the table. 'If you don't mind, I'd like a minute. Dolly, will you excuse me, Jess, Meg, Polly?'.

He walked outside into the garden, pulling a pack of cigarettes from his pocket and lighting one. The night was dark and moonless, with stars carpeting the inky sky, but he didn't notice. Instead, he paced, digesting the information, trying to find an alternative, but nothing came. Wood smoke wafted on a breeze, and he inhaled it with the smoke from his cigarette.

Polly was right. Julia killed his father. His own grandmother was responsible for his mother's death, and his unhappy childhood, and he can't understand why it's not more devastating. Perhaps it just hadn't sunk in yet.

As he walked back to the veranda steps, he realised the mystery of his father was resolved, but he was strangely detached as if it was not related to him. The murderer was his grandmother. She had motive, more motive than he could see his grandfather having.

Robin wanted revenge. Imprisoning Jake was both revenge and convenient. It stopped Jake from exposing him as Mugabe's collaborator before he could get his family out of Rhodesia. Christ, if the Rhodesian command had found out, he'd have been lynched. Gaoling Jake also prevented him from trying to find Celia.

He took out another cigarette and sat down on the lower step of the veranda. His grandparents were treacherous people. That was why they let George abuse him and his mother. Obviously George knew too much.

Matt had another insight. How did George die? It was soon after Matt enrolled in boarding school. Less than a year later, George died in Germany in an army vehicle accident. Matt wondered how much of an accident it was. Perhaps it was Robin's way of removing another threat.

A movement caused Matt to turn around.

Polly sat on the top step. 'I'm sorry Matt. I shouldn't have said what I did about your grandmother. It's nonsense, and I didn't think.'

He shook his head. 'No, you may be right. It never occurred to me. One member of my family killed my father. If it was Robin, George, or Julia, it doesn't matter, but I'm certain now that they were all in it together. It's just a shock.' Drawing on his cigarette, he lapsed into silence, aware of Polly's closeness.

She slid her bottom down the steps until she sat on the step above him, her feet next to his thigh, her legs within inches of his arm. 'You don't really know anything, Matt, it's all just conjecture.'

Matt shook his head. There was something else he should tell Polly. He owed it to her at least. 'Polly.' He stared at her bare feet next to his leg, wanting to touch her.

'Yes.'

'I have some other information.'

'What?' There was surprise in her voice and a hint of fear.

'I know what happened to your painting.'

An intake of breath made him glance up at her.

'It was removed by ah... some people.'

'Why?'

'Well, because my face was splashed all over the media, and well, they're idiots, that's why. They thought it was a bit of a lark. They should have just asked you to take it down instead of the silly antics.'

'Why? Why do you have to keep your face from the press?' Polly's face looked guarded.

'I'm really sorry Polly,' he paused, then added, 'for everything.'

She nodded but said nothing.

'They took it because it's a convention for us not to have our photos in the paper or on public record. It creates problems, for both me and my family. It can also create problems for people who have helped us on ops. Their cover is blown and so is ours, but for them it's worse.' He made a slight gesture with his thumb across his throat. 'Revenge can take a lifetime, so it's never over or forgotten.'

Polly said. 'I still don't understand.'

'I was in the Special Air Service. It's not supposed to be known outside my close family. I told you I was in the Para's, and I was. My home regiment is the Para's. I just did a couple of three-year stints with the SAS, black-ops and counter terrorism, mostly.'

'But why would they steal it? Surely you could have just told me.'

'I was too late. I figured if I lay low for a few days, it would be old news. That's why I came to Zimbabwe earlier than planned. My friends are idiots. I didn't know what they were planning. I'm sorry to put you through all the grief with the police and everything, but at the time I had no idea they'd done it.'

'Where is it now?'

'It's on a base in Australia, an Island somewhere. The police were told to drop the investigation. But my old CO promised to fix it. I rang him before I came, and he said he'd sort it out. You'll get it back.'

Matt stared out into the garden. She most likely thought he was as big an idiot as his mates. Dew fell, dampening his shoulders. He took a deep draw on his cigarette. 'We should go back into the house.' He flicked his cigarette away into the night, its red glow arching into the darkness, and felt something pushing under his thigh. Polly's bare toes. He straightened his back and moved his hand to cup the back of her ankle, his thumb stroking her anklebone. He didn't turn around, but he was supremely aware of her and a surge of happiness washed through him.

Chapter Thirty-Seven

The morning light flooded in through the bedroom window, making lacy patterns on the bedspread. Matt was aware of Polly breathing next to him. He rolled on his side, watching her eyelids flickering as she dreamed, her mouth a little open, lying on her back, arms flung out above her head, one leg hooked outside the blanket. She looked utterly abandoned to the innocence of sleep.

His throat tightened and leaning towards her, he placed his lips against her forehead. With his voice low, he said, 'Unless you want the entire house to know what we've been up to, you might want to go back to your room.'

She opened her eyes and stretched, her breasts popping out from beneath the sheet.

'In a minute.' He pulled her to him, feeling her warm softness as she snuggled in closer.

Yesterday evening had seemed endless while they sat waiting until everyone went to bed. He was not letting her go again without something to carry him through the day. He has a meeting with Tom at six thirty, but they have time.

Last night, Tom took Matt aside saying, 'Come with me in the morning to check out the operations base. I'd really value your expert opinion, son.' Matt hesitated, but Tom said, 'just to look at it and give us some advice.'

Now running his hand down Polly's belly, and along her thighs he concentrated on her warm softness, and the curve of her bum pushing against his hands. All thoughts of meeting Tom disappeared, lost in the feel of her, the tender trace of her warm breath. His lips trailed across hers, savouring her moist mouth loose beneath his. He slid his hands down her slippery smooth thighs.

Her breath quickened, her mouth demanded, her back arched, breasts pressing against his chest. She groaned, eyes flying open and gazing into his. Afterwards, she snuggled down in the bed, watching him dress. 'Where are you going? Come back to bed Matt, it's too early.'

'I have to go Polly. Tom will be waiting. I promised. We'll be back by breakfast. It's Dennis's birthday party today so everyone will be busy. Perhaps we can sneak away again later unless you want to tell them.'

Polly shook her head.

He grabbed his towel and a change of clothes. 'I have to shower, but I'll see you at breakfast.' As he bent to kiss her, her arms slid around his neck, pulling him back to the bed. He withdrew from her embrace and walked from the room, closing the door soundlessly behind him.

Polly lay luxuriating in his lingering warmth. She was not sure how she could remain strong enough to let him go when she returned home, but she was determined not to let the future interfere with her joy now. If this was just a temporary thing on Matt's part, she won't be saying anything that will put him under pressure. After all, she is supposed to be flying back to Australia in a couple of weeks, and he will go back to the U.K. She was resigned to a last fling; happy her heart was not aching anymore.

If he wanted more of her, he would have to come to Australia to get her. Twice she had made all the moves. Now it was his turn. Although he suggested they tell the family, she can't let Dolly, Jess and Fletcher think that she's so shameless she would fall into bed with the man just for a few days, even if that was exactly what she was doing.

A vehicle scrunching on gravel told her it was time to get up. She checked the corridor to see if it was empty, before skipping back to her room with only a towel to cover her. She clutched her clothes from last night in her hand. With a last glance behind, she crept into her bedroom, shutting the door and jumped into her own bed, snuggling into cold sheets. She lay remembering Matt's hands on her body.

Twenty minutes later, Tom and Matt drove along a dusty road, with Tom pointing out landmarks. They passed antelope and buffalo and a family of giraffe browsing tree top branches. Baboons squatted on the side of the road. They crossed a causeway and Tom pointed to large grey lumps in the river. 'Hippos.'

The place was teaming with game, and Tom kept up a constant patter of names and information. After thirty minutes, they arrived at a gate with a sign saying Private Property, No Unauthorised Entry. A thrill of anticipation ran across Matt's shoulders.

'We had to put that up and keep the gate closed, or tourists would be all over the operations area.' Tom's elbow hung out the window as he waited for Matt to open the gate. As Tom drove through, Matt lifted his face to the winter sun. It was a balmy 12 degrees Celsius, and the air crackled with dry static. Dust coated everything. A cloudless sky domed across the vast plains. Dense forests flanked the left side of the road, leafless now and twiggy, with bare branches casting cross-hatchings against the sky. Kopjes jutted up from the forest and along the other side of the road, fat-trunked baobabs raised their stumpy branches.

A kilometre along the road, a line of kopjes concealed the camp, and camouflage netting covered the infrastructure. There had been no expense spared in setting up this place. A building stood beyond a circular drive on both sides of which were barracks. On the right, a parade ground, and in the distance, playing fields. To the left, an excavator dug up dirt.

Tom said, 'It will be a swimming pool.'

'How many men do you have here?' The place was impressive.

'About twelve hundred, but we plan to recruit more. You can see over there we are building more barracks. We divide the men into six companies of two hundred, each commanded by a captain and the lot overseen by Lieutenant Colonel Jama Khumalo.'

'Jesus,' Matt was stunned. 'How the hell have you kept it a secret?'

Grinning Tom said, 'Who are they going to tell? It's not like they can get out of here easily, and anyway, we have recruited carefully. Every man here wants to be, and is committed to, what we are aiming for. There are no tsotsis—bad guys, here. It's a good reason for an army, Matt, to protect the innocent and vulnerable and to bring democracy instead of oppression. I hope all the people here believe in that.'

'How long have they been here?'

'No one stays here for over six weeks before returning to their regular barracks. We have a resort on the coast in Mozambique. They go there to get drunk and laid regularly. We're pretty strict, don't want them getting AIDs or talking out of school when they're pissed, so we control everything. No one's a prisoner and if they are married, their wives and families can live here too. We have married quarters. If they want to leave, they just have to say. So far, no one has. The pay is good, and the conditions are mostly good. Our biggest problem is keeping them occupied. They're itching to get out and fight someone. We have them doing anti-poaching patrols, but no poacher worth his salt will come anywhere near this place. That's what will make this entire operation fail. If Mugabe keeps going for too long, they'll get bored and fight each other.'

'Have you thought of a coup? It might be less bloody and get it over with quickly.'

'Ja, but the trouble with a coup is that it's an illegal overthrow of an apparently democratically elected government. Although, the May election this year was a farce. Everyone knows it was rigged, most people weren't allowed to vote, or their names weren't on the roll, but the names of dead people were. We even know the company who rigged the roll. Mugabe paid the bastards millions, but he'll claim it was free and fair. If we attempt a coup, it would never be a legit exercise. In the meantime, no one will condemn an anti-poaching campaign. If the worst comes to the worst, all we plan is to protect people if they need it.'

'That makes sense.' As they walked towards the administration building, Matt observed the men lolling about sloppily, drinking tea, watching listlessly as the two of them pass. The place is untidy and there's litter on the ground. The soldiers hang with their mates, but he sees it's racially aligned. Not healthy. They need a proud team spirit with blacks and whites mixed, so they become one unit.

Dog and Brander sauntered towards them warily, not sure what the lay of the land is, but determined to speak with Matt.

He introduced them to Tom and explained he had an advisory role. After chatting a while, Matt promised to catch up later, and followed Tom through double doors into the administration centre. In an office towards the rear of the building, he introduced Lieutenant Colonel Jama Khumalo, the man in charge of the battalion.

Matt was fascinated to hear the Lieutenant Colonel was a direct descendant of Lobengula Khumalo, the last king of the Ndebele from whom Cecil Rhodes bought the land.

'Cheated out of his land, you mean?' Jama smiled.

Tom said, 'Ja, cheated if you like, but its history now, hey. Now the tables are turned, and we've all been cheated.' Tom laughed and turned to Matt. 'We have this argument all the time, but it's a moot point.'

The Lieutenant Colonel impressed Matt with his calm and intelligently curious character, reminding him of Livingston in some ways.

Khumalo was interested in Matt's background and pumped him for information about the British Army. He seemed desperate for help and nodded when Matt talked about keeping the men occupied, forming multiracial squads, developing pride and other observations.

Matt explained how developing a culture of intolerance to any kind of dishonesty, sloppiness, corruption, or pragmatism was just as important as fighting spirit. They needed to instil a culture of ethics, professionalism, and pride in their jobs. He talked about developing a focus on results, building a healthy rivalry between companies through sport, in the absence of taking their aggression to the enemy.

He suggested they consider forming commandos instead of companies, breaking them down into squads and sticks of men who would learn to trust each other with their lives.

'How strong are the Zimbabwean Armed Forces?' Matt asked.

The Lieutenant Colonel said, 'Approximately 30,000, less perhaps about four or five thousand are air force, the rest army.'.

'What about the police and the war veterans?'

'Twenty thousand police and possibly forty thousand war veterans.'

'Those are long odds.'

'Yes, but we will recruit more. We are working on officers who are for democracy, and who will train here and go back to infect the army with good purpose. But they will not interfere in politics or join in civil war. They are professionals. It's the younger war veterans who are a problem. They have only ever fought defenceless civilians, and even then, many need dagga to operate.'

'What's dagga?' Matt said.

'Gunja,' Tom said.

'Marijuana,' Jama said. 'They force some into the war veterans program against their will, but they join because otherwise they have no money, no jobs. We will recruit the good ones.'

'What kind of informer network have you established?' Matt asked.

Jama shrugged.

Matt said, 'Has anyone developed a hearts and minds and misinformation strategy? What about the Chinese? What will they do? It's unlikely they'll interfere, but they may supply weapons to whichever faction will support their continuing exploitation of Zimbabwean resources. What kind of firepower does the air force command?'

Tom looked helplessly at Jama, and Matt realised he was expecting too much. At this point, they had no chance, despite their clear purpose. The entire operation looked bleak.

Later, driving back to the homestead, Matt remained pensive. Clearly they needed help, and it was help he could give them, but did he want to get involved? The odds were stacked against them, and this was not his fight, nor his problem. The country was a basket case, the rest of the world hardly noticed. Amnesty International didn't even focus on Zimbabwe much, not by comparison with other countries.

Mugabe was cunning, having created the smoke screen of democracy. Besides the country was miniscule in the grand scale of things. Aid agencies were everywhere, and North Korea, Gaza, Chechnya, Afghanistan, and Syria, among others, were much greater threats for the world to worry about. In any event, Matt didn't want to be involved in any more fighting.

Tom said. 'Well, what do you think?'

'I don't know Tom, let me think about it, will you? It needs work, that's for sure, but it looks like an impressive start.'

'I'm not sure what we do about Fletcher. Do you think we should trust him with this information, my son?'

Matt glanced at Tom. The wily old bugger. In one fell swoop, he had branded Matt on his side. 'Your call Tom but I reckon I would trust Fletcher.'

'What about Polly?'

'What about her?' Heat crept up his neck, and he looked out the window at the river in the distance.

'What d'you think she would say about this operation?'

'Christ, I don't know. Why ask me, I hardly know her. Ask her what she thinks.'

'I think you know her well enough, Matt, and I would like to know if we should tell her or not. Basically, if we tell Fletcher we tell her, but you may not want her to know.'

'Why wouldn't I?'

'Come on, Matt.'

Matt searched Tom's face, wondering if there was any point denying it. Polly didn't want to tell them, but he was okay with them knowing.

'How do you know?'

'Well, for one thing, I saw Polly practically butt naked, skittering down the hallway from your room this morning. It was pretty obvious last night, the way you two studiously ignored each other. Except for a brief sojourn on the veranda, you hardly said a word, avoiding eye contact and generally behaving weirdly. Either you're planning on robbing a bank, murdering someone, or planning some other hanky-panky.' Tom laughed. 'You must think we were born yesterday. Really, what we all want to know is how serious is it?'

'What do you mean, all?'

'Dolly guessed ages ago, and then Meg worked it out when Polly came back from Vic Falls. Women are better at this than us blokes. Don't know if Fletcher knows, but I suspect he does. So ja, we all know.' Tom paused. 'Although no one knows yet about Polly in your room last night. I haven't had time to tell them. But don't worry, they'll all know by breakfast.'

For a moment, irritated by their interference in his life, Matt stared out the window. Then an image of Polly scampering back to her room butt naked made him smile. He said, 'I hated all the sneaking around, but Polly didn't think it wise to fess up yet. I don't think she sure about me. Wouldn't blame her. Anyway, don't say anything until I have time to warm her, please. He got out of the car and walked toward the house

Tom called after him. 'You haven't answered my question yet.'

'What question?' Matt turned to look back at Tom.

'How serious is it?'

'Fuck off Tom,' he said, and walked into the house and went in search of Polly.

She was sitting alone at the breakfast table, gazing out the window. The empty eggshell on her plate, evidence she had already eaten breakfast. She had a coffee cup in her hand and was busy scooping the crema off and licking the spoon.

Matt watched her from the doorway, following her gaze outside. The morning colours of the veldt beyond the window sparkled with dewy, wheat coloured grass, washed out in the brilliant light. In the distance was a line of trees running along a riverbank.

Matt heard Tom walking down the hallway and said softly, 'Polly.'

Her face lit up.

'Polly, I need to speak with you.' He beckoned her to follow him and then disappeared before Tom arrived.

Moments later, his bedroom door opened, and Polly walked in, her eyes searching his. He pulled her into his arms and kissed her, tasting the coffee on her lips.

'God, I'm starving, but first you should know they know.' Matt said.

'What?' Her eyes were wide and worried.

'About you and me.'

She inhaled sharply. 'How?'

'Tom saw you this morning, running down the hallway naked.' He chuckled, unable to help the image in his head.

She said, 'I was not naked. I had a towel wrapped around me, although it wasn't a very big towel, but I didn't think anyone saw me.'

'Well, too late now. We may as well tell them.'

'Tell them what? That you're fucking my brains to mush in their guest bedroom. I don't think so.'

'No.'

'Well, what then?'

'Tell them you're going to stay in Zimbabwe with me. Stay here at the farm.'

'What, for how long?'

'For however long it takes.'

'Matt, you're talking in riddles, and I told Poppa I would go with him to South Africa to see his friend Annie.'

'He doesn't need you, Polly. Annie can look after him, but I need you here with me.'

'I thought you were going back to the U.K. in a week.'

'I was, but things have changed, and I might stay.' He looked into her eyes, his arms loosely about her waist, wondering when he made up his mind to stay and help Tom. Then he realised she couldn't stay here, not once they become operational. It would be too dangerous. He didn't want her in harm's way. 'Or do you want to come back with me to London?'

'Ha! What about you coming to Oz?'

'Okay. I can do that too, but I may have to be here for a while, just a few months.'

'Matt, you're not making sense. Tell me everything.'

'I can't Polly. It's not my story to tell. Come, let's go through to the dining room. Tom will tell you about it, okay? But I need you with me at least for a little while in the beginning. I haven't got enough of you to carry me through, not yet.'

Kissing her again, he stood back, opening the door for her to leave. He followed her down the hallway to the dining room.

Tom was sitting at the table, dishes of bacon, eggs, baked beans, mushrooms, and tomatoes steam in the table centre. Coffee warmed on the sideboard, and four slices of toast popped up as they entered the room.

'Ah Matt, I wondered where you got to. Morning Polly, sleep well?' Tom took bacon from a dish. 'Help yourself Matt. Have you already had breakfast, Polly?'

Polly's face was pink, still focussing on his reference to her sleeping well last night, knowing he had seen her semi naked. 'I ate with Poppa and Dolly, but he's gone for a walk and Dolly, Meg and Chris are busy arranging things for tonight.'

'I told Polly you'd explain things to her, Tom. I would like her to stay with me at least for a while before things get hot, then she needs to go home to be safe from all this.'

'Safe from what? I don't understand what you're talking about.'

Tom said, 'Sit down Polly and I'll tell you. I am trusting you with all our lives and I need assurance that you won't betray that trust—you and Fletcher.'

'What about me?' Fletcher walked in the door. 'Oh, good, there's some coffee left. Morning Matt, morning Tom. What's this about then?'

Matt glanced at Tom's face, but the man merely helped himself to eggs.

Matt followed suit, sitting down and scooping eggs from the dish.

'Do you want coffee Tom? Matt, can I pour you one?' Fletcher poured three coffees, passing each cup to the table as he did. 'Poll, you want another?'

She shook her head.

For the next minute everyone, but Polly, became busy organising their food and drink.

Polly said, 'Tell me what's going on?'

Tom chewed thoughtfully for a moment and then placed his knife on his plate. 'Okay, I'll tell you everything, but like I said, I am placing a trust in you that is frankly foolish. Despite our long history, we don't know each other well. Matt said I can trust you, and I trust him. I have to tell you I have misgivings because you're a journo, Fletch. If I take the gamble, and I'm wrong, then we're all dead. So, are a lot of other people. Either you have that on your conscience, or you tell me now not to entrust this information to you.'

'Christ, what is it? Don't tell me you're about to stage a coup, Tom?' Fletcher laughed at his joke.

Tom picked up his knife and cut into the egg. 'It's not a coup exactly. It's peace keeping in case the country breaks down in civil war once Mugabe pops his clogs.'

'What? You're kidding me, surely not, you... how... okay sorry... explain.'

Tom talked, explaining most things, but he left out the bit about the camp and its operations.

Polly stared at Matt. 'That's where you were this morning? That's why you're staying?'

Matt nodded, willing her to understand, hoping she wouldn't hate him.

Fletcher watched the exchange and then turned back to Tom. 'Where is this operation?'

Tom said, 'I can't tell you that, Fletch.'

'It's here!' Polly said angrily, glaring at Tom. 'I saw the men. Dennis told me they were tourist, but they weren't, were they Tom? They're soldiers, mercenary soldiers.' Her eyes filled with tears, and she turned to Matt. 'Is that what you'll be, Matt, a mercenary?'

'Christ,' he put his head in his hands. 'It's not like that Polly.'

'What is it then?' Her mouth twisted with bitter disappointment and grief.

'These men are trying to prevent wholesale slaughter. They're trying to protect the innocent and bring about free and fair elections, to re-establish the rule of law.'

'But they'll do it at the point of a gun. What's stopping them from taking over? They can just replace Mugabe with another dictatorship. Violence begets more violence, and you can't guarantee innocents won't get hurt.'

'How else don't you see it's the only way to save these people? The bastards in power couldn't care less about anything other than their own greed?' He stretched over the corner of the table to take her hand. 'Please Polly, I love you, and I need you with me on this?'

She snatched her hand away. 'No, you just want a fuck buddy while you're stuck in this godforsaken country doing what you know best, and that's killing people.'

She got up and stomped out of the room. Matt heard her footfalls all the way along the corridor before she slammed the bedroom door.

Matt remained rigid. Struck by indecision. She was right. It was all he knew, other than, he couldn't lose her. Saying he loved her came out without him thinking, but it was true, and now he didn't know what to do. Either he helped his family, or he left and hoped Polly could forgive him.

'Jesus!' Fletcher said. 'It's like a flashback to the past. They reckon history repeats itself, but I never thought to take it so literally. Did you mean that, Matt?'

Matt turned to Fletcher. 'Mean what?'

'Did you mean that about loving her?'

Is that all the bloke took out of that exchange? He got up. 'I'm going for a smoke.'

'You haven't eaten your breakfast, Matt.' Tom said.

'I lost my appetite.'

Fletcher can't let it go. 'Matt, stop, I'm serious. Did you mean it when you said you loved her?'

Glowering at Fletcher, Matt said, 'What d'you think I fucking meant,' and walked out through the French doors.

'That went well.' Tom sighed and wiped his mouth on a napkin.

Fletcher said, 'Why are you doing this really, Tom?'

'I told you, mate. There is no hidden agenda. This is our country and we're concerned citizens, black and white. Mugabe's done untold damage to this place, but it's nothing to what could happen if he dies. We're trying to prevent civil war breaking out.'

'Will Livingston be in the running for the presidency?'

'No, he's already ruled that out, saying it would seem like he was setting up this army for his own benefit. I'm telling you, Fletcher, that man is more righteous than any other human I know.'

'Okay, given I believe you, and I understand your need for secrecy, you can rely on my discretion, but I want the entire scoop at the end. Oh, and I want to help. I can place the right stories in the right places. Good media can do a lot for your credibility?'

Tom chuckled. 'I thought you'd retired Fletch, once a journo, always a journo, hey? Anyway, there might be nothing to report in the end. If there is a peaceful transition, well, we'll disband and melt back into the night. The men will be back in the army and at least we will have trained and educated them well. If not, we're here and might do some good. We needed a misinformation strategy. We also need an information strategy. Both need contemplating?'

They lapsed into silence. Then Tom asked, 'What about Polly? Will she be all right, man?'

'She'll be fine. I'll talk to her.' Fletcher said. 'She doesn't understand the stakes, and she doesn't get that this might be a good thing, unlike war. But it's deeper than that. She's heart sore. She doesn't believe Matt loves her. Calling him a mercenary was just to hurt him. A kick below the belt because she's hurting. But I believe him, and I will convince her. If she knows Matt loves her, she'll be fine.'

'Ja, a man would have to be deaf, blind, and dumb not to see that he loves her, but women are mysterious beasts. What did you mean by history repeating itself?'

Fletcher closed his eyes. 'Nothing really, just that I was once a witness to a similar quarrel between Jake and Celia. Polly will be fine, although I don't want her in any danger or in the country when it all goes off. Can you guarantee me that, Tom?'

Tom nodded. 'I'll make sure she's safe.'

'Okay,' Fletcher sighed, getting up from the table. 'I'll talk to her.'

Later that same day, as the western sun pointed accusing fingers across the dust-hazed landscape, guests arrived for the party. They flew in on light planes, some piloted by Tom and Chris, some in their own planes, others on charters from Chiredzi. They filled the lawn outside the house with colourful costumes, from little black cocktail dresses to traditional and colourful African and Indian designs.

Across the garden, beneath the trees, Fletcher sat with Polly on a bench, holding her hand. She had calmed down after her teary moment in the bedroom earlier, and he said, 'We should join the party, Poll.'

She nodded. 'I'll be with you in a minute, Poppa, and thanks. Sorry I was a witch.'

He smiled. 'You're all right, Poll. You're all right.' He walked toward the party and through the clustered guests.

Polly could see Matt with Livingstone's family. She should mingle, but she needed a minute to bolster her courage. While she sat, her artist's eye took in the colours, the light and shadow, the flickering torches, and the fairy lights in the trees. Above her pinpoint, stars blinked on through the mantle of darkening sky, and she wondered if she could ever capture the colour and feel of Africa on canvas.

An owl screamed in the distance, the night alive with other sounds that Polly couldn't distinguish, the rising cacophony of night birds, frogs, and insects, interrupted occasionally by the distant cackle of what might have been hyenas and the cough of a lion. It was a background orchestra to the murmuring crowds of guests before her, and the muted music drifting from the house. The scent of perfume, damp lawn, flowers, dust, and soap on the crisp dry air would endure forever in her senses.

She rose to join the guests, fingers trailing lightly across the bark, a last glance at the setting sun, glowing volcanically on the darkened horizon. The palate of splashed reds and purples and greens across the sky illuminated the yellow dust haze that hung above the parched land. Its sublime beauty stole into her soul, and its tentacles of entrapment held her in awe. She turned away from the setting sun to return to the party and shivered in the cool of early evening. The country was dying under tyranny, but surely only its own people could fix that. It was not up to foreigners to interfere. Yet, if Matt could help them help themselves, perhaps he should give it a shot, but only if that was what the people wanted.

Livingston took Matt's arm as he introduced his father, the chief, and his uncle, the local N'anga or witch doctor. The two old men stared at him in silence. Matt was a little disconcerted by their scrutiny.

Livingston's uncle said something in his language, and the Chief nodded. Livingston translated. 'My uncle said *his spirit has come home, and you will lead us to prosperity.*'

Matt frowned but remained silent. He would need to learn their language if he was going to stay here.

As if reading his mind, Livingston said, 'For now, we will speak in English.'

Bridie stood close to Livingstone, shyly outshining them all with her traditional dress and turban. Her ears dripped and her fingers sparkled.

Matt asked her, 'Are these Marange diamonds?'

She leaned into whisper in his ear. 'They are cubic zirconia from Johannesburg. Livingston thinks if I wear them, pretending they are diamonds, everyone will know we are loyal supporters of Mugabe, and just as corrupt.' She placed a conspiratorial finger to her lips. 'But you mustn't tell.' Her finger waggled back and forth. 'This is family business only.'

Matt stopped what he was about to say. This was his family. For better or for worse. When he set out on this journey, he hadn't bargained for what he'd found. Now he not only had found his father but had gained more than he could have possibly imagined—a new father and more family than he was comfortable with. And then there was Polly. Would she agree to be included in the whole confusing mix?

As night deepened, waiters walked between the guests, offering platters of finger food, wine, and beer. Dennis and Dolly appeared on to the veranda, and a cheer rippled around the guests as Dennis waved. Still, Matt couldn't see Polly. The crowd sang happy birthday and raised their glasses to Dennis's health. Matt realised the man had witnessed the birth, transformation, rebirth, and death of this nation. Would another rebirth be possible?

He spotted Polly at the far edge of the lawn. She smiled and waved tentatively. Matt excused himself from the group and strode towards her. When he reached her, he stopped and took her hand. 'Polly. I love you. I want to marry you. I just wanted you to know that. You don't have to say anything now, but I also wanted you to know that if you decide to marry me, you will have this goddam complicated family and my duty to them to contend with. Not an easy challenge, I know. But once my obligations are done, we can go where you like, live where you want, but please give me a few months to do what I have to do.'

Polly smiled. 'Dolly told me the Ryder men were soul stealers, and I still have to get the African landscape right, so I'll be here for a while. We can see how that goes and take it from there.' She moved into his arms and over Matt's should she smiled at Fletcher, who had lifted his glass in her direction.

About the Author

Gillian Long has a PhD in creative writing, and a background in publishing, psychology, politics, and executive leadership in both civil service and the not-for-profit sector. She has lived and worked in Africa, and Europe and now lives on a farm in the Australian Wet Tropics of Far North Queensland. Her previous novels, short stories, forthcoming titles, and other writing can be seen athttps://gillianlong.wordpress.com

An Uncivil War

Book 1 in the Mark Anders Series
Gillian Long
978-1-7638041-2-8

In 1937, Mark Anders, an Australian photojournalist, heads for the Spanish Civil War intending to expose the truth. He soon finds truth is a slippery fish. Sometimes a man must resort to dirty tricks to achieve his aims, and he must do that before the conflict sets fire to Europe's fragile peace.

A Wilderness of Mirrors

Gillian Long

978-0-9945598-7-6

When Harvey Kashton, a billionaire investor in a bauxite mine, is found dead in the gentlemen's withdrawing room of Bancroft House, the housekeeper Susan Ainsworth acts swiftly to prevent a scandal. Yet within days, his death will bring police, spies, and gangsters all traipsing through the gracious old hotel, but they underestimate Susan's ability to deceive and misdirect. That is, until the unassuming intelligence officer, Chris Davis arrives in this wilderness of mirrors.

The 9th District.

Book 1 in the Mark Anders Series

Gillian Long

ISBN 978-0-9945598-3-8

This historical novel is based on real events set in North Queensland during the great depression, when men's lives are cheap, immigrants are expendable, and a mysterious disease is sweeping through the cane fields.

Mark Anders has had enough. He challenges the powerful sugar industry, and the fight becomes brutal. But Mark's weakness is Beatrice, the daughter of his nemeses who will stop at nothing to discredit a godless Bolshevik.

Disgraced and driven from his home Mark discovers his real heart's desire. It's not his farm or the woman he loves, but does he have the courage to leave everything he built behind to bear witness to the truth?

Greenwash

Gillian Long

ISBN 978-0-6455760-5-4

Set in Queensland this global conspiracy acts out through a local crime, and an environmental disaster as Dr Jack Fallon races against time to expose the truth before catastrophe destroys all he loves.

Jack is often accused of being a loner, but that suits his role as a mining engineer, who spends most of his time in the outback. His mother disappeared under strange circumstances when he was a child, and he took solace in the riches of the earth. But its geological structures are notoriously unstable and may yet take everything he now holds dear including Sophia, the woman he loves.

Becoming Helen

Gillian Long

ISBN 978-0-6455760-0-9

Becoming Helen is a 1930s tale of deceit, disillusionment, and retribution after a British Intelligence Officer compromises a young German girl into spying on her own country, expecting her to lie, cheat and bed chosen German military targets for the Allied cause.

Magdalena von Herff barely knows what name to use before men begin to exploit her beauty, intelligence, and talents, but she soon realises that none are there to help her, except perhaps one—her enemy. Set in Europe, Britain, and America.

Dying Days

Gillian Long

ISBN 978-0-9942671-1-5

Three generations of murder, scandal, and intrigue is uncovered when Matt Reid, an ex-British Special Forces soldier, arrives in Australia in search of his biological father.

He meets Alan Fletcher, a retired war correspondent, whose story about the disappearance of a Rhodesian SAS soldier in 1980, sends Matt off to Zimbabwe on a mission to find the truth.

What he doesn't plan is to become a person of interest to paranoid secret police or to uncover plots of treachery and revenge and a half century old family feud.

This is a story about discovering family, falling in love and finding redemption.

The Trouble with Maggie

Gillian Long

ISBN 978-0-9942671-8-4

Maggie had everything she wanted; a wonderful husband and two gorgeous kids. Her life was perfect, until the fateful moment she ignored her dead grandmother's warning, and her life changed forever.

Set in rural Australia, this story is about the trials of marriage; secrets, guilt, love, and temptation, but most of all, it is a story about Maggie's journey to redemption, while filled with heroism, hedonism, hanky-panky, and hocus-pocus.

Watershed

Gillian Long

ISBN 978-0-9942671-4-6

It's the end of the 2020s and Australia struggles under tyranny. The economy has collapsed as terrorism escalates. Conscript Blake Lincoln returns from an endless Middle East war, wounded and a national hero. When he meets Charlotte, all he wants is to have his old life back. Instead, he uncovers secrets that will blow the government apart.

Watershed is set in Brisbane, Sydney, and Canberra, and takes in the vast wilderness of Cape York, and the raw beauty of the Kimberly region.

It is a story about the insidiousness of political corruption, the dangers of social injustice, the fragility of democracy and the power of family, as one man prepares to abandon all he believes in to save the woman he loves.

Gillian Long